Under a
Lakota
Moon

A Novel

I'm grateful to my family for their encouragement. Thanks to my critique-group sisters, who had faith in my talent. And to Linda Prince, who gave me a chance.

Walnut Springs Press, LLC

110 South 800 West

Brigham City, Utah 84302

http://walnutspringspress.blogspot.com

ISBN: 978-1-93521-718-3

Female cover image courtesy of www.ladiesemporium.com.

Under a Lakota Moon

A Novel

Deborah L. Weikel

For the Lord seeth not as man seeth; for man looketh on the
outward appearance, but the Lord looketh on the heart.

1 SAMUEL 16:7

Chapter One

Rosalynn McAllister scanned the horizon, then sighed and paced the train landing again. She glanced at her children, Joshua and Hannah, who played with some marbles while Rosalynn's aunt Dorothy sat patiently on one of their steamer trunks. Rosalynn craned her neck as she tried to get a better view of Peaceful, but all she could see from the landing was one dusty street that led through the center of town. She was running out of patience. They had traveled for days on the train with little sleep, and they had been waiting for several hours. The children were hungry, and Aunt Dorothy needed a place to rest.

Unconsciously, Rosalynn exhaled another exasperated sigh. Opening her handbag, she drew out a letter from her sister, Susan, and read it again.

January 7, 1870

Rosalynn and Aunt Dorothy,

I'm having a baby and need your help. I want you to move to Peaceful, Minnesota as soon as you can. My husband owns a large farm so there is plenty of room for all of you.

Susan

Five years previously, Susan had abandoned her parents and sister, leaving a hastily scribbled note that she was eloping. Rosalynn and her parents didn't know anything about the man Susan was marrying—or even where he lived, for that matter. Then, out of the clear blue sky, Susan had sent this letter demanding that Rosalynn and their aunt Dorothy drop everything and move to Minnesota. It was just like Susan to be inconsiderate. Crumbling the note, Rosalynn shoved it back into her handbag.

Susan had always been fickle. As a small child, she was selfish and conceited. When their parents died, Dorothy offered to take them in. Her house was small, and there wasn't much money, but Rosalynn was happy. She loved her aunt dearly and appreciated the sacrifices she made for them. Susan, on the other hand, constantly complained and bickered.

"Rosalynn, dear, how many times are you going to pace back and forth?"

Rosalynn heard her aunt's gentle voice and heaved another dejected sigh. Glancing down the street, she noticed some movement; Peaceful was finally waking. The train had arrived at 7:00 a.m., and Rosalynn knew it had to be at least 8:00 by now.

She gave her aunt a weak smile. Joshua and Hannah were getting bored playing on the landing, and Rosalynn knew her aunt must be tired of sitting so long on the steamer trunk.

"I thought for sure Susan would be here by now," Rosalynn said. "In my letter, I told her the exact day and time we would arrive."

"Well, I suppose something came up. Or maybe she simply forgot about us," Dorothy responded, sounding tired and slightly annoyed. "Surely, she would have been here by now if she or her husband were coming—"

"Ma, I'm hungry," Joshua interrupted.

"Me too, Mama," Hannah mimicked her older brother.

Reaching down, Rosalynn picked up her daughter and balanced her on her hip. She absently kissed Hannah's forehead and tousled Joshua's hair as she canvassed their surroundings.

"Why don't we take our food basket and a blanket and sit beneath that big willow tree over there?" Rosalynn tried to keep her voice bright. "We can have a picnic."

They all looked at the large weeping willow on the other side of the road. The tree seemed to beckon them with its protective branches and the cool, inviting shade that lay underneath it.

"Yes, Mama!" Both children chimed in unison.

"That would be wonderful," Dorothy said with a sigh of relief. "I would love to stretch out."

Rosalynn put Hannah down and picked up the food basket. *Thank goodness we packed plenty of food for the trip,* she thought, pursing her lips. After handing Joshua the water jug, Rosalynn grabbed the quilt and passed it to her aunt.

"I help, Mama?" Hannah asked, pulling on her mother's skirt.

"You can help carry the basket." Rosalynn smiled at the three-year-old. "It's too heavy for me to carry alone."

Grateful that Hannah was content to assist, Rosalynn grabbed one of the handles. It was a slow walk, but they finally made it to the tree.

Rosalynn watched her aunt from a distance and couldn't help but chuckle. Dorothy spread the blanket in the shade and waited for Rosalynn and Hannah to arrive before carefully sinking to the ground. Then the older woman scooted around until she found the perfect spot to recline. Taking off her brown, homespun jacket and matching bonnet, she placed them neatly beside her.

"Oh, this is heavenly!" Dorothy remarked. "Can you feel that breeze? I bet I could lie here and take a nice nap."

Rosalynn slipped her hat and jacket off. "That's a wonderful idea, Aunt Dottie," she said. "Why don't we all lie down for a little while after we eat?"

"No, Mama, me no nap," Hannah protested, her lower lip protruding.

Joshua crossed his arms as he plopped down next to Rosalynn. "Me neither, Ma," he said. "I'm eight years old now. That's too old for naps."

Rosalynn smiled when she saw the stubborn tilt of her son's jaw. She opened the basket and removed the food.

"How about if we just take a little rest then, after we eat?" she suggested. "You two got up extra early this morning and none of us got very much sleep on the train."

"Do we have to go to sleep?" Joshua asked, letting his arms relax in his lap.

Rosalynn knew that if her children slowed down for five minutes, they would fall asleep.

"No, son," she answered. "I'll be content if you just rest. I'll tell you a story."

"Yes, Mama, story!" Hannah clapped her hands with excitement.

Joshua frowned at his little sister. "Golly, Ma, I'm always outnumbered by girls. I wish I had a brother."

"That would be nice, darling, but I'm afraid you're stuck with Aunt Dottie, Hannah, and me," Rosalynn responded.

Joshua's comments reminded her how desperately the young boy needed a male figure in his life. There was nothing she could do about that right now, although she hoped Susan's husband could help fill the void for the short time the family would be in Peaceful.

After they ate, Rosalynn put the remainder of the food in the basket. Then the children curled up on the quilt, Joshua hiding a sleepy yawn behind his hand. Rosalynn swallowed a grin and started her story. Before she could get far, both children and Dorothy were fast asleep. Rosalynn laid her head down to rest a few minutes before deciding what to do next.

—————

Rosalynn awoke sometime later, bewildered. *Where am I?* she wondered as she opened her eyes. As her eyes focused, she found herself staring up into the branches of a tree. Yes, they were branches, and there was the sky.

Bolting upright, it took her a few seconds to examine the vicinity. Next to her, she discovered her family still sleeping and in the distance, she heard a hubbub of activity. Then it dawned on her. She was in Peaceful, Minnesota. They had arrived by train. *My goodness, how long did I sleep?* she thought. She found her handbag and pulled out her father's gold watch. Half past nine— it couldn't be! She had slept for over an hour. Thank goodness the tree was at the edge of town so they didn't attract too much attention.

Reaching over, Rosalynn lightly tapped her aunt on the shoulder. Once she could tell that Dorothy was coherent, Rosalynn whispered, "Auntie, I'm going to find a ride to Susan's for us. I'll be back as soon as I can."

Rosalynn slipped her simple gray hat over the wisps that had escaped from the bun at the nape of her neck. She stuck the hat pin into the hat, brushed the wrinkles and grass from her outdated, dove gray traveling suit, and replaced her white kid gloves. Satisfied that she was presentable, Rosalynn headed back to the train station.

She approached the ticket office and asked the man on duty if he knew Susan Larson. He said he hadn't lived in Peaceful long enough to recognize the name, and he suggested that Rosalynn try the livery stable up the street. Rosalynn thanked him and made her way toward the stable.

Her spirits rose as she realized that if nothing else, she could rent a wagon and drive her family to Susan's house. But to Rosalynn's regret, the livery stable didn't rent wagons.

"What would I do that fer?" the man asked. "Everyone in Peaceful owns a wagon. Renting . . . that's fer city folk."

Rosalynn was determined to get to her sister's house before dark.

"Is there anyone who could take me to the Larson farm on Willow Creek Road?" she asked. "I would be happy to pay them for their trouble."

"You might try that man over there in the wagon," he said, pointing toward a feed store. "Jeb Swift lives on Willow Creek."

Rosalynn thanked the man and headed for the feed store. Eventually she'd run out of streets and ticket offices and livery stables . . . and feed stores. What a miserable thought that was.

As Rosalynn drew near, the sight of the grizzled old codger sitting on the wagon seat made her hesitate. He looked to be in his early fifties and was the most unkempt man she had ever laid eyes on. The flannel shirt he wore had more patches than fabric, and his brown felt hat had certainly seen better days. He needed a shave, and his salt-and-pepper hair was well below his collar.

Rosalynn craned her neck back to get a closer look and plucked up her courage. Pasting on her friendliest smile, she asked, "Excuse me, sir. Are you Mr. Jeb Swift?"

"Yep," he answered nonchalantly.

Relieved that she had approached the right man, Rosalynn continued. "The gentleman at the livery stable told me you live on Willow Creek. Is that correct?"

"Maybe." The man looked at Rosalynn as if he were sizing her up. "Who wants to know?"

"I'm kin to Susan Larson," Rosalynn said, not feeling the need to go into too much detail.

The man appeared satisfied. "Yup, I live on Willow Creek."

"Thank goodness." Rosalynn breathed a sigh of relief. "My name is Rosalynn McAllister. I was hoping I might be able to hire you to drive me out that way."

Jeb's brows scrunched together. He pulled his hat off, swiped his forehead with the back of his hand, and then scratched his head before replacing the hat. "What you want to do that fer?" he asked.

This could take all day, Rosalynn thought with a forced grin on her face. This man was slower than molasses in January! "I have family out that way—the Larsons. Do you know them?" Rosalynn was doing her best to be tolerant, but Mr. Swift was trying her patience.

"Yup," the grizzled man replied.

"Well, can I hire you to drive me and my family out there?" Rosalynn asked again. *For pity's sake!* She was beginning to think Mr. Swift was addle brained.

"I dunno 'bout that," Jeb drawled. Scratching his chin whiskers, he added, "How many are there?"

"Two adults and two children," Rosalynn replied. "We also have our luggage."

Scratching his shoulder, Jeb seemed to mull it over. Rosalynn wondered if no one had ever told him it was impolite to scratch in public. Suddenly, she had an uncontrollable urge to scratch. *It must be contagious,* she thought with a smile.

"Well, I can't promise, but I'll try. I gotta load some feed sacks first. Where can I find you?"

"At the train station." Rosalynn felt elated. "I can't thank you enough, Mr. Swift."

"It won't be too long, miss. Like I said, I can't promise I'll have room." Scratching his side, Jeb climbed down from the wagon seat.

Rosalynn started for the train station. *Praise the Lord!* She had found a ride for them. Jeb Swift may be a bit peculiar, but at least he was willing to help.

When Rosalynn arrived at the willow tree, Aunt Dorothy and the children were ready to leave. Rosalynn explained that a neighbor of Susan's would be taking them to the farm. "Now, Aunt Dottie, this man is a bit earthy but seems perfectly harmless."

"What do you mean a bit earthy?" Dorothy threw Rosalynn a suspicious glance.

"You'll see," Rosalynn said with a smile.

They only had to wait about ten minutes before Rosalynn saw Jeb Swift climb onto his wagon and lead his team down the street. The tired-looking horses plodded along as though Jeb had all the time in the world.

"He doesn't get in much of a hurry, does he?" Dorothy commented as she watched the horses meander down the road.

"Let's just say we won't have to worry about being thrown from a runaway wagon as long as Mr. Swift is driving," Rosalynn remarked.

"Rosalynn, that's not a very nice thing to say!" Dorothy reprimanded. "It's not like you to poke fun at someone."

"Oh, Aunt Dottie, I wasn't poking fun at him. Swift is his name—Jeb Swift." She broke out laughing as she watched her aunt's expression change from confusion to amusement.

"Oh, my!" Dorothy placed her hand over her mouth to stifle a giggle. "This is the first time we've laughed since this wretched trip began."

Rosalynn watched in amusement as Jeb Swift aligned the wagon with the landing and pulled on the reins. She waited until he finished fiddling with the reins before starting the introductions. "Mr. Swift, may I introduce my aunt, Miss Applegate, and my two children, Hannah and Joshua."

Eyes pinned on Dorothy, Jeb's chest puffed out as he stood gallantly in the wagon. He reminded Rosalynn of a strutting rooster, and apparently, Aunt Dorothy was the new hen in the barnyard.

Jeb lifted his hat, scratched the top of his head, and then replaced it again. "Miss? Did I hear right, yer a miss?"

Dorothy lowered her eyes and then lifted them ever so slowly. "Why, yes, Mr. Swift, I'm afraid I am Miss Applegate." A gentle laugh rang from her lips.

Rosalynn couldn't believe it! Was her aunt actually flirting with this old cuss?

"My, my, my, Miss Applegate. It's a real pleasure to meet you," Jeb cooed sweetly. Stumbling as he went, he jumped from the wagon onto the landing. He took Dorothy's hand in his and shook it profusely. "A real honor, miss." He smiled, still shaking her hand.

Rosalynn bit her bottom lip to keep from grinning. While she was amused by his antics, she also realized that there could be no harm in her dear aunt attracting a possible beau. This was a new life for all of them, after all. Just because it was too late for *her* to find true love, didn't mean it was too late for Aunt Dottie.

Jeb finally tore his attention from Dorothy long enough to size up the situation. Rubbing his hand along his grizzled jaw, he muttered aloud, "I reckon I can get the trunks in the wagon. Mind you now, you and the young'uns will have to sit in the back. Miss Applegate can sit up front with me." Off came his hat for another scratch.

"That's fine, Mr. Swift, we don't mind sitting in the back." Rosalynn declared, relieved that their ordeal was almost over.

The trunks were loaded and everyone found a place to sit. Rosalynn was glad she didn't have to ride on the wagon seat with

Mr. Swift, since her mind was too busy to carry on a conversation. Her thoughts turned to Susan. Was she just being irresponsible or was something wrong? Maybe Susan's husband didn't want them here. For the hundredth time, Rosalynn prayed that she had done the right thing in moving her family to Minnesota. *At least Jeffery will never find us here*, she thought with a shudder. She never wanted to face him again.

In no time at all, the town of Peaceful was behind them as they made their way down a well-worn road. The gunnysacks filled with grain were anything but comfortable, and Rosalynn's back began to ache.

The wagon slowed as Jeb Swift turned onto a narrow, rutted road. Rosalynn's spirits started to brighten at the thought of a hot bath and a soft bed. She arched her back to get a better view, and then gasped in surprise.

Stretched below them was a beautiful valley with a creek snaking across the basin floor and then disappearing into the distant horizon. A copse of trees stood on the west end of the property, and rich fields fit together like quilt blocks on the eastern side. Pillowed in the center of the valley were a farmhouse and outbuildings.

Never had Rosalynn seen a prettier prospect. *Susan must be so happy*, Rosalynn realized with a pang of jealousy. Her sister had what she herself wanted so desperately—a husband and a home for her and the children. *Please, Lord, take away the bitterness in my heart. I will be content to have a home for us. I know no man will ever look at me with love in his eyes, but that's all right, Lord. I have Thee and my self-respect. I did the right thing by divorcing Jeffery. I'd rather be alone than be beaten by my husband, Father.*

"Well, there's the Larson place. They own the valley below and the forest yonder," Jeb explained, pointing to the stand of trees.

With his hat in hand, he swabbed the beads of moisture from his forehead. He replaced the hat and scratched the back of his neck. "My place can be reached through the woods by foot or horseback."

Clicking his tongue, the horses started down the incline. It was a gentle slope and the children enjoyed the ride immensely. At the end of the hill, they crossed a small bridge and Rosalynn thought. *And a creek on the property, too!* All those years on the dirt farm in Missouri—lugging water to her garden and livestock—had made Rosalynn appreciate the luxury of a creek.

As they neared the farmhouse, Rosalynn spied a small fruit orchard with trees in full bloom. They drew nearer, Rosalynn inhaled the blooms' sweet fragrance, trying to calm her racing thoughts, to relax and enjoy the surroundings.

When the house came into view, Jeb stopped the wagon. The spacious, two-story farmhouse was a welcome sight. What caught Rosalynn's eye first were the two verandas. They both ran the length of the house, one on the ground floor and one across the second story. A white picket fence enclosed the yard. It was the perfect place to raise a family.

Rosalynn had never lived in such a big house before. No wonder Susan said there was room for them all.

Jeb drove the wagon around back. Up close, Rosalynn could tell that the house was a bit run-down and needed a coat of paint, but she thought the structure itself looked solid. Then, glancing around at the overgrown weeds that covered the yard and the neglected outbuildings, Rosalynn felt a niggling of doubt creep in. The fields were neat and well cared for, but the rest of the farm seemed to have been neglected for some time.

Rosalynn felt the wagon jerk to a stop and watched as Jeb jumped from the seat to the ground. He quickly went around to the other side and offered Dorothy his hand. Dorothy's face brightened at the attention.

"Are you sure this is the Larsons'?" Rosalynn inquired as she scrambled from the wagon unattended and lifted the children out. "The place looks abandoned."

"Yup, I'm sure. I've lived here nigh on 30 years. It's a shame how the place has gone to rack and ruin since old Adrian passed on. I did hear the Larsons have been having a hard time lately." Without pausing, he continued, "Do ya want me to carry yer trunks into the house?"

Rosalynn shook her head, wondering what he meant by "hard times." "No, thank you, Mr. Swift. If you would just unload them by the gate, I'd appreciate it. How much do I owe you for bringing us out here?"

Jeb waved his hand in answer as he strode to the back of the wagon and started to unload the trunks. "That's city doings. We don't charge to help folks 'round here. We don't call our friends Mister, neither. Call me Jeb."

"What kind of troubles have the Larsons been having, Jeb?" Rosalynn tried to sound nonchalant as she helped him remove their things from the wagon. A funny, nagging feeling was starting to creep into her stomach. *Please, Lord, forgive my anger with Susan. I pray she and the baby are all right.*

"I don't listen to town gossip, miss."

Rosalynn didn't pursue the conversation. Instead, she tried to calm the feelings of dread that were sneaking into her mind.

Jeb finished unloading their belongings, tipped his hat to Dorothy, and climbed back onto the wagon seat. "Now, don't be 'fraid to holler if ya need anything. I'll come back in a couple days to see how yer gettin' along."

Rosalynn and Dorothy thanked Jeb for his kindness. Jeb returned Dorothy's smile, then turned the wagon around and headed back up the hill to the main road.

Feeling alone and frightened, Rosalynn looked at the house, which suddenly took on a sinister look. The dark windows felt like eyes glowering down on them. "Beware, beware!" they seemed to whisper. *Dear Lord, what if this place isn't Susan's farm after all? Something is wrong; I can feel it in my bones. Please give me the courage to continue and the strength to be brave for my family.*

Chapter Two

Rosalynn shuddered and turned from the house. Examining the immediate surroundings, she saw several small buildings fairly close by. She also spotted a chicken coop, a huge barn, and a silo in the distance.

"Now what do we do, Rosalynn?" Dorothy asked. "We certainly can't stay out here until Susan decides to return home."

Rosalynn heard the undertone of sarcasm in her aunt's voice and couldn't blame her for being a bit agitated. Susan had better have a good reason for treating them this way. Again, the feeling of foreboding filled Rosalynn's heart. *Have faith,* she silently scolded herself.

"Why don't you and the children stay here, and I'll go see if anyone's home." Rosalynn tried to sound upbeat. "Please don't let the children go into the yard. The grass is so high and overgrown with weeds, there may be snakes."

"Whatever you think is best, dear." Dorothy bit her bottom lip and glanced around. "Is it just me, or does it feel creepy around here?"

Rosalynn didn't want to worry her aunt needlessly, but she had always been honest with her. "I feel something too, Aunt

Dottie, but I want to make sure this is Susan's house before we go any further."

"And what if it's not?"

"Let's not court trouble, auntie. Just say a little prayer that it is Susan's house."

Rosalynn gave her aunt a reassuring smile and affectionately squeezed her arm. Taking a deep breath, she opened the gate. When she released it, the gate slumped against the wooden picket fence. The leather hinge on the bottom of the gate was the only thing that kept it from falling to the ground.

Gathering her skirt, Rosalynn held it tight against her body. Tall weeds grabbed at her, and in her state of mind, she almost felt they were trying to stop her from entering the house. She finally made it to the steps and was about to climb them when a horrible stench reached her nose.

Rosalynn quickly retrieved the embroidered lace handkerchief she kept tucked in the bodice of her dress. The subtle fragrance of roses wafted from the linen fabric as Rosalynn placed it over her nose and mouth.

"Are you all right, Rosalynn dear? What's the matter?" Dorothy called from the gate.

Rosalynn turned toward her aunt. "I'm fine, auntie. There's a terrible smell. I think it's coming from the back porch. You and the children please stay back."

Luckily, Hannah and Joshua were actively playing tag and not paying any attention to her. Rosalynn reached for the screen door with her free hand, making sure the handkerchief was still in place over her nose. Slowly she pulled the screen door open, or rather the frame of the door. The screen was torn and dangling by just a few threads.

As she popped her head through the doorframe, Rosalynn immediately discovered the cause of the foul odor. Hanging on a nail inside the door was a half-decomposed rabbit. On the floor, below the rabbit, was a pail of soured milk. Rosalynn stared at the bloated body of a dead mouse as it floated in the clabbered milk.

Rosalynn's stomach rolled and heaved, and she clamped her mouth shut against the bile that rose, burning her throat. She tried to peer through the windowpane, but an old towel dangled across the window on the inside.

Rosalynn banged on the open door and waited several seconds. Then she swished the flies away and knocked again, this time with more vigor. Still no answer came. Rosalynn wasn't sure what to do. Suddenly, something scampered across the floor behind her on the porch. Suppressing a scream, she shoved on the door. It gave way to her weight and she dodged inside and slammed it shut. As she leaned her weight against it, she felt her body start to relax. Her heart pounded at the near miss with the nasty mouse.

She forced herself to calm down before going any further. With a giant sigh, Rosalynn cautiously opened her eyes and found that she was in the kitchen. The room was dark and dreary and had an odious smell of rotten food.

With the scented handkerchief still shielding her nose, Rosalynn quickly scanned the kitchen. Never in her life had she seen such a hovel. Every dish, pot, and pan was dirty, and rotten food lay on the counters. Kettles and cast iron skillets with hardened food still in them covered the cold cook stove. The once-pretty curtains, strung across the cupboards and windows, were nothing but soiled rags. Surely, not even Susan could live like this.

Cautiously, Rosalynn craned her neck as she tried to see beyond the kitchen. She called out Susan's name but the house remained silent. Taking a few steps into the dining room, Rosalynn called out again, "Is anyone home? Susan, it's me, Rosalynn."

There was no answer.

Rosalynn wasn't convinced that her sister lived there at all. As she looked around the dining room, she was disgusted to see the table piled high with papers, clothing, and dirty dishes. Despite her ill feelings of intruding, Rosalynn searched among the papers and letters for any clue. Finally, she recognized the handwriting on one of the envelopes. It was the letter she had written to Susan. At least there was proof Susan knew they were coming and that she actually lived here.

Rosalynn heaved a sigh as tears of relief filled her eyes. *Thank you, Lord, for guiding us to the right farm.*

"It's all right, auntie. Susan lives here," Rosalynn called from the back porch.

"Praise the Lord," Dorothy answered. "I was beginning to worry."

When Rosalynn approached Dorothy, she saw a look of relief wash over her aunt's serene countenance. "I have to admit, so was I." She managed a little laugh and a reassuring smile. "No one is home so I'm at a loss about what to do. Any suggestions, auntie?"

"I'm sure Susan and her husband wouldn't mind if we waited inside for them. After all, Susan asked us to come."

"True," Rosalynn murmured, deep in thought.

Watching her children play in the dirt, she realized for the first time what a chance they had taken in coming here. She honestly thought Susan might have changed over the years; most people do grow up, after all. However, the condition of the house proved Susan hadn't changed one bit.

"Aunt Dottie, the house is a pigsty. I can't believe Sue allowed her home to become so filthy. I know we pampered her, but I assumed she would have more pride in herself."

"Maybe the baby came early and she didn't have anyone to

care for her," Dorothy offered.

Rosalynn tried to think optimistically, but after seeing the state of the house, she doubted that an early birth was the reason. She knew it had taken more than weeks, for the home to reach its current state.

"Well, do we go in or camp out in the yard?" Dorothy asked.

"I guess it'd be all right to go in the house. No telling when Susan will finally show up, and I don't want us stuck out here after dark. But I caution you, it's bad in there." Rosalynn gave Dorothy a warning glance.

Rosalynn carried Hannah while Dorothy took Joshua's hand. They carefully approached the back porch, quickly passed the dead rabbit and the soured milk, and bolted into the house. As Rosalynn secured the back door, the children began to fuss because of the terrible smell. Soothing them as best she could, Rosalynn tried to divert their attention by asking them to help her look around. This seemed to appease them, for the moment, anyway.

"I thought I had prepared myself for the mess you spoke of, but I feel near apoplexy witnessing it firsthand," Dorothy replied, holding the skirt of her dress close to her body. "Never have I seen such clutter! It's unhealthy to live like this. Is the entire house as bad as this room?"

"I don't know," Rosalynn replied as she opened a door off the kitchen. "I didn't venture past the dining room." She paused, and then added absently, "Here's a nice pantry, and so handy right next to the kitchen."

"Where does that door lead?" Dorothy asked, pointing.

"I don't know, auntie, let's find out," Rosalynn answered, following Dorothy's gesture. The closed door was next to the back door. They opened it and found that it was a root cellar. "I'm not going down there. There are probably mice." Rosalynn shuddered and quickly closed the door.

As they continued to explore the main floor, they discovered two nice-sized parlors with fireplaces, a large bedroom with a sitting room, and a locked room off the dining room. They didn't even venture upstairs.

In the larger parlor, they found a picture of Susan posing with a tall, blonde young man. They looked so happy and in love. *Perhaps everything was going to work out after all,* Rosalynn mused, then placed the picture back on the dust-covered piano.

She looked around the parlor, thinking that it could be a pretty room if it were cared for. The wallpaper featured delicate pink roses and vines, and the hardwood floors, now grimy with neglect, would be beautiful when polished and accented with bright scatter rugs. The furniture was old fashioned and the rose-colored fabric was dusty, but Rosalynn knew it would clean up well. The white lace curtains, now tinged with dust and cobwebs, must have added elegance to the room at one time. The fireplace was small but elegant with a beautiful hand-carved mantelpiece depicting flowers and birds.

"What a nice room to have tea and visit in, Aunt Dottie." Rosalynn's thoughts carried her to a more carefree, cultured life.

"It will be nice once we clean it," Dorothy answered, taking a closer look around the room. "Odd though, there aren't any other pictures besides Susan's. With all of these beautiful shelves, it looks like there once were some knick-knacks of some sort."

Before Rosalynn had a chance to reply, they heard the children scream. As she ran out of the parlor, she called out, "Joshua, where are you?" She heard the children yell out again and ran to the second parlor. To her relief she found them standing in the middle of the small parlor, unharmed. "What in the world is wrong? Why did you scream?"

Without speaking, both children pointed across the room as

they moved closer to their mother. Rosalynn could sense that they were frightened, but why? Her gaze moved in the direction they indicated and Rosalynn saw a small, furry animal cowered in the corner. The poor little thing looked more scared than they were. Then Rosalynn spotted the broken window.

"I was afraid you saw wild Indians," Dorothy said, a bit shaken.

"There are no wild Indians around here, remember, Aunt Dottie? This is 1870." Rosalynn threw her aunt a warning glare. The last thing she needed was for Joshua and Hannah to be scared to death.

"Of course not." Dorothy clearly realized her mistake, and she tried to comfort the children. "It's okay, chickens," she soothed, "it's only a baby raccoon." She then pointed to the window. "See, he came in through the broken window. I think you scared him, too."

The two women guided the children out of the parlor and shut the door.

"Now, the poor little thing can crawl back out of the window. Don't you two go in that parlor until I make sure he's gone, though," Rosalynn warned.

"But, Mama, he come back." Hannah's eyes were huge in her small elfin face.

"Don't worry, darling. I'll put something over the window after he leaves. Besides, I bet he would be too frightened to come back again."

"He didn't look scared to me, Ma. He looked mad! He was growling like a mean dog and showing us how big his teeth were." With that, Joshua demonstrated how the raccoon looked while growling.

Rosalynn laughed at her son's expressive face. "I'm sure the raccoon can be mean, but we'll leave him be, and he'll find somewhere else to live. I promise."

"I don't like Aunt Susan's house, Ma. It stinks here, and it's dirty. Can we go back home now?" Joshua asked.

"Yea, Mama, scary. I wanna go home." Hannah's lower lip jutted out into a pout and her large blue-green eyes were glassy with unshed tears.

Rosalynn gazed down at her children. They were serious. They wanted to leave, and she couldn't blame them—not one bit.

"Come here, children." Rosalynn bent down, and both children ran into their mother's arms. "I know it's been difficult for us since we left St. Louis. You two have been so brave and such a big help to Aunt Dottie and me. I don't know what we would have done without you." The children's faces brightened at the compliment. "But we can't go back home. This is our home now. Remember how we all prayed about what we should do when Aunt Sue wrote asking us to move to Minnesota?" Joshua and Hannah both nodded their heads. "We all felt that Heavenly Father wanted us to come here, remember?"

"I remember, Mama," Hannah chirped.

"I remember too, but maybe He doesn't want us to anymore. I bet God didn't know Aunt Susan lived in a dirty house with wild animals living in it. I bet God knew we wouldn't like to live with her."

Rosalynn suppressed the laughter she felt churning inside her. Her gaze met Dorothy's and she knew her aunt was also having trouble keeping a straight face. "God knows everything, Josh, you know that. Maybe God thought Aunt Susan needed our help or maybe God wants us here for some other reason."

"Like what?"

"I don't know. We need to have faith that everything will be okay. God is very wise." Rosalynn's smile was soft and loving. "I promise you both that if we don't like living with Aunt Susan, we'll move into town. How does that sound?" Rosalynn looked at Dorothy for support. "What do you think about that, auntie?"

"I think it's a good idea, dear," Dorothy replied. Then she hugged the children and added, "We would still be close to your Aunt Susan if she needed us. But we need to give it a chance."

Joshua and Hannah looked at each other and then smiled. "Okay, we'll give Aunt Susan a chance. But do we have to live in a dirty house?" Joshua's face crinkled with disgust as he looked around them.

Rosalynn tousled her son's hair. "Maybe we can do some cleaning now. I'll tackle the kitchen if you two will help Aunt Dottie with the bedroom. Wouldn't that be a nice surprise for Aunt Susan when she comes home?"

"Do you think we should do anything while Susan is away?" Dorothy asked, a brow darting up.

"I'm sure Susan wouldn't object to us doing housework for her. By the looks of things, that's why she asked us here. Besides, I'm not cooking in a dirty kitchen. And, as far as the bedroom goes, it doesn't appear as though anyone has slept in it for some time. We're all going to welcome a good night's sleep tonight."

"I know you're right, dear." Turning to the children, Dorothy asked, "So, do I get any help cleaning the bedroom?"

Both children agreed to help and headed for the bedroom.

Dorothy then turned to Rosalynn and whispered, "I trust your instincts, Rosalynn dear. If you feel it's acceptable to clean the house, then we'll clean it. I'm tired and dusty and the last thing I expected to do when we arrived was clean a bedroom before we could sleep in it. But, as always, we will trust in the Lord."

Rosalynn smiled at her weary aunt and placed a kiss on her soft cheek. "That's right, Aunt Dot, we should always trust in the Lord."

Upon entering the bedroom for the second time, they all took a more critical look at the task before them. The bed, floor, and dressers were piled high with clothes and bedding. Old boots and shoes were scattered all over the floor. Stacks of papers and books lined the walls.

"What a mess!" Dorothy exclaimed. "You don't suppose this is Susan's room, do you?"

"I don't think so, Aunt Dottie. I don't see any signs of a woman sleeping in here. I'm sure she and her husband sleep upstairs or in the locked room off the dining room. I mean, look around. There are no signs of anyone preparing for the arrival of a new baby."

"Well, I'd hate to think we imposed on someone's privacy by taking over their bedroom," Dorothy exclaimed.

"It looks more like a junk room to me," Rosalynn volunteered. "My goodness, the clothes are rags! Perhaps someone was keeping them for quilt making or something."

"I'm sure you're right, dear," Dorothy replied, holding up a pair of holey bib overalls. I can't imagine anyone wearing these."

"Those are perfect, Aunt Dottie! Now find me a shirt to wear."

"What are you doing, Rosalynn McAllister?" Dorothy screeched when Rosalynn grabbed the bibs from her hand. "You can't wear those grimy, ratty bibs! No telling who wore them, and they may be unclean."

Rosalynn ignored her aunt's ranting and laughed as she stepped behind the dressing screen. "I'm not about to ruin my only halfway decent traveling suit cleaning that dirty kitchen. Did you find me a shirt, auntie?"

Dorothy shook her head in defeat. "I can't believe you are actually serious, Rosalynn. Here I thought I raised a lady." Stooping down, she picked up an old flannel shirt with holes where the elbows used to be. "Why, I do declare. I think this will look lovely with your bibs, dear!"

Rosalynn peeked over the screen and giggled. Her aunt held the shirt with her thumb and index finger as though afraid to touch it. "Okay, wiseacre, no comments on the new ladies' fashions."

When Rosalynn stepped out from behind the screen she was met with a peal of laughter.

"Mama's funny," Hannah giggled.

"Funny? I'll make you think funny!" Rosalynn joined the laughter. Picking Hannah up, she plopped her on the bed. "That deserves a tickle."

"Me too, Ma. I wanna a tickle too," Joshua yelled, laughing.

"Okay, young man, you asked for it." Rosalynn chased the giggling Joshua around the room until she finally caught him. She plunked him down on the bed next to his sister and tickled them both until they yelled, "Uncle!"

Soon Rosalynn stood in the middle of the kitchen with her hands on her hips. "Where in the world do I start?" she asked aloud. "I'll need hot water, lots of hot water."

She removed the dirty dishes and rotten food from the cook stove and then brushed the dried food and debris onto the floor. Finding a broom in the pantry, she swept the bulk of the garbage into a corner to contend with later. At least she wouldn't be tripping over it as she worked. She discovered with relief that the wood box was full of kindling and wood.

Next, Rosalynn went into the dining room and picked up all of the old newspapers she could find and started a fire. Once the kindling caught hold, she focused on the water pump. Again, she was reminded of how fortunate Susan was to have running water in the house.

Rosalynn needed water to prime the pump and went outside. She returned with the jug of water they had brought with them. After the pump was primed, she filled two large kettles she had found in the pantry and set them on the stove. The stove was a newer four-burner model with a reservoir on the side for keeping water hot. A large warming oven sat above the stove, with a heating gauge on the oven door. All the stove needed was a good cleaning and it would work like new.

While she waited for the water to heat, Rosalynn stacked all the dirty dishes next to the sink. Then she forced herself to remove the dead rabbit and the soured pail of milk from the back porch. Hopefully, Susan and her husband wouldn't mind her dumping the offensive items back by the woodshed.

Next, Rosalynn took down the soiled and tattered curtains, then discarded them along with the spoiled food and the rest of the rubbish. She swept the floor in the dining room and the kitchen, deciding that mopping would have to come later. She uncovered a small table in the kitchen and cleaned it off; it would come in handy while she prepared the meals. Susan hated cooking and Rosalynn had a feeling she'd be elected to the job.

Rosalynn was used to hard work. She worked as hard as any man did when she lived on the dirt farm in Missouri. When she lost the farm and had to move in with her aunt Dorothy, she took on the household chores, along with the gardening, so that her aunt could focus on making cosmetics. That was their bread and butter.

When the water was finally hot enough for Rosalynn to wash the dishes, she grated lye soap into a wash pan and then filled it with hot water. She put the dishes in the wash pan and then filled another wash pan she found in the pantry for the rinse water. Putting them side by side in the large sink made it much easier for her to wash such a large amount of dishes.

Rosalynn took some of the wash water and scrubbed down the counter where she planned to lay the clean dishes. She couldn't find a clean kitchen towel anywhere so she used some old flour sacks she found stacked in the pantry. The pantry was already proving to be indispensable.

Not wanting to take the time to see if the water reservoir was usable, Rosalynn refilled the kettles to heat more hot water. She made a mental note to check the reservoir later, hoping that Susan hadn't left water in it to rust.

Rosalynn tackled the dishes with gusto, using all of her pent-up frustrations. While the dishes were drying, she scrubbed the rest of the counters and both tables. Stepping back to view her handiwork, she called to her family to come and see the kitchen.

"Oh, my, you've done a wonderful job, Rosalynn dear!" Dorothy blurted out as she stepped into the room. "It's a nice kitchen and will be very pretty when you're finished."

"Yes, I agree with you, auntie. I'm a bit surprised at how it turned out too! I couldn't believe the dishes were Blue Willow, and everything else is high quality too. It's such a shame to see such pretty things neglected like this."

"Yes, I agree. We need beeswax to polish the dining room furniture. And look at the floors! I didn't even notice they were hardwood floors," Dorothy said, glancing around the kitchen.

"Mama, I'm hungry," Hannah whined, blinking tired, red eyes.

The toddler rubbed her eyes with tiny fists, smearing a streak of dirt across her face. It had been a long day for them all. Rosalynn asked Joshua to bring in the basket of food. After they had eaten, Rosalynn gave the children each a sponge bath and put them down for a nap. Dorothy decided to rest with the children, which freed Rosalynn to finish the kitchen and start on the dining room.

Rosalynn felt so blessed to have her aunt with her. A home with two women usually courted trouble, but with them, it had been a blessing. Dorothy couldn't do the hard, laborious jobs, and Rosalynn didn't have time to do the little things in the house plus all of the outside chores. Moving in together had been a wise decision.

Soon it was late afternoon, and still no sign of Susan. Rosalynn had been so busy cleaning that she'd momentarily forgotten about her sister. As she gave a quick look around her, she started to feel nauseous. It was strange being in a house without the people who lived there.

Rosalynn had just started cleaning the table from the noon meal when she heard the screen door flap shut. Susan was finally home! Filled with relief, Rosalynn headed for the kitchen to greet her sister.

"Well, it's about time, Susan!" Rosalynn forgot the anger she had felt earlier. She was just relieved that everything was all right.

As Rosalynn came around the corner from the dining room to the kitchen, she collided with a solid force. Confused, she opened her eyes and found herself pressed against a man's chest. He was the tallest man she had ever seen and she had to crank her head back to look at him. When she did, she let out a blood-curdling scream.

Rosalynn pushed away from him and then screamed again. "Indians! Aunt Dorothy, get the gun!" She grabbed the broom as it leaned against the wall and struck the tall, broad-shouldered Indian over the head. Her second strike came to a stop in his powerful grip.

Dorothy ran into the dining room, a gun in one hand and a fireplace poker in the other.

"Shoot him!" Rosalynn's voice sounded shrill and hollow in her own ears.

"Do not shoot. I am unarmed." The tall, bronzed man protested calmly, raising his hands in the air. There was no fear on his lean countenance. "I have no desire to die in my own home."

His stance was commanding, and his dark, eyes moved from Rosalynn to Dorothy.

Slowly, the words sunk into Rosalynn's rattled brain. *This is his house? Impossible!* He wasn't the tall, blonde man in the photograph with Susan.

"This house belongs to my sister, Susan, and her husband Mike Larson. What have you done with them?" Rosalynn's body was taut, but she was trying hard not to show the fear she felt.

Please, sweet Jesus, protect us from this heathen. Please, I pray that Susan and her family are alive. Rosalynn's silent prayers screamed within her, and her heartbeat sounded like a drum in her ears.

The copper figure loomed before Rosalynn and Dorothy, dignified and proud. The muscles in his jaw flexed. "Mike Larson was my brother—my half brother."

Was? How could this be? Mike was clearly white. "I don't believe you," Rosalynn stated, clenching her teeth.

Reaching out to her aunt, Rosalynn demanded the gun, her eyes never leaving the intruder.

"Now, I'm not going to let you shoot him, dear. We need to find out what's going on before passing judgment." Dorothy then directed her attention back to the Indian. "Can you prove who you are?"

"I am Lone Wolf, a Lakota brave. My mother, Pale Flower, married my father, Adrian Larson, after his first wife died. Susan McAllister married my half brother, Mike, about five years ago."

Apparently taking the man at his word, Dorothy let her arm drop to her side.

Rosalynn wasn't convinced. "Anyone could know that kind of information. You're going to have to do better than that before I believe you. Where are my sister and her baby? What have you done to them?"

"I have done nothing with that lazy wasichu—white woman."

Lone Wolf clearly didn't like Susan, but his daunting expression showed no emotion. Still, Rosalynn could feel the undercurrents snap in the air like lightning shocks. Lone Wolf slowly moved to the sideboard, opened the top drawer, pulled out a folded piece of paper, and handed it to Rosalynn.

Rosalynn leaned the broom against the table, still leery of the towering, bronze Indian. She took the paper and unfolded it. Feeling weak, she sat down at the dining table. *Please, Lord, let it be good news.* But almost as soon as she uttered the prayer, she knew the news wasn't good.

Chapter Three

Rosalynn read the letter twice before reality sunk in. Her body and mind felt numb. *Why, Lord? What are we to do now?*

"Rosalynn, dear, what's the matter? Has something happened to Susan?"

Rosalynn stared into her aunt's ashen face. She then glanced at Lone Wolf, expecting to see triumph smeared across his hard, unmoving features. Instead, she met solemn, dark eyes in a face that showed no emotion.

"Aunt Dottie, please sit down, and please put that silly gun away."

Dorothy obeyed and slipped the gun onto the table, then sank into a chair across from Rosalynn.

"Please, Mr. Larson, sit down," Rosalynn mumbled, ashamed of herself. She had never struck a person in her life, not even to defend herself from Jeffery's wrath. Even worse, she had judged Lone Wolf because he was an Indian. Silently, she prayed that God would forgive her for such deplorable behavior.

Lone Wolf pulled up a chair and sat down. His body was tense and alert, his shoulders straight and his jaw set in a harsh line.

"I'm very sorry for the way I've treated you. Please forgive my rudeness. I'm normally not judgmental of people; you just caught me by surprise. It's been a long, trying day for us." Rosalynn sighed and tried to compose herself before continuing. "I'm Susan's sister, Rosalynn McAllister, and this is our aunt, Dorothy Applegate. I hope we can start over." Rosalynn offered a feeble smile and was relieved when Lone Wolf nodded in agreement.

Rosalynn sensed that Lone Wolf was a man of few words and even less emotion. With a dejected sigh, she directed her attention to her aunt. "Aunt Dottie, I need to read Susan's letter to you." Her voice was low and full of emotion, and it sounded hollow and faraway to her own ears.

Lone Wolf,

Now that Mike is dead, I'm leaving this horrible place with someone I've loved for a long time. Don't try to find me. I'll never agree to come back. I'm too young to have two brats saddled to me and live out in the middle of nowhere. If you want the kids, I left them with the minister and his wife in town.

Susan

Rosalynn slumped down in her chair, trying to make some kind of sense of the letter. She glanced at her aunt for moral support, and noticed the older woman's pale cheeks and crinkled brow. *I feel like such a fool to have trusted my sister and put my family in danger! Yet, Lord, when I prayed to Thee for answers, I felt strongly that this was what Thou wanted us to do. Was I mistaken? Did I want a new beginning for us all so much that I put my family in peril? Dear Lord, don't forsake us now!*

"I can't believe Susan ran out on her husband and children. She's always been unreliable, but to abandon her family is unconscionable. I feel as though I don't even know my own sister anymore." Rosalynn felt her heart harden against Susan and she didn't like the feeling. "We didn't know Sue had two children. Are they safe?"

Lone Wolf stared back at Rosalynn, apparently unwilling to offer the information she was so desperate to hear.

"Are they still with the minister?" Rosalynn stared earnestly into Lone Wolf's dark eyes.

No answer.

A frustrated groan escaped Rosalynn's lips. "Are they safe?" Her voice grew louder with each question he ignored. "At least tell me if they're safe, Mr. Larson. Please!"

Lone Wolf finally replied somberly, "The children are safe with Reverend and Mrs. Baker. Gretchen is four. The baby is a boy. He has no name."

"Sue didn't name the baby?" Rosalynn couldn't believe she had heard Lone Wolf correctly.

"Why should she care to name a baby she did not want?" Lone Wolf's smoldering stare made her squirm in her chair, wishing for an escape.

"Just because Susan's my sister doesn't mean I accept her behavior, Mr. Larson. I'm just as angry with her as you are."

Tension filled the room, and the silence was deafening. Rosalynn's chin jutted out with determination, while Lone Wolf's intimidating profile seemed to dare Rosalynn to submit.

Rosalynn saw Dorothy look from her to Lone Wolf.

"Why would she ask us to come live here only to leave like this? I don't understand, dear." Dorothy's voice quivered with emotion. "Can you explain what is going on, Mr. Larson?"

Lone Wolf pulled his eyes from Rosalynn. "For the past five years I have come to help my brother till the land and plant the crops. I help with the winter wood for the fires and then harvest the crops and do the fall butchering. The rest of the time, I live up north with my mother's people.

"When I returned this spring, Mike was very unhappy. He did not share his troubles and I did not pry. Your sister hated me. I did not want Mike to feel he had to choose between us, so I stayed in the old log cabin our father built when he came to America.

"When I came in from the fields two weeks ago, I found Mike . . . he hanged himself in the barn. I cut him down, but it was too late. He was dead."

Rosalynn and Dorothy's gasps reverberated through the room. Unfazed, Lone Wolf continued.

"Later, I found a note he had left for me in the log cabin. He couldn't live with the constant bickering and the insults Susan screamed at him every waking hour. He loved her, but could no longer live with her constant threats to divorce him and take his children from him. When he mentioned leaving her, I did not think he meant to leave her by death."

Lone Wolf's voice dripped with anger, and Rosalynn couldn't blame him. She had been on the receiving end of Susan's unchecked tongue many times.

"This last baby was not wanted by Susan, and she blamed Mike from the beginning. Her tongue was sharper than a warrior's lance. I know, for I heard her many times screaming obscenities at him. My brother was not hard like me here," he said, hitting his fist against his chest. "He was gentle and kind. He adored his daughter and was happy Susan was bringing another life into this world for him to love. He gave up everything for her, but Susan was born with a heart that could not love."

Rosalynn felt shame again. Here she was, concerned with her problems, while Lone Wolf had suffered so much more from her sister's selfishness. Lone Wolf kept his countenance well guarded, but she heard the spirit of love in his words. He didn't have to tell them that he loved his brother deeply, and that he was suffering inside.

Rosalynn felt a strong desire to hold Lone Wolf in her arms and comfort him—not as a woman holds a man, but as a mother holds a child. It surprised her, since she was usually so frightened of men that she felt uncomfortable even shaking hands with them. Yet something inside her sensed that Lone Wolf was not like most men— that his spirit was different. Even so, she was afraid to trust him.

"No words can express my sorrow for you, Mr. Larson." Rosalynn reached out and touched his hands as they rested clutched together on the table. "I know how it feels to lose a loved one."

Lone Wolf drew his hands back as though Rosalynn had burned the flesh from his bones. "Why are you here?" he asked bluntly.

Rosalynn pulled her hands back and laid them in her lap. She tried to read his thoughts, but Lone Wolf's expression was impassive. She looked at her aunt for help, but Dorothy only waved her on.

"You explain, dear. I think I'll put some water on for tea."

Rosalynn folded her arms in front of her on the table. She could feel Lone Wolf's stare burning into her, and she averted her eyes to avoid his scrutiny.

"Susan sent a letter several months ago, insisting that we move here. She mentioned that she was going to have a baby, but not that she already had one child. She assured us her husband would welcome us on the farm. We wrote back and told her we were coming and the date we would be arriving. When she didn't pick us up at the train station, your neighbor, Mr. Swift, was kind enough to bring us here."

Rosalynn glanced up and found Lone Wolf staring at the food

on the table. She forgot she hadn't cleaned up after the noon meal. "Please, forgive me, Mr. Larson. You must be starving after working all morning in the fields." Rosalynn grabbed a clean plate from the table. "I'm sorry, it isn't much, but there's no food in the kitchen. I'm afraid these are leftovers from our trip here on the train."

Rosalynn cut off several thick slices of bread from the loaf and stacked them on the plate. She then added several generous slabs of ham, along with a large wedge of cheese. Opening a jar of pickled eggs, she stabbed two eggs with a fork and piled them beside the ham. "I only have oatmeal cookies for dessert."

Rosalynn placed the heaping plate in front of Lone Wolf, but he pushed it away. She stubbornly pushed the plate of food back in front of him. Dorothy fixed them each a cup of tea and sat back down at the dining table.

"I will bring fresh milk for you tonight." Taking the ham, Lone Wolf placed it between the slices of bread.

"Thank you," Rosalynn replied. "That would be nice if you can spare the extra milk." She was happy that he had decided to eat, but was careful not to show it on her face. He was proud and might feel uncomfortable if she made an issue of it.

Lone Wolf shrugged. "I pour it to the hogs. It will be good that you take it."

"Pouring good milk to the hogs? Whatever for?" Rosalynn then remembered the soured milk on the porch. "Are you the one who left the pail of milk on the back porch?"

Lone Wolf nodded, and then swallowed the food in his mouth before continuing. "After Mike died, I brought fresh milk and meat to your sister every day. When I saw the milk and the rabbit still on the porch, I thought she had gone into town. When she did not return, I came into the house and found the note on the table."

Rosalynn shook her head in disgust. "Susan has never lived in a finer house than this. I can't believe she let it get in this condition. Was it because of the baby?"

"No, she has always been this way," said Lone Wolf.

"Well, it'll have to be scrubbed completely before I bring her children here to live with us."

Lone Wolf's dark brows darted together and he stared at Rosalynn, unflinching. "There is no need to clean the house. You will not be here long."

"What do you mean, we won't be here?" Rosalynn panicked. "We sold everything we owned for the tickets to come here. We have no home left in Missouri. No, we will stay here in Susan's house."

"This is not Susan's house. Our father willed the farm to Mike and me together. Now that Mike is gone, the farm is mine. You are welcome to stay until you make other arrangements, but you must leave soon. I will raise my brother's children here on the farm."

"You want to raise the children?" Rosalynn couldn't believe such a foolish notion.

"Of course I want my brother's children." Lone Wolf's smoldering eyes challenged Rosalynn.

"Well, I want my sister's children, and I will raise them in this house. I'm sure the minister will agree with me that they need to be with their mother's kin." Rosalynn felt her voice rise with agitation, but she didn't care. The gall of this man, to tell her she couldn't have her own flesh and blood!

"You think they should not be raised by a savage," Lone Wolf replied harshly, pushing the plate away and rising from the table.

Rosalynn flinched at his bluntness, but she couldn't avoid the dark eyes that bore through her. "No, Mr. Larson, that's not what I think. You are a man. Men, regardless of race, should leave child rearing to women. Women are more capable of raising children, the same as men are better at plowing fields than women."

Rosalynn could feel her heart pumping fast, but she refused to let Lone Wolf bully her. She had heard Indians respected bravery, and though she was terrified, she straightened her shoulders in an attempt to look brave.

Shaking his head, Lone Wolf declared, "We will take a trip into town tomorrow and talk with the minister. He is in charge of the children at this time."

"That would be fine with me, Mr. Larson," Rosalynn replied stiffly, but inwardly she felt a measure of relief. Surely a minister would realize that she was the best person to raise her niece and nephew. After all, she would raise the children as Christians, and as a woman she could make sure they felt wanted and loved.

"I will come for you after the noon meal. I need to work in the fields in the morning while it is still cool," Lone Wolf said brusquely.

"Whatever is convenient for you is fine with me," Rosalynn stated, trying to make her voice sound light.

"There is food in the cellar and meat in the smokehouse. Take what you need while you are here."

"That's very kind of you, Mr. Larson, but we can take care of ourselves. We don't need your help." Refusing to meet his gaze, Rosalynn lifted her chin in defiance.

"I know that you do not need my help," Lone Wolf replied unyieldingly, "but you cleaned the kitchen. Consider it payment for your work."

Lone Wolf's dark eyes seemed to penetrate into Rosalynn's soul. Feeling a flutter in her stomach, she realized her apprehension wasn't just about Susan's children. There was something about this man. . . . Finally, she answered him, "I'll use the food only if you eat with us."

"I work long hours. I have food in my cabin."

Rosalynn started to protest, but Lone Wolf left before she had a chance to argue.

Once Lone Wolf was gone, Rosalynn turned to her aunt. "Aunt Dottie, what are we going to do now? Susan's husband committed suicide . . . Susan ran off with another man . . . Susan's children . . . no house . . ."

Dorothy clasped Rosalynn's hands in hers. "Everything will work out, dear, just have faith."

"Oh, auntie, what would I do without you?" Rosalynn exclaimed, pulling her into a hug. "Of course, the Lord will take care of us. I'm sure the minister will realize the children would be better off with us, and I'll seek legal advice about the ownership of the farm. Mr. Larson may be mistaken about Susan not having lawful rights. What judge is going to throw out two helpless women with four children?"

When Lone Wolf saw smoke coming from the farmhouse, he left the fields to investigate. Seeing the trunks outside the gate, he assumed that squatters had thought the place abandoned. He entered the house expecting to find the squatters making themselves at home. Instead, a skinny white woman dressed in his brother's old clothes attacked him with a broom.

As soon as the woman claimed to be Susan's sister, Lone Wolf knew that Susan must have had something to do with them being there. But she had never mentioned that her family was coming. *She was too busy planning her departure after the baby was born,* he thought bitterly.

When this woman, this Rosalynn, tried to comfort him, Lone Wolf felt that she was sincere. It was difficult for him to speak of his brother without feeling deep anguish. Ever since that terrible day when he found Mike dead in the barn, Lone Wolf had been alone. He had no one to share his grief, and he certainly would not show the white woman—a stranger—his grief.

Lone Wolf remembered the feel of Rosalynn's hand on his. Because he drew only disdain and fear from the white world, he was not accustomed to having a white woman touch him. Susan had beguiled Mike with sweet talk and feminine wiles. Was Rosalynn sincere or just crafty like her sister? *They are sisters, cut from the same blanket,* Lone Wolf thought.

Spending time alone with white women was a big gamble for an Indian. All they had to do was say that Lone Wolf had assaulted them, and the town of Peaceful would hang him. The wasichu had tricked him in the past, and he could not trust them. The white women must leave, Lone Wolf decided. Soon.

Red Cloud's warriors had left a bitter path of mistrust in Peaceful. It didn't matter to the wasichu that they had lied to his people and taken everything away from them, including their dignity. Now Red Cloud and his tribe lived on a reservation not fit to sustain a herd of goats, let alone a tribe of hungry people. There was no fight left in the old chief. He only wanted his people fed, clothed, and kept warm in the cold months. The old ways were gone along with the buffalo and their sacred grounds.

The sooner the white women accepted the fact that the farm was his, the faster they would leave. He would not give up Mike's children easily, either. The Great Spirit would not allow him to lose his brother and the children also. The Great Spirit was merciful.

———

When Rosalynn woke the next morning, she went to the back porch, where she found not only a pail of fresh milk, but also a string of fish and a basket of eggs. She strained the milk first, then cleaned the fish and put them in a bowl of cool water. They would have fish for dinner.

For breakfast, Rosalynn scrambled some eggs and fried the last of the ham they had brought with them. Then she cut thick slices of bread and toasted them on the top of the stove. Tomorrow they would have butter from the cream she skimmed from the milk. The best treat was the fresh milk; they hadn't had milk since they sold their cow to come to Minnesota.

Rosalynn wanted to tackle more of the house, but when she realized that Aunt Dorothy and the children were still exhausted from the day before, she agreed that they should all rest. As she soaked in a tub of hot, steaming water scented with Dorothy's rose water, Rosalynn thought about the events of the day before.

Lone Wolf had frightened her when she had first seen him standing there. He was well over six feet tall in his moccasin boots, and he had broad shoulders and a chest of iron. His hands were very large and masculine—not the hands of a banker or a river boat gambler, but rather the strong and calloused hands of a laborer.

Coarse, black hair hung to Lone Wolf's waist, and he wore a broad-rimmed hat with a single feather tied on the side with a strip of leather. With features sharp and finely proportioned, his striking visage left a vivid impression in Rosalynn's memory. The coppery skin, flawless and taunt over high cheekbones and a broad nose, and eyes like obsidian—dark and brilliant. His lips were full and yielding, and his voice deep and haunting. Lone Wolf was magnificent, ethereal, a soul from a different time and a different place.

Her heart ached for the handsome stranger. How would he and his kind survive in a world that didn't seem to want them? Would all mankind ever find a way to live in harmony?

After her bath, Rosalynn combed her long, nut-brown hair. As her hair dried, she dressed, choosing a simple calico frock made of sky blue fabric sprinkled with small red flowers. It was a bit faded but clean and freshly ironed, and the red belt she wore accentuated her small waist. She knew she was too thin—a scarecrow, Jeffery had often called her. Working long, hard hours on the farm had taken its toll on her health.

Once her hair was dry, Rosalynn combed it into a soft bun high up on her head, leaving tendrils curling along the nape of her neck. She pinned a red bow beneath the bun to help keep it in place. Her hair was naturally wavy and therefore difficult to manage, and if she had been young she would have left it down.

Rosalynn looked at her reflection in the mirror. Staring back at her were blue-green eyes in a heart-shaped face. Already, she saw wisps of hair falling from the bun. "What's the use?" she muttered.

By the time noon came, Rosalynn was ready for her trip into town. She made out a list and tucked it into her handbag. She explained to the children that Lone Wolf was an Indian, but they should not be frightened of him. Disappointed that he had missed meeting Lone Wolf the day before, Joshua refused to take a nap. He would nap after seeing his first real Indian.

When Rosalynn heard a knock on the back door, she quickly ran to answer it. The last thing she wanted was to have Lone Wolf bombarded by two pint-sized, quizzical children. She had already whacked him with a broom. Laughing at the remembrance, she flung open the door.

Standing tall and proud before her was Lone Wolf. Gone were the soiled work clothes and the wide-brimmed hat. He was wearing soft buckskins beautifully decorated with red, blue, white, and teal seed beads. On his feet were knee-high buckskin moccasins with fringe up the side and beaded work on the top of each foot. His blue-black hair was clean and damp and hung loosely to his waist. In place of the hat, he wore a leather thong around his forehead, tied in the back. He smelled fresh and clean with a hint of mint. He reminded Rosalynn of a wild animal . . . fearsome yet beautiful.

Looking into a face chiseled with generations of a proud race, Rosalynn was lost in his striking eyes. They were a warm brown, flecked with black, and surrounded with thick, black lashes. Never had she ever been so attracted to a man. What was this she felt for Lone Wolf?

Embarrassed by her own ogling, Rosalynn brought her hand to her throat, fearing that Lone Wolf would hear the pounding of her heart. Finally, she found her voice.

"Mr. Larson, please come in." She reached for his hand and pulled him into the kitchen.

"My name is Lone Wolf. My father was Mr. Larson." Lone Wolf eyed her intently.

Laughing, Rosalynn agreed to call him Lone Wolf. "You must call me Rosalynn, then. After all, it's only fair."

What's wrong with me? Am I flirting? she thought. She had never flirted before, not even when Jeffery was courting her. But around Lone Wolf she felt different—she felt free and uninhibited by the constraints of proper society. In fact, she suddenly felt happy for the first time in years.

Rosalynn thanked Lone Wolf for the food he had left earlier, but he didn't answer. He appeared to be deep in thought, so she decided that he must not have heard her. When she again thanked him for the food, Lone Wolf opened his eyes and mumbled something incoherent. He then quickly pointed to the fish soaking in a bowl of water on the counter. "You need to put the fish in the cellar. They will spoil in the heat."

Rosalynn felt her face redden. "I'm embarrassed to say I'm

afraid to go down to the cellar. After seeing a mouse scurry across the porch yesterday, well, I . . ." her voice trailed off.

Lone Wolf's brows darted up with curiosity. "That is hard to believe. A woman who attacks Indians with brooms is afraid of a mouse?"

Rosalynn watched a smile slowly melt across Lone Wolf's lips. The even, white teeth against bronze skin were enough to make any woman swoon, and Rosalynn felt herself blush again. "Spiders . . . there may be spiders, too," she breathed out in almost a whisper.

Lone Wolf's smile broadened and his brilliant brown eyes grew darker, captivating Rosalynn's senses. Opening the cellar door, he retrieved a lantern that hung just inside, then grabbed a match from a box on the floor and struck it against the door jam. He lit the wick and stepped aside so that Rosalynn could look into the cellar. She peeked around the corner and was relieved to see that the lantern lit the entire room below.

Lone Wolf went down the stairs first. "I see no mice or spiders," he called up to her. "I think you will be quite safe."

Rosalynn heard a hint of amusement in his voice. She looked above her head to make sure a rogue spider wasn't lurking in the shadows. Exhaling a deep sigh, she ventured down the stairs, holding up her skirts to keep from tripping. Lone Wolf reached out to take her hand. When their fingers met, Rosalynn felt a surge of excitement bolt through her body. She shuddered, then mentally scolded herself.

The air below ground was downright chilly, and Rosalynn was grateful for the chance to live in a house that had a cellar. She had always wanted a cellar on the farm in Missouri, but Jeffery had refused to dig one.

"There are still some potatoes, onions, carrots, and cabbages left from last fall. Over in that corner are pumpkins and squash.

Your sister did not cook much."

Along the wall were empty shelves. Lone Wolf explained that the shelves were for butter, cream, or whatever else that required a cool environment. Below the shelves were crocks of lard and molasses.

"Do you think you will be brave enough to come down here when I am not with you?" he asked.

"I think so," Rosalynn said with a smile.

"Good. If you go up first, you can hand me the fish, then the milk and the eggs. They will keep longer down here."

After the food was safe in the cellar, Lone Wolf closed the door. "Are you ready to go into town, Roz-lynn?"

Her name sounded foreign coming from his lips, but Rosalynn felt her heart skip a beat and her pulse quicken. When he said her name, it sounded like sweet music to her wounded soul. *Father, this is so strange. Why do I feel so giddy inside?* "Yes, Lone Wolf, I'm ready. I just need to fetch my shawl and handbag."

———

While Lone Wolf waited for Rosalynn, he noticed again how clean and tidy she had made the kitchen. It was obvious that Rosalynn was better at housework than her sister. In fact, he was beginning to see many differences between them.

Lone Wolf had been surprised by Rosalynn's carefree spirit when she greeted him earlier. His eyes had trailed from her rosy red lips to her smoldering, turquoise eyes. Her beautiful, alabaster skin and cherry-tinted cheeks captivated him. A dirty cloth didn't hide her chestnut hair today, and he had to fight the urge to touch the wisps that danced around her sweet face, teasing him. She was dressed in a simple frock, but her womanly frame needed no extra adornment.

Lone Wolf was speechless when Rosalynn gave him

permission to call her by her Christian name. Never had a white woman given him permission to speak to her, let alone address her so informally. His heart wanted to soar, but the pain of the wasichu burned deep into his soul. *Great Spirit, speak to me. Is this white woman my destiny? I asked for a mate, but my heart is afraid to love a wasichu. What good can come from such a union? You are all powerful and good. If You want this woman to be my mate, You must show me the way to her heart.*

A loud ruckus from the front house and then the sound of running feet interrupted Lone Wolf's thoughts. Two rambunctious children came zipping around the corner from the dining room to the kitchen. When they saw him, they came to a screeching halt. Four curious blue-green eyes stared at him.

"Are you really an Indian?" the little boy asked first.

"You nice?" the little girl chimed in, staying hidden behind the boy.

"Okay, you two, where are your manners? Lone Wolf, I would like to introduce my children to you. This little guy is Joshua," Rosalynn said, placing her hands on her son's shoulders. "And this little minx is Hannah." Rosalynn picked her daughter up and swung her onto her hip.

Lone Wolf stared from Rosalynn to the children. Rosalynn had children? Where was the fortunate husband? Lone Wolf tried to put his feelings aside and looked at the children. They both had their mother's eyes and dark brown hair. "How!" Lone Wolf held up his hand in greeting. He felt like a cigar Indian he saw once in St. Paul.

"He really is an Indian, Ma!" Joshua couldn't contain his excitement. "Do you have a bow and arrows? Can you teach me to shoot an arrow? Do you have a horse—"

"Whoa, Joshua," Rosalynn interrupted her son with a giggle. "You're going to frighten Lone Wolf."

"Indians don't get scared, Ma. They're braver than anything."

Lone Wolf clearly had to struggle to maintain a serious face. "Indians are brave. We only fear women with brooms."

Rosalynn laughed. Handing Hannah to Dorothy, Rosalynn placed her shawl over her shoulders and picked up her handbag. "I don't know how long we'll be, Aunt Dorothy. The fish is in the cellar if you decide to start dinner. Is there anything you need in town?"

"No, dear, I don't need anything," Dorothy replied, then smiled at the children. "But if you happen to run across any peppermint sticks . . ."

Rosalynn chuckled as she hugged the children and her aunt goodbye. "I'll see what I can do about the peppermint sticks if you two behave for Aunt Dorothy."

Lone Wolf had the wagon hitched and ready when Rosalynn came out the back door. He helped her onto the wagon, then walked to the other side and climbed in next to her. "I smell roses."

Blushing, Rosalynn explained, "I bathed in rose water. Aunt Dottie makes women's toiletries from rose petals."

"I like it," Lone Wolf stated as he picked up the reins.

Chapter Four

Lone Wolf couldn't concentrate on the road, not with Rosalynn sitting so close to him. Glancing sideways, he studied her profile and then turned his attention back to the road. On the second glance, he noticed that she sat stiffly at his side, hands in her lap, clutching her handbag.

She wore a straw bonnet adorned with tiny blue and white dried flowers, shielding her fair complexion from the afternoon sun. A white lace shawl draped gracefully across her shoulders.

Why did she not mention yesterday that she was married with children? *Great Spirit, what a joke You play on me. I asked for a mate and You brought me a wasichu who is married. I am confused, Great One. My heart tells me Rosalynn is my destiny, but this cannot be.*

Lone Wolf glanced again at Rosalynn, his mind in turmoil. "Roz-lynn, you did not mention yesterday that you had children."

"Our first meeting wasn't exactly under normal circumstances," Rosalynn replied with a gentle smile on her soft lips.

Lone Wolf had to admit she was right. There wasn't anything normal regarding the events that had taken place in the last twenty-four hours. "You did not mention you were married, either. Why is it you came here without your man?" Lone Wolf knew he was being overly personal, but he didn't care. He was not one for white man's fancy speeches and intrigue. If one wanted answers, one needed to ask questions.

When Rosalynn didn't answer, Lone Wolf cast her a perplexed look. The rosy glow had faded from her cheeks. Her angst-ridden eyes darted anxiously to her lap, where she twisted the strings on her handbag.

"Roz-lynn, are you ill?" Heaving on the reins, he pulled the team to a stop. "Do you need to rest? You are very pale."

Rosalynn shook her head in short, jerky motions. "No, I'm fine. Please, let's just continue on to town."

Something was obviously wrong, but Lone Wolf complied with Rosalynn's wishes and urged the horses into a brisk walk. She looked frightened and reminded him of a wild doe—alert and ready to spring from danger. Was she frightened of him? Perhaps he was merely a savage to her after all.

They entered Peaceful on the west end of town, where the train station was located. As Lone Wolf drove the wagon over the tracks onto Main Street, Rosalynn could see the livery and the feed store on a side street to the left.

Peaceful was larger than Rosalynn had imagined. In the first block alone she saw a telegraph office, a dry goods store, a bakery, and a large mercantile. On the left side of Main Street stood a small café, a millinery shop, a boarding house, and a small redbrick schoolhouse. On the corner of Main and First Street was a quaint little church.

Lone Wolf pointed out the café and the mercantile and explained that friends of his owned them. Surprised at how busy the town was, Rosalynn looked around with great interest at the horses and buckboards that lined the streets and the people that filled the boardwalk. On the north end of town, fancy carriages and buggies lined the finer establishments.

Rosalynn noticed that Lone Wolf and his passenger drew a lot of attention from patrons walking along the boardwalk, and she smiled as they drove down the block. Children laughed and played along the street. Groups of boys huddled together playing marbles, and little girls used long sticks to roll hoops down the side streets. It seemed to be a nice town—a good place to raise a family.

After turning left at the church onto First Street and then left again onto Lilac Lane, Lone Wolf pulled the wagon to a stop in front of a charming white house with a picket fence. The exterior of the house was immaculate, and Rosalynn noted the budding flowers lining the well-manicured lawn and walkway. Lilac trees encircled the yard, and Rosalynn knew that in the spring the purple blossoms would permeate the air with a wonderful scent.

"This is where Reverend and Mrs. Baker live," Lone Wolf explained as he set the brake and jumped down from the wagon seat.

Rosalynn started to climb from the wagon, but Lone Wolf caught her around the waist and swung her to the ground. His large hands spanned her slender waist and lifted her as though she were a small child. Rosalynn could feel her cheeks redden when Lone Wolf plunked her down in front of him. Gone was the teasing she had seen when he came into the house earlier that afternoon. Instead, his countenance reflected a gentleness no man had ever shown her before.

"Thank you, Lone Wolf," Rosalynn managed to say in a hushed tone. What was this feeling—admiration? She felt starved for attention and thought herself silly to conjure up fantasies about

Lone Wolf when he was merely being kind. *Get hold of yourself, Rosalynn. Don't dream of things that can never be.*

"Are you ready to meet your niece and nephew, Roz-lynn?" Lone Wolf's words broke the trance, his voice washing over her like a caress.

Rosalynn couldn't trust herself to speak, so she nodded her head in response. As Lone Wolf escorted her up the sidewalk, she noticed that his face looked pinched. Was he afraid that he might lose his niece and nephew? Rosalynn shook off her concern for him, knowing she had to focus on doing what was best for her sister's children.

They stepped onto a little lattice porch with white wicker furniture that looked inviting and cozy. A rag doll, a spinning top, and some blocks lay in a small toy chest in one corner of the porch. Lone Wolf rapped on the door, which was soon opened by a middle-aged woman with graying hair. She wore a burgundy day dress with rows of white lace at the throat. The dress's three-quarter-length sleeves were adorned with wide rows of lace and trimmed with burgundy satin ribbons. As she stared at the beautiful dress, Rosalynn felt frumpy and tried to smooth the wrinkles from her simple, homemade frock.

"Why, Mr. Larson, I wasn't expecting you today. You usually visit the children on Saturdays." She then noticed Rosalynn for the first time. "Oh my, I didn't see you brought a friend. You didn't sneak off and get married, did you?" The woman's mouth broke out in a smile, and her china blue eyes twinkled with mischief.

Lone Wolf gave Rosalynn a smoldering gaze as he clasped her elbow. "I am sorry for visiting unannounced, Mrs. Baker. This charming lady is Mrs. Roz-lynn McAllister. She is Susan's sister. We were hoping to visit Gretchen and the baby."

Rosalynn overlooked Mrs. Baker's comment about marriage and was glad that Lone Wolf ignored it as well. Instead, she gave

Mrs. Baker a polite smile and extended her hand in greeting. "It's a pleasure to meet you, Mrs. Baker. I can't express my gratitude enough to you and your husband for caring for my niece and nephew."

"You're quite welcome, Mrs. McAllister," Mrs. Baker said warmly. "It's our Christian duty, and our pleasure, to help those in need. Please come in, both of you." The older woman guided Rosalynn and Lone Wolf into an elegant parlor.

"I hope our visit hasn't inconvenienced you, Mrs. Baker. If it's not a good time, we can call back later."

"Not at all, Mrs. McAllister. The children are napping, but we can get acquainted over tea until they wake." Mrs. Baker's warm smile was reassuring. "Please sit down," she offered, ringing a small bell.

Rosalynn chose a wing-backed chair with embroidered roses in deep, vibrant greens and shades of pink. Rich mahogany furniture adorned the room. Glancing around the parlor, Rosalynn admired the warm greens and soft rose colors, and the creamy beige wallpaper dotted with tiny rosebuds.

Soon, a pretty, blonde-haired, blue-eyed girl of about sixteen entered the room. "Hilda, please tell cook we need tea and scones for four," Mrs. Baker said. "Then I want you to run over to the church and tell Reverend Baker we have guests."

"Yes, ma'am," Hilda replied, giving a little curtsy before dashing from the room.

"She's a good girl. We hired Hilda as a nanny for the children, but she helps the cook and housekeeper as well." Mrs. Baker smiled. "So, Mrs. McAllister, you are Mrs. Larson's sister. She never mentioned she had family the entire time she lived in Peaceful."

"That doesn't surprise me, Mrs. Baker. Susan was always a little self-absorbed." Rosalynn tried to keep the resentment from her voice, but her laugh sounded loud and forced. She didn't know how much she should tell the Bakers about Susan, so she prayed for guidance.

Mrs. Baker directed her attention to Lone Wolf. "How's the planting coming along, Mr. Larson?"

"Slow without Mike's help. I have the oats and the barley planted, but I still need to plant the corn and potatoes. We planted alfalfa last winter and it is coming up now."

"That's wonderful. Are you going to hire out for help now that you're alone?" Mrs. Baker's seemed concerned.

"There is no one in Peaceful who would agree to work for a half-breed savage." Lone Wolf responded with a touch of bitterness. "The farmers I do know are busy planting their own crops."

"Perhaps if you dressed like us and cut your hair, you would be more accepted by the residents of Peaceful," Mrs. Baker suggested. Then, turning to Rosalynn, she asked, "What do you think, Mrs. McAllister?"

Rosalynn fastened her eyes on Lone Wolf. He sat taut, his back not touching the chair. His proud face showed no emotion, and Rosalynn wondered what he was thinking. She turned to look at the reverend's wife.

"Well, Mrs. Baker," Rosalynn's voice was slow and deliberate as she chose her words with care, "I believe a person should please himself instead of trying to appease hypocrites who judge others." Rosalynn looked at Lone Wolf and blushed when he winked at her. "I wouldn't have any respect for Lone Wolf if he dressed like us and cut his hair against his own wishes. In fact," she turned back to Mrs. Baker, "I like Lone Wolf just as he is. I've never met a more considerate person in my life, except for my Aunt Dorothy."

Rosalynn paused and then continued, relying on the Holy

Ghost for guidance. "If people are going to judge Lone Wolf by the clothes he wears and his long hair, I think they need to read the Bible more. The Bible clearly states that God made us in His image. I would assume that includes all races, including Indians." Then she smiled and asked, "What do you think, Mrs. Baker?"

"I don't know how my wife feels," a male voice interjected, "but I agree with you wholeheartedly, young woman."

Startled, Rosalynn turned. Standing in the archway was a short, chubby man with gray hair—what little he had left. His blue eyes twinkled when he smiled, and Rosalynn decided that all he'd need to be Santa Claus was a beard and a red suit.

Reverend Baker strode into the parlor, grabbed Lone Wolf's outstretched hand, and shook it profusely while he pounded Lone Wolf on the back with his other hand. He then walked over to Rosalynn, took her hand in his, and gave it an affectionate pat. "I don't know who you are, young woman, but I'm Reverend Baker. You just summed up an hour sermon for me in about two minutes flat," he guffawed. "It seems some folks around here need a good dose of humility, and I think you're just the one to give it to them."

"Really, Mr. Baker," Mrs. Baker reprimanded, clearly embarrassed. "For pity's sake, calm down. I was merely trying to help Mr. Larson be more accepted in Peaceful." Her nervous fingers fluttered over the lace at her throat.

"Lone Wolf isn't the one who should change, my dear. It's the hypocrites this young lady spoke of who need help." Reverend Baker was obviously passionate about the subject.

"The young woman has a name, Reverend Baker," Mrs. Baker commented dryly. "Her name is Mrs. McAllister, and she's Mrs. Larson's sister."

"Welcome to Peaceful, Mrs. McAllister," Reverend Baker said with a grin. "I can always use a fresh recruit to proclaim the good word." Then, winking, he added, "I also need a good, strong voice for the choir."

Rosalynn smiled in response. She liked the reverend very much, even if he was a bit overzealous.

Hilda brought the tea and scones and placed the tray in front of Mrs. Baker. The girl curtsied and then scurried from the room.

Reverend Baker sat next to his wife on a rose-colored velour sofa. As he sipped the tea, he studied Lone Wolf and Rosalynn. Rosalynn could feel his eyes upon her and wondered what he was going to say next.

"Are you here to visit the children, Mrs. McAllister? Or are you here for more important matters concerning Mrs. Larson's children?"

Rosalynn replaced the fragile teacup on the saucer and held it in her lap. "Both, actually, Reverend Baker. I would like to raise my sister's children. I can provide a loving home for them and see that they are raised as Christians." Rosalynn bit her lower lip, examining the reverend's expression. *Please, Lord, soften his heart.*

Reverend Baker placed his teacup on the table and leaned against the back of the sofa. He clasped his hands in front of him and twiddled his thumbs as though in deep thought. Then leaning forward, he spoke. "That's what I thought you'd say, and I respect your desire to take them in and raise them as your own. It's commendable of you. They are sweet children and need to be placed in a permanent home as soon as possible."

The reverend paused and sat back against the sofa. Rosalynn could feel her heart pumping fast. Instinct told her that the reverend was trying to cushion her for bad news.

"However, I do have some distressing news, Mrs. McAllister. I wrote to the circuit judge about the placement of the children. I explained to Judge Warner that Lone Wolf wanted the children and was trying to prepare a home for them."

Rosalynn's heart fluttered with trepidation. *I'm not going to get discouraged, Father. I have faith in Thee to do what's best for all of us.*

Reverend Baker offered Rosalynn a kind smile, then paused as if to draw strength from within. "I received a letter from the judge yesterday. He'll be in Peaceful on Thursday and will consider all applicants desiring to adopt the children. He'll let me know his decision before he leaves town on Friday."

Rosalynn's throat felt tight. "You mentioned applicants, Reverend Baker. Am I to understand there are other people interested in raising Mike and Susan's children?"

"Yes, that's correct, Mrs. McAllister," the reverend answered sympathetically. "There are several families in Peaceful willing to take on the responsibility of raising them."

Rosalynn looked at Lone Wolf and wondered what was he thinking. Was he just as disheartened as she was?

Lone Wolf then asked, "Do you think the judge will consider family before strangers, Reverend?"

"I would imagine he'd choose family first. Judge Warner is a fair and just man." Reverend Baker smiled. "Well, you know that, Lone Wolf. You've known him since you were a child. We need to have faith that the children will live where God wants them. He works in mysterious ways and with various instruments." Reverend Baker looked at Lone Wolf and then at Rosalynn. "I'm trying my best to be honest with both of you."

"What other issues will Judge Warner feel are important, Reverend Baker?" Rosalynn asked.

"I don't think you have anything to fear, Mrs. McAllister," declared Mrs. Baker. "You appear to be a good Christian, married woman. I'm sure you and your husband can provide for the children. Would you raise them here in Peaceful? By the way, where do you live, Mrs. McAllister?"

Rosalynn's mind raced. Married? They thought she was a married woman! What would they think of her when they found out she was divorced?

Rosalynn tried to focus her thoughts and calm herself. There would be time later to think about the mess that she was about to create. She pasted a smile on her face and answered Mrs. Baker. "No plans have been set yet, Mrs. Baker."

Rosalynn didn't feel like she was speaking a falsehood, since they really hadn't made any plans yet. *Lord, don't forsake me. My life is confusing right now and I have no answers, only faith in Thee. I'm relying on Thee to help me make the right decisions.*

"Well, enough speculating," Reverend Baker's words broke through Rosalynn's thoughts. "We'll leave the matter in the Lord's hands. He knows what's best."

Rosalynn smiled at Reverend Baker, wondering if he could read her mind.

Everyone seemed to be in deep thought when a small child stumbled into the parlor carrying a rag doll. Rubbing her sleep-filled eyes, she started for Mrs. Baker.

"Gretchen."

The little girl turned when she heard her name. All of a sudden, her bright blue eyes lit up and a grin spread across her small features. "Uncle Gabe!" she squealed, running pell-mell toward Lone Wolf.

Lone Wolf smiled at his niece as his outstretched arms grabbed her and tossed her into the air. Gretchen laughed with delight, begging for more. Rosalynn had never seen Lone Wolf so happy. His grim expression changed into a smile and his chocolate brown eyes filled with affection. It was clear that he and his young niece were crazy about each other.

Reverend and Mrs. Baker excused themselves. "We'll see if

the baby is awake," Mrs. Baker said with a smile as she closed the parlor doors.

Lone Wolf settled his niece on his lap. Gretchen wrapped her arms tightly around his neck, the rag doll forgotten.

"I missed you, Uncle Gabe. I wanna go home with you. Take me home, please," Gretchen begged, her eyes misty with tears.

Rosalynn's heart nearly broke as she witnessed the devotion between uncle and niece. Tears slipped from her eyes. The small waif didn't just like Lone Wolf; she *loved* him. Any fool could see the bond between them.

How did they become so close when Susan hated Lone Wolf? Rosalynn wondered. Regardless, he would make an excellent guardian for his brother's children,

"I'm sorry, tiny rabbit, not today, but soon," Lone Wolf said tenderly. "The Great Spirit knows how much my heart cries for you and the little one." Lone Wolf gently brushed the golden curls from the petite face. "I brought you a surprise."

"What, what, Uncle Gabe?" Cheered up in an instant, Gretchen bounced on Lone Wolf's knee excitedly.

Lone Wolf turned Gretchen so that she faced Rosalynn. Rosalynn offered an affable smile. "Hello, Gretchen."

Gretchen's brows crinkled with confusion, and she turned to Lone Wolf.

"This is your aunt Roz-lynn, Gretchen. She has come a long way to see you and the little one."

Gretchen frowned at Rosalynn again and then at Lone Wolf. "You married a wasichu, Uncle Gabe."

Lone Wolf laughed aloud.

"What's a wasichu?" Rosalynn asked.

Lone Wolf smirked as he watched Rosalynn's face turn crimson. "Wasichu means 'white man' in the Lakota language. In this case, 'white woman.'" Looking at Gretchen affectionately, he explained, "Your aunt Roz-lynn is not my wife, tiny rabbit. She is your mother's sister."

Gretchen's eyes widened as she desperately clung to Lone Wolf. "I don't like her, Uncle Gabe! Make her go away!"

"Shh," Lone Wolf soothed. "Do not be frightened, Gretchen. Roz-lynn is nothing like your mother. She will not harm you, I promise."

Rosalynn felt the meaning behind Lone Wolf's words, and she knew he would protect Gretchen at all costs. *I knew Lone Wolf was special. Father, why couldn't Jeffery love Joshua and Hannah like Lone Wolf loves Gretchen?*

"Darling, your uncle is right. I would never harm you or your baby brother. I love children. In fact, I have a son and a daughter. They are your cousins. Won't you give us a chance to get to know you?" Rosalynn smiled at the child and offered her hand in friendship.

Gretchen looked at Lone Wolf as if seeking reassurance. He smiled at her and gave her a gentle push with his knee. "Go see your aunt Roz-lynn, tiny rabbit."

The young girl twined her fingers together as she slowly approached Rosalynn. Head down, eyes on her fingers, she stopped just within her aunt's reach.

Rosalynn reached for her niece and cautiously wrapped her arms around the child, closing her eyes in a silent prayer of thanks. After several seconds, Gretchen put her little arms around Rosalynn's neck.

When the embrace ended, Gretchen smiled shyly at her aunt. Head tilted down, blue eyes glancing over long lashes, Gretchen murmured, "You smell good."

Rosalynn laughed softly, opened her handbag, and removed a small heart-shaped bottle and drew the purse strings closed. "You smell roses, Gretchen." Rosalynn opened Gretchen's hand

and placed the bottle on her palm. "Here's a bottle of rose water for you."

Gretchen gasped. "For me? For my very own?" Her eyes were huge and expressive. "How do I put it on?"

Rosalynn removed the lid and gently placed Gretchen's finger over the opening. She turned the bottle upside down and then upright. Rosalynn took Gretchen's finger and dabbed the rose water behind each ear.

"You must promise me, Gretchen, to ask permission from Mrs. Baker before opening the rose water," Rosalynn cautioned as she replaced the lid.

"I promise, Auntie Rosalynn! Thank you for giving it to me." Gretchen hugged her aunt and ran to Lone Wolf.

"Smell me, Uncle Gabe!" Gretchen demanded, stretching her neck until Lone Wolf took a good sniff.

"Mmm." Lone Wolf smiled, his eyes locked on Rosalynn's. "I have something for you also." Opening a leather pouch, he removed a circular wooden object about six inches long. He brought the object to his lips, positioned his fingers over the tiny holes, and blew into one end.

As she heard the sound of the hand-carved wooden flute, Gretchen squealed and jumped up and down. She placed the rose water in the pocket of her pinafore and held her hand out for the flute. She blew into it and a faint melodious sound escaped, so she tried it again with more force. This time a long, harmonious note filled the room. Gretchen then placed her fingers over the holes, pumping her fingers up and down as she blew into the flute.

"I'm playing a song!" Gretchen announced with glee.

Mrs. Baker knocked lightly on the parlor door before entering with a small bundle in her arms. "I'm sorry I took so long. The baby was wet and Hilda needed to bathe and redress him." With great care, she placed the baby in Rosalynn's arms. "He doesn't have a name," the woman said tersely. "I'll be happy when the judge makes a decision regarding who is to raise these two little darlings," she continued. "They deserve better than what they've been through." Then she gave Rosalynn an anxious smile and added, "I'm sorry, Mrs. McAllister. That wasn't a Christian thing to say."

"No apology necessary, Mrs. Baker. I know what Susan is like."

Mrs. Baker smiled and then left the parlor, leaving Rosalynn to coo over the baby. He was alert and bright-eyed. Both children had fair complexions, blonde hair, and blue eyes.

As she studied the baby, Rosalynn felt contempt for her sister. How could Susan abandon her beautiful children? *Please forgive me, Father, for being judgmental. I pray Susan realizes what course her life is taking and desires to change.*

When Rosalynn handed the baby to Lone Wolf, the baby pulled on his uncle's long, raven hair and played with the beaded fringe on his jacket. Lone Wolf's countenance was soft with unspoken emotion. Rosalynn knew it must be hard for him to look at his brother's children knowing that Mike was gone from this world. *Oh, Father dear, is there any way Lone Wolf and I can both win guardianship? Please help the judge to make the right choice!*

———

Leaving Gretchen and the baby brought great pain to Lone Wolf. He despised Susan for the hurt she had caused Mike and his mother, and for her neglect of her children. It was a blessing that she left, because now Gretchen and the baby would have a chance at happiness and loving care.

On more than one occasion, Reverend Baker had explained to Lone Wolf that God didn't want His children to hate one another—that he should forgive Susan and pray for her. But he found it difficult to pray for someone who caused so much devastation for those whom she should have watched over and protected.

When Rosalynn defended him to Mrs. Baker, Lone Wolf felt stunned. He knew Mrs. Baker didn't mean to sound condescending, and that it was just her way of trying to help. However, when Rosalynn came to his defense, Lone Wolf's heart leaped with joy. He felt that Rosalynn could see into the deep recesses of his heart as if it were a window. How could a wasichu understand a Lakota's spirit so well? He admired Rosalynn and had to keep reminding himself that she was a married woman.

"I am hungry," Lone Wolf stated as he turned the wagon towards First Street. "Are you hungry, Roz-lynn?"

Rosalynn nodded. "Yes, I do believe I am hungry. I was so nervous about meeting Gretchen and the baby that I couldn't eat much this morning."

"I knew something was bothering you. You did not look well earlier. I was afraid you were frightened to be with me alone."

Rosalynn gasped. Her touch was as gentle as a wisp of air on Lone Wolf's arm. "I'm sorry, Lone Wolf, if I gave you that impression. It's odd, for I don't know you very well, but I feel I could trust you with my life."

Lone Wolf smiled with relief. He looked into Rosalynn's sweet face and saw no deception. "I would never let any harm come to you, Roz-lynn. You are a kindred spirit."

"Thank you, Lone Wolf."

Lone Wolf turned onto Main Street and headed the wagon to the south end of town. He glanced at Rosalynn and watched her mouth melt into a smile. His heart beat faster and his breath caught. She was indeed a beautiful woman.

Lone Wolf stopped the team in front of a small café and jumped from the wagon. "There is a rich man's restaurant at the north end of town, but they do not allow Indians to eat there."

Rosalynn cast a smile at Lone Wolf as he came to help her down. "Surely you jest, Lone Wolf. You shouldn't tease about something so serious.

"It is no joke, Roz-lynn." Lone Wolf said earnestly. "I eat at the café. It's small, but the food is very good. The owners, Todd and Arlene, are my friends."

Rosalynn looked down at Lone Wolf. "Well," she declared as he lifted her from the wagon, "I shall never eat at the rich man's restaurant, as you call it! I don't care how fancy it is. I'd rather eat at your friends' cafe."

Lone Wolf frowned. "Because Todd and Arlene are former slaves, most of the residents will not eat there."

Rosalynn smoothed her skirt. "Then we shall give them our patronage. It doesn't matter what color their skin is. We're all God's children, aren't we?"

Lone Wolf watched in astonishment as Rosalynn marched toward the café, her back ramrod straight and her head held high. He couldn't help but admire her conviction.

Rosalynn looked around the quaint little café. "I have to admit it's nicer than I expected."

Lone Wolf followed her gaze. The café was small but clean, and it seemed homey with its freshly starched white curtains and yellow-checked tablecloths.

"Lone Wolf, what brings you to town? It's not Saturday," a man wearing an apron called out.

"I missed Arlene's cooking," Lone Wolf responded. He escorted Rosalynn to a table by a window and pulled a chair out for her, then waited for her to sit before choosing a chair across from her.

The man hurried to their table carrying two glasses of water, two menus slung under his arm. "You've got the place to yourselves. Dinner's over and it's too early for supper. We still have some of today's special left if you're interested. It's chicken and dumplings."

"Thank you, Todd. Please give us a minute to decide." Then Lone Wolf motioned Todd back. "Before you leave, Todd, meet Mrs. McAllister. She may be moving to Peaceful."

"Glad to meet you, Mrs. McAllister. I was hoping you were hitched to this old army scout, but I guess you're taken." Todd laughed, tossing his head toward Lone Wolf. "I met Lone Wolf during the war. He was a scout for the north. When I settled down and jumped the broom with Arlene, I was hoping Lone Wolf would do the same."

"Jumped the broom?" Rosalynn inquired, grinning at Lone Wolf as he squirmed in his chair.

"Married," Todd said with a wink. "Slaves jump a broom and that makes them married. Arlene and I moved to Peaceful after the war. There wasn't anything for us in the south, and Lone Wolf was nice enough to loan us the money to buy the café." Todd's face grew serious. "Some folks here don't cotton to blacks, but it's like that everywhere. The immigrants treat us real nice, though."

"Well, I'm sure we'll be friends if I decide to stay in Peaceful," Rosalynn replied. Then she laughed. "I've never been on the society list in the past, and I'm sure I won't be here."

After Todd left, Rosalynn studied the menu. "What can you recommend? Everything sounds good."

"Everything is delicious. Arlene is a good cook," Lone Wolf answered, and then took a drink of water. His thoughts drifted to Todd's comment. He was the second person to ask if Rosalynn was his wife. Rosalynn was beyond his reach in many ways, but at least he had today. He would cherish the memories.

Todd returned to their table carrying a small china teapot, a cup, and a pot of honey. "Here's some hot water for your Injun tea. How about you, Mrs. McAllister? Can I get you something to drink?"

Rosalynn thought a minute. "Do you have any lemonade?"

"Sure do." Todd grinned from ear to ear.

"Wonderful. I'll take a tall glass of lemonade." Then handing Todd the menu, she said, "I think I'll try your wife's chicken and dumplings. My dumplings never turn out right."

"Arlene was the cook for a large plantation in South Carolina. She can cook the best chicken and dumplings you ever tasted. They're so light and fluffy they'll melt in your mouth."

"You do not have to convince me," Lone Wolf said. "I want the fried chicken with mashed potatoes."

Todd turned toward Rosalyn. "Arlene makes the best fried chicken, too. She gets a good scald every time. What's funny is that fried chicken, and chicken and dumplings, was slave food. The white folks wouldn't touch it until they were near starving during the war. Eat slave food?" Todd snorted, then left for the kitchen.

"The only problem with eating here is listening to Todd brag about his woman," Lone Wolf chuckled.

"I heard that, Injun Scout," Todd bellowed from across the room. "You're just jealous I got a woman and you don't."

Lone Wolf laughed. "They are very happy . . . here," he said, pointing to his heart.

"Well, there's certainly no sin in that!" Rosalynn smiled warmly. "It's nice they can overcome the pain they've suffered in the past and start a new life."

"They are very happy to be free from bondage. They overlook many things."

"Bondage comes in many forms," Rosalynn replied, her eyes cast down.

"Are you in bondage, Roz-lynn?" Lone Wolf leaned closer,

keeping his voice low so that Todd couldn't hear.

Rosalynn's bit her lower lip.

"Do not answer me, Roz-lynn. When you are ready, you will tell me what troubles you."

Lone Wolf smiled at Rosalynn and was relieved when she smiled back. He removed from his waist a leather pouch decorated with beads and fringe, then opened it. He pinched some fragrant substance between his fingers and dropped it in the teapot.

As the concoction brewed, Rosalynn drew in a deep breath. "There's mint in the tea, isn't there?"

"Yes," Lone Wolf answered softly, happy to see Rosalynn herself again. "Among other herbs in nature."

"It smells good," Rosalynn remarked, then thanked Todd as he placed a glass of lemonade on the table.

Lone Wolf let the tea steep a few minutes, then poured some of the brew into a cup through a tea strainer. He took a dollop of honey and stirred it into the tea. Tasting the tea, he smiled. "Would you like to try it, Roz-lynn?" He didn't know if she would drink from his cup.

Without hesitating, Rosalynn took a sip from his cup. Her brows raised in surprise. "It's good. I can taste chamomile, lemon balm, and mint."

"You know the herbs of the earth."

"A little. I've helped Aunt Dottie with some of her infusions. Have you tried lemonade?" Rosalynn asked with a quizzical expression on her face.

"No, Roz-lynn." He, wrinkled his nose.

Rosalynn laughed and pushed her glass toward him. "Try it, it's good."

"No."

"That's not fair, I tried your tea."

'No."

"'Fraidy cat!"

With a reputation to uphold, Lone Wolf finally took a big gulp of the lemonade. The minute the tart juice hit his tongue, the taste buds seemed to explode in his mouth. He couldn't spit it out, not in front of the laughing Rosalynn. Lone Wolf had no choice; he had to swallow the stuff. His eyes began to water and his face screwed up into a twisted pucker.

"How can you drink such a sour concoction?" Lone Wolf breathed out laboriously, then gulped down some water to wash the taste from his mouth.

"Can't handle it, eh?" Rosalynn laughed until her sides ached.

"You tried to poison me, Roz-lynn!" Lone Wolf laughed back.

Todd brought their meals, giving them a curious look. "I don't know what you're doing, Mrs. McAllister, but I haven't heard Lone Wolf laugh so much since I've known him. It's about time he loosened up a little."

———

Todd was right. The dumplings were light and fluffy, and the sample of fried chicken Lone Wolf shared with her was tender and moist with a crispy coating. The potatoes and chicken gravy were creamy and buttery. But the best part of the meal was sharing it together.

Rosalynn's thoughts drifted to the man in front of her. He was so kind to Gretchen and the baby boy. He helped Todd and his wife buy the café. Was there no end to his goodness? *Why didn't I meet Lone Wolf before Jeffery, Lord? He could have been my children's father. Would Lone Wolf have married a wasichu? I'll never know now,* she thought with regret, glancing at Lone Wolf.

Chapter Five

As they left the café, Lone Wolf asked Rosalynn where she wanted to go next. He watched her glance down Main Street, then noticed several people stopping to stare at them both. When he was alone, people would either watch him carefully out of the corner of their eyes or just pretend he wasn't there, but he wasn't used to having them stop and point. Clearly, it was because of the beautiful white woman on his arm.

"I need some cloth," Rosalynn replied. "There's a dry goods store across the street."

Lone Wolf walked Rosalynn across the street, wondering if being seen with him would embarrass her. He studied her facial features, trying to discern her thoughts. She marched past the staring, whispering townspeople, chattering away as she focused her attention on him. Once again, Rosalynn rose in his estimation.

When they reached the dry goods store, Lone Wolf pushed opened the door for Rosalynn. He stepped inside and stood next to the door. They didn't allow Indians in this establishment, but he didn't want to spoil Rosalynn's outing.

Rosalynn gasped with delight when she saw the bolts of fabric arranged on shelves along the walls and heaped on tables down the middle of the store. Obviously, she hadn't expected such a large selection in Peaceful.

"Where do I begin?" Rosalynn flashed Lone Wolf a brilliant smile that made his heart flutter.

He watched as Rosalynn made her way around the store. She chose several bolts of cloth and stacked them on the counter. She then selected sewing needles and several spools of white thread. When she set them on the counter, a clerk entered from the back of the store.

"Oh, I didn't hear you come in." With raised eyebrows, the clerk scanned the pile of fabric on the counter. Then she grabbed the top bolt and asked Rosalynn how many yards she needed.

Before Rosalynn had a chance to answer, the clerk turned and saw Lone Wolf, "Get out of here, you heathen murderer!" she yelled. "Get out and let decent folk shop!"

Rosalynn's head snapped back at Lone Wolf standing next to the store entrance. "I beg your pardon, madam. Whom are you speaking to?" Rosalynn's voice was terse.

"Oh, not you, ma'am. It's that mangy redskin." Then, looking at Lone Wolf again, she hollered out, "I told you to scat! Are you deaf or just stupid?"

"How dare you speak to another human being in such a degrading fashion!"

Lone Wolf saw Rosalynn's face turn red with anger. He marveled that such a small woman was so full of fire.

"I've changed my mind. I wouldn't buy so much as a spool of thread from you!" Rosalynn grabbed her skirts and flounced to the door.

"Injun lover," the woman spat out with disgust.

Rosalynn turned to face the woman. "That's right. I'm an Indian lover and proud of it," she said flippantly. Then she turned to Lone Wolf. "Come on, Lone Wolf. I'll not waste my money here."

Once outside, Lone Wolf hurried after Rosalynn. No one except his family had ever defended him with such conviction. Rosalynn was standing next to the wagon when he finally caught up with her. Lone Wolf almost laughed when he saw her still fuming and muttering to herself.

"The nerve of that woman! If I wasn't a lady and a Christian . . ."

"Calm down, Roz-lynn," Lone Wolf implored.

"Don't you dare tell me to calm down, Mr. Larson! The audacity of that woman! How dare she speak with such disrespect to you! What makes her think she is better than you in God's eyes?"

Lone Wolf didn't realize that Rosalynn was drawing a crowd of spectators until he saw her stiffen. He turned in the direction she faced and saw a man from the telegraph office approaching her. Lone Wolf drew closer to Rosalynn.

"Don't you dare ask me if this Indian is bothering me, mister," Rosalynn fumed, waggling her finger at the man. "He's a friend!" She stamped her foot and stiffened her body with her fists against her sides.

The man raised his arms in surrender and stalked back across the street, mumbling as he shook his head. Slowly, the rest of the crowd dispersed.

"You must calm down, Roz-lynn. You cannot change the contents of a person's heart. I am used to people treating me with disgust and hatred. It is the way things are." Lone Wolf gently took Rosalynn's arm and guided her closer to the horses, then continued. "When I was a small boy, the children were very cruel and teased me because I was a half-breed. The wasichu didn't accept me, and I felt out of place among my mother's people as well because of the white man's blood that flowed in my veins.

"One day when I came home from school in Peaceful, I was brokenhearted and crying with anguish. The children had ganged up on me and beat me badly. Mike tried to intervene, but there were too many of them. We both came home a bloody mess."

Lone Wolf tried to keep his voice steady but the emotion flowed with his words. "As I cried on my mother's lap, she read a scripture to me from my father's Bible. That scripture is still with me today, Roz-lynn." His voice a thread above a whisper, Lone Wolf placed his hand over his heart. "That scripture is what makes me strong and proud of who I am. Would you like me to quote it for you, Roz-lynn?"

Rosalynn nodded her head as she stared into Lone Wolf's deep brown eyes.

"It is 1 Samuel 16:7. It says, 'But the Lord said unto Samuel, Look not on his countenance, or on the height of his stature; because I have refused him: for the Lord seeth not as man seeth; for man looketh on the outward appearance, but the Lord looketh on the heart.'"

"That's beautiful, Lone Wolf. It's true. God doesn't measure us by the color of our skin or by what we acquire in wealth. He looks into our hearts and judges us by our actions and our thoughts." Their eyes locked. "It's nice that your mother loved you so much that she took the time to heal your soul with God's words of comfort."

Lone Wolf only nodded at Rosalynn in response.

"I'm sorry if I embarrassed you, Lone Wolf," she said quietly. "I can't abide narrow-minded people. If a person harms someone I care for, I lose control. Perhaps we should just head home before I get us into trouble."

Rosalynn's voice faded, and the only words Lone Wolf heard were *someone I care for.* "You care for me, Roz-lynn?"

Her cheeks pinked as she squirmed under Lone Wolf's scrutiny. "Of course I care for you, Lone Wolf. I was hoping we could be friends. I know we both want custody of Susan and Mike's children, but I'd still like to be friends."

Friends. That's all she wanted from him. What did he expect when she belonged to another? "I will always be your friend, Roz-lynn."

"Thank you. Can we return to the farm now?"

"What about your list, Roz-lynn? Do you not want to fill it? I need to go by the mercantile for supplies anyway. They have cloth—not as much as the dry goods store, but they may have what you want."

"Are they going to chase you out like a stray dog?" Rosalynn demanded, arms akimbo.

"No, Roz-lynn," Lone Wolf answered with a wide grin. "The Olsons are not like most wasichu. They are friendly like Big Todd and Arlene and the reverend and his wife."

"All right then," Rosalynn laughed. "I'll shop at the mercantile."

They headed back across Main Street and down the block to the mercantile. Sitting on a corner lot across from the church, the store looked enormous with its large false front.

"How 'bout a haircut, redskin?" someone sneered from the direction of the barbershop.

Lone Wolf noticed Rosalynn hesitate as she walked beside him. He gently pressed his hand to her back, felt her relax, and then escorted her into the store.

Everyone turned as Lone Wolf and Rosalynn entered the building. Lone Wolf guided Rosalynn to the dry goods section. "I need to fill an order as well. Do not leave without me." He didn't want her subjected to the locals' hostilities because she was with him. He knew how things could escalate. "Promise me, Roz-lynn."

"I promise, Lone Wolf," Rosalynn replied, then added with a chuckle, "I'm not accustomed to being protected."

That is strange, thought Lone Wolf. *Surely, her husband cares for her enough to keep her safe. But then where is the husband?*

"Hello."

Rosalynn looked up and found a young blonde woman standing on the opposite side of the table. "Hello." Rosalynn returned the smile.

"My name is Ida Olson. My husband and I own the merc."

"How nice." Rosalynn immediately felt at ease with the woman with dancing blue eyes and a Swedish accent. "My name is Rosalynn McAllister."

"Darn, when I saw you walk in with Lone Wolf, I was hoping he finally settled down and married a pretty young woman." Ida laughed.

"Have you known Lone Wolf long?" Rosalynn asked,.

"My husband's family came to America with the Larsons before he was even born."

Rosalynn glanced just beyond Ida and noticed a group of women congregated together. One would look up, glare at them, and then duck her head back into the huddle. "I must be the talk of the town today," she whispered to Ida and nodded at the circle of women.

Ida turned and looked behind her. On the other side of the room, the women glared back at them and then marched out of the store.

Rosalynn felt her smile droop into a frown. "I'm sorry, Ida. I just lost some customers for you."

"Nonsense, they'll be back. Hurry with your shopping, Rosalynn, and then come in the back for a cup of tea before heading home. I have a feeling we are going to be good friends."

Rosalynn continued shopping, eager to visit with Ida. She chose red-and-white gingham cloth to make curtains for the kitchen, white cotton to make aprons, and tea towels to embroider.

Then she selected some embroidery floss and several spools of white thread. She and her family had left everything they owned except their clothes and a few personal items in St. Louis, but she was relieved that they had been able to bring their patterns and sewing notions with them.

After depositing her goods on the counter, Rosalynn went in search of cleaning supplies. She ended up with half a dozen bars of lye soap, a new broom, and several large scrub brushes. She decided on beeswax and linseed oil to polish the furniture and hardwood floors.

Rosalynn also bought work clothes for herself and the children. Joshua was a farm boy now and couldn't wear a Buster Brown suit for collecting eggs or carrying stove wood. After seeing the condition of Hannah's dress when the girl had played in the dirt, Rosalynn thought bib overalls and work shirts were in order for her as well. Rosalynn also grabbed a felt hat for Joshua on the way to the counter.

Checking her list, Rosalynn saw that all she needed now was the food supplies. She filled a small sack with penny candy for the children and then waited for someone to help her with the food.

Ida returned and told Rosalynn to leave her list on the counter. The two women headed for the living quarters in the back of the store. "Swede will fill it when he finishes with Lone Wolf. When those two get together they are like two old hens."

Rosalynn felt right at home sitting in Ida's cheerful kitchen. She could hear children playing in the backyard. "How many children do you have, Ida?"

"We have five children." Ida laughed when Rosalynn's eyes widened. "Swede's first wife died and left him to raise two girls alone. He wrote back home to Sweden begging anyone to come to America and marry him. My family knew his, so it seemed natural for me to come to Peaceful. That was ten years and three children ago," Ida laughed. "I have no regrets. Swede is a good man and a good provider."

"There seem to be a lot of Swedish people in Peaceful." Rosalynn sipped her tea and nibbled at a cookie.

"The Swedish colonized Minnesota. There were a few Germans and Dutch, but mostly Swedish. It's good, rich farmland, and most of the Swedish immigrants were farmers in the old country. Of course, most of the high mucky-mucks in town turn their noses up at us immigrants. It doesn't make sense—we're all immigrants except for the Indians, and they're treated worse than we are."

"Did you know Lone Wolf's mother?" Rosalynn asked.

"Pale Flower? Yes, she is a wonderful, caring person," Ida replied. "She mostly kept to herself, like Lone Wolf does. She lived here almost thirty years and people were still horrible to her."

Rosalynn's eyes widened. "Are you saying she is still alive?"

"Yes, didn't Lone Wolf tell you?" Ida's brows shot up with surprise.

"No, but I've only known him since yesterday. My sister was married to his brother, Mike. I arrived yesterday with my aunt and two children. We were hoping to make a life here, but with Mike dead and Susan gone . . ." Rosalynn's voice trailed off.

"You're Susan's sister?" Ida stared at Rosalynn. "Well, bless my soul. You're nothing like her, and believe me, that's a compliment." Then Ida brought her hand to her mouth and shook her head. "Oh, I'm sorry, Rosalynn. That wasn't a very nice thing to say. She is your sister, after all. Please forgive me. I spoke out of turn."

Rosalynn reached across the table and patted Ida on the hand. "There's nothing to forgive. I know Susan for what she is. I take it she wasn't well liked in Peaceful."

"On the contrary, Susan rubbed elbows with the best of them.

She didn't socialize with poor immigrants like me. Snob Hill was more to her liking."

"Snob Hill? What's that?"

"It's what we commoners call Nob Hill Boulevard, where the rich and elite live. Susan was part of their crowd. They believed every ridiculous lie she spread. In all honesty, I feel that's one of the reasons Lone Wolf is having such a hard time with the residents of Peaceful."

"What lies did she spread?"

"Oh, that Pale Flower didn't want her on the farm and was poisoning her. She told everyone that Mike was beating her and that Lone Wolf bullied her. Susan had everyone convinced she was from a wealthy family back East. Mike, of course, told us differently."

"No wonder Lone Wolf hates Susan. Where is his mother now?"

"On the Indian reservation. Susan demanded that she leave and threatened to divorce Mike if she didn't. Susan wielded that threat against him like a weapon. Mike loved her, but he was frightened she'd take the kids from him. Since Mike's death, Lone Wolf has been workings hard planting the crops. He was hoping to provide a good home for Gretchen and the baby, and to bring his mother home. I guess you and your husband will take the children. Poor Lone Wolf! He doesn't stand a chance at getting the kids, but I'm not the one who's going to tell him."

Rosalynn knew she should explain that there was no husband, but she just couldn't get the words out, not yet. *What will people think when they find out I divorced Jeffery? More importantly, what will Lone Wolf think?*

Soon Lone Wolf was ready to leave, so Rosalynn said goodbye to her new friend. "I'm not sure what's going to happen until I speak with the circuit judge on Thursday. I'll try to let you know if I have to leave town."

When Rosalynn reentered the store, she noticed her purchases were gone. "Did you tally my bill, Mr. Olson?"

"Please, call me Swede—everyone does." Swede smiled. "Lone Wolf paid for everything and we loaded it on the wagon."

Rosalynn gave Lone Wolf a glowering look, but didn't want to argue with him in public. With the last of the farewells said, Lone Wolf escorted Rosalynn to the wagon and helped her onto the seat.

"I see you moved the wagon closer to the merc."

"Swede and I didn't want to haul everything so far," Lone Wolf said with a wink.

"My goodness, you certainly had a large order, didn't you?" Rosalynn couldn't believe how full the back of the wagon was.

"As you said, Roz-lynn, the house was bare of food, and I also needed feed for the animals."

After they were on their way out of town, Rosalynn could have sworn she smelled food. She kept sniffing and looking behind her until her curiosity got the better of her. "I smell fried chicken." She looked at Lone Wolf and watched his mouth twitch into what she thought might have been a smile. "I really do smell fried chicken," she insisted stubbornly.

Rosalynn watched as Lone Wolf struggled to maintain a somber countenance. She crossed her arms over her chest and jammed her chin out in defiance. All of a sudden, Lone Wolf burst out laughing. His fathomless, obsidian eyes danced against his dark skin. Rosalynn felt her body tingle with goose bumps. *He is so handsome!* she sighed to herself.

"I'm sorry, Roz-lynn." Lone Wolf cast Rosalynn a droll look from the corner of his eye. "I am teasing you. I bought a large order of fried chicken from Arlene before I came to get you. I thought you might be too tired to cook dinner when you got back to the farm."

A smile crept across his full, generous lips, and suddenly Rosalynn was at a loss. How could she stay angry when her heart was thumping so fast it caused her breath to catch in short jerks? *How considerate of Lone Wolf.* She was speechless.

"Are you mad at me, Roz-lynn?" Lone Wolf's dark brows drew together. "I was only teasing you."

Rosalynn had to say something. She felt like a silly schoolgirl carrying a crush for a naughty little boy. "Yes . . . no . . ." she stammered. Rosalynn could feel Lone Wolf's eyes upon her. "Yes, I am upset with you, Lone Wolf. Not for the chicken—that was very nice of you to think of me . . . us."

"Why, then?"

Rosalynn drew in a deep breath. It was difficult to be exasperated with Lone Wolf when he was so close. The wagon seat was narrow and she could feel the heat of his body as he pressed against her. Never had a man affected her like this before! She sighed again and forced herself to focus on the conversation.

"You paid for my things at the mercantile," she said. "I told you before that we are not a charity case, and I am not the type of person to take advantage of someone."

"I am sorry if I wounded your dignity, Roz-lynn." Lone Wolf's mouth curved into a gentle smile. "I admire your self-respect, but I have pride also.

"You are a good woman, Roz-lynn, but the things you were buying were to benefit my house. It was not fair for you to do the work plus pay for the supplies. Would you want to make me feel like a man who takes advantage of a woman?"

Rosalynn frowned. "Well . . . no, but I wish you would have consulted me. Everyone will think I'm using you."

"Now, you are being self-conscious and stubborn. How will anyone find out I paid for your things? Only Swede knows, and he does not gossip about his customers.

"Remember, we made a deal yesterday," he stated carefully. "I was to buy the supplies and you were to clean the house. We both want Gretchen and the baby. Neither of us wants them given to strangers. I would rather give you the house and let you raise the children than have both of us lose them."

"I promise, Lone Wolf, if I'm blessed to raise Susan and Mike's children, you can see them anytime you wish. I would never keep them from you."

"Do not make promises you cannot keep, Roz-lynn. You do not have the only say over the children, since you have a husband."

Rosalynn lapsed into silence. What would Lone Wolf say when he found out that she had divorced Jeffery? Would he think she was like Susan? How could she explain to him that she had no choice, when she was ashamed to let a living soul know how Jeffery had treated her? She had to hide behind the shame if she wanted to keep her self-respect.

Lord, why should I care what Lone Wolf thinks of me? I just met him. Yet, I feel a bond with him. Is it because we are both loners, misfits in a world that doesn't want us? Is it pity or something stronger I feel? What difference does it make, Father? I'm doomed to be alone. What man wants damaged goods?

That night as Rosalynn tried to sleep, the day's events swirled in her mind. Then plans for the house loomed before her. She only had three days to make the abandoned farmhouse into a happy home, and she was determined to do it.

Then what was bothering her deep down in her heart? Her stomach wrenched. *Jeffery.* He was no longer a part of her life, but he still affected her. As long as narrow-minded people judged others, she would never totally be free of him.

She had married Jeffery McAllister when she was twenty. He was very attentive, and Rosalynn was thrilled to have such a dashing man court her. Susan was two years younger than her and was jealous that Rosalynn had found a beau of her own. Susan went out of her way to attract his attention, but Jeffery just laughed at her girlish attempts to be flirtatious.

Shortly after they were married, Jeffery started to change. He was young; he didn't want to break his back being a farmer. He was a dreamer, and a lifestyle as a river gambler was more to his liking. The longer he stayed on the homestead, the more moody he became. Rosalynn had never seen his temper before, and it scared her.

Rosalynn had prayed that she would be able to help Jeffery. She just needed to be patient and understanding. Isn't that what Jesus taught? However, Jeffery didn't want anything to do with the church—or God, for that matter.

Then Jeffery started to abuse her. At first he yelled at her when he drank, blaming her for everything that went wrong. She couldn't do anything right in his eyes. Then he slapped her once, and she blamed it on the whiskey. When the slapping became a daily habit, she realized he wasn't going to change. Rosalynn wanted to move in with Aunt Dorothy, but by then it was too late—she was pregnant. When she told Jeffery that she was going to have a baby, he was furious.

Jeffery accused her of trapping him into a marriage he didn't want. He screamed, saying she and the baby were like a millstone around his neck. Then he took his riding crop and struck her several times. She pleaded for him to stop, but the more she cried out the harder he hit her. Mercifully, Rosalynn fainted from the pain, and when she awoke, her husband was gone.

Part of Rosalynn was relieved that Jeffery had left, and part of her was terrified of being alone and with child. She never confided in anyone that he had abused her. Her shame kept his secret.

For the following three years, Rosalynn worked hard on the

small dirt farm. All she had to do was live on the land and make improvements, and the deed would be hers. She took care of her son alone. She planted a garden in the summer and sold what she could spare. When the hens were laying, she traded eggs for supplies she couldn't grow herself. She preserved the rest of the harvest with great care for the winter.

The Lord blessed her with a few sheep. She sheared them herself, then carded the fleece and spun it into warm, thick wool. In the evenings, while her son slept and the loneliness of the nights engulfed her, she knitted socks and warm mittens, hats and mufflers, shawls and baby clothes. She eked out a meager existence, but her faith and determination were growing stronger.

During the fourth year she was on the land, Jeffery returned home, hat in hand, begging for mercy. When Rosalynn was a child, her aunt had taught her the importance of forgiveness, so Rosalynn gave Jeffery another chance.

Jeffery worked hard making the improvements necessary for them to acquire the deed to the property. He planted fruit trees and erected a barn, and he even built an addition on the one-room cabin so they could have a bedroom and a kitchen. How wonderful it was to cook on a cook stove instead of the fireplace! Jeffery bought a cow so their son could have fresh milk. It was such a blessing to have so many improvements accomplished in such a short time.

Rosalynn was the happiest she had ever been. Jeffery was gentle and loving, and soon she found herself pregnant again. She decided to wait a while before telling him about the baby. After his reaction to her pregnancy with their son Joshua, she was a little apprehensive. He tolerated Joshua now, but there was no bond between them.

Jeffery started to drink again. Rosalynn pleaded with him to stop, but he would just get angrier. During one of his drinking bouts, he told her that he had extended credit for the lumber he had used for the improvements. He also told her he charged at the mercantile. He blamed the mounting debts on her, and soon he began abusing her again.

Rosalynn prayed for a miracle. She prayed for the safety of her son and the unborn baby she carried. She prayed that Jeffery would just give up and leave again.

Rosalynn thought things couldn't get any worse until Jeffery told her he had sold the homestead. That's why he had come back in the first place—to improve the land so he could sell it. He gave her two days to pack what she wanted before she had to leave. When Rosalynn started to protest, he snapped his riding crop at her in warning. She had felt the sting of his crop on more than one occasion, and the crazed look on his face frightened her. She sensed that her life and the lives of her children were in danger, so she backed down.

When Jeffery left for town, Rosalynn knew it was over. Never again would he beguile her with his broken promises and superficial affection, nor would he get the opportunity to abuse her again. She packed a few of her belongings, loaded her sheep and a few chickens in a wagon, and left for town. She knew her aunt Dorothy would take her in.

For the next two years, Rosalynn and her two small children lived in her aunt's tiny house. Somehow, the Lord always provided for them. Rosalynn continued selling woolen items and her aunt made women's toiletries from home.

When Rosalynn divorced Jeffery, the community ostracized her. A divorced woman couldn't be trusted with decent menfolk. She was now a sullied woman—branded, like Hester, who wore the scarlet letter.

Aunt Dorothy didn't fare well with the women in town either.

Still a beautiful woman in her forties, women didn't trust her. But ladies of high society purchased her toiletries. The hypocrites would secretly send their maids to the back door.

When the letter came from Susan, Rosalynn recalled how she and her aunt were eager for a new beginning. They both prayed about the matter and felt that going to Minnesota was the right choice. Dorothy sold her house and furnishings, and Rosalynn sold everything but their clothes and a few personal items. There was no turning back; there was nothing to go back to now.

Rosalynn finally dropped off to sleep asking God to bless them with a future to look forward to and a home to call their own.

Chapter Six

Rosalynn arose earlier than usual, despite the restless sleep she had the night before. Thinking of Jeffery always made her feel infinitely worse, and now she had an additional problem. She felt horrible at the thought of taking Susan and Mike's children away from Lone Wolf; after all, he had little family left. Yet Rosalynn was torn, because she knew in her heart that she was meant to come to Peaceful. God must have known what Susan was plotting, and He needed her and Aunt Dottie there to care for the children. Why else would He have wanted her to come?

After saying her morning prayer, Rosalynn read several passages from the Bible. She found her day went much better when she devoted it to the Lord. In fact, scripture reading was the only thing that had gotten her through many days in the past.

Rosalynn dressed in her new bib overalls and work shirt, careful not to wake Dorothy and the children. She brushed her hair and then meticulously twisted the shiny mane into one long rope. Then she coiled the rope of hair into a bun and tucked the end through the center to secure it. It was an easy solution when she was in a hurry or didn't want to mess with her hair.

Slipping from the room she shared with her aunt, she tiptoed through the adjoining sitting room, where the children were fast asleep. Once in the kitchen, she started a fire in the cook stove and put a pot on to boil for tea, then headed off to the smokehouse.

When she entered the little shed, the delicious aroma of smoked meats engulfed her. She glanced around the dark room and saw large picnic hams and slabs of bacon hanging from the rafters by long cords. Packages of neatly wrapped meat filled the shelves along the walls. Rosalynn picked through the packages and chose sausage for breakfast and a pork roast for supper.

She returned to the house and rekindled the fire before frying the sausage for gravy. Then she made buttermilk biscuits and placed them in the oven. Her goal was to have breakfast ready by the time Lone Wolf arrived with the morning milk.

When Rosalynn heard Lone Wolf whistling on his way to the house, she quickly ran to the back porch, hoping to catch him before he headed off for the fields. As he approached the steps, a look of surprise crossed his handsome features. "Good morning," she said, smiling. "I hoped I'd catch you before you left for the fields. I have breakfast ready."

A perplexed look crept across his face. Before he had a chance to refuse her, Rosalynn spoke again. "I made extra just for you."

"Thank you," Lone Wolf responded solemnly.

Shaking off the notion that something was wrong, Rosalynn took the basket of eggs he offered her and returned to the kitchen. Lone Wolf followed her and placed the pail of milk on the counter, along with another basket.

"I found some morels when I took Bessie out to pasture this morning," he said. "I thought you and your family might enjoy them."

Rosalynn removed the sausage gravy and biscuits from the warming oven and placed them on the table. "What are morels?" Rosalynn sat down and motioned Lone Wolf to join her. She scooped up two bowls of oatmeal and placed one in front of Lone

Wolf at the head of the table.

Lone Wolf reached for the brown sugar and the cream pitcher.

"You have never eaten morel mushrooms, Roz-lynn?"

"No, I'm afraid I know very little about mushrooms. Are you sure they're safe to eat?"

Lone Wolf nodded. "My mother's people have been eating them for centuries."

Rosalynn offered the blessing over the meal and then dished Lone Wolf a large helping of biscuits smothered with sausage gravy. When she handed the plate to Lone Wolf, her hand brushed against his. A feeling akin to a lightning bolt surged through her body and she gasped softly. She felt her face redden when Lone Wolf scrutinized it.

"Does my touch offend you, Roz-lynn?" Lone Wolf's voice was despondent and his chocolate brown eyes held a tinge of sadness.

Rosalynn tried to answer, but only managed a string of incoherent words, unable to stop the trembling in her body at the sound of his voice.

Lone Wolf reached for her hand and gently held it in his large, calloused one. "I am half Lakota, Roz-lynn. The Lakota are very passionate, honest people. I am also half Swedish. I feel the same as the wasichu, a bit more untamed, perhaps, but with compassion and yearnings." Lone Wolf took her small hand and placed it against his cheek. "See, I am a man made of flesh and bones." He then placed her hand over his heart. "My heart pumps the same as yours. It has the same feelings a white man's does, but with more passion, for the Lakota is not ashamed of showing his emotions. Because I respect you, my feelings sleep. Do not fear me, Roz-lynn. I would never harm you."

Rosalynn was stunned. Never had a man spoken so eloquently to her, or with such honor and respect. She felt Lone Wolf's heart beat within his breast as he kept her hand pressed against him.

She pulled her hand away and then gently brushed it against his soft cheek. No stubble, just smooth, golden skin taunt against a firm jawline. She heard Lone Wolf take a sharp breath and felt his body shudder under her touch.

"I . . . I don't fear you, Lone Wolf," she whispered, and then pulled her hand back. "I can't explain my feelings—I don't understand them myself." For the first time, Rosalynn was relieved Lone Wolf thought she was a married woman. "I guess I'm just curious. You are the first Indian I've ever seen."

Rosalynn looked into Lone Wolf's alluring, dark eyes and felt her body melt. She needed a diversion. "How—" her voice squeaked out. She cleared her throat and tried again. "How do I prepare the mushrooms?"

Lone Wolf smiled. Not just any kind of smile but one that jarred Rosalynn to her very soul. "Someday, Roz-lynn, you will share your feelings with me. But for now, I will teach you how to cook mushrooms."

Rosalynn felt tiny sensations twirl down her spine. Lone Wolf was so handsome, but more importantly, he was kind and gentle. It took all her strength just to keep her feelings in check.

"First, you must rinse the mushrooms in cool water and then let them soak in saltwater. This helps remove any insects and dirt."

Rosalynn tried to keep her attention on what Lone Wolf was saying, but her mind kept traveling back to his touch.

"Rinse off the saltwater and gently pat them dry with a cloth. After they are dry, cut them in half and dip them in a mixture of milk and eggs beaten together."

Rosalynn was lost in his eyes, from which radiated a benevolence she could not resist. And his smile . . . white teeth against full, kissable lips . . . What was she thinking! She was a mature Christian woman of twenty-eight, mooning like a lovesick calf. Was it wrong to have such thoughts?

I admire Lone Wolf, Father. I could so easily fall in love and spend the rest of my life here on this farm with him.

Rosalynn cleared her throat and sat straight in her chair. Shaking the romantic thoughts from her mind, she forced herself to focus on Lone Wolf's words.

"Next, dredge them through dried bread crumbs or flour. Fry them in lard until they are golden brown and crispy. They are very good. My father used to say they tasted like pork chops."

"They sound delicious. I'll fix them for the noon meal. What time will you come in from the fields?"

"I will not come in for the noon meal." Lone Wolf bent his head down and continued to eat his breakfast.

Rosalynn felt puzzled by Lone Wolf's response. "Then I'll bring dinner to you in the fields around noon."

Lone Wolf shrugged his shoulders and continued to eat in silence.

"I brought a pork roast in from the smoke shed for supper tonight," Rosalynn went on. "I hope that's agreeable with you."

"It does not matter to me what you cook. I will be eating in my cabin." Lone Wolf averted his eyes, his cordial mood suddenly gone.

"Why?" Rosalynn's asked softly.

"It's for the best," Lone Wolf answered gruffly, rising from the table. "I have work to do."

As Rosalynn watched him leave, she wondered what had happened to cause him to revert to his sullen ways. Was it because she let him peek into her heart and he felt repulsed by what he saw? After all, she was supposed to be a married woman. Perhaps he regretted his offer to let them stay there. Maybe they were more of a burden than he had anticipated. *That's just how Jeffery felt.*

Lone Wolf walked briskly to the barn, the imprint of Rosalynn's small hand still tingling on his skin. He hated treating her so coolly, and he couldn't bear to see the hurt in her beautiful, turquoise eyes. But he didn't trust himself to keep hidden the feelings that were growing inside him for her.

When they returned from Peaceful the night before, Lone Wolf noticed that Rosalynn went quiet when he mentioned her husband. It was then he realized that his growing feelings were wrong. Rosalynn was married. Period.

The night before, Lone Wolf had fallen into a melancholy mood when he returned to his cabin. It had been nice to spend the day with Rosalynn and then to have dinner with her and her family, but then he had to return to his lonely existence.

He loved children, and seeing Rosalynn with her family was like a knife in his heart. *Why, Great Spirit? Why did You send Roz-lynn here? To torment me, Great Spirit? To show me how lonely I am?*

Rosalynn was out of his reach. Lone Wolf knew he had to distance himself from her to save his heart from breaking in the future. It was going to be difficult enough when the infamous husband decided to show up. Lone Wolf knew he couldn't witness Rosalynn's eyes fill with love for another. It would hurt too much.

It would be hard, but Lone Wolf was determined to stay away from the farmhouse and his guests. He felt guilty for coveting his neighbor's wife—for breaking one of the Ten Commandments. He was ashamed to be jealous of a man he had never laid eyes on. How could he speak to Rosalynn about what was in his heart? She would find it repulsive if she knew how he felt. Soon she would be gone, and his lonely life would continue.

For once, Lone Wolf was grateful for the hard work that waited for him. He would plow and seed until he no longer felt any longing, any pain, only bitterness and loneliness. He was accustomed to that

Lone Wolf harnessed the team, hoping Rosalynn wouldn't make good on her promise of bringing the noon meal, and praying that she would, all in the same breath.

——•——

Rosalynn tackled the housework with renewed gusto. She was hurt and confused at Lone Wolf's behavior, or lack of it. Biting her lower lip to keep from crying, she wondered what happened to the Lone Wolf she had spent the previous day with. Was he beguiling her for motives of his own? She didn't enjoy having negative thoughts about Lone Wolf, nor did she enjoy placing him in the same class as Jeffery. But what else was she to think?

When she took Lone Wolf his dinner in the fields, he didn't stop long enough to thank her. Instead, he waved from the field and called to her that he would eat later. Rosalynn was dejected. She had hoped to see if he liked the fried morels and to talk with him. *Please, Father, tell me what to do.*

As Rosalynn walked back to the house, she felt her hurt turn to anger. She wouldn't give Lone Wolf the satisfaction of knowing how his rejection affected her. She could be cool and impersonal, just like he was, if she put her mind to it.

Rosalynn decided to make a boiled supper from the pork roast she brought in from the smokehouse. She cut the meat into bite-sized pieces and then browned it in a Dutch oven. Next, she added diced onions and chunks of carrots, cabbage, and potatoes. Once the pot began to boil, Rosalynn placed it on the back of the stove to simmer until dinnertime. She didn't have time to bake a loaf of bread, so she decided to make a quick batch of crusty cornbread instead.

She gathered the ingredients, still marveling at the amount of food in the kitchen and pantry. Lone Wolf had bought so much food in Peaceful that they had a hard time finding room in the kitchen cupboards and pantry to hold it all. Thank goodness someone had built bins in the kitchen to hold all the flour and sugar.

Since she knew Lone Wolf would not eat with them, Rosalynn scooped some of the boiled supper into a smaller covered pot. She remembered the mouse floating in the clabbered milk, and she covered the cornbread as well before placing the food on the back porch.

All through dinner, Dorothy and the children chatted about how the house was coming along.

"Rosalynn, you're not very talkative tonight," Dorothy observed with a frown. "You're not ill, are you?"

"I'm just a little tired, Aunt Dottie, that's all."

"I imagine you are, dear. I wish you would let me help more. I feel lazy just watching the children and sewing while you do all of the hard labor."

"You're far from lazy, Aunt Dot. Besides, I told you how much help you are, taking care of the children. I can't care for them properly plus do all of the cleaning. And look at the lovely aprons and curtains you've made. That is a laborious job in itself."

"As long as I'm some sort of help to you, Rosalynn dear."

Rosalynn stretched her arm across the table and grasped Dorothy's hand. "Just give me moral support, Aunt Dot. That's what I really need right now."

Lone Wolf left the fields, fed and watered the animals, and then milked the cow. He was bone weary. Night had fallen by the time he left the milk on the back porch. When he spied the covered pots, he grew curious and peeked under the lids. The tantalizing aroma caused his stomach to growl. He hadn't expected Rosalynn to save him any dinner after the way he had treated her.

The day had been hot and Lone Wolf, tired as he was, went to the small pool below the waterfall to bathe. He sat next to a large boulder close to the pool and ate the delicious meal. *Rosalynn is certainly a good cook,* he mused as he devoured the food.

He rinsed the cooking pots in the creek and then placed them on the boulder. Standing next to the inviting water, Lone Wolf recalled how his family had bathed and swam there throughout the years.

Within seconds he was standing under the cascading falls and letting the water pound on his aching muscles. He felt relief come to his muscles but not to his heart.

Lone Wolf stepped out from the falls, grabbed his loincloth, and put it on. He never dressed after his evening bath. Why bother when he went alone to his cabin every night?

Reaching down, he grabbed a handful of mint that grew along the bank. He rinsed it in the cool water and then popped it into his mouth. The taste was fresh and invigorating and reminded him of the iced mint drink his mother used to make when he was a child.

Pale Flower, his mother, was his only refuge now that Mike was gone. His half-sisters hadn't kept in contact with either of them after their father died.

Lone Wolf grabbed his clothes and the cooking pots and headed back toward the cabin, his path guided by the light of the full moon. Suddenly he saw a dark figure standing next to the rail fence near the garden area. As Lone Wolf crept closer to the figure, he heard a feminine voice singing. It sounded like Rosalynn, but he wasn't positive. He had never heard her sing.

The voice was sweet and gentle as it floated across the meadow in the night's breeze. By the words he could make out, she was singing a love ballad. He waited until the song was over before announcing his presence.

"Roz-lynn, what are you doing out here alone?"

Rosalynn turned suddenly, screamed, and then jumped from the railing where she had been perched. She froze, staring into the night shadows and clutching her throat.

"It is me, Lone Wolf. Do not be frightened." Lone Wolf dropped his clothes and the cooking pots and headed for Rosalynn.

Within seconds, he was by her side. He saw the terror in her huge, radiant eyes and watched her tremble with fear. He grabbed her by the shoulders and leaned close so she could see him in the moon's rays. The delicate scent of roses wafted in the breeze. "It is me, Lone Wolf."

"Lone Wolf?" Rosalynn's voice quivered as her eyes locked with his.

A smile played across Lone Wolf's lips and he sighed with relief. "Yes, Roz-lynn. I am sorry, I did not mean to frighten you. Are you better now?" He released her and then stepped back to get a better view of her face.

Rosalynn let out another screech and turned her back on Lone Wolf. "Lone Wolf, you're naked!"

"Naked?" Lone Wolf frowned in confusion. "I am not naked, Roz-lynn. I am wearing a loincloth." Lone Wolf couldn't help but chuckle.

"That's pretty close to naked for me, Lone Wolf Larson! Why, I've never seen so much skin on a man before in my life."

Lone Wolf thought Rosalynn's comment was odd for a married woman, but he was enjoying teasing her too much to concern himself. "Most of the Lakota braves only wear a loincloth."

"Well, it's indecent where I come from. Now put some clothes on so I can head back to the house."

Lone Wolf relented. He went back to the spot where he had dropped his clothes and put his buckskin britches on. "I'm decent now, Roz-lynn. You can turn around."

He watched Rosalynn slowly turn her head to face him. "I declare, Lone Wolf, you exasperate me. My face must be ten shades of red. Not to mention my heart is in my throat." Rosalynn huffed indignantly, then brushed a strand of hair from her face. Her eyes darted back and forth from him to the empty air around them.

Lone Wolf couldn't help but see the humor in the situation and tried to suppress his amusement. Finally, he couldn't contain himself any longer and let out a loud, rolling laugh.

Rosalynn stared at him, her hands on her hips, a smile twitching on her rosy lips. Lone Wolf could tell she was having a hard time keeping a straight face. He laughed and laughed. Rosalynn pursed her lips together and then rolled her eyes. A little chirp escaped her lips, then a giggle, and soon she laughed just as heartily as Lone Wolf. Finally, she swiped the tears from her cheek with the back of her hand. "Stop! I can't laugh anymore," she demanded. "My sides are aching and you've got me crying."

Lone Wolf settled back against the fence and folded his arms across his bare chest. He watched Rosalynn push the tendrils from her face. "What brings you out here after dark?"

Rosalynn turned her body toward the fence and folded her arms across the top rail. She then rested her chin on her arm. "I was hot and needed some fresh air after washing the dinner dishes. How about you?"

"I, too, was hot and bathed in the creek. I ate the supper you saved for me. Thank you for thinking of me."

Lone Wolf watched Rosalynn shrug her shoulders and gaze into the starlit sky. The evening was warm and the air fresh and clean.

"It's so beautiful here," Rosalynn remarked. "I never noticed the starry sky and the gorgeous moon before. It's not at all like this in St. Louis. It's nice to take a moment and enjoy what God has created for us."

Lone Wolf turned and faced the same direction as Rosalynn. He leaned his body against the fence and gazed into the inky sky. The stars were brilliant tonight, not a cloud in sight to detract from their beauty, and the full moon beckoned him.

"It's a sweetheart's moon tonight," Lone Wolf said softly.

"Sweetheart's moon?" Rosalynn stared up into the inky heavens.

"Perhaps I will explain it to you someday," Lone Wolf sighed.

"It must be some kind of Indian folk tale." Rosalynn grinned, glancing briefly toward him.

"Something like that," was Lone Wolf's only response.

"Tell me about the Lakota and how you came to be here." Rosalynn turned to face Lone Wolf.

"It's a long story, Roz-lynn. Are you sure you want to hear it?" Lone Wolf smiled and then raked his hand through his long, damp hair.

"I'm in no hurry, are you?" Rosalynn asked, throwing Lone Wolf another brilliant smile.

When Rosalynn tried to climb back onto the fence and slipped, Lone Wolf picked her up like a rag doll and gently seated her on the top rail. Then he immediately backed away, not trusting himself in such close proximity.

"My father came from Sweden with many other Swedish families to settle land in the remote northwestern corner of the state. The Swedish immigrants migrated to this area because of the fertile land and the abundant forests. Father had no idea when he chose this section of land that it was the summer camp of the Lakota Sioux and the Ojibwa Indian tribes."

"If the settlers took over the Lakota's land, then what happened to the Lakota?" Rosalynn asked.

Lone Wolf continued. "The Lakota were chased from the wooded northwest, near Canada and Lake of the Woods, and were forced to live in the southeast corner of Minnesota. The land was then populated and made into towns like St. Paul and Lake Pepin. The government forced the Lakota from the land again. The wasichu wanted the Lakota punished even more and sent them to a small ten-mile wide area on the southwest side of the Minnesota River. The land was not large enough to contain all of the Lakota, and the hunting was very poor. They did not have the abundant woods of the north to sustain them, and many starved."

"How horrible for the Lakota. What happened next?"

Rosalynn seemed genuinely interested in the plight of his people. Lone Wolf shifted on the ground, leaned his back against a fence post, and then continued. "Red Cloud could not stand to see his beloved people starve, so he disbanded the tribe. My mother was among those who went with him. They followed the Minnesota River north along the state lines. By the time they reached their summer grounds, they were too weak to continue into Canada and safety.

"Red Cloud knew his people could not fight for their birthright any longer. His people were dying from starvation and the elements. Some of the Sioux went into Canada, but Red Cloud stayed on the reservation with the sick, the old, the children, and the women. He wanted to make sure his people were cared for and that the government kept the promises they had made to the Sioux. There he remains, no harm to anyone. He stayed to fight the father of the wasichu in Washington, but only with words."

"And your mother? What happened to her? When did she meet your father?"

Lone Wolf laughed and then stood up next to the fence. He flexed his sore muscles and then helped Rosalynn from her high perch. "Not tonight, Roz-lynn. It grows late and we are both tired. Your aunt will be worried." Lone Wolf walked over to the place where he had dropped his clothing and then went back to where Rosalynn stood. "Thank you again for the supper. It was very good."

Rosalynn took the pots from Lone Wolf. "I hope you'll eat with us from now on, but if you feel uncomfortable, I understand. I'll continue to leave your food on the porch."

Before heading for his cabin, Lone Wolf watched as Rosalynn returned to the house. It was nice having someone to talk to for a change; he had been so lonely since Mike died. He missed his mother and Black Hawk. Every year he returned to the hated reservation for the winter to care for his mother. Since Susan was gone, he hoped Pale Flower would return to the home she had loved. However, if the judge gave Rosalynn custody of the children, Lone Wolf vowed that he would give her the house. Maybe in time, Pale Flower would return and live with him in the cabin. So much depended on what the circuit judge decided on Thursday.

Rosalynn had one more day to complete the housework. The downstairs was finished, but she still needed to tackle the upstairs. She cringed to think what waited for her on the second floor, but she planned to stay busy enough to keep thoughts of Lone Wolf at bay.

The previous night still burned in her mind. It had been difficult to pay attention to Lone Wolf's words and not his broad, chiseled chest. Every time he had crossed his arms, his well-muscled biceps rippled in the moonlight, and her heart skipped a beat. She couldn't stop herself from thinking how wonderful it would feel to have Lone Wolf hold her close.

Grabbing a broom, Rosalynn started up the stairs, muttering, "This is ridiculous!"

"Rosalynn dear, you didn't hear a word I said," a voice called.

Rosalynn shook her head to clear her thoughts, and then peeked over the railing to the floor below. "Did you say something, Aunt Dottie?"

"My goodness, darling, where is your mind these days?" Dorothy's gentle reprimand was followed by a smile. "I was telling you that I want to help clean the upstairs with you. Hannah is napping, and Joshua went out to help Lone Wolf."

Rosalynn shook her head. "No, auntie, I don't want you wearing yourself out cleaning Susan's mess."

"I refuse to take no for an answer, Rosalynn." Dorothy headed up the stairs with a bucket of cleaning supplies and a mop. "Now, don't upset me by treating me like a child. If we both work at it, we can have the upstairs done in no time."

Rosalynn looked into her aunt's determined face. Her usually soft lips were pursed together, and a frown creased her brow.

"Okay, Aunt Dottie, I know when I'm licked," Rosalynn laughed and gave her aunt a hug. "But remember, I warned you." Rosalynn's eyes squinted at her aunt as she wagged her finger.

When Rosalynn and Dorothy reached the landing, they saw that a long, wide corridor ran the length of the house, with rooms on both sides. There was a window at each end of the house, which allowed sunlight to filter into the hall. Rosalynn had expected it to be dark and dreary, and she was pleased that it wasn't. The corridor was wide, with an oil lamp on a small table at each end of the hall.

Rosalynn opened the first door on the right and peeked inside. Toys, children's clothing, and bedding were strewn all over the floor of the large room. A small bed and a crib sat along one wall.

"This must have been the children's room," she sighed.

"Oh, the poor dears." Dorothy clicked her tongue. "To live this way is so sad."

The room next to the children's was just as cluttered. "This has to be Susan's room," Rosalynn commented dryly as she looked at the pile of women's clothing scattered all over the floor and any other place that afforded a small ledge to heap them on.

"What is that horrible odor?" Dorothy asked, covering her nose with her hand.

"I don't know," Rosalynn gasped for air and slammed the door shut.

Across the hall, they found a huge bedroom with an adjoining sitting room and a small fireplace. As in the other bedrooms, the wallpaper featured blue wisteria with delicate, climbing green vines. A small balcony outside the sitting room overlooked a beautiful meadow.

Rosalynn opened a door, expecting a changing closet, and found it led to a smaller room. "I wonder if this was an office or a nursery for a baby."

"I would think a nursery," Dorothy offered, glancing around the small room. "I wonder why Susan didn't take this nice, big room for herself and fix this little room for the baby?"

"There's never any rhyme or reason to what Susan does."

The two women ventured to the other end of the corridor

and discovered three more bedrooms. One had obviously been Mike's room; it was the only bedroom in the house that was neat and clean.

"The first thing we need to do is open all of the windows and let in some fresh air up here," Rosalynn said with hands on her hips. Next, she called Joshua from the barn to help her haul off the trash. She then swept and mopped the floors while Dorothy went through the clothing and toys, discarding what was unusable.

When they came to Susan's room, they discovered the source of the stench. Four chamber pots filled to the brim sat under the bed. "How disgusting!" Rosalynn exclaimed, appalled at the laziness of her sister.

In one of the bedrooms, Rosalynn came across several wooden crates. She opened them and found dozens of beautifully carved wooden animals inside. The carvings looked incredibly lifelike, and Rosalynn knew it took great talent to capture the animals' spirits so accurately. In the other crates, she found delicate china figurines, gorgeous hand-woven rugs, and furniture throws in bright colors and unusual geometric designs. Joshua carried the boxes of knickknacks downstairs for Dorothy to dust while Rosalynn finished the bedrooms.

Rosalynn decided the girls would use the children's old room and that Joshua would get Susan's room. She wanted to use the one with the sitting room for herself and make the small bedroom adjacent to it into a nursery for the baby. *But it all hinges on what the judge decides,* she thought grimly.

Rosalynn moved the furniture into the appropriate rooms, re-hung the curtains, and placed scatter rugs on the hardwood floors. Then she grabbed the mattress from Susan's bed, dragged it to the room across the hall, and slung it over the balcony railings to air out.

When she returned to Susan's room, she discovered a small,

burgundy book wedged under the bed railing. Opening the book, she quickly scanned the pages and saw that it was Susan's diary.

Rosalynn glanced at a few of the entries, then plopped down in a rocking chair. Hoping to find out where Susan went and why she would leave her children in the hands of others, Rosalynn flipped to the back of the diary to the last entries.

In one of the final entries, Susan described how she had watched in the night shadows as Mike hung from the rafters. She made no attempt to help him, and, in fact, she was elated. Rosalynn felt nauseated at the heartless, sinister ramblings of her sister, so she closed the book. "I can't read anymore," she whispered to herself. *Why, Lord? Why did Susan turn out so evil and cruel?* Shaking her head, Rosalynn threw the diary into one of her dresser drawers, praying she would never have to read it again.

By bedtime, the entire house was spotless and shone with a woman's loving touch—except for the locked room off the dining room. It remained locked at Lone Wolf's request.

When Rosalynn snuggled beneath the clean sheets and quilts that night, she felt satisfied with a job well done. Almost any woman would be proud to call the beautiful house her home. It was starting to feel like home to Rosalynn and her family already, and a pang of despair filled her at the thought of leaving. *I pray, dear Lord, that tomorrow brings good news and relief to all.*

Chapter
Seven

Rosalynn waited by the gate for Lone Wolf to pull the wagon to a stop. He jumped from the seat box and offered his hand to her. "Please, take this," Rosalynn said as she handed him a basket. Puzzled by her curt tone and the sour frown on her face, Lone Wolf took the basket and placed it in the back of the wagon. Rosalynn held out her hand, and he helped her onto the seat. He waited patiently for Rosalynn to smooth her skirt and settle in before releasing the brake. When she was ready, he snapped the reins, setting the horses in motion.

Lone Wolf stole a glance at Rosalynn and decided she was beautiful despite her stern expression. How prim and proper she looked with her tiny hands covered with white crocheted gloves and folded in her lap. The Confederate-blue skirt with matching waistcoat over a lacy white blouse accentuated her blue-green eyes, and a blue bonnet, adorned with clusters of red cherries and blue and white dried flowers, sat at a haughty angle on her well-groomed head.

"I knew you didn't take time to eat the noon meal so I packed a basket for you," Rosalynn replied, interrupting Lone Wolf's silent musings.

"I cannot eat and drive the wagon." Lone Wolf took a quick glance at her, hoping to read her thoughts.

"I'm very capable of managing a team, Mr. Larson." Rosalynn's voice sounded sharp as a knife.

He took another quick look at Rosalynn. He assumed she was upset because of his cool attitude yesterday, and he couldn't blame her.

Lone Wolf shrugged his shoulders in response and handed the reins to her. Reaching behind them, he grabbed the basket and sat it on his lap. *It is difficult, Great Spirit, to stay aloof from Rosalynn when she is so thoughtful and kind. Please bless this food so that I may be strong in wisdom.*

Lone Wolf opened his eyes and found Rosalynn staring at him with a perplexed expression. "Why do you look at me so, Rozlynn? Do you not think a heathen blesses his food?"

Rosalynn shot Lone Wolf an angry scowl. "I've never thought of you as such, and you know it, Mr. Larson! I was merely thinking how you are like a diamond in the rough. There are many sides to you. I wish you would make up your mind who your enemy is and stop acting so childish. Oh, why explain anything to you? I'll probably be gone tomorrow and you won't even remember me by next week."

Lone Wolf didn't know what to say. She was right except for one thing. He would never forget her.

The remainder of the trip to town was solemn and quiet. When they approached Peaceful, Rosalynn handed the reins back to Lone Wolf. Today of all days, Lone Wolf chose to be moody. *Actually,* she fumed to herself, *he has acted strange since our last trip to town. He was fine until we returned home.* Something was amiss, but what?

Rosalynn's heart began to beat faster and her throat felt tight and dry as they entered Peaceful. *Oh, Lord, I'm frightened. What will the judge decide today? Please, let Thy Spirit be with me and soften the judge's heart. All depends on Thee; I put my trust in Thee.*

The wagon jerked to a stop and Rosalynn's eyes popped opened. Lone Wolf jumped from the wagon seat and offered to help her down. Rosalynn accepted his hand and carefully climbed from the wagon.

She felt a little overdressed, considering that she usually wore only a simple frock. She hadn't worn so many petticoats in ages, and they made her feel heavy and sluggish. Ten petticoats plus a crinoline. What was she thinking?

Rosalynn stared at the courthouse, which sat snug between the sheriff's office and the post office. It was a nice redbrick building on the north side of town. As Lone Wolf escorted her inside, Rosalynn felt her heart quicken.

"May I help you?" A clerk from behind the counter asked Rosalynn, ignoring Lone Wolf.

The clerk was a weasel of a man with beady little eyes and a long, droopy mustache. Rosalynn noticed that he had more hair on his face than his head.

"Please inform Judge Warner that Mr. Larson and Mrs. McAllister are here to see him." Rosalynn glanced at Lone Wolf. She might be a little miffed at him for his childish attitude of late, but she refused to allow anyone to degrade him in her presence.

"Is Judge Warner expecting you?" the clerk asked, his eyes pinned on Rosalynn.

"Yes, he is." Rosalynn stared back, unmoved.

"What is the nature of your business?" The clerk's mouth was set in a firm line.

"It's a private matter." Rosalynn stated defiantly.

The clerk cleared his throat, embarrassment smeared across his red face. "I'm sorry, but the judge is busy."

Before Rosalynn had time for a rebuttal, the judge's door opened and a distinguished older gentleman stepped out. "Any appointments, Horace?"

"Yes, sir," Rosalynn interjected quickly. "Mr. Larson and I have an appointment to see you, but this man says you're too busy."

"Well, I just un-busied myself," Judge Warner replied dryly, casting a scowl at the clerk. "Please come into my chambers, Miss . . ."

"It's Mrs. McAllister, actually," Rosalynn said with a smile of relief.

"Oh, Reverend Baker mentioned you would be coming to see me." Then, turning to Lone Wolf, Judge Warner offered a genuine smile. "Lone Wolf, it's been a long time. How's your dear mother?"

Rosalynn couldn't help but smirk at the surprised expression on the clerk's face when Judge Warner openly expressed friendship toward Lone Wolf. She watched as Lone Wolf accepted the friendly handshake before they followed the judge into his chambers.

"Please sit down." Judge Warner pulled up a chair for Lone Wolf before circling his desk and sitting down in his chair.

"Well, let's see," the judge said almost to himself as he rustled through a stack of papers on his desk. "Ah, here they are," he said, looking up with a smile. "I knew I had the letters somewhere."

"Let's start with you, Lone Wolf." Then more seriously, he added, "I was sorry to hear about Mike. He was a good man and he will be missed."

Lone Wolf nodded.

"Reverend Baker wrote to me saying you would like to raise

Mike's children."

"Yes, sir." Lone Wolf sat ramrod straight. Rosalynn knew he was nervous by the way he fidgeted in his chair. He wrung his hands, and his eyes kept darting from her to the judge.

"Can you explain to me how you intend to raise them? I know how demanding farm life can be—I grew up on a farm myself. I never saw my father during the spring planting or the fall harvest. With Mike gone, your workload has doubled, I'm betting. Children need love and attention. They also need supervision." Judge Warner seemed to study Lone Wolf carefully.

"What you say is true."

Hearing the quiver in Lone Wolf's voice, Rosalynn sensed it was difficult for him to succumb to the wasichu's laws. *How his very soul must scream for independence,* she thought.

"I do work hard on the farm, but I intend to bring my mother home to care for the children and the house. I also have a friend on the reservation who wishes to learn how to farm. I hope he will come with Pale Flower and help me as I teach him the ways of the white man."

"And is Pale Flower in agreement with you on raising Mike's children?"

Lone Wolf looked away at the mention of his brother. "Pale Flower does not know Mike is dead."

"I see. So you haven't seen her in some time?" The judge asked, peeking over his wire spectacles.

"Not since last winter."

Judge Warner continued to write as Lone Wolf sat in silence. He then turned to Rosalynn and said, "Now for you, Mrs. McAllister." Judge Warner's voice was warm and friendly.

Lone Wolf stood and walked to the window.

"Reverend Baker tells me you are Mrs. Larson's sister. Is that correct?" the judge asked.

"Yes, sir, I'm Susan's sister." Rosalynn felt her stomach twitch with anxiety.

"Good," Judge Warner mumbled as he continued to write. "I've also been told that you have two children of your own and a maiden aunt living with you."

"Yes, sir." Rosalynn glanced at Lone Wolf and felt some relief when he smiled at her. Suddenly, she felt foolish for treating him so badly on the way into town.

"If you win custody of the children, do you plan on living in Peaceful or returning to—where do you hail from, Mrs. McAllister?"

"St. Louis, Missouri, Your Honor. But we would live in Peaceful." Rosalynn tried to focus her mind on the judge.

"I see." Judge Warner continued to write on his little pad. "When does your husband plan on joining you here?"

Rosalynn made no response.

Judge Warner glanced up and asked again. "When does Mr. McAllister plan to arrive in Peaceful, Mrs. McAllister?"

Rosalynn's eyes darted from the judge and then to Lone Wolf, her fingers nervously intertwining with the drawstrings on her handbag. She prayed silently for guidance. *What do I say, Father? The truth?*

"Are you ill, Mrs. McAllister?" Pouring a glass of water, the judge pushed it across the desk to her.

Rosalynn took a sip of the water and felt her stomach rebel. "I . . . I . . ." She stammered and placed a gloved hand over her mouth. *I don't want to cry, Lord. Please, don't let me cry.*

Regaining her composure, Rosalynn looked at the judge. "I'm not married, Your Honor." The words were barely above a whisper.

"Excuse me, Mrs. McAllister, did I hear you correctly? Did you say you're not married?" Judge Warner's eyebrows cocked up, forming deep lines across his forehead. "Is your husband deceased?"

Both the judge and Lone Wolf stared at her, waiting for a response.

Rosalynn felt her face grow pale and her throat constrict. She placed a gloved hand over her mouth, praying she could maintain her emotions. She shot a quick glance at Lone Wolf and immediately felt guilty for not telling him the truth earlier.

Lone Wolf's expression was one of disbelief. His usual relaxed stance was now ridged, his muscles taut, and a scowl marred his coppery features.

Rosalynn silently prayed for strength, and after a few moments drew up her courage. She replied in a clear voice, head held high, but spirits low. "I'm divorced, Judge Warner." She felt her shoulders sink with defeat.

"You are not married, Roz-lynn?" Lone Wolf asked, clearly stunned by the announcement. He sat down with a thud in a chair next to her and tried to make eye contact. "Why did you not tell me?"

Silence filled the small office.

Judge Warner looked first at Rosalynn, and then at Lone Wolf. He cleared his throat and continued with his inquiry. "Are you legally divorced, Mrs. McAllister, or just separated from your husband?"

Rosalynn tried to maintain some decorum as she explained, "I'm legally divorced. I divorced my husband, Jeffery, almost four years ago."

"I see," Judge Warner commented. He removed his spectacles and placed them on his desk. Rubbing his eyes, he leaned back in his chair. Closing his eyes, he twiddled his thumbs over his rotund belly as though in deep thought.

"Your marital status does change things, I'm afraid." Judge

Warner leaned forward in his chair and placed the spectacles back on his nose. He folded his hands together on the desk and looked straight at Rosalynn, who braced herself for bad news.

"I had my mind made up, more or less, but this puts a new light on the case," Judge Warner said. Looking at Lone Wolf, he continued, "I was leaning toward granting custody of the children to Mrs. McAllister, Lone Wolf. I was under the impression that she was married.

"My first responsibility is to the children. They are my main concern. I feel that placing them in a stable home with a mother and a father who can provide for them is a priority. Since you are both unmarried, I have no choice but to place them with one of the families that has demonstrated an interest in them." Judge Warner breathed a dejected sigh. "Now I must rethink this case."

"I'm sorry, Judge Warner, I don't mean to be disrespectful, but I feel you are being unfair." Rosalynn tried to keep her voice calm and her feelings in check. "Just because I'm not married doesn't mean I can't take care of Susan's children. I've supported my own two children just fine by myself. Also, I think it's unconscionable to place them with strangers when there is family on both sides who are willing to raise them." Rosalynn's eyes darted to Lone Wolf, then back to the judge. "Shouldn't family connections come before materialistic concerns, Your Honor?"

"Mrs. McAllister, can you afford to feed, clothe, and care for two more in addition to the two children you already have?" the judge asked. "How would you support them?"

"The same way I support my two children, Your Honor—by selling homemade goods and homegrown vegetables. My aunt made a living selling her homemade toiletries in St. Louis. Between the two of us, we were able to make ends meet."

"Yes, but, Mrs. McAllister, this isn't St. Louis. This is little Peaceful, Minnesota. You'll have to admit the sales will be much less here. In addition, you don't have the convenience of your own home to rely upon here, do you? You'll have to rent, and that costs money."

Rosalynn sighed. "I suppose you're right, Judge Warner. But what about Lone Wolf? It would be a sin to take Gretchen from him. He is a kind and loving uncle and has a wonderful farm. And from what I've heard about his mother, she would love the opportunity to be with her grandchildren."

"That's true, Mrs. McAllister, but as Lone Wolf stated, he hasn't even informed Pale Flower that Mike is deceased. I can't gamble the lives of two children on a 'maybe.'"

Rosalynn slunk back in her chair and bit her lip in consternation. "It isn't fair. There has to be a way for me or Lone Wolf to adopt our family's children."

"If the little girl is as attached to Lone Wolf as you say, how will your having custody help her get over missing her uncle, Mrs. McAllister?"

Rosalynn raised her chin. "I made a promise to Lone Wolf that if I was the fortunate one to gain custody of Susan's children, he could see them anytime he wished. I would never keep him from his brother's children."

"I also told Roz-lynn that if she won custody, I would let her have the farmhouse to raise the children in," Lone Wolf interjected.

The judge smiled. "I've been a judge for twenty-plus years, and during that time, I've learned to analyze people. I can tell when someone is lying, and I can discern people's innermost feelings." He wagged his finger at them.

Rosalynn and Lone Wolf exchanged quizzical glances. Judge Warner sat back in his chair and studied them. "There is a way . . ."

"I will do anything you ask of me, Judge Warner," Lone Wolf declared. "I will do anything for my niece and nephew."

"So will I, Judge Warner," Rosalynn broke in, silently praying for a miracle.

"Marry, then," the judge stated simply, eyeing them both.

"I beg your pardon?" Rosalynn frowned, certain that she had misheard him.

"Who?" Lone Wolf wondered.

"Each other, Lone Wolf," the judge chuckled, obviously enjoying the stunned looks on their faces.

Silence engulfed the small room. Judge Warner leaned forward, his hands splayed in front of him. "Look, you both want the children. You're both single. And, my guess is that you like one another a lot. I propose that you marry."

Rosalynn and Lone Wolf stared at each other.

"We can't marry. We barely know each other!" Rosalynn stammered. "What kind of life would that make for any of us?" She looked away from Lone Wolf when she felt her face grow hot with . . . was it excitement?

"I've seen worse beginnings, and they worked out fine. And, as I said earlier, I have a sixth sense about such things. But it's up to you." Judge Warner pulled his gold pocket watch out of his pocket and looked at it. "I leave on the noon stage tomorrow. You bring me a marriage license, and I'll award custody of the children to both of you. Otherwise, I'll choose one of the other families before I leave town." Then, frowning at both Rosalynn and Lone Wolf, he added, "Mind you now, it has to be a real marriage. If I hear that you've divorced or annulled the marriage or are living separately, I'll pull those kids out of your home before you have time to spit. Do I make myself clear?"

In a daze, Rosalynn mumbled that she understood, and she heard Lone Wolf do the same.

The minute Rosalynn left the courthouse, she dashed down Main Street, her blue skirt kicking up to display a lacy white petticoat and trim ankles.

"Roz-lynn, where are you going?" Lone Wolf called after her.

"I need to see Ida," Rosalynn replied as she continued to run.

Lone Wolf ran to catch up with her and caught her by the arm. "Please, Roz-lynn, we need to talk."

Rosalynn could not look at him. "I can't talk about it now, Lone Wolf. I need to see Ida."

"Why, Roz-lynn, what is wrong?"

"I . . . I have a female complaint," she blurted out before she realized what she had said. It wasn't totally a lie, she thought miserably. She was a female and she had a problem.

"I will wait for you in the wagon," Lone Wolf called out as Rosalynn hurried down the street.

The instant Rosalynn entered the mercantile, she scanned the building for Ida and found her stocking shelves with canned goods. Ida looked up when the bell above the door rang, and Rosalynn watched as her smile froze on her face. Ida immediately put the cans down and went to meet her. "You look like you need a strong cup of tea!"

Ida guided Rosalynn to the living quarters behind the store. She sat Rosalynn down at the small kitchen table and then poured them each a cup of hot tea. Then she sat down and waited.

Rosalynn sat with her head cupped in the palms of her hands. Tears threatened to burst out, but she forced them back. "Oh, Ida, I'm so confused. I don't know what to."

"Perhaps if you talk about what is troubling you, it will help you feel better," Ida suggested sympathetically.

"Nothing can ever make me feel better. How can one change the past? How can one change—" Rosalynn's voiced cracked with emotion, then tears broke through the strong will that had kept them dammed. Her body quaked with sobs until she couldn't cry anymore.

Absently, Rosalynn reached for the scented handkerchief tucked in her bosom, but discovered that she couldn't reach it with her jacket on. Instead, she fumbled in her handbag for another one. Then she removed her gloves and stuffed them in her bag. She blew her nose and then dabbed the wetness from her pale cheeks.

"Thanks, Ida. I guess I've needed a good old-fashioned cry for a long time." Rosalynn tried to smile but her heart ached beyond endurance.

"What are friends for, Rosalynn?" Ida smiled as she affectionately patted Rosalynn on the arm. "It's a woman's right to cry."

Gratefully, Rosalynn attempted a weak smile. She inhaled deeply and slowly let the air out. "I'm not a married woman, Ida. The truth is out. I'm divorced."

Rosalynn waited for the usual gasp of disdain, but none was forthcoming. She glanced at Ida and was relieved to see a smile on her face.

"Is that what's so horrible, Rosalynn? You are a divorced woman? That's not so bad."

"Ida, that makes me a wanton woman—a threat to any other woman's husband who comes within hugging range of me." Rosalynn slumped back into her chair.

"Where did you get such a notion?" Ida queried with a hearty laugh. "Being divorced is no different than being a widow."

Rosalynn lifted her chin and crossed her arms. "Well, it mattered in St. Louis, and it will matter here when word gets out."

"Is that what's bothering you—what others will think?"

"Well, not exactly, but what they think will affect how they treat my children. I don't want my children growing up ashamed of me."

"Sounds like you need to get remarried." A mischievous smile danced across Ida's lips. "And I think I have the perfect man in mind."

"Now you sound like Judge Warner," Rosalynn said with an exasperated sigh.

"Judge Warner?" Ida inquired. "What did he say about Susan and Mike's children?"

"The judge won't let Lone Wolf or me have custody of the children unless we marry each other. He wants the children to have a mother and a father."

"I think it's a wonderful idea!" Ida came back. "The judge and I think alike." Then she giggled at Rosalynn's surprised expression. "Lone Wolf would make you a wonderful husband. I've know him for a long time, and he is a remarkable person."

"But we barely know each other! Anyway, he told me how he hated Susan for threatening Mike with divorce. Can you imagine what he thinks of me now?" Rosalynn buried her face in the palms of her hands as tears threatened to break free again.

Ida pulled Rosalynn's hands from her face and looked her straight in the eye. "First of all, we all know that if you divorced your husband, you must have had a good reason to do so. Second, I think you have stronger feelings for Lone Wolf than you realize, dear friend. Is that why you kept the truth from him? To protect your heart?"

"At first my marital status wasn't an issue. Then I thought I'd keep my personal business to myself. After all, I didn't know if I'd be here much longer, and I just didn't feel like airing my dirty laundry in public." Rosalynn paused and then continued. "I guess you're right about Lone Wolf. I really do respect him and I guess I was ashamed to tell him the truth."

"That makes sense to me. But now that Lone Wolf knows,

why don't you start at the beginning and tell him everything?"

Rosalynn's eyes grew large. "Tell him why I divorced Jeffery?"

"That would be a good start."

"Absolutely not. I've never even told my Aunt Dorothy, and she's closer to me than anyone. No, I can't tell Lone Wolf. I just can't." Suddenly, hysterical tears streamed down her cheeks. "I can't tell anyone, I can't."

"It's okay, Rosalynn," Ida soothed as she put her arms around Rosalynn. "I'm sorry, I didn't mean to upset you. I can see that the pain is still too fresh. Perhaps in time you will be able to talk about it. For now, what does Lone Wolf think of the judge's idea?"

"I don't know." Rosalynn sniffed as she wiped the tears from her face. "I couldn't even look at him after he found out I was divorced. I couldn't bear to see the look of disgust on his face."

"Give him a chance, Rosalynn. Lone Wolf's not like other men. He's kind and compassionate. He's had a hard time of it also, and I'm sure he sympathizes with you more than you realize."

"How did you do it, Ida . . . marry someone you didn't know? Weren't you scared? Didn't you have reservations?"

"I'd be lying if I said no," Ida chuckled. "Of course, I was frightened, but I read Swede's letters to his family and I could feel his pain. I prayed about it and knew he was for me."

Rosalynn snorted. "In my case, the question is, would Lone Wolf marry me? I'm divorced. I have two children and a maiden aunt to support. Millstones . . . I'm a wasichu or whatever it is that Lone Wolf calls white man. I'm the enemy." Rosalynn pounded her chest with her fist.

"Lone Wolf doesn't look at you like an enemy," Ida replied with compassion. "Nor does he speak of you as an enemy." Ida winked over the rim of her teacup.

Rosalynn felt herself blush.

"Go home, my friend. Pray about it and then speak to Lone Wolf. Let your heart guide you."

Rosalynn wanted to say that she had followed her heart once before, and it had lied to her.

On the way home from Peaceful, Rosalynn refrained from looking at Lone Wolf. A million things crammed her head, giving her a dreadful headache.

"Roz-lynn, we need to talk," Lone Wolf spoke quietly.

"Please, not now. I need to think," she replied, rubbing her temples.

As soon as the wagon pulled to a stop in front of the house, Rosalynn climbed out before Lone Wolf could walk around to help her down. Then she ran inside and went straight to her room.

Chapter Eight

When Rosalynn woke sometime later, it was dusk. She lit the candle on her dressing table, then poured water from the pitcher into the bowl. Looking into the mirror, she choked back a gasp. Her eyes were red and swollen, and most of her hair had fallen from the neat bun she had worn earlier. She splashed the cool water across her flushed face, then brushed and plaited her hair into a thick braid down her back and secured it with a ribbon.

Lone Wolf seemed like a nice, genuine person, but Rosalynn had reservations about marrying a man she barely knew. In fact, marriage was the last thing on her mind since she had arrived in Peaceful. Yes, it would be nice to marry, but Rosalynn wanted to be sure this time. She didn't want another Jeffery on her hands. She shuddered and the muscles in her stomach tensed. Just the thought of marriage sent a foreboding chill down her spine.

It would be a gamble. Was it worth risking her happiness to have a chance to raise Susan's children? Rosalynn knew she was frightened—frightened to trust, to love again.

Kneeling beside the bed, Rosalynn offered a prayer. Tears slipped down her cheeks as she poured out her heart and soul. *Father, I will do Thy will. If Lone Wolf agrees to marry, then I will take it as a sign of Thy will. If we aren't to marry, then I pray Thou will touch Lone Wolf's heart and tell him it's not to be. Amen.*

Rosalynn found her aunt downstairs in the small, cozy parlor, sitting in her rocking chair and reading Bible stories to the children. Flames flickered in the fireplace, casting a soft glow on the room.

"My dear, you're awake. Are you feeling better after your rest?" Worry lines marred Dorothy's usually smooth face.

Rosalynn walked over and kissed her aunt on the cheek. "I'm sorry, Aunt Dottie. I needed to be alone for a while and think about a few things."

"Mama," Joshua and Hannah chimed in unison.

"Aunt Dottie is reading us a story about Daniel and the lion's den." Joshua smiled and sidled up next to his aunt.

"That's wonderful, darling." Rosalynn smiled down at her son and then placed a kiss on the top of his head. "Aunt Dottie, have you seen Lone Wolf?"

"Yes, dear, he's been here several times inquiring about you. He asked for you to come out on the front porch when you woke." Then with a smile, she added, "I think he's concerned about you, dear."

"Thanks, Aunt Dottie. I do need to talk with him. When the children go to bed, I'll explain everything to you."

Rosalynn grabbed her shawl and threw it over her shoulders as she walked out the front door. Her heart felt heavy in her chest. She didn't want to face Lone Wolf and tell him about her marriage.

It was a beautiful evening, and Rosalynn admonished herself for not enjoying them more often. The stars twinkled brilliantly against an inky sky as the moon stretched its glittering beams across the horizon. "If I could have just one wish, Lord," she whispered gazing skyward.

"What would you wish for, Roz-lynn?" Lone Wolf stepped out of the darkness, joining her on the porch.

"Oh, Lone Wolf, you frightened me!" Rosalynn gasped, clutching her throat.

"Are you well, Roz-lynn? I was concerned." Lone Wolf's facial features were obscured by the shadows, but his voice was gentle and caring.

Lone Wolf stood so close that Rosalynn could smell the sweet fragrance of mint on his breath. She looked up and tried to read his thoughts, but his face melted into the evening dusk. "I'm better, thank you."

"Good." A sigh of relief echoed in the silence of the night. "Let us sit and talk."

Lone Wolf guided Rosalynn to the porch swing. He sat next to her and the swing slowly rocked back and forth. A lamp's flame filtered through the window, casting a soft glow over them. The buzz of fireflies and the occasional hoot of an owl filled the silence. Under different circumstances, it would have been a night for sweethearts.

Muffled voices seeped through an open window as Dorothy read to the children. The chilly air seemed to penetrate Rosalynn's very soul, and she shivered under her thin shawl.

"Are you cold, Roz-lynn?"

Rosalynn nodded, not trusting herself to speak.

Lone Wolf removed his buckskin jacket and placed it over her shoulders. Rosalynn immediately felt the warmth of his body permeate from the garment. She sighed and then snuggled deeper into the warm coat. She could smell Lone Wolf's scent in the leather—mint, sage, wood smoke, and sweat, all mingled together in an intoxicating fragrance.

"We need to talk, Roz-lynn."

"I know," Rosalynn replied softly, glancing at him.

Lone Wolf paused as though in deep thought, then began, "I was shocked when you told Judge Warner that you were divorced. All this time you gave the impression that you were married. Why?"

It was Rosalynn's turn to pause. How could she explain without saying all that was in her heart? Snuggling deeper into Lone Wolf's jacket, Rosalynn wanted to hide, but she silently prayed for guidance.

"I guess I am ashamed of being divorced."

It was the truth, or at least a half-truth. She couldn't bring herself to tell him that she was afraid of men, afraid to trust. No one must ever know what Jeffery did to her, mentally and physically.

"Ashamed?"

Rosalynn felt her throat constrict. Her heart beat fast against her chest and her palms began to sweat as she nervously clenched Lone Wolf's coat close to her chin. "Yes, ashamed. I've lived with people treating me like a leper for the past four years, and I didn't want it to start all over again here. When you told me that Susan threatened to divorce Mike, I saw your contempt. I didn't want you to think I was like Susan."

Rosalynn could feel the side of Lone Wolf's warm body pressed against hers in the narrow swing. Normally, she felt repulsed when men came too close, but she enjoyed sitting close to this man. She exhaled the breath she had been holding and tried to relax.

"There is truth in your words. When you first arrived, I was wary because you were Susan's sister, and because you were a wasichu. But I do not understand why you should care what I thought. Can you tell me why?"

Rosalynn glanced at Lone Wolf. He appeared sincere, and though Rosalynn knew that a man could deceive her, her heart wanted to trust.

"I just did, that's all," she blurted out, sounding harsh even to her own ears.

Silence engulfed them.

Lone Wolf finally spoke, his deep, melodious voice soothing her troubled spirit. "I will not speak of it. You will tell me when you are ready."

Tears stung her eyes at the tenderness in his voice. It had been a long time since a man had treated her with such kindness. *Please, Lord, help me trust.* "Thank you," she said.

"But we must speak of what is to be done with Gretchen and the baby. The judge leaves tomorrow. Have you thought about his suggestion, Roz-lynn?"

Rosalynn was afraid to look at Lone Wolf, afraid of what she might see in his eyes. "Yes," she whispered.

"Are you willing to marry a savage for the sake of the children?" Lone Wolf's countenance looked sad in the dim light.

"You are not a savage to me, Lone Wolf, and you never will be." Then more quietly, she asked, "How about you? Are you willing to marry a tainted woman?"

"I do not know what a tainted woman is." Lone Wolf inched closer to Rosalynn. He took a loose strand of her hair and wrapped it around his finger. Then, in a husky whisper he asked, "So, do you think we should marry?"

Tingles coursed through her as his soft voice washed over her like angel dust. Harsh, demanding, threatening—she could deal with those traits, but this . . . how could she defend herself against an unpretentious, humble man like Lone Wolf? And did she really want to?

Rosalynn found it difficult to speak, and when she did her voice quivered. "W—What do you think? Are you willing to marry without love? You would be sacrificing yourself and may regret it later. I couldn't bear to go through that again."

Lone Wolf shifted his body as he tried to get a better look at Rosalynn. "I would never divorce you. If we marry, you must understand, it will be for always."

Rosalynn tensed. She grabbed the arm of the swing, trying to keep her body from shaking. Was she signing her own death warrant? Jeffery forfeited their marriage without a struggle. Lone Wolf wasn't Jeffery, and Rosalynn sensed that Lone Wolf's convictions ran deep.

"I'm frightened of remarrying. I don't know if I can fully trust a man again . . . or do all the things that married people do . . ." Rosalynn gripped the jacket closer to her body. She suddenly wanted the darkness to swallow her.

Lone Wolf reached over, took Rosalynn's cold hand in his warm one, and gently clutched it. "I will not expect you to make love with me just because we are married, Roz-lynn. I give my word. I have faith in the Great Spirit. He will guide us. It is not easy for me to trust either, but I am willing to have faith if you are."

Rosalynn listened carefully. Could she trust Lone Wolf? She admired him, but she had admired Jeffery at first, too. *Lord, help me to trust and love again. If Lone Wolf is willing to try, I will try also. This is a risk I must take for the children.*

"Will you marry me, Roz-lynn?" Lone Wolf asked, breaking the silence.

"Yes, Lone Wolf, I will marry you," Rosalynn murmured softly. As she said the words, she felt a heavy weight lifted from her shoulders.

Lone Wolf sucked in a deep breath. "You honor me, Roz-lynn. I will never forget you sitting here under the sweetheart's moon and agreeing to be my wife. The Great Spirit is already blessing us."

Rosalynn's heart leapt within her chest. "What's a sweetheart's moon?" Still holding her hand in his, Lone Wolf explained softly,

"The sweetheart's moon is out on nights like this." Looking up into the twinkling sky, he continued, "The Lakota warriors and young maidens sneak out on nights when the moon is full of romance. We will have many chances to be together when the moon calls us, Roz-lynn. You will know it in your heart when the sweetheart's moon is upon you."

Rosalynn could not speak, and her heart pumped so loudly that she was sure Lone Wolf could hear every beat. What was it about Lone Wolf that made her heart leap? Was it his innocence, his integrity, his native bearing as a Lakota warrior? Whatever the reason, the intimacy between them confused her. *Father, I pray Lone Wolf is what he's portraying himself to be. Please don't let him be a wolf in sheep's clothing.*

Rosalynn could feel his eyes upon her even in the semi-darkness and tried to remove her hand from his. She couldn't let him know how she felt, when she wasn't sure herself. She needed time to think.

"You are quiet, Roz-lynn. Does the sweetheart's moon have you under its spell?" She detected a hint of amusement in his voice.

"You are a silly romantic, Lone Wolf," Rosalynn reproached playfully. "Next, you'll tell me you believe in fairies."

"I do not know these fairies you speak of, but one day I will hear you admit that you found love under the sweetheart's moon, Roz-lynn."

"Until then, we need to make plans," Rosalynn said, changing the subject but laughing nervously.

"Yes, Roz-lynn." Lone Wolf joined in with a chuckle. "We will leave for town early so I can return in time to do the chores."

"Do you have a preference as to which bedroom we use?" Rosalynn paused, relieved that the dim light concealed her deep blush.

Lone Wolf appeared deep in thought. "If we use the largest bedroom upstairs, I can sleep in the adjoining parlor. Is that agreeable with you?"

"Yes. In fact, I had hoped to use that bedroom if I stayed. But are you sure you're willing to sleep in the parlor?"

"Yes, Roz-lynn," Lone Wolf whispered, causing Rosalynn to fidget next to him. "I will sleep in the parlor until you no longer fear me. When the time comes, you will tell me when we can live as husband and wife."

Rosalynn knew that not many men would be so considerate. "Thank you," she responded. "That helps me feel better."

Lakota men probably feel the same way as white men do about divorced women, Rosalynn thought, *so Lone Wolf may not ever be romantically attracted to me.* She prayed that God would help things to work out.

Lone Wolf rose early the following morning, prayed to the Great Spirit, and finished his chores before bathing in the creek. The water was cold and invigorating, his senses keen and alert.

Today was his wedding day. Lone Wolf couldn't believe he was going to marry Rosalynn. He still felt shocked that she wasn't married. Why the secrecy? What was behind her fear? *Great Spirit, help me heal Roz-lynn's heart.*

When Lone Wolf parked the wagon in the back of the house, he noticed Jeb Swift pulling into the driveway.

"Well, howdy, Lone Wolf," Jeb greeted. "I didn't know you were still around. I don't get out much during planting season, I told the ladies I'd check on them on my next trip into town. They're still here, aren't they?"

Lone Wolf had to look twice to make sure it was actually Jeb. The usually scruffy bachelor was all scrubbed up like a Sunday preacher and wearing a new Sunday suit. His craggy old face was clean-shaven, and his freshly cut, slicked-back hair smelled like spicy cologne. Gone was the tattered old hat, replaced with a brand-new one.

Lone Wolf let out a long, low whistle. "Is that really you, Jeb? Did someone die?"

"Nah. This is my courting suit." Jeb stuck his thumbs under his lapel and strutted like a bandy rooster.

"Courting suit?" Lone Wolf's lips curled into a smile.

"Yup, I come a-callin' on the pretty Miss Applegate. She's here, ain't she?"

"Yes, she is here. I am to marry Roz-lynn today." Lone Wolf puffed out his chest with pride.

"You don't say? I thought she was already hitched."

Lone Wolf heard the screen door slap shut and glanced toward the house. Joshua stood on the top step in a little Buster Brown suit. Hannah stood next to her brother in a frilly little frock with pretty spring flowers and a white pinafore. Her long, honey-colored hair was pulled back in braids with bright blue ribbons tied on the ends. Lone Wolf felt his heart skip a beat. They would be his children now—a family of his own.

"Are you really going to be our pa, Lone Wolf?" Joshua asked.

Lone Wolf smiled into four big blue-green eyes. "Yes, Joshua, I am going to be your pa, if that is what you wish."

"Is it ever!" Joshua shouted. "Oh boy, Hannah, we're going to have a real pa just like other kids!"

Hannah stood slightly behind Joshua and peeked at Lone Wolf. "You nice pa?"

"Are not all fathers nice?" Lone Wolf asked, grinning from ear to ear.

"No, some are mean and—"

"All right, Joshua, that's enough." Rosalynn shouted from an upstairs window. "Why don't you two get the quilts and lay them down in the back of the wagon?" Then, glancing at Lone Wolf, she smiled. "We'll be out in a minute."

Rosalynn closed the window and went back to her room. Joshua's words echoed in her mind: "Some are mean . . ." Did he remember how violent Jeffery had been? He had been young at the time. *Please, Father, don't let him remember those terrible times. I promise that this marriage will be different.*

Rosalynn gave herself one more glance in the dressing mirror. Since this was a second marriage, she had decided to dress less formally, choosing a dress that Susan had left behind. It was an outdated ball gown, a creamy beige silk gown with short, puffy sleeves that fell softly off her shoulders.

She had forgotten how many layers of clothing a lady wore. First, came the baggy knee-length chemise, then the corset and the corset tournure to puff the dress out without wearing ten petticoats. The camisole and calf-length pantalets came last.

Grabbing her shawl made of delicate off-white crochet thread, Rosalynn placed it over her head to serve as a veil. Wisps of hair struggled free, framing her face. Then she pulled on her crocheted white gloves and picked up her purse.

Dorothy gasped when Rosalynn descended the stairs. "What a beautiful bride you make."

"You're the one who would make a beautiful bride, Aunt Dottie. I'm nothing special to look at and I know it." Rosalynn placed a kiss on her aunt's smooth cheek.

"Nonsense, child, and I'm sure Lone Wolf would agree with me." Dorothy hugged Rosalynn close.

"Speaking of Lone Wolf, he's waiting for us in the wagon, and Jeb is here as well." A small smile played across Rosalynn's lips as she raised her brows at Dorothy.

"Oh, my. May I invite him to the wedding, dear?" Dorothy asked. "He is a friend of Lone Wolf's after all, and we can't pick up and leave just when he's arrived for a visit." Dorothy smoothed her hair and then brushed the invisible wrinkles from her dove gray silk gown.

"Yes, auntie, by all means, invite him."

When Rosalynn and Dorothy stepped outside, they found Lone Wolf and Jeb standing by the wagon, talking. Joshua and Hannah sat on the quilt in the back of the wagon.

Jeb rushed over to Dorothy, grabbed her right hand, and pumped it enthusiastically. "I'm plum honored to see you again, ma'am."

Dorothy drew her left to her chest. "Why, Mr. Swift, how nice to see you again. My, don't you look handsome today."

"Aw, it's nothing, ma'am. I just thought I'd gussy up a bit when I came callin'." Jeb gazed at Dorothy with a look of pure adoration.

Rosalynn had to suppress a giggle. "Since you're all dressed up, Mr. Swift, why don't you come with us into town? Lone Wolf and I are getting married today." Rosalynn paused. "If it's okay with you, Lone Wolf."

Lone Wolf returned Rosalynn's smile, then turned to Jeb. "Yes, Jeb, you are welcome to join us."

"I'd be honored," Jeb replied as he gazed at Dorothy. "But it's Jeb, remember?"

"Wonderful. Why don't you ride with Jeb, Aunt Dottie?"

Dorothy glanced demurely at Jeb through lowered lashes. "Why, if Mr. Swift—I mean, Jeb— doesn't mind, I would be delighted to ride with him."

"I'd be right pleased to have your company, Miss Applegate," Jeb cooed.

"Now who's being formal?" Rosalynn laughed, then winked

at Jeb. "We're friends, remember?"

"Yes, ma'am, we are." Jeb returned the wink and held out his arm for Dorothy. "Come, Dorothy, let me escort you to the wagon."

Lone Wolf stared at Rosalynn as the wagon rattled down the dirt road. "You are very pretty today, Roz-lynn."

"Not really, but thank you. It's just the dress." Rosalynn laughed nervously and felt the heat creep up her neck. "It's one of Susan's castaways. I can't see throwing away good clothes." *Why are you rattling away? Calm down before you make a fool of yourself!*

Lone Wolf studied Rosalynn. "No, it is not the dress. You smell good, too. Like roses again."

Rosalynn glanced away, not wanting to pursue the conversation. Lone Wolf was as strikingly handsome as ever in his fringed buckskins. "You look very nice in your buckskins. I haven't seen you wear these before."

Lone Wolf touched his sleeve. "They are very special. I wear them for ceremonial occasions only, such as weddings. My mother made them for me long ago."

"Well, they're beautiful. I've never seen white buckskins before, but I'm not an expert by any means."

"My mother bleached the skins in the sun to make them white and then worked with them until they were very soft. The process isn't very appealing."

Rosalynn returned Lone Wolf's smile. "The bead work is exquisite. I've never seen patterns like this before except in the rugs I found in the house."

"They are Lakota, and the colors symbolize what we believe. The color red is the color of Wi, God of the sun. Green is Maka, the earth, and yellow is Inyan, the rock. The Lakota are thankful for Mother Earth. She provides everything we need to survive."

Rosalynn pondered Lone Wolf's words. Was he a Christian? Why hadn't she asked him before now? "So you believe the Lakota way of life and not the way of the wasichu?"

Lone Wolf paused in thought. "I respect the Lakota and their beliefs, but I believe what my father read to us from the Bible. I am a Christian. I believe in Jesus Christ and His Father, the Great Spirit."

Relieved, Rosalynn smoothed her dress and then folded her hands in her lap. "It takes conviction to stand by your principles. I admire you for honoring your mother's people and your father's beliefs. It isn't easy being different."

Lone Wolf focused his attention on the road, and Rosalynn studied him. Long, blue-black hair still damp from bathing trailed down his back. Two long braids wrapped in fur framed his face, while a single feather adorned one braid. His face was lean, masculine, and ruggedly handsome, his cheekbones high. His firm jaw, straight nose, and copper skin completed the perfect profile. When he turned toward her, Rosalynn stared into dark, mysterious eyes.

"You study me, Roz-lynn." Lone Wolf's deep, voice snapped Rosalynn from her silent reverie.

"I'm sorry, I didn't mean to stare." She turned to hide her embarrassment.

"Do you find me unattractive, Roz-lynn?" Lone Wolf's words reverberated with a trace of sadness.

Rosalynn was surprised by Lone Wolf's candidness. She had never met a man so open and honest.

"White women find my looks savage. Indian women find me too tall and big-boned. I get my size from my father. I hope you can accept me in time."

Rosalynn occupied herself by smoothing her veil. "I accept you as you are now or I wouldn't marry you."

"You did not answer my question. Do you find me unattractive?"

"Of course not, Lone Wolf. In fact, I find you uncommonly handsome. You are like no one I've ever met before. I find you very intriguing." Rosalynn smiled at Lone Wolf and then lowered her gaze.

"Truly, Roz-lynn?" Lone Wolf's face lit up. "You do not mind my dark skin and long hair?"

"There's nothing I dislike about you. I'm lucky to be marrying a proud and honorable man such as you. I want this marriage to work, and I'm hoping you'll be patient with me. There are a few things I need to work out myself."

"Do you want to tell me what hurts you so?" Lone Wolf asked.

Rosalynn saw a look of genuine concern in his dark eyes. "Maybe someday, Lone Wolf. I need to face the ghosts alone right now. Please try to understand."

"I understand, Roz-lynn, and I will wait until the sun no longer shines and the water no longer flows. I will wait forever."

Chapter Nine

Rosalynn was grateful for the children's endless chatter during the remainder of their journey to Peaceful. She listened halfheartedly to their questions about what kind of flowers grew along the roadway, which family lived on each farm, and what grew in the fields they passed. She was grateful for Lone Wolf's patience in answering the children as she endeavored to stay calm.

She was going to marry Lone Wolf! She only wished the marriage had been initiated by love and not convenience. After all, Lone Wolf wanted the marriage to be permanent, but there was no mention of love. Still, Rosalynn would put her faith in God, and she would pray that the marriage would succeed. So why did she feel turmoil inside? Her heart told her to trust Lone Wolf, her brain told her to be wary, and her body . . . her body hungered for affection and love.

Glancing at Lone Wolf, she caught her breath. Dressed in his ceremonial buckskins, he was magnificent. Black hair, long and flowing, fluttered in the wind like the mane of a stallion—proud and free. His chiseled profile was that of an ancient and dignified people.

When they reached Peaceful, Rosalynn noticed that Todd and Arlene's restaurant was dark. "Why is the café closed?"

"Something important must have come up." Lone Wolf shrugged as he focused on the team of horses.

He pulled the wagon to a stop in front of the church. As Jeb pulled in behind them, Rosalynn glanced across the street. "The merc is closed also. I hope nothing is wrong." Disappointment washed over Rosalynn. It would have been nice to have a few friends at the wedding.

"I am sure everything is fine, Roz-lynn," Lone Wolf called out as he jumped from the wagon seat.

He reached for her hand to help her down, and the children jumped from the back of the wagon onto the dusty street. Rosalynn's stomach tensed, her face felt flushed, and she had a hard time keeping her hands from trembling.

"Are you ailing, Roz-lynn?" Worry lines creased Lone Wolf's face. "Your face is very pale." He took her arm gently as though she was made of china.

"Oh, I'm just being silly. I don't know why I'm so nervous. This is just a little country wedding with only Jeb, Aunt Dottie, and the Bakers in attendance." She tried to sound light, but she could hear the anxiety in her voice and knew that Lone Wolf heard it also. "We should have had a quick ceremony at the Baker's rather than a wedding in an empty church."

Lone Wolf smiled, then tucked a rebellious tendril behind Rosalynn's ear. "It will be over soon, I promise. I wanted a church wedding, Roz-lynn. I intend to do this only once."

Rosalynn looked intently at Lone Wolf, wishing she could read his thoughts. Then she heard her children shouting; apparently, they didn't want to dilly-dally while their mother contemplated her fate.

When they entered the church, Rosalynn stopped and gaped, not trusting her eyes. The Bakers and the children were not the only ones present; in fact, half of Peaceful seemed to be in attendance. Todd and Arlene, along with Ida and Swede and their children, filled the front pews. She didn't recognize the other faces, but she was sure Lone Wolf did.

Rosalynn turned to Lone Wolf. "How did all of these people find out we were getting married today?"

"I told them." Lone Wolf was grinning from ear to ear, clearly enjoying her astonishment. "I told Todd when you were talking to Ida, remember?"

I hadn't agreed to marry you yet—we hadn't even discussed it! What made you think I'd marry you?"

"I was praying you would," Lone Wolf responded sheepishly. "Now, come. Reverend Baker is waiting for us."

Rosalynn peeked past him and saw Reverend Baker motion for them to approach the front of the church. She grabbed Lone Wolf's hand and squeezed it tightly. "Let's get this over with before I change my mind."

In a daze, Rosalynn said her vows, blocking out everything else. The only thing she was aware of was the man holding her hand and the final words of the minister. "I now pronounce you man and wife." *Please, God, sanction this marriage with Thy love.*

When Reverend Baker told Lone Wolf to kiss the bride, Rosalynn held her breath, anticipating their first kiss. She turned to him, tilted her head back, and closed her eyes, then felt a soft brush of warmth on her cheek and sensed the fragrance of mint and sandalwood. She opened her eyes just as Lone Wolf pulled back. He had brushed his cheek against hers, but he had not kissed her. Rosalynn felt like weeping. *Dear Lord, Lone Wolf can't bring himself to kiss a wasichu. Please, Father, I can't take rejection again.*

Everyone congratulated the bride and groom. The men slapped Lone Wolf on the back and shook his hand, while the women kissed and hugged Rosalynn. But the happiness she had felt earlier had dissipated into thin air. She pasted a smile on her lips, but her heart ached.

"Were you surprised to see all of us here?" Ida laughed and linked her arm through Rosalynn's.

Rosalynn smiled and nodded her head. "I was wondering why the café and the merc were closed."

"I'm Todd's wife, Arlene. I didn't get to meet you the other day," said a pretty black woman. "Congratulations and welcome to Peaceful."

"Thank you, Arlene."

Rosalynn then introduced Dorothy to everyone.

A few minutes later, Judge Warner winked at Rosalynn and then pressed a kiss to her cheek. "Well, you did it," he declared. "I brought the papers giving you and Lone Wolf legal custody of the children. I hope it works out for the both of you."

"Thank you, Judge Warner, for all of your help and for coming to the wedding," Rosalynn replied sincerely.

After what seemed like hours, they were ready to head for home. The surprise reception at the café had been wonderful, and there was a great show of love from the community. Rosalynn and Lone Wolf thanked everyone for making their wedding special. They were especially grateful to Reverend and Mrs. Baker for taking care of Susan and Mike's children.

"We would like to repay you for all you've bought for Gretchen and the baby," Lone Wolf offered, shaking Reverend Baker's hand.

"No," Mrs. Baker responded with a smile. "Everything was donated or made for the children, and we want it all to go with them. I hope you will bring them to church."

"We will," Rosalynn promised.

She hugged Mrs. Baker and then took the baby in her arms. As she looked down at the gurgling infant, tears threatened to give away her emotions. How could a mother abandon a gift from God? Rosalynn touched the chubby little cheek with her lips and then kissed him. The baby looked at her with deep blue eyes. A bubble escaped his mouth and then dribbled down his chin. Rosalynn wanted to laugh and cry all in the same breath. In the end, all she could do was hold him tight, vowing to be the best mother she could.

Joshua and Hannah approached Rosalynn with Gretchen in tow. Rosalynn knelt down to show the baby to them. "Look, Josh and Hannah, isn't he darling?" She then directed her attention to Gretchen. "How are you, Gretchen? I see you've met your cousins."

Gretchen smiled, holding onto Hannah's hand. "Me and Hannah are going to be sisters now. I promised to share the baby."

Rosalynn swallowed a grin. The girls were friends already.

Hannah pumped her head up and down. "My sister and baby, Mama." She reached over and kissed the baby's cheek. "Hi, little baby. Come home now."

Rosalynn kissed her daughter and stood to leave. Noticing Lone Wolf looked forlorn Rosalynn handed him the baby. Lone Wolf's face brightened as he took the baby and carefully placed him in the crook of his arm. He rubbed the baby's cheek with his finger and then took the chubby little hand and held it. How small it looked in his huge hand. Rosalynn, touched by the display of affection, felt hot tears sting her eyes.

The baby gurgled and crooned as Lone Wolf nibbled on his fat little fingers. His chubby little legs pumped under the blanket with excitement. Clearly, the baby recognized his uncle.

Lone Wolf's expression calmed many of Rosalynn's fears. *Yes, Father, I did the right thing. At least the right thing for Lone*

Wolf and the children. Was this marriage going to be worth it a year from now, five years from now? Would she regret marrying for the sake of the children and not for love? Rosalynn suddenly felt very tired.

———

"Roz-lynn, we are home," Lone Wolf whispered. Rosalynn's head rested on his shoulder and he hated to disturb her. It was nice to feel her warmth and smell the sweet scent of roses.

"Roz-lynn. Sweet Roz-lynn, wake up," he repeated, touching her warm cheek.

He watched her long lashes flutter open. When her sight focused on him, she jerked her head upright.

"Oh, my, did I fall asleep?" She looked around. "We're home already?" Glancing into the back of the wagon, she noticed that the children were gone. "Where are the children?"

"Dorothy and Jeb carried them into the house." Enjoying the close proximity with Rosalynn, Lone Wolf was in no hurry to get out of the wagon.

"Well, my goodness, I best help her." Rosalynn scrambled from the wagon, not waiting for Lone Wolf to assist her. "Two more children to prepare for bed—"

"I will unharness the team and milk the cow before I come in. I fed the rest of the animals before we left, so they are fine until morning." Lone Wolf's words were lost on the retreating Rosalynn, and he smiled to himself.

By the time Lone Wolf finished the chores it was sundown. It had been an eventful day. Though their marriage had not been conceived through love, it was still important to him. His only regret was that his mother and his friend Black Hawk had not been in attendance.

Rosalynn was beautiful and kind. Lone Wolf marveled at how

the Great Spirit had brought them together. *She is my destiny, Great Spirit. I pray we will have a loving marriage in time. Please give me the patience to wait for her heart to heal.*

Lone Wolf had vowed not to pressure Rosalynn into a relationship she wasn't ready to have, and he would keep his promise. He would wait for her to invite him into her heart and embrace him. It would be difficult not to touch her, hold her, to express his feelings of adoration.

The evening was warm and still with only the crickets making music somewhere in the distance and fireflies dancing in the fading light. Lone Wolf watched the orange and red sunset burst over the hills as the sun said good night. The moon stood out against the fading sky. A sweetheart's moon. It was a time for sweethearts to meet in secret and express their love and devotion. "Someday, my Roz-lynn will express herself to me under such a moon," he whispered as he faced the heavens. "I, too, will express my love the Lakota way, beneath the moon for sweethearts."

The next morning, Rosalynn had to force herself to get out of bed. The past week had taken its toll. Her entire body ached, and she felt physically and emotionally drained.

Rosalynn and the children had slept upstairs for the first time. She was grateful that Dorothy had insisted on keeping the baby with her at night until the older children became more accustomed to sleeping in their own rooms.

Rosalynn had waited up as long as she could for Lone Wolf to retire, then finally gave up and went to bed. Perhaps he had changed his mind and decided not to sleep in the adjoining sitting room. Part of Rosalynn was disappointed, and part of her was relieved. It wasn't going to be easy having a man in her life again.

She didn't take the time to dress; instead, she quickly grabbed her shawl and wrapped it around her shoulders before going downstairs. The mornings were still cool, and the warmth of a fire and a cup of steaming tea sounded good.

Soon a fire crackled cheerfully in the kitchen as the sun rose across the scarlet sky. It was going to be another beautiful day, Rosalynn decided as she sipped her tea by the window.

When she heard the baby cry, she took Dorothy a bottle of warm milk, then returned to the kitchen. *What a blessing that Reverend and Mrs. Baker provided so much for the children.* Rosalynn thought, relieved that she didn't need to rush into town for baby supplies and clothing.

She was still daydreaming at the kitchen window when she heard the screen door slam shut. She hurried to the back door and stepped out, her heart racing. Lone Wolf was striding away from the porch, and Rosalynn noticed a pail of fresh milk and a basket of eggs near her bare feet.

"Good morning, Lone Wolf. You're up earlier than usual, aren't you?" Rosalynn tried to smooth her wild hair with one hand, while the other clutched the shawl closer to her chest. How embarrassing to be caught in her nightgown!

"Good morning, Roz-lynn. I am behind with the chores and the planting, so I thought I had better get an early start."

He didn't appear shocked by her appearance, so Rosalynn ventured on, hoping he might change his mind. "Can't you at least take time to eat? It wouldn't take me long to fix breakfast."

Lone Wolf stopped for a moment and then started back toward the house. "All right, Roz-lynn, I will eat breakfast with you."

As Rosalynn scooted aside for Lone Wolf to pass, she felt her face redden under his gaze. "I'm a little embarrassed to be running around in my nightgown and—" Her voice trailed off.

"You look like an angel with your white nightgown and flowing hair."

Rosalynn gulped down a gasp when Lone Wolf reached out to touch her hair, and he drew back his hand. She stood silently, waiting for his next move. With feather-like gentleness, he touched the shiny brown hair that framed her face. "Your hair is as soft as a baby kitten's, Roz-lynn." He then reddened beneath his coppery skin. "I am not very romantic, am I? I have spent too much of my life in a Lakota camp wrestling with my brothers and racing our ponies against the wind. My parents did not speak much English at home. My father taught my mother Swedish, and my mother taught my father Lakota. So I am not a very eloquent speaker."

"You have nothing to be ashamed of, Lone Wolf. I find your speech and mannerisms very pleasing. In fact, no one has ever paid me such pretty compliments." Rosalynn's breath caught at the intimacy between them.

"Your first husband must have been a very foolish man not to see you for who you are. Someday, I wish to hear about this man who took your love so lightly."

Rosalynn lowered her head.

"For now, I wish you to wear your hair down. Will you do that for me, Roz-lynn? It is too pretty to hide in a bun."

"We'll see. I'm a bit old to be parading around like a lovesick schoolgirl." Rosalynn tried to keep her laugh light and friendly, but she could hear the trembling in her voice. "I best get started with breakfast. Aunt Dottie and the children will be demanding food the minute their feet hit the floor."

Rosalynn didn't wait for an answer from Lone Wolf and started for the cook stove. When he didn't enter the kitchen behind her, she turned, wondering why he hadn't followed. The look on his face startled her. He stood staring as though in a trance. "Lone Wolf, are you all right?"

No response came.

Rosalynn stepped back and kept quiet as Lone Wolf looked

around the kitchen. Then she remembered that he had grown up in the old farmhouse. She tried to see the house through his eyes and realized it must have been a long time since he'd seen it cared for.

Silently, she watched Lone Wolf walk into the dining room and touch each piece of furniture with loving care. He stopped in his tracks when he entered the company parlor. Rosalynn inhaled as he stared at the intricate carvings she had found stored in the crates upstairs. *Please, Lord, don't let him be upset with me for putting out the beautiful treasures I found.*

Rosalynn wondered what Lone Wolf's thoughts were as he reached for a carving and rubbed his thumb over the small deer. His low breathing echoed in Rosalynn's ears.

She didn't know what expect. Was he angry with her for snooping in his family's possessions? Her heart thumped hard against her chest when Lone Wolf faced her, his eyes glistening with emotion. Rosalynn's throat constricted.

Lone Wolf laid the carving down and approached Rosalynn. He took her small hands in his large, calloused ones. "Roz-lynn . . ."

Lone Wolf's voice cracked, and he met Rosalynn's gaze.

"Are you angry with me, Lone Wolf?" Rosalynn craned her neck back so she could search his visage. "I know this is your family's house and those are your personal belongings. I had no right to open the crates. I'll pack them away, I promise." She tried to pull away.

Lone Wolf stood in silence before her, then leaned over and gently rubbed his cheek against hers.

"Roz-lynn, you have made me very happy." His voice was a low, husky whisper.

"I have?" Rosalynn felt her body relax. *He isn't mad, Father.*

"Yes, you have." He released her hands and looked around. "My mother loved this house. She kept it spotless. She took pride in her family and herself. I cringed every time I came in here when Susan moved in."

"Susan hated my mother, and when she forced us from our home, she removed everything that reminded her that Indians had lived here. I always thought she destroyed all those things."

Rosalynn felt anger boiling up inside of her like a teapot ready to spout steam. How could Susan treat Lone Wolf and his mother with such hatred? She vowed to make it up to them somehow. "So you don't mind that I brought the things downstairs?"

"No, Roz-lynn. I do not mind. I like it, for it reminds me of my family and how happy we were in this house. I see my mother's colorful Lakota rugs on the polished floors. All of the trinkets and gifts we gave in love are scattered around as reminders that I did once have a family."

"These small wood carvings are the most exquisite figurines I've ever seen." Rosalynn picked up the carved deer that Lone Wolf had placed on the table and gently rubbed her fingers over the smooth wood.

"My mother loves animals of the forest. They remind her of happier times among the Lakota. Ever since I was a small boy I've carved them for her during the long winter evenings by the fire."

"You carved them?" Rosalynn's eyes were wide. "You're very talented. I have never seen such detail. They are all so realistic."

Lone Wolf's face lit up with boyish charm, and Rosalynn couldn't help smiling at him.

"Will you come in for dinner?" Rosalynn asked as Lone Wolf finished his breakfast.

"No, I will stay in the fields." Lone Wolf took a sip of hot mint tea. "I need to finish planting before it is too late for the seeds to mature." While what he had just said was true, he was secretly afraid that if he came in for the noon meal, he wouldn't want to leave Rosalynn again.

Rosalynn sat down across from him. "You still need to eat. I'll send Joshua out with a food pail. Then this afternoon I think I'll start clearing the garden area for planting."

"That is too much work for you to do alone. If you wait, I will help you when I finish the plowing for the day."

"Nonsense." Rosalynn waved her hand in the air. "I've planted a garden every year since I can remember. If I find something too challenging, I'll let you know."

Lone Wolf leaned back in his chair and placed his hands on his hips. "Roz-lynn, the garden has not been tilled for many years. The work is too hard for a woman. Let me help you."

"Listen here, Lone Wolf Larson." Rosalynn said, pointing her finger at him. "I have Joshua to help me, and besides, I'm used to hard work. You have enough to do without mollycoddling me."

Lone Wolf watched with a boyish grin as Rosalynn rose from the table and went into the kitchen. How could a woman be so beautiful dressed in a nightgown with her hair cascading wildly down her back, and be so stubborn at the same time? He had to admit he admired her spunk.

Lone Wolf's thoughts were jarred back to the present by a woman's scream. Taking the few steps to the kitchen doorway in one leap, he watched as Rosalynn scrambled onto a countertop and perched precariously. He ran to her side, his eyes darting around the room.

"Roz-lynn! What is wrong?" Lone Wolf saw that her face was as white as snow. "Roz-lynn, answer me. Are you hurt?"

Rosalynn stared at the floor, her body shaking involuntarily. "No!" She wiped a wisps of hair from her cheek and then pointed toward the pantry.

With a long shuddering breath, she whispered, "A . . . a mouse."

"A mouse?"

"It ran into the pantry!"

Lone Wolf tried to stifle a smile. "It is gone now. Come down from there before you hurt yourself."

Rosalynn shook her head.

"It is safe to come down, Roz-lynn, I promise." Lone Wolf held out his hand.

"No!"

"Roz-lynn, the mouse is more frightened of you than you are of it."

"No, it's not," Rosalynn replied stubbornly. "It ran across my foot. I'm not coming down in bare feet."

Laughing heartily, Lone Wolf gathered Rosalynn in his arms and carried her up the stairs, ignoring her protests. Without ceremony, he plopped her on the soft feather bed, then reassured her, "You are safe now. I will see what I can do about ridding the house of man-eating mice." Then he winked at her and left the room.

Lone Wolf still chuckled as he walked to the field. He tried to keep his mind on the planting, but the furrows weren't as straight as they usually were. His thoughts kept drifting back to Rosalynn, and he'd snap back to the plowing only to see the horse meandering. He tried not to think about how Rosalynn felt in his arms—so soft and desirable. The scent of roses still lingered with him.

Words could not describe how he had felt when he walked into the house and found his mother's things displayed and everything neat and clean. Rosalynn was everything she portrayed and more. She was kind and considerate and a loving mother. She had high moral standards and strong Christian values. If only she would trust him! Her first husband must have done something unforgivable to her to make her so afraid.

—••—

"Well, how does it feel to be married again, dear?" Dorothy asked Rosalynn as they shared tea together. "You look happy."

"I am. For the first time in years, I have hope for the future. I don't mean financial security, but hope for happiness. I feel like I've been carrying around a boulder on my shoulders ever since I married Jeffery. Now, I feel free again."

"I'm so happy for you, dear. I could just cry." Dorothy sniffed and then blew her nose. "I can see now that it truly was meant for us to move here, and I truly think Lone Wolf was meant for you."

"Oh, Aunt Dottie, I feel the same way. I was so confused about who God wanted to raise Gretchen and the baby, and He found a way for all of us to be together as a family. I still marvel at His miracles."

Rosalynn hummed as she tidied the upstairs after breakfast. When she entered the little sitting room, her fears were confirmed. There were no signs of Lone Wolf anywhere. Obviously, he hadn't slept in the house on their wedding night.

Why is he still sleeping in the cabin? Rosalynn thought as her heart fell. Maybe the relationship was one-sided after all. Maybe he was just looking for a housekeeper and nanny. Maybe he couldn't get past the thought of her being a divorced woman. Maybe he just plain disliked the wasichu.

Chapter Ten

Over the days that followed, Rosalynn kept busy in the garden, taking her frustrations out on the hard, baked soil and the overgrown weeds. Close to the house and well situated in the full sun, the garden was enclosed by a tall, white picket fence to protect the plants from forest animals. While she worked, Rosalynn welcomed the sun's heat that penetrated into her bones.

As she pulled the weeds and removed most of the sod, Rosalynn was delighted to find rhubarb and strawberry plants already green and starting to leaf. She also discovered a small grape arbor, several raspberry bushes, and a few blueberry bushes. In the corner of the garden, asparagus peeked above the dry weeds.

One afternoon, sitting back to admire her work, Rosalynn made a mental note to tell Lone Wolf that she was ready for the soil to be turned and disked. Her thoughts drifted to her new husband. He was so kind to her, and so loving and gentle with the children. Every evening after dinner, they read scriptures together as a family, and then he played with the children until they were exhausted. Joshua was especially fond of Lone Wolf and tagged along after him as often as Rosalynn permitted. In fact, Joshua left with his new father each morning to help feed the animals and gather the eggs, then went with him to the fields. Rosalynn had gotten into the habit of taking their dinner to them at noon. Only to herself did she admit that seeing Lone Wolf at lunchtime was a highlight of her day.

Every night while Rosalynn and Dorothy prepared the children for bed, Lone Wolf slipped off into the darkness, leaving Rosalynn to go to her bedroom alone. Day after day, the same scenario played out, and Rosalynn wondered how she and Lone Wolf were to become better acquainted if they never spent any time alone together. She had pictured them talking together in the sitting room off her bedroom, then him sleeping in the sitting room, just as they had planned. Because Lone Wolf never stayed or tried to talk privately with her when everyone else had retired for the day, she often felt hurt and rejected, and her prayers were fervent.

Just the night before, when Lone Wolf again disappeared after scripture study, Rosalynn had prayed, *Dear Lord, what shall I do? I cannot just blurt out my feelings to Lone Wolf. What would he think of me? Please help us make this marriage work, Father.*

Rosalynn sighed as she came back to herself in the garden. She picked some asparagus for dinner and headed for the house. Filthy and covered in perspiration, she desperately needed a bath before dinner.

She hated the thought of bathing in the small, cramped tub in the house. *Where does Lone Wolf bathe?* He always came to dinner with damp hair, so she knew there must be a nice spot somewhere along the creek that ran through the valley floor. Certainly, she could find another good spot for bathing. Why, she and Aunt Dorothy could take the children there to play when the summer grew warmer!

Overcome by the thought of cooling off in the creek, Rosalynn hurried to the house, placed the asparagus on the counter, and checked on the beef roast in the oven. Thank goodness she had made the bread and the custard pies that morning while the kitchen was cool.

She ran upstairs and grabbed her rose soap, a towel, and a clean frock. When she came back down the stairs, she went to tell Dorothy where she was going, but found her fast asleep with the girls and the baby.

Once outside, Rosalynn headed for the creek just beyond the small fruit orchard and the garden. She could see where irrigation lines ran from the creek to the garden and was delighted that she would not have to haul water in the heat of summer.

As she followed the stream, Rosalynn ran across the cabin where Lone Wolf stayed. It sat in a secluded field filled with lupine, balsam root, and wild daisies. She was tempted to go up to the cabin, but thought better of it and continued downstream.

She was about to give up on finding a suitable place to bathe when she heard rushing water. Cupping her hand over her eyes to shade them from the sun, she saw what looked like a small waterfall in the distance. As she drew closer, she saw water spilling into a beautiful blue-green pool. Soon she stood next to the pool, inhaling the intoxicating fragrance of the mint that grew along the banks. It appeared that someone had banked the sides with rocks and blocked the stream with logs.

Rosalynn went immediately to the waterfall and stuck her arm into the cold water as it rushed down the bank. Giggling like a small child, she placed her clean clothes under a bush near the falls and draped the towel over the branches.

After making sure she was alone, Rosalynn took the pins from her hair, stuck them in her pocket, and removed her bib overalls. She peeled off her shirt, but decided to leave her pantaloons and chemise on just in case. She stepped into the cool water, steadying herself as she clung to the damp rocks that formed the pool. Soon, her entire body was submerged under the cascading water. It felt wonderful as it pelted down on her sore muscles. For several minutes she stood there, letting the water soothe her aching body.

Finally, when her body started to feel numb, she decided to step away from the falls. Pushing her hand through the waterfall, Rosalynn expected to brace herself on a rock wall, yet her hand touched nothing but air. Surprised and curious, she plunged through the cascading water.

The cave she stood in was about fifteen feet in diameter and was completely concealed by the waterfall. The cold air inside the cave made her shiver, and she decided to share her discovery with the children—on a warmer day.

In the meantime, she needed to wash up and get back to the house before her aunt started to worry. She reached through the pounding water and grabbed the bar of soap from the bank. When she glanced up, a movement caught her attention. Rosalynn pushed the hair away from her face and rubbed her blurry eyes. Was she imagining it, or had she seen something move?

When her eyes cleared, Rosalynn let out a strangled cry and ducked her head back under the falls, almost drowning in the process.

Lone Wolf! She held her breath and drew her face close to the water. Through the rippling blue torrent, she could barely make out a masculine body. "Oh my stars!" she muttered aloud. It *was* Lone Wolf and he was undressing!

"You found his bathing spot all right, you ninny," Rosalynn scolded herself. "Okay, calm down." But her mind raced as fast as the rushing water. How could she let Lone Wolf know that she was there before he . . . She did not want to think beyond that!

"You can do this," she whispered under her breath.

By now Rosalynn had goose bumps the size of boulders and was shivering so hard that her teeth chattered loudly. Mustering her courage, she crossed her arms over her chest, took a deep breath, and then popped her head through the once-invigorating waterfall. She opened her eyes and saw—to her horror—that Lone Wolf was down to just his leather loincloth.

"Stop, Loon Woof," she sputtered as the water pounded over her face, distorting her speech. Through the pelting water, she watched Lone Wolf and realized that he had not heard her and was about to remove the tiny cloth.

Rosalynn frantically pushed her body through the falls, her feet slipping on the wet rocks. "Stop!" was all she could muster.

The last thing Rosalynn saw before plunging into the cold pool was Lone Wolf turning in alarm, springing backwards, and falling over a large boulder. Rosalynn sank to the bottom of the pool, then used her feet to spring back to the surface, sputtering and coughing and flinging her arms about like a wild woman.

When her brain finally told her to swim, she relaxed enough to keep afloat, but it was too late. Lone Wolf jumped up and dove into the icy water. Within seconds, his arms were around her. Their faces were only inches apart, and Rosalynn wished she could crawl under a rock.

Lone Wolf's arms held her like a vice and made her skin prick under the thin fabric of her chemise. She grabbed his waist to keep from reeling back and couldn't help but feel the warmth of his body.

"Roz-lynn, are you all right?" Lone Wolf's coppery skin glistened as droplets of water coursed down his face and onto his firm chest. His long, raven hair clung to his back like a cloak. He released one arm from Rosalynn's waist and brushed the wet hair from her cheeks. His embrace tightened and Rosalynn could feel his heart pump against her skin.

All at once, the proximity was more than Rosalynn could bear. She placed her small hands on his massive chest and pushed away from him, grateful that the water reached to her neck.

"I'm f–f–f–f–fine," she managed, catching her breath. "You just startled me, that's all."

Lone Wolf released her and paddled his arms backward until several feet separated them. "I startled you? My heart is still racing from seeing a wood sprite come charging out of the falls!" His laugh resonated across the water. "This is my personal sanctuary, and finding someone here was the last thing I expected."

"I'm sorry if I intruded." Rosalynn kept her arms crossed in front of her and tried to keep her voice as normal as possible.

This wonderful, unpretentious man—her husband—was the most virile man she had ever encountered, and he was clearly unaware of his own charisma. Rosalynn found it hard to breathe knowing that he was so close, and so unclothed.

"I . . . I wanted to bathe in the creek and just followed it to this spot," Rosalynn stammered, more nervous than cold. "I won't come back again, I promise."

"Please, come here anytime you wish, Roz-lynn. This place holds many special memories of happy times with my family. We came here often throughout the years. My father, Mike, and I dug a twelve-foot hole where you fell in so that we could dive into the water from above the falls. The water is much more shallow at the other end."

"Yes, I know it's about twelve feet deep. I found out the hard way." Rosalynn could not help but laugh.

"What should we do now, Roz-lynn? Do you want me to wash your back?" Lone Wolf winked and grinned saucily. Rivulets of water cascaded down his face—the face she was growing to love so well.

The sound of his voice was enough to send her into ecstasy,

and her heart almost stopped at the thought of his hand on her bare skin. "No," she managed to croak out, holding out her hand in protest. "I'm perfectly capable of bathing myself, Lone Wolf Larson. Don't you dare come any closer!"

Lone Wolf chuckled, then raised his brows. "Then you can wash my back. I am not as agile as you, my little fairy."

"Don't give me that innocent act, mister. Now, if you will turn your back, I will quickly wash and get out."

"If that is your wish, Roz-lynn." Lone Wolf let out an exaggerated sigh.

"Don't turn around until I say. Promise?" Rosalynn kept her eyes pinned on Lone Wolf's back.

"I promise," Lone Wolf called out without turning.

Rosalynn watched as he stepped out of the water. His brown skin glistened in the sun as he walked to where he had placed his clothes. The black mane that hung below his waist was as glossy as a jeweler's stone, and his broad chest and shoulders tapered to narrow hips and long legs.

Rosalynn turned and looked away, reprimanding herself for coveting her own husband. Surely, it must be a sin to have such fervent feelings even for one's spouse.

She grabbed the rose-scented soap and hastily washed her hair and body. Dunking under the water, she popped back to the surface, gasping for air.

"Are you all right, Roz-lynn?"

"Yes, I'm fine. I'm getting out, so don't turn around."

"I gave you my word," Lone Wolf answered with a hint of sadness. "You need not be frightened of me."

Rosalynn quickly dried and then slipped on the clean frock. "I'm decent. You may turn around now." She gathered her soiled clothes and started to leave. "I'll head home and give you some privacy."

"Please, do not go, Roz-lynn. I promise to be respectful."

Rosalynn glanced back at Lone Wolf and found him watching her. His countenance was sincere, his voice tender and pleading. How could she tell him it wasn't him that she did not trust, but her own feelings?

"All right, Lone Wolf. I would enjoy chatting for a while."

Rosalynn dropped her soiled clothing on the grass next to the large boulder where Lone Wolf had undressed earlier. She scrambled on top of the rock and tried to keep her attention on smoothing her hair with her fingers, but her gaze kept creeping to Lone Wolf as he slipped back into the water.

It was hard not to stare. He dipped into the water with great ease and came back up in the center of the pond. When he turned to face her, Rosalynn heard a gasp escape her throat. Finely chiseled muscles bulged from his biceps as he took the lye soap and began to lather his well-defined chest. There wasn't an ounce of fat on his lean form. Feeling the heat rise to her face, Rosalynn quickly averted her eyes and again directed her attention to her tangled hair.

A few minutes later, she heard Lone Wolf step from the water. She offered him her towel and he accepted it.

"I usually dry in the sun, but I do not think you will look at me until I am dressed," he said teasingly.

"I'm respecting your privacy as you respected mine," Rosalynn answered, not daring to tell him that she desired him as a wife was meant to desire her husband.

Lone Wolf had never approached her romantically, and if she succumbed to him without provocation, he might think she was a wanton woman. His opinion of her mattered to her more than anything, she suddenly realized.

"Lone Wolf?"

"Yes, Roz-lynn?"

"What should we name the baby? We can't continue calling him 'baby' forever."

"I'm dressed, Roz-lynn."

As she turned to look at him, their eyes locked. How beautiful his brown eyes were! How she longed to touch him!

"You name him, Roz-lynn." Lone Wolf used the towel to dry his long hair, then bent down, picked some mint from the creek bank, and stuck it in his mouth.

Rosalynn cleared her throat. "What was your father's name?"

"Adrian. Why?" Lone Wolf asked as he chewed the mint leaves.

"I thought maybe we could name him Michael Adrian Larson. How would you feel about that?"

Silence.

Rosalynn's brows crept together. "I know Gabriel is your Christian name . . ."

Lone Wolf's head shot up.

"When I heard Gretchen call you Uncle Gabe, I asked Ida about it. She explained that Gabriel is your Christian name and that only your family used it. I wasn't prying, honestly. Anyway, I was hoping . . . hoping someday we might have a son. I would like our son to have your name, but if you prefer Mike's baby to be named Gabriel, I understand."

Rosalynn bit her lip and looked down, waiting for Lone Wolf's reply. Suddenly she felt his gentle fingers tilt her chin until their eyes met. She wished with all her heart that she could express her love to him. Yet, she must respect him and allow him to grow accustomed to the idea of being married to a wasichu.

"Roz-lynn, you make my heart sing. Never have I met a person more pure of heart than you. Thank you for the generous offer, but what about your father's name?" Lone Wolf stood eye level with Rosalynn as she sat on the boulder.

"I'll reserve my father's name for my son, along with my husband's name."

Rosalynn felt Lone Wolf brush the side of his face against her cheek. His skin was still cool from his bath.

Lone Wolf took Rosalynn's small hands in his. "Then he will be named Michael Adrian."

"Lone Wolf, I need to ask you something personal. I hope you don't get upset with me." Rosalynn's heart quickened. *Help me, Lord, to say the right thing.*

"You can ask me anything, Roz-lynn. I have nothing to hide from you."

Rosalynn searched her husband's face. Asking him was a gamble, but something inside pushed her to continue.

Her stomach tensed with apprehension, and for a moment she thought she would be ill. *Lord, I can't live in limbo; I need to see into Lone Wolf's heart. I can't let this fear that Jeffery instilled in me rule my life. Help me be strong. I would rather face rejection now than live with hope for something than can never be.*

"I was wondering why you didn't kiss me at our wedding. Is it because I'm a wasichu?"

Lone Wolf smiled warmly. "I did kiss you, Roz-lynn."

She started to protest, but he interrupted. "I kissed you in the way of the Lakota. Like this." Lone Wolf brushed his cheek against hers. "That is how the Lakota show affection."

"Is it?" Rosalynn sighed. "Have you ever kissed the way the wasichu kiss?"

Lone Wolf fastened his gaze on her. "No, Roz-lynn. You are the only woman I've ever wanted to kiss the Lakota way."

"You've never been with a woman before?" Rosalynn gasped.

"No. An honorable Lakota brave would never disrespect a

maiden by compromising her before marrying her. Marriage is sacred."

Rosalynn looked away. "I agree. I wish it were so with all of the wasichu."

"Will you teach me to kiss like the wasichu, Roz-lynn?" Lone Wolf came closer and tilted her chin with his hand.

"I can try," Rosalynn giggled nervously, "but I don't have a lot of experience myself."

Rosalynn felt Lone Wolf's warm, minty breath on her face, and her stomach filled with butterflies. She took a deep breath. "First, we bring our lips together like this." Rosalynn placed the palms of her hands on Lone Wolf's cheeks, brought her lips to his, and then brushed them across his lips.

"I like that, Roz-lynn. Show me again."

Rosalynn smiled. This time she wrapped her arms around his neck and hungrily brought her mouth down on his. The kiss lingered, and Rosalynn could feel Lone Wolf's lips surrender to hers.

"Again, Roz-lynn," Lone Wolf's demanded huskily. "Let me try." Following Rosalynn's lead, he embraced her and brought her tight against his chest. His lips sought hers with as much vigor as Rosalynn's had his. She felt her head reel as their lips joined in perfect unison.

Several seconds later, Rosalynn backed away from Lone Wolf, fanning her face with her hand as she tried to catch her breath. "I think that's enough practice for one day!"

"Do the wasichu kiss often?" Lone Wolf asked with raised eyebrows.

Lone Wolf looked like a child with a new toy, and Rosalynn stifled a giggle. "Whenever they want to, I guess."

He liked her kisses! Rosalynn thought her heart would burst with happiness.

"Good. It will be often with us, Roz-lynn," Lone Wolf said with a determined expression.

Rosalynn suddenly came to her senses. "Dinner is probably burned to a crisp! We'd better head back to the house."

As they walked side by side, Rosalynn summoned her courage again. "Lone Wolf, would you mind sleeping in the sitting room from now on? I don't think we are ever going to get better acquainted unless we start spending time together. It would be nice if we could talk in the evening after everyone has gone to bed. I really do want to know you better."

"I was only waiting for your invitation, Roz-lynn."

"My invitation?" Rosalynn studied Lone Wolf with a quizzical frown.

"Yes, I promised to give you time, remember? I will make no overtures to you without being invited to do so."

Rosalynn smiled. "Well, I'm inviting you."

"I will be honored, Roz-lynn." Lone Wolf laced his fingers through hers, and they walked back to the house hand in hand.

Chapter
Eleven

Lone Wolf loved to play with the children in the evenings and then listen to Rosalynn and Dorothy read from the Bible. The women would help Hannah, Joshua, and Gretchen each read a verse by placing a finger under each word and then whispering the word to them. It reminded Lone Wolf of his own childhood and sitting on his father's lap while he read to his family from the Bible.

The evening of Rosalynn's discovery of the waterfall, she and Lone Wolf and the family discussed the events of the day—a usual practice after scripture study. On this particular evening, the main topic was, of course, the naming of the baby. Everyone was delighted with his name, especially Gretchen.

Later, while Rosalynn and Dorothy tucked the children into bed, Lone Wolf checked on the livestock. When he returned, Dorothy had retired with the baby, whom they would call "Mikey" while he was an infant.

When he returned from the barnyard, Lone Wolf found a wedge of pie on the small table next to his favorite chair in the family parlor. Rosalynn stood by the fireplace stirring the fire.

"This is good pie. What kind is it?" Lone Wolf took another bite with relish.

"It's just a custard pie. There aren't any fresh berries or fruits this time of year, but we do have an abundance of eggs and cream."

"I like it," Lone Wolf said with his mouth full.

"I can see that." Rosalynn smiled.

For several seconds, the only sounds were the crackling of the fire and the ticking of the clock on the mantle.

"Lone Wolf," Rosalynn began, "tomorrow is Sunday, and Aunt Dorothy and I would like for all of us to attend church. How do you feel about that?"

Lone Wolf thought a moment. It had been many years since he had gone to church. He had attended for a while after his father passed away, but it wasn't the same. Soon, both he and his mother thought it best if they stayed away from church, since their attendance caused friction between Mike and the Swedish families who defended them against the rest of the town. Lone Wolf and Pale Flower decided to worship in their home, where the Spirit dwelled in abundance.

Lone Wolf thought of Rosalynn and the rest of the family. They needed to be in church, and it was their right to be there. He would put aside his own feelings for them. "I have not gone to church for a long time, but I will go if you wish."

"That would be wonderful." Rosalynn picked up Lone Wolf's empty plate and headed for the kitchen. "It'll be so nice to go to God's house again."

Rosalynn returned with two mugs of hot tea, sitting one on the table next to Lone Wolf's chair. Then she sat across from him, close to the warm fire. "If you're not too tired, Lone Wolf, I thought we might talk a while."

Lone Wolf drank in Rosalynn's beauty. The firelight danced on her mahogany tresses, turning them into burnished bronze. It took all of his self-control to keep from reaching out and touching her locks and caressing them between his fingers.

"Did you hear me, Lone Wolf?" Rosalynn fidgeted in her seat.

Lone Wolf cleared his throat. "I am not tired, Roz-lynn. We can talk if you wish. Do you want to retire upstairs?"

"I thought we might just sit here in the parlor for tonight and talk. There's no fire in the sitting room upstairs and it's a bit chilly."

"I can build a fire for you." Lone Wolf started to rise.

"Not tonight, Lone Wolf. We have to get an early start in the morning, and I thought we could just sit here for a while and talk. There are a couple of concerns I'd like to clear up. How about if we start talking in the sitting room upstairs tomorrow night?" Rosalynn took a sip of tea.

"That is fine with me. What concerns do you have?" Lone Wolf's brows knit together. Did he do something wrong? Now that they were married, was Rosalynn going to place impossible demands on him as Susan had on Mike?

"Nothing to be worried about," Rosalynn laughed as she snuggled down deep in her chair. "I'm mostly concerned about how hard you work. I would like to lessen your load. Joshua can feed the chickens and gather the eggs on his own now. I think he's old enough to fill the wood boxes, too."

Lone Wolf silently chastised himself. He should know by now that Rosalynn wasn't like her sister! But he was so happy that he almost *expected* something terrible to happen. "Yes, I agree with you. It is important to teach children responsibility. This is the same with my mother's people."

"Good. I'd like to start milking the cow, too. I've done it before and it'll be one less thing for you to do." Rosalynn's bright eyes searched his.

"No, Roz-lynn," Lone Wolf answered softly, "I will milk the

cow. The planting should be finished soon. Besides, Joshua comes out and helps me. He is a good boy. I am proud to be his pa."

A gentle smile formed on Rosalynn's lips. "He admires you very much. He asked me the other day if he could call you Pa, so I told him to ask you. Did he?"

"Yes," Lone Wolf beamed with pride. "I told him I would be honored."

A sigh of relief escaped Rosalynn's lips and her face softened. "I've noticed the girls are starting to call you pa also. Gretchen has called me Mama a couple of times—she is such a sweet girl. She wants to help me all of the time, but I keep telling her she needs to be a little girl."

"She will adjust in time. She had a lot of responsibilities when Susan was here." Lone Wolf's tone was harsher than he intended, and he decided it best to change the subject. "How is your garden coming?" If Rosalynn caught the bitterness in his voice, she didn't acknowledge it.

"It's ready for you to disk. Then I can plant the seeds."

"I can disk it tomorrow after church."

"No, not on Sunday, please. You need a day of rest and so do your horses." Rosalynn looked determined.

"As you wish, Roz-lynn," Lone Wolf said with a chuckle. It was just like her to think of the animals. "I will disk it on Monday. Make a list of the seeds you want, and I will pick them up at the merc."

"I already made a list," Rosalynn said excitedly, then went to a small desk, pulled out a slip of paper, and handed it to Lone Wolf.

Lone Wolf read in silence. "You do not need to plant potatoes. I planted fifty acres."

Rosalynn's brows arched. "Why so many?"

"I sell them to a broker who ships them East." Lone Wolf

scanned the rest of the list. "I can get some of these vegetables as plants."

"That would be wonderful!" Rosalynn plopped on the floor in front of Lone Wolf's chair and gazed up at him with twinkling eyes. "Once I get the garden planted, I'd like to start on the yard. I can see new plants peeking up through the weeds."

Lone Wolf bit his lip. Rosalynn was close enough that the fragrance of roses wafted in the air, and it stirred something deep within him. How he wanted to press his cheek against hers! Clearing his throat, he tried to focus on the conversation. "Yes. My mother loved to work with the soil also."

Rosalynn moved closer and laid her hand on his knee. "Can you tell me about your mother? I mean, I don't want to pry, but I would like to learn more about her."

A shiver passed through Lone Wolf's body at Rosalynn's touch. He searched her pretty, upturned face and knew she was sincere. Very few wasichu cared to hear about his Lakota mother and her ways. He silently thanked the Great One for bringing such a woman to him. But if he wanted to keep his word and wait for Rosalynn to invite him to stay with her, he needed to keep some distance between them. "Tomorrow night I will talk of Pale Flower. Tonight, we need our rest if we are to rise early for church."

Lone Wolf and Rosalynn climbed the stairs together. They checked on the children and then entered her bedroom. Rosalynn lit a lamp and placed it on a small writing desk, then went into the sitting room and lit a lamp, placing it on the hearth.

Lone Wolf followed her. It had been years since he slept in the house—since Susan came and demanded that he and his mother leave.

Rosalynn touched his arm. "Are you okay? You look as though you are a million miles away."

"I was thinking how strange it feels to be in this house again. It has been a long time." As Lone Wolf spoke, he turned away, afraid to seem vulnerable. "This room belonged to my sisters. Mike slept in Joshua's room, and the girls have my old room."

"I didn't know you had sisters!"

"Yes, I have two half-sisters from my father's first marriage. They went back East to boarding school and decided to stay there when our father died. I never hear from them." Lone Wolf went to the cold hearth and leaned against it. Rosalynn followed, sitting on the arm of a chair next to the fireplace. "So the locked room downstairs belonged to your parents?"

Lone Wolf stared into the hearth, visions of the past filling his mind. "Yes. This room belonged to my father and his first wife. The little room next door was a nursery. When my mother first came here, she refused to share a bedroom where his first wife's memory still lingered, so my father added on the bedroom and sitting room downstairs."

"What about Aunt Dorothy's rooms?"

Lone Wolf pushed his long hair back with his hand. "Those rooms were reserved for company after my father's parents died."

"It's a nice house. I didn't realize how nice it was until after I cleaned it." Rosalynn laughed softly.

"Yes, there are many happy memories for me here. This is the only place where I ever truly felt loved."

Rosalynn bit her lower lip. "Why do you go by Lone Wolf instead of Gabriel?"

"Enough questions for one night, Roz-lynn," Lone Wolf laughed. "We need our sleep."

"You're right." Rosalynn smiled and rose to leave.

Lone Wolf caught her by the arm. "We must kiss good night, Roz-lynn."

The dim light cast a shadow across Rosalynn's face, but Lone Wolf could still see her reddened cheeks. He drew her to him and gathered her into his arms. Bending down, he kissed her gently, then kissed her again with more urgency. Rosalynn circled her arms like a halo about his shoulders, returning his kiss. When they finally parted, they were both out of breath. They said good night, and Rosalynn left the sitting room.

Glancing around him, Lone Wolf saw a stack of quilts and pillows. He proceeded to make a bed on the sofa, then realized that it was too short. *Rosalynn is just a wall away, climbing into a nice, big bed,* he thought with a wry grin, then shrugged his shoulders and started making a bed on the floor. Soon he blew out the lamp and crawled into his makeshift bed. He had just finished saying his prayers when he heard voices coming from Rosalynn's room. He cocked his head to one side, straining to listen. The door creaked open, and Joshua stuck his head into the darkened room. Before Lone Wolf had a chance to speak, the boy was gone.

Lone Wolf smiled and then placed his arm under his head. He heard Rosalynn ask Joshua why he was up so late. It reminded him of his own youth when he would come into his parents' room if he was frightened or had a bad dream.

He had just closed his eyes when he heard Joshua ask his mother why she didn't sleep in the same room as Lone Wolf, since they were married. Lone Wolf popped up from his sleeping position, his heart racing.

"Lone Wolf is like a brother or a father to me. I like him, son, but . . ."

Swallowing hard, Lone Wolf stared into the darkness. How could she kiss him with such passion and not love him? *Please, Great Spirit, give me hope that Roz-lynn will learn to love me. I need patience. I must not give up, Great Spirit. I will show Roz-*

lynn I am worthy of her love. She will learn to trust me.

Lone Wolf eased his back against the cool sheets, a fervent prayer still swirling in his mind. After a while, he let his feelings ebb like a flurry of snow settling on a carpet of brown earth. He had to have faith in the Great Spirit. That was his only hope.

When Rosalynn woke the following morning, Lone Wolf was already attending to the morning chores. She kneeled beside the bed and prayed, *Please, Lord, as we go to Thy house this day, let it be a happy experience for us.* Then she donned her robe and hurried to wake the children and start breakfast.

Lone Wolf had a fire going in the cook stove, so Rosalynn put on a kettle of water to heat. She quickly prepared oatmeal and toast, and the children ate hurriedly. Then Rosalynn and Dorothy teamed up to get the children ready for church. Dorothy bathed and dressed Mikey, while Rosalynn dressed the girls and then braided their long hair. Joshua insisted that he was old enough to dress himself and headed back upstairs.

Rosalynn finished dressing the girls and then cleaned up the breakfast mess, leaving the oatmeal on the back of the stove to keep warm for Lone Wolf. Then she ran upstairs to get ready. As she brushed her hair, Lone Wolf knocked on the door.

"Come in," Rosalynn called. He entered the room just as she started to coil her hair into a bun. She took a quick glance at him in the mirror and felt giddy inside. "Good morning."

"Good morning, Roz-lynn."

She turned and noticed that he looked pale and had dark circles under his eyes.

"You look like you had a terrible night's sleep. Is it because we're going to church today? We can stay home if it's upsetting you, or I can just take Aunt Dorothy and the children."

Her heart struggled between rushing to him and waiting until he was ready to speak. She hated to see him battle with demons of the past; she knew too well how the past could dictate the future.

"I didn't sleep well last night, but I am fine. I do want to go to church today." Lone Wolf ran his hand through his hair, a gesture Rosalynn knew meant that he was worried or upset.

"Do you want to talk about it?"

Lone Wolf shook his head. "Like you, I have to work some things out for myself. I have called on the Great Spirit to help me."

Rosalynn smiled sympathetically. "I understand. Please know that I am always here if you need to talk."

Lone Wolf stepped closer. "There is something you can do for me."

"What is it?"

Her husband shifted his weight from one foot to the other, then thrust his hands deep into his pockets. "Please wear your hair down for me."

Turning back to the mirror, Rosalynn released her coiled hair and let it fall over her shoulder in one big curl. Then she turned in her chair and looked at him directly again. "You want me to wear my hair down for church?" she laughed. "I'm too old to canter about town like a schoolgirl."

Lone Wolf did not smile. "You are beautiful, Roz-lynn. Please wear it down for me. You told me once that you would."

"Yes, I did, but I meant around the house, not in town."

Lone Wolf's face fell.

"All right, you win," she conceded. "But I warn you, my hair has a mind of its own."

Rosalynn turned to brush her hair, but Lone Wolf took the brush from her hand. She watched him through the mirror as he gently brushed it for her, fingering the long tresses as he went. "You have beautiful hair. It is so soft. I have desired to touch it since I first met you. Look how it curls around my finger."

"I told you it had a mind of its own," Rosalynn laughed, enjoying the gentle strokes. Then, looking at the clock, she exclaimed, "We're going to be late if we don't get going."

Lone Wolf handed the brush back to Rosalynn. "I will hitch the team. I rode over to Jeb's earlier and asked him to stop by and pick up your aunt. I hope that is all right with you."

"That's fine. I know Aunt Dottie will be pleased."

Lone Wolf left the room and Rosalynn glanced at her reflection in the mirror. She sighed, wondering how she could help Lone Wolf feel wanted. She pulled her hair back and secured it with wooden combs, then tied a black ribbon with a cameo in the center around her throat.

She went to the closet and chose a blue dress with short, puffy sleeves. Delicate, white lace trimmed the collar and sleeves. After she dressed, Rosalynn turned before the dressing mirror, relieved that her five petticoats held the skirt out nicely. She pulled her shawl from the peg, grabbed her handbag, and looked at her hair once more. Wisps of hair were already escaping and forming soft curls around her face. When she met the family outside, Lone Wolf gave her an approving smile.

As they journeyed to town, Rosalynn couldn't help but admire Lone Wolf. He looked so ruggedly handsome in his dress buckskins and bright red shirt.

"I hope you are not ashamed of me, Roz-lynn, for wearing buckskins and long hair."

Rosalynn's gaze met his. "On the contrary. I think you are very handsome. I hope you never change."

Lone Wolf smiled as he continued to guide the team down the dirt road. "I am happy you accept me as I am. I do not think I could ever cut my hair like the wasichu. The Lakota believe our spirit is in our hair. If we cut our hair, we lose our spirit."

Rosalynn admired Lone Wolf for standing by his convictions, knowing herself how difficult it was to be the outsider. "I had no idea long hair was so important to you. You must never conform to all of the wasichu's ways. We all need to live in peace, but we all have the right to our beliefs."

<hr />

When they arrived at the church, Lone Wolf pulled the horses to a stop. Just behind them, Jeb stopped as well, and both men jumped down to help the ladies and children from the wagons. The streets were crammed with carriages and buggies, while people dressed in their Sunday best mingled together in small groups before entering the church. When Lone Wolf finished securing the horses and joined Rosalynn and the rest of the family, many of the churchgoers stared and whispered rudely. Rosalynn thought fervently, *I'm not going to let anyone spoil our time in Thy house, Lord. I'll let Thee judge those who persecute us.*

Rosalynn smiled at Lone Wolf and placed her hand in the crook of his arm. "Remember Daniel and the lion's den." Lone Wolf smiled back and patted her small hand.

Inside the church, Rosalynn scanned the chapel for an empty pew. She saw Ida and waved, heaving a sigh of relief. She pointed toward Ida as she whispered to Lone Wolf, and then headed for the Olson's pew.

Ida stood and hugged Rosalynn. "Here, sit in front of us. There should be plenty of room for all of you, but if not, we have some room back here with us."

Soon Todd and Arlene joined Ida, Swede, and their children. Across the chapel, Rosalynn spotted Mrs. Baker and gave her a discreet wave. Then Rosalynn glanced at the children to make sure they were being reverent and smiled at Dorothy and Jeb as they sat together at the other end of the pew. Mikey slept peacefully in the crook of Lone Wolf's arm.

We are here in Thy house, Rosalynn prayed with her head bent. *I pray that Thy Spirit will be with us. Please comfort Lone Wolf; I know this is difficult for him. Amen.*

Rosalynn peeked at Lone Wolf from the corner of her eye. His stiff posture revealed his unease, but he looked proud and majestic in his buckskins and flowing black hair against his bronze skin. Noticing that his hands were clenched under the baby, she reached over, unfolded them, and held his hand in hers. She felt the warmth of his fingers through her gloves as he rubbed his thumb over the back of her hand.

She glanced up, found his gaze on her, and smiled reassuringly. "We are in the Lord's house. He welcomes everyone, even if some of the parishioners don't."

Reverend Baker offered an opening prayer, after which the congregation sang "Onward Christian Soldiers." The reverend greeted all newcomers and visitors and asked them to stand and introduce themselves. When their turn came, Rosalynn stood confidently and introduced Lone Wolf as her husband. She could feel stares burning into her back, but she was determined not to be intimidated.

Reverend Baker began his sermon, "The Importance of Forgiveness," and Rosalynn reflected on his words.

"To heal ourselves and come closer to God, we all must be able to forgive one another.

"God cannot forgive us if we refuse to forgive those who trespass against us. Many confuse forgiveness with weakness. If a neighbor uses you, forgive him and then walk away. Forgiveness doesn't mean you have to continue to let someone hurt you or use you disadvantageously. Nor does it mean you have to like the person. But if you carry the hate around with you, it will eat at your soul and you will become an embittered shell."

Reverend Baker looked out at the congregation. "Who wins then? The offender goes on unfettered, and most likely doesn't even care how affected you are by the ordeal. You are the one who is suffering. Let God judge the offender and mete out the punishment. Your job is finished once you have forgiven the offense.

"I tell you this, brothers and sisters, not to judge or condemn you, but to save you from an everlasting hell. I care for each and every one of you and pray you will heed my word."

Rosalynn's mind raced to Jeffery. She knew she needed to forgive him for the pain and suffering he had caused her and the children. Never had she thought about forgiving him and then just letting the pain go. Somehow, the reverend's words made sense to her.

Jeffery certainly wasn't suffering from his actions. *She* was suffering. Their children were suffering. Did Jeffery care? No. The reverend was right. She was so consumed with bitterness that she allowed her fear to control her life with Lone Wolf. It had to stop. *Please, dear Heavenly Father, forgive me for my bitterness and pride. Forgive me for keeping the pain Jeffery caused deep inside me, preventing me from forgiving him and from healing. I now know I'm the one who is suffering, not Jeffery. I give the pain to Thee, Father. Let Thou judge Jeffery for his sins. Amen.*

Rosalynn felt the burden of despair begin to lift from her soul. Suddenly, the sound of the piano interrupted her silent meditation. Lone Wolf handed her a hymnal and she sang along with the congregation.

Jesus, my Savior true,
Guide me to thee.

Help me thy will to do.
Guide me to thee.
E'en in the darkest night,
As in the morning bright,
Be thou my beacon light.
Guide me to thee.

Reverend Baker offered a closing prayer and then it was time to leave. As the congregation dispersed, some of the Swedish families and poor farmers approached Rosalynn and Lone Wolf, welcoming her to Peaceful. Lone Wolf had never met many of them before, and Rosalynn was glad that they were cordial to him. The majority of the parishioners glared at them from afar, but Rosalynn didn't care. It was a beautiful day full of promise.

"Rosalynn, you and your family are eating in the park today, aren't you?" Ida asked as they walked out of the church together.

"I didn't know anything about a picnic in the park," Rosalynn replied with a quizzical look. "I'm afraid we didn't bring any food with us."

Ida smiled. "That's okay, we have plenty. We gather after church on Sunday and have a potluck. It gives all of us time to visit."

"Yes, you must stay, Rosalynn," Arlene joined in. "Many of the parishioners live so far out that we never get an opportunity to visit. It's a nice time for all of us. The children play, the women talk and share recipes and such, and the men play horseshoes or discuss the crops and weather."

Rosalynn wanted to stay, but was afraid Lone Wolf might have had enough church for one day. "Oh, it does sound like fun, but I don't want us to be a burden . . ." Her words trailed off as she looked at Lone Wolf and Dorothy.

"Nonsense. Your family isn't a burden," Ida answered with a grin, then glanced at the more elegantly clad church members. "We poor folk eat potluck while others have their fancy tea parties."

"We always have tons of food left," Arlene added.

Rosalynn bit her lower lip. "Lone Wolf, what do you want to do?"

"I think it's a nice way for you and Dorothy to get acquainted with your new neighbors," he said with a wink.

Rosalynn then looked at Dorothy and Jeb. "Aunt Dottie, Jeb, what do you want to do?"

Dorothy smiled at Jeb as he scratched his neck. "I agree with Lone Wolf. What about you, Jeb, would you like to stay and eat and visit for a while?"

"Eating someone else's vittles sound good to me," Jeb replied, smacking his lips.

The decision was unanimous, Rosalynn and Lone Wolf headed for the wagon to get the quilts. As they walked across the well-manicured lawns next to the church, she noticed that the park was overflowing with people. Every person in Peaceful must have attended church that day.

While Lone Wolf was busy watering the horses, Rosalynn scrambled into the back of the wagon. She was about to jump down when Lone Wolf darted in front of her.

"Roz-lynn, what are you doing crawling in the back of the wagon in your good church dress?" Lone Wolf stood in front of her, crossing his arms over his massive chest.

Accustomed to doing things herself, Rosalynn had automatically retrieved the quilts without asking for help. "I can fetch things on my own, Lone Wolf Larson. I've been doing it for quite some time."

Lone Wolf crept closer to the wagon.

With her legs dangling in front of her, Rosalynn felt quite unladylike. She smoothed her dress and then looked into Lone Wolf's brown eyes. She felt her pulse quicken as he inched closer and closer until their faces were nearly touching. The scent of mint and sandalwood hypnotized her senses. "Are you going to let me down?" Her voice caught in her throat.

Lone Wolf's eyes never left hers. He placed his hands on her knees, and she jumped as though a surge of lightning had entered her body. Her breath quickened and she felt her face grow hot.

A wicked smile slowly melted across Lone Wolf's face. "For a price, I will get you down, Roz-lynn."

"A price?" Rosalynn squeaked.

"Yes, a price." Lone Wolf moistened his lips with his tongue. "A kiss for your freedom."

With wide eyes, Rosalynn glanced around them and then looked back at Lone Wolf. "You want me to kiss you here . . . in front of the church . . ." Her voice escalated with each syllable. "With people milling all around?"

Lone Wolf grinned.

"You've got to be kidding!"

He shrugged his shoulders and tightened his grip on her knees. "Unless you are ashamed to kiss me in front of the wasichu . . ."

Rosalynn decided to call his bluff. She took her hands, placed them on his cheeks, and gave him a light peck on the lips. "There, you got your kiss, now let me down."

"That is a kiss for a brother or a father, not for a new husband." Lone Wolf's eyes smoldered.

Rosalynn was enjoying the flirtatious teasing, and the casual mention of a father or a brother surprised her. Wasn't that what she had told Joshua last night—that Lone Wolf was like a father or brother to her? She passed it off as coincidence. "And how did you become an expert so quickly, I'd like to know?"

Lone Wolf placed his arms around her waist. "I had a good teacher. Now, where is my kiss?"

Rosalynn thought her heart would stop, but she managed to say, "You're the expert, Lone Wolf. If you want a kiss, come and get it."

Lone Wolf grinned and tightened his arms around her. He brought his mouth close to hers and kissed her cheek and then careened down and nibbled on her chin.

Rosalynn couldn't wait any longer and brought her lips down on his. She put her arms around him and dragged her fingers through his long, flowing hair.

It lasted only seconds, but it felt like eons before Lone Wolf pulled away. He looked into her eyes, and a look passed over his face that Rosalynn hadn't seen before. Was it desire?

"Now I will put you down, Roz-lynn, but you have a hungry look in your eye and lips that show you've been kissed."

Rosalynn's hand flew to her mouth and she knew Lone Wolf spoke the truth. Her lips felt swollen and tingly.

Lone Wolf put his hands under her arms and picked her up as though she were one of the children. He held her suspended in the air and then slowly lowered her, pressing her body next to his. "I warned you, Roz-lynn, that we would kiss often. Are you mad at me?"

She wanted to say yes, but how could she when he looked at her with those big, dark eyes and that irresistible smile? "No, I'm not, but I may get even," she warned, scooting away. She grabbed the quilts and started toward the park. "Everyone is probably wondering what's taking us so long."

"I do not think so." Lone Wolf let out a chuckle as he hurried to catch up with her. "They know we are newlyweds."

Rosalynn's mouth flew open. "Lone Wolf, don't you dare say a word. For pity's sake, of all the places and times to want a kiss."

"You have corrupted me, Roz-lynn." Lone Wolf laughed again, grabbing her arm.

"Corrupted you, indeed. I think you crave nothing but kisses and sweets." Rosalynn tried to appear angry, but a giggle rose up from inside her.

After taking the quilts from her and putting them under one of his arms, Lone Wolf took her hand and escorted her to the picnic. Under a tall tree, they stretched the quilts out next to Ida's and Arlene's. Then Rosalynn left the children in Lone Wolf's care while she helped with the food.

"This is such a good idea," Rosalynn said later with a mouthful of Arlene's fried chicken. "We'll be prepared next Sunday, I promise."

As Rosalynn glanced around, she noticed that Reverend and Mrs. Baker didn't stay with one group of picnickers but tried to mingle with everyone.

"Good, maybe you can bring some of that custard pie Lone Wolf was bragging about," Ida said with a wink. "I think you need to share the recipe, don't you, Arlene?"

"Of course. I'm always looking for new recipes for the café."

Rosalynn blushed, grateful the men were eating a safe distance away. "It's just a simple custard pie. I think Lone Wolf has been deprived of a woman's cooking for too long."

"Now don't downgrade your cooking, dear. You are an excellent cook," Dorothy replied, then turned to the ladies. "Rosalynn used to sell her baked goods in St. Louis, and she always sold out."

Ida swallowed her food before speaking. "We have a farmer's market every Saturday during the summer months here in Peaceful. Why don't you bring in some of your baked goods and sell them?"

"I have way too many mouths to feed now to sell baked

goods." Rosalynn laughed, glancing down at the sleeping Mikey. "But I might bring in some surplus eggs. I also have oodles of asparagus right now. I plan on preserving some, but I have plenty to spare."

"It's too early for the farmer's market, but I could sell it at the merc," Ida offered.

"I can use it at the café, too. I never have enough eggs, and fresh asparagus would be a nice treat." Arlene popped a donut hole in her mouth.

Rosalynn shifted her weight and took a peek at Mikey to make sure he was still sleeping. "Great, I'll bring some to town this week. What else, besides the farmer's market, is there to do in Peaceful?"

"We have a quilting group that meets every other week," Arlene offered. "Each meeting takes place in a different home, and the hostess provides a light luncheon."

"Oh, that sounds like fun. When can Aunt Dottie and I join?"

"We meet next Wednesday at the merc. We usually get started about nine in the morning," Ida explained. "We all chip in and pay Hilda to watch the younger children."

"Is she the girl who works for Mrs. Baker?" Rosalynn asked.

"Hilda was helping Mrs. Baker out when she had Gretchen and the baby, but she doesn't need her help any longer," said Ida. "This helps her earn a little money of her own."

"It would be well worth paying her to watch the children so Aunt Dottie and I could attend your quilting bee," Rosalynn said happily. It was nice to have new friends and be part of a community again.

Rosalynn glanced around the park, hoping to spy Lone Wolf among the crowd of people. Most of the children were finished eating and were playing tag and marbles. Some of the men played horseshoes while the women visited. She finally spotted Lone

Wolf with a group of farmers along with Jeb, Todd, and Swede. Tears swelled in her eyes. She was so happy that Lone Wolf was accepted in the small circle.

"Rosalynn dear, are you ill?" Dorothy sounded concerned.

Everyone turned to Rosalynn and she blushed. "I'm fine, Aunt Dottie."

"Are you crying, Rosalynn?" Ida inquired, moving closer to her.

Rosalynn glanced toward Lone Wolf. "I'm just happy for Lone Wolf. He was so lonely and had no one. Now look at him. He's much more at ease with the wasichu."

"The wasichu?" Arlene's face screwed up with curiosity.

"White man," Rosalynn laughed, but then grew serious. "He still misses his brother terribly."

Ida glanced at the group of men. "His family was very close. They coddled Lone Wolf from day one, according to Swede. I'm sure he misses having a family."

"Well, he has a family now," Dorothy replied. "Our home is brimming with family."

Later that evening Rosalynn slipped upstairs while Lone Wolf checked on the livestock. The children were all fast asleep and Dorothy was exhausted, so she had retired early to read in her little sitting room.

Rosalynn combed her hair and let it cascade down her back. She removed her clothing and donned a long, flannel nightgown with pink flowers scattered over the fabric. Shivering from the evening chill, she wrapped a shawl around her shoulders, then built a fire in the sitting-room fireplace. When Lone Wolf entered the room, she had just sat down by the fire.

"I knocked, but there was no answer," he said.

"I didn't hear you." Rosalynn smiled and asked Lone Wolf to join her. "It's a little chilly tonight, so I built a fire."

Lone Wolf headed for his favorite chair. "The nights in Minnesota are chilly in the spring."

The room fell silent, and Rosalynn glanced at Lone Wolf out of the corner of her eye. He sat still in the rocker, staring into the flames in the hearth.

"Why don't you sit down here, Lone Wolf, beside me. It's nice and warm by the fire."

"You do not mind, Roz-lynn?"

"Of course not. Here, let me remove your moccasins." She scooted closer to him and unlaced the knee-length leather boots. When she pulled them off, she noticed a knife concealed inside one of the moccasins. "You carry a knife inside your boot?"

Lone Wolf nodded. "It is customary with my mother's people."

She hoped he never had a need to use it. The knife was wickedly long and very sharp. "Oh." Rosalynn placed the boots off to the side. "Moccasins look comfortable."

"They are." Lone Wolf slid onto the floor next to Rosalynn, resting his back against the hearth.

Rosalynn cocked her head to one side, a teasing smile playing on her lips. "Are you ready to tell me about your mother?"

Lone Wolf started to protest, but Rosalynn interrupted. "You promised, Lone Wolf."

He folded his arms over his chest and stretched his long legs out, crossing them at the ankles. "My father came from Sweden with my two older sisters and his first wife. They and many other Swedish families settled land in the remote northwestern corner of the state. As I told you before, he had no idea this section of land was the summer camp of the Lakota Sioux and the Ojibwa tribes.

"My father's first wife arrived in America ready to give birth, but she lost the baby. The voyage was hard on her and she never fully recovered from the miscarriage. Over the next couple of years, she had several more miscarriages before she finally carried Mike full term. Father had the house built by then and his parents had arrived from Sweden. They tried to help, but they were very old. My father's wife died after Mike was born. He was lost without her. He had three children to care for as well as his aging parents."

Rosalynn listened intently to the melodious sound of Lone Wolf's voice. "Is that when he met your mother?"

Lone Wolf stared into the fire. "My father found a small band of Lakota Sioux hiding out on his land. He did not know what to do. There had been a lot of raiding and burning all over Minnesota, but the Indians he found were mostly elderly or women with children. They were cold, tired, and hungry."

"Is this the band of Indians you told me about who were with Red Cloud?"

"Yes, my mother was among them. Pale Flower was a young maiden of sixteen when she met my father. She did not know anything about the wasichu except that they took our land. But she felt a special bond with the lonely widower."

Lone Wolf paused. Rosalynn kept her gaze pinned on him in the dimmed room. The only light came from the fire, and the sound of crackling wood filled the room. The warmth from the fire felt good against her skin.

Rolling over on his side, Lone Wolf, cradled his head against the palm of his hand. "When my father asked for help from Red Cloud, he had no idea he would be blessed with a young Indian bride. Those were hard times, thirty years ago on the prairies of Minnesota. Pale Flower agreed to help him with the children, and they ended up falling in love."

Rosalynn smiled at the mental picture of a young Indian maiden and a tall, handsome Swede. The fire between them must have burned bright.

Lone Wolf pushed the hair back from his face. "My father let the small band summer on his property. He learned a lot from the Sioux about the land and what it offered. They lived on fresh walleye, pike, and trout that they caught in the creek. They gathered wild rice, morels, and black walnuts when the season permitted it. The Indian women made pemmican for the long winter months."

Rosalynn frowned. "What is pemmican?"

Lone Wolf smiled and reached out to brush a curl from Rosalynn's cheek. "Pemmican is a type of food that kept many Indian tribes from starving during the long, harsh winters here. It is made from ground wild cherries, pits and all, and then added to bear grease along with finely ground jerky.

"Red Cloud and his people taught my father how to grow corn and beans and how to gather the wild rice for the winter."

"I find this fascinating." Rosalynn smiled down at Lone Wolf. "Can you tell me how they preserved the food?"

Lone Wolf grinned at her eagerness and continued. "They steamed the corn first by placing water in a large leather pouch. Then they dropped several hot rocks from the fire into the pouch to bring the water to a boil. The women put the husked corn into the pouch, and once it was steamed, they left it in the sun to dry hard.

"Later, the women removed the corn from the cobs by rolling the kernels with their fingers. The dried corn was carefully stored and used later when food was scarce. They either used the corn in soups and stews or ground it into meal and made small cakes that they baked on rocks or placed in the fire."

"How very industrious the Lakota are. I never thought of

Indians growing or gathering food. How do you harvest wild rice?"

Lone Wolf sat up, crossing his legs before him. "When the wild rice is ready to harvest, the Lakota take a canoe and gather it from the waters. They knock the rice from the shaft into the bottom of the boat. It is then gathered and dried. If the sun is not hot enough to dry the rice, the women strip the bark from the trees to make long trenchers. They place rice in the trenchers and use sticks positioned over a low burning fire to dry it. They watch the rice carefully and turn it often to keep it from burning. When the rice is dry enough, they place it in birch-bark baskets. The baskets are covered and buried under the teepees for the winter. The dried beans, walnuts, berries, and mushrooms are stored the same way."

"We could learn a lot from the Lakota." Rosalynn sat in deep thought. "I can see why this area is so important to your mother's people. It's like the Garden of Eden—filled with everything you need to survive."

Lone Wolf took the poker and stirred the dying fire, then grabbed a few chunks of wood and placed them over the hot coals. The greedy fire licked at the logs, engulfing them in bright red and orange flames. "I agree with you. We can learn much from each other. The woods here are overflowing with whitetail deer, elk, black bear, moose, and rabbits. There are also wolves, foxes, and otters. The Lakota hunt and trap for meat. The tribe eats some of the meat, but most of it we preserve for the winter. We save the skins and turn them into leather or furs. Nothing is wasted."

Rosalynn's eyes grew wide. "You preserve meat also?"

"Yes, we dry the meat and store it as well. We also dry wild apples by cutting them into circles and then stringing them on sinew in the hot sun until they are like leather. They make very good pies in the winter."

"You must show me how to preserve when the time comes. It would be nice if Pale Flower were here to help me and to be in her own home again. By the way, where is Pale Flower?"

Lone Wolf crossed his legs again and placed his hands in his lap. After several seconds of silence, he went on. "My mother lives on the Indian reservation. When Susan kicked us out, the reservation was the only place I could take her. A friend of mine, Black Hawk, cares for her when I am here on the farm.

"Usually, I would come here in the spring and stay until after the crops were harvested and the butchering was over. I would then return to the reservation to care for my mother through the harsh winter months."

"What is the Indian reservation like?" Rosalynn wondered softly.

"It is a bad place to live. The wasichu did not build good houses, and the people freeze in their houses all winter. The land is no longer good for hunting, so the government distributes food, but it is never enough.

"The young men are angry, for they cannot care for their families like they did before the wasichu came. They cannot hunt to fill the bellies of their children or to make clothing, bedding, and teepees. Some have turned to alcohol for comfort."

"It's sad that people can't live together in harmony. I'm sure it saddens God to see us fighting like children. Why don't the Indians learn to farm the land like you do?"

"Black Hawk is trying to learn the ways of the wasichu, but it is difficult when there is no one to teach him and no money to buy seed and plows. Chief Red Cloud fights for the rights of the Lakota instead of making war, but little progress is made."

"Can't you teach your friend to farm?"

"Yes, but I have been needed here during planting season. Mike and I owned the farm together and shared the work and profits. I banked my money, for I had no family to keep until now."

Rosalynn looked earnestly into Lone Wolf's eyes. "Why don't you have your mother and Black Hawk come here? I'm sure your mother would love to return to her home. And Black Hawk could help you while he learns to farm. You could share the crops with him and then maybe he can help those on the reservation or buy a farm of his own."

"That would be nice, Roz-lynn, but I do not think they would come. My mother is proud and she was ridiculed by Susan so much, I do not think she will ever trust the wasichu again."

Lord, there has to be a way. Help me think of a way to bring Lone Wolf and his mother together.

Rosalynn noticed Lone Wolf's bleak expression and wished she could console him by holding him close in her arms. Instead, she decided to change the subject.

"Tell me about your Christian name."

Lone Wolf smiled as though the remembrance was bittersweet. "When my mother gave birth to me, she knew what my life was going to be like. She knew I would not be Lakota or wasichu. She named me Lone Wolf. My father wanted me to have a Christian name. My full name is Gabriel Lone Wolf Larson."

"Are you named after the angel in the Bible?"

Lone Wolf nodded. "Yes. My father was a good man, a man of God. He told me once, after I had a terrible day at school, that I was like the angel Gabriel. He said my destiny was to protect. I asked him who was I to protect, and he said the Holy Spirit would reveal all to me when the time came."

Rosalynn held her breath. "Has he told you yet?"

Lone Wolf searched Rosalynn's face. "Yes, Roz-lynn."

"Who, then?"

"You, Roz-lynn. It is my destiny to protect you."

Chapter Twelve

When Rosalynn woke the following morning, she immediately thought of Lone Wolf, and her heart filled with joy. He had said she was his destiny! *Lord, I pray that I am Lone Wolf's destiny and that he is mine. I want so much for this marriage to work and for Lone Wolf to love me.*

Rosalynn brought her hand to her lips and recalled vividly the good-night kiss she had shared with Lone Wolf the night before. *He is an astute learner,* she thought with wonderment.

As she dressed in a crisp, white waist shirt and a dark blue skirt, she thought of Pale Flower and Black Hawk. There had to be a way to get them to the farm. Rosalynn knew that once they were there they would want to stay, because she would make sure they felt wanted and needed.

Rosalynn combed her long mane, braided the sides, and secured them in the back with a barrette. It felt odd having her hair down, but she would do it to please Lone Wolf.

By the time Lone Wolf finished milking the cow, breakfast was finished. Rosalynn placed the platter of ham and eggs on the table, then sliced some bread and browned it on top of the cook stove. The corn meal mush was ready just as the screen door slapped shut.

Rosalynn turned toward her husband and heard a strange noise. "What is that?"

Lone Wolf grinned, then proudly held out two small kittens for Rosalynn's inspection. "Here are the mousers I promised you."

"Mousers? Why, they're not much larger than the mouse I saw." Rosalynn giggled, taking the tabby kitten Lone Wolf offered.

"They will know how to work for their keep, you will see." Lone Wolf laughed as he rubbed the gray and white kitten behind the ear.

Clearly not used to being handled by humans, the kittens snarled, scratched, and hissed.

"They sound half wild to me," Rosalynn exclaimed as she tried to pet the snarling feline. "Ouch, it bit me!"

"They will tame down once they are accustomed to being around people. They are barn cats and have not had much attention other than the milk I gave them every day."

"Well, we'll see," Rosalynn said skeptically.

Lone Wolf took the kitten from Rosalynn, put both kittens on the back porch, and shut the door. "Once they are familiar with their new surroundings, you can let them in the house to catch mice. You only need to leave a window open for them."

"The children will be ecstatic when they hear that we have kittens." Rosalynn poured Lone Wolf some of his Indian tea.

Lone Wolf sat down at the table. "The girls will be, but Josh needs a dog of his own. Every boy needs a dog."

Rosalynn shrugged her shoulders. "You're his pa, Lone Wolf. If you think Joshua needs a dog, then get him one."

"You do not care, Roz-lynn?"

"Of course not. This is your home, Lone Wolf."

Rosalynn offered the blessing over the food. As they ate in silence, Rosalynn reflected on how blessed she was. Her world was nearly perfect. When she had first arrived in Peaceful, she had so many doubts. But now God's plan for them was obvious—so obvious that she felt like laughing for not seeing it sooner.

"You smile, Roz-lynn. What makes you so happy?"

"Everything! I remember how filled with despair I was when I came here and found Susan gone. Now I have so much to be thankful for."

A shy smile snuck across Lone Wolf's face. "I feel the same way. I was so lonely after Mike died. I needed someone to care for the children and the house and I prayed to the Great Spirit. I got more than I asked for."

A nanny and a housekeeper. Was that all she was to him? Rosalynn was afraid to look at Lone Wolf, afraid she would read on his countenance what he had implied. *Am I just fooling myself, Heavenly Father? Is that all Lone Wolf sees me as?*

Rosalynn's throat tightened and throbbed from holding in her tortured feelings. She bit her lower lip, demanding her spirit to hide the pain that ached in her heart. Her pride would never allow her to tell Lone Wolf how she felt if he didn't feel the same way about her. His kindness wasn't necessarily an expression of love, and she would have to keep reminding herself of that.

Fortunately, the children began to stir, and Dorothy brought Mikey into the dining room. Absently, Rosalynn prepared the children's mush and then fixed a plate of ham and eggs. She poured the children each a glass of milk and then took the baby so Dorothy could eat.

Rosalynn could feel Lone Wolf's eyes on her as she fed Mikey his mush. When she finished, he took the baby. How gentle and loving he was, she thought as she watched the tall man coo to the tiny infant.

How could she be mad at him just because he didn't love her? Most men would feign love merely to impose on a woman, and she was grateful that at least he was honest.

"He will be a big man like his father was. He's from hearty Swedish stock." Lone Wolf remarked, handing the baby to Rosalynn and asking Joshua if he was ready. Rosalynn felt her heart sink.

Lone Wolf stood and then cleared his throat. "Roz-lynn, I need a kiss good-bye." An impish grin flashed across his handsome face.

Rosalynn looked up at him, surprised. Everyone's eyes were pinned on Lone Wolf and her. Rosalynn tilted her head back and Lone Wolf planted a kiss on her lips.

The girls huddled together giggling, while a disgusted look crossed Joshua's face. Dorothy merely smiled.

"Now we can leave, Josh," Lone Wolf said, as though kissing Rosalynn was an everyday occurrence.

As Lone Wolf and Joshua were about to leave, they all heard a loud commotion on the back porch. Everyone ran to see what had happened. There in the middle of the floor were the two kittens growling and snarling as they fought over a mouse. The tabby pulled with all his might, the mouse's head in his mouth. The gray and white kitten had the mouse by the tail and was not about to give up.

Everyone laughed at the funny display. "I told you they were natural mousers," Lone Wolf laughed, his arm around Joshua. "Come, son, we have chores to do."

Joshua beamed at Lone Wolf's words. "Yes, Pa. Let's go."

Rosalynn held her breath as she witnessed the show of affection between her son and Lone Wolf. Tears threatened to expose her happiness as she watched father and son set out for the barn in deep conversation. *Lord, I thank thee for sending us here. I will be satisfied with Lone Wolf's friendship, but if Thou canst help him love me, I would be the happiest of women.*

Rosalynn closed the back door under protest. "Girls, you can see the kittens after you have breakfast and they eat theirs. Chores need to be done and you need to be dressed before going out to play."

Gretchen and Hannah downed their breakfast and headed upstairs to make their beds and dress. Rosalynn buttered a bread pan and poured the leftover cornmeal mush into the pan. She would slice it and fry it for the noon meal.

While Rosalynn washed the dishes and tidied the kitchen, Dorothy changed Mikey's diaper and placed him in a nearby cradle to play with his toys.

"Come sit with me, dear," Dorothy said. "We haven't sat and had a nice cup of tea together since you married Lone Wolf."

Rosalynn poured herself a cup of tea and sat next to Dorothy at the table.

"You really like Lone Wolf, don't you, dear?"

Taking a sip of hot tea, Rosalynn thought for a moment. "Yes, I do, Aunt Dottie. I do like him."

"That's marvelous, dear. I'm so happy you found someone to love. Isn't the Lord wonderful? I mean, in St. Louis we both were resolved to live our lives alone. Then we moved to Peaceful and we both found someone to fill our hearts." Dorothy dabbed the corner of her eye. "It's such a miracle."

Rosalynn looked at her aunt, unprepared to tell her that Lone Wolf only wanted friendship and someone to care for the children. It was hard enough for her to accept it without sharing the truth with everyone. "You found love, Aunt Dottie?"

"Yes, dear, I have. At least I hope I have! Jeb hasn't declared his feelings yet."

"Oh, yes he has, auntie. He does that every time he looks at you." Rosalynn laughed, reaching over to pat her aunt on the shoulder.

Dorothy giggled. "Our lives are turning out so wonderfully, dear. I thank God daily for the precious blessings He's given us." Dorothy patted Rosalynn's hand. "Thank you for allowing me to care for little Mikey. I always wanted children of my own, and Mikey fills that little hole in my heart. All of the children do, but Mikey is so small and depends on others for everything. It's nice to be needed."

"Yes, it's nice to be needed and appreciated." Rosalynn hoped her voice didn't sound dejected.

"You've never told me what happened between you and Jeffery, and I'm not prying now. However, I see a big difference in the way you act toward Lone Wolf. Even your attitude is more positive. The Lord knew our men were waiting here for us."

"Yes, He must have known, Aunt Dottie. Lone Wolf has done so much for us. I'd like to repay him for his kindness. I want to bring his mother, Pale Flower, here to live with us. What do you think of the idea?"

"I didn't know his mother was still living until I heard her mentioned on Sunday at the picnic. Of course, she needs to live with us here. Where is she now?"

"She lives on an Indian reservation up north. Lone Wolf told me Susan kicked her out when she married Mike. I just don't know how to get her here."

Both women sat in deep thought.

"Why don't you telegraph her?"

"That's a great idea, Aunt Dottie. Lone Wolf doesn't think she will ever come back here because of the way Susan treated her, but I think she will once she realizes we aren't like Susan."

"Of course she would stay. Her son and grandchildren are here. You need to send a telegraph as soon as possible."

"I'm going to town today to sell our surplus eggs and asparagus. I'll talk to Ida and see what she thinks. She knows Pale Flower personally. Did you want to go to town with me?"

"No, dear, I'll stay home with the children. I'm really enjoying just being a woman of leisure. I enjoyed making my toiletries, but I enjoy being with the children more. Besides, Jeb said he might stop by today."

"I don't miss the hours of crocheting either," Rosalynn laughed. "It'll be nice to just make things for my family—although it would be nice to make some extra money to stick back for Christmas."

"What a wonderful idea. Ask Ida about my toiletries. I wouldn't mind selling a little to make a nest egg for Christmas."

"I will. Do you want me to take the girls or Mikey to give you a break?"

"Heavens no, dear. We're fine together. The girls are no bother to me. I enjoy them. You go have a nice visit with Ida."

Rosalynn packed the eggs carefully in a basket cushioned with straw and covered them with a clean tea towel. She cut fresh asparagus to sell and some to cook for dinner. She hoped she was home in time to prepare dinner.

After she hitched the team, Rosalynn headed for town. The solitude was nice, but she wished Lone Wolf were with her. She found she ached for his presence more and more every day.

When she pulled into Peaceful, Rosalynn headed straight for the merc. Carrying in the eggs and asparagus, she moaned over the strain. She had been accustomed to carrying heavy loads and doing hard work, but Lone Wolf wouldn't allow her to do anything strenuous. It felt nice having someone pamper her after what she suffered over the last several years.

"Rosalynn, I didn't expect to see you in town so soon!" Ida greeted as she helped Rosalynn with her baskets. "My, what did you bring?"

"Eggs and asparagus," Rosalynn replied, heaving the heavy baskets onto the counter. "I had such a large surplus, I thought I'd bring it in today. Besides, I have a secret mission to perform and I need your assistance to pull it off."

"Oh, I love a good intrigue. Did you want me to find out if Arlene needs any eggs and asparagus before I buy it all?"

"Yes, and please put all of the money on my account. I'll need it when Christmas approaches."

"That's a great idea," Ida replied, and then called for her oldest daughter to count the eggs and weigh the asparagus.

"Why don't Todd and Arlene build a hen house and plant a garden?" Rosalynn asked. "They have plenty of room behind the café. It sits on the outskirts of town, so there shouldn't be any complaints from the neighbors. That's how Aunt Dorothy and I made a living in St. Louis."

"I don't know why. I'll mention it to them," Ida said.

Rosalynn followed Ida to the living quarters in the back of the merc and sat down at the table. "Before I forget to ask, Aunt Dorothy wanted to know if you would be interested in selling her rose water toiletries."

Ida nodded. "I'm sure they would sell. I don't carry very much in the line of women's toiletries, so they would be something new."

Ida poured the tea and sat down next to Rosalynn. "Now, what dastardly deed do you have cooking in that little head of yours?"

Rosalynn chuckled. "Nothing sinister, I assure you."

"Darn," Ida feigned disappointment. "Then what good deed can I help you with?"

"I want to bring Pale Flower and Lone Wolf's friend Black Hawk here to live on the farm. However, I don't know how to go about it. I'd like to send a telegram to save time."

"Does Lone Wolf know what you are planning?"

"No, I want to surprise him. Lone Wolf really needs help, and Black Hawk wants to learn how to farm. And I think Pale Flower deserves to get her life back."

"Let me think a minute," Ida paused for a few seconds, then went on. "They would have to travel by stagecoach. The train doesn't go that far north. It should only take them a couple of days to get here."

Grabbing a pencil and paper from her desk, Ida asked Rosalynn to write the telegram. "Be sure to request confirmation and also include the estimated arrival date." Then she added matter-of-factly, "You know you'll have to pay the fare."

"That's fine, I can pay for their trip here." Rosalynn handed the note to Ida. "I signed it 'Lone Wolf.' I hope he won't be upset I'm doing this without his approval, but I feel very strongly that it's what I'm suppose to do. Call it feminine intuition," she laughed.

Ida read the note. "Let's send it off right now and then buy the stagecoach tickets."

Rosalynn stared wide-eyed at Ida. "The stage line will let them ride, won't they? I've seen firsthand how some people feel about Indians."

"They'll let them ride, all right. It's money in their pockets."

After Ida sent the telegraph, they headed for the stage line office. Rosalynn paid the fare and then Ida asked for a receipt.

The clerk grunted and then turned away.

Both women glanced at each other. The door behind them opened and they turned just as the sheriff entered the building.

"Sheriff Lord," Ida greeted as the sheriff approached them. "Let me introduce a new resident of Peaceful. This is Mrs. Larson, Lone Wolf's new wife."

The sheriff's brows tilted up. "I just arrived back from St. Paul and hadn't heard the good news yet." He extended his hand to Rosalynn. "Congratulations, Mrs. Larson, and welcome to Peaceful. I've known Lone Wolf since he was a scrawny little kid."

"Thank you, Sheriff Lord." Rosalynn returned his smile.

"Are you leaving already?" Sheriff Lord inquired, pointing to the clerk.

"No, I'm sending for Pale Flower, but the clerk here won't issue me a receipt as proof that I paid for the fares. I would hate to be charged twice."

The sheriff looked at the clerk. "Give the lady her receipt. And there better not be any foul play because Pale Flower is an Indian, hear me?"

"Yes, sir," the clerk stuttered and quickly handed Rosalynn the receipt.

Rosalynn thanked the sheriff, grateful to find another ally in Peaceful.

"That's okay, Mrs. Larson. It's my job to keep the peace and also to keep some honest people honest," he glared at the clerk. "Tell Lone Wolf I said hello."

"I will, Sheriff, and thanks again."

Once outside, Ida warned Rosalynn to keep the receipt in a safe place. "If I hear anything, I'll send one of the boys out to the farm and let you know."

"Thanks, Ida. I appreciate all of the help you have given me today."

The next day, Ida's son delivered a message from Pale Flower. It read: Will arrive Friday noon.

Chapter Thirteen

Lone Wolf and Joshua entered the kitchen just as Rosalynn was setting the table. Hannah and Gretchen ran to Lone Wolf and jumped into his arms. Both girls were talking so fast that Lone Wolf could barely understand them. *So, this is what it feels like to have a family of my own, Great Spirit? It is good to be loved and wanted.*

Was he loved? Obviously, the little girls adored him, and Joshua regularly thanked him for being his pa. But what about Rosalynn.

She is beautiful, Lone Wolf thought as he sat back in his chair. With her hair down, she looked younger, softer. He couldn't help but smile at the tiny wisps of hair that framed her flushed cheeks. She glanced at him and he smiled. When she returned his smile, his heart nearly melted. He couldn't wait for the day to end so they could talk alone in the sitting room off her bedroom. Every day, he prayed that she would learn to trust him in time.

Rosalynn hummed as she placed the food on the table. Dorothy blessed the meal, and then Rosalynn served the children. Lone Wolf looked at the unfamiliar food. He didn't want to hurt Rosalynn's feelings, so he took a small bite and then smiled at her. "This is good. What is it called?"

"It's just hash made from the leftover beef roast, vegetables, and gravy," Rosalynn said as she buttered a piece of bread and gave it to Hannah.

"I like it." Lone Wolf answered, then poked the fried mush with his fork. "What is this?"

"It's fried mush. Try it."

"Fried mush?" He gave her a sour look.

Rosalynn laughed. "I took the leftover cornmeal mush from breakfast, sliced it, and then fried it in bacon drippings."

"It's good, Pa," Joshua coached. "Put butter and syrup on it."

After watching Joshua slather butter and syrup on the golden brown mush, Lone Wolf did the same. He cut off a small piece and stuck it in his mouth. "Mmm, good and sweet. I like your fried mush, Roz-lynn."

"I think you're addicted to sweets, Lone Wolf." Rosalynn said, taking a bite of food.

"That reminds me, what is for dessert tonight?" Lone Wolf smiled, his mouth full.

"See, I told you," Rosalynn laughed. "I made rice pudding with raisins."

Lone Wolf's brows rose. "Rice pudding?"

"Don't worry, you'll love it."

Lone Wolf finished the noon meal, wishing he could linger but knowing he needed to get back to the plowing. He glanced around the table. Joshua was explaining to Rosalynn how he helped with the plowing and the animals. Rosalynn listened intently, asking questions and giving him her full attention. The girls giggled as they sneaked tidbits of food to the kittens under the table. Dorothy fed the baby with a spoon, making *choo-choo* sounds to try to convince him to take another bite. Mikey smiled and squirmed at the attention. Lone Wolf thanked the Great Spirit again for his many blessings.

The next several days went by quickly. Rosalynn wanted the house to be perfect when Pale Flower and Black Hawk arrived on Friday. It had been difficult to keep the secret from Lone Wolf, and there were times when Rosalynn wanted to tell him, but she decided against it. If Pale Flower didn't come for some reason, he would be disappointed. It was best to wait and make sure that Lone Wolf's mother and his best friend were actually on that stagecoach.

Thursday dawned bright and beautiful, and Rosalynn hurried as she dressed in a worn frock. Today was her last opportunity to finish the housework. She wanted to mop and polish all of the floors and dust every room. She needed to wash clothes, too, but that would have to come later. Everything must look nice for Pale Flower's homecoming.

After preparing sausage gravy and biscuits, Rosalynn put some rice on to boil for hot cereal. She was pulling the cinnamon rolls from the oven when Lone Wolf came in with the milk.

"Good morning," he greeted. "Something smells good." Lone Wolf sniffed the air as he placed the pail on the counter.

"I made cinnamon rolls," Rosalynn informed him. "I think you could smell sweets from a mile away."

She inverted the cinnamon rolls onto a platter so the hot syrup could drizzle over the buns, then took one and placed it on a small plate for Lone Wolf. Once she had blessed the meal, Lone Wolf started on the cinnamon roll first. He took a big bite and then washed it down with ice-cold milk from the cellar. Then he smiled. "This is much better than Arlene's."

"Thanks for the compliment . . . I think." Rosalynn laughed happily. "I make my cinnamon rolls different than most women do."

Lone Wolf gobbled down the last of the cinnamon roll and then piled his plate high with biscuits and gravy. Rosalynn dished up a bowl of rice, added butter, cream, and honey, then passed it to him.

"Roz-lynn, you will make me fat and lazy with so much good food." He grinned and took a big bite of the biscuits and gravy.

"The way you work, I doubt you'll gain weight, Lone Wolf," she answered. "Do you want me to pack a snack for you and Joshua?"

Lone Wolf waggled his brows at Rosalynn. "If you include some cinnamon rolls, I do."

Rosalynn made two sandwiches from the biscuits and sausage patties, then wrapped them in a napkin. Next, she wrapped several cinnamon rolls and placed them in a basket with the sandwiches. She filled the water jug with fresh water and a smaller jug with milk. She went into the cellar, brought back a half dozen boiled eggs, and placed them in the basket as well. "This should tide you two over until noon."

The girls came racing into the dining room, their bare feet pattering on the hardwood floors. They headed straight for the back porch. Joshua came in next, filled a plate, and started eating so he could leave with Lone Wolf.

Rosalynn called the girls back into the house and placed their plates of food on the table. "Okay, you two. You know the rules. Eat, dress, chores, and then you can play with the kittens."

"Okay, Mama." Hannah grinned, taking her place at the table.

"Okay, Auntie Rosalynn," Gretchen chimed in with a shy smile.

Rosalynn returned the little girl's smile. Gretchen seemed happy with her new family, and she never mentioned Susan.

Dorothy walked into the dining room and handed Mikey to Rosalynn, then poured herself a cup of mint tea. "Lone Wolf, we are out of your Indian tea, dear. I sure do miss it."

"My mother makes it for me, and I do not know when I will see her next," he said sadly, then pushed his plate away. Just as Rosalynn started to wonder if she should tell him her secret, Dorothy let out a squeal.

"A mouse! I just saw a mouse squeeze under Pale Flower's bedroom door."

Rosalynn threw Lone Wolf a beseeching look. He sighed with an amused smile on his lips. "I will see if I can find it."

Lone Wolf went to the closed door and turned the knob.

Rosalynn stared at him. "I thought you kept your mother's room locked?"

"I did when Susan lived here. Things had a habit of coming up broken or missing. I no longer feel I need to keep it locked. I trust everyone here."

Rosalynn felt elated. *He trusts us!* It was high praise, indeed.

Lone Wolf searched in vain for the mouse.

"Do you mind if we air your mother's room, dear?" Dorothy asked when he returned, winking at Rosalynn.

Lone Wolf looked confused. "If you wish, but I see no need to go to the trouble. Mother will not come back here to live."

"Well, you know Rosalynn. She likes everything neat and tidy."

"Am I that bad, Aunt Dottie?"

Dorothy smiled. "Well, the room may be infested with mice. We can't let them chew up and destroy all of Pale Flower's things, can we, dear?"

"Infested?" Rosalynn exclaimed, her eyes pinned on Pale Flower's door. She could feel the color drain from her face.

Lone Wolf and Joshua left to work in the fields, the girls

finished their chores and went outside to play with the kittens, and Dorothy took baby Mikey into her room. Meanwhile, Rosalynn tidied the kitchen and then put a ham on to boil for dinner. After she got a pot of beans cooking as well, she sat down at the table and tried to enjoy a hot cup of mint tea.

Dorothy entered the dining room and plopped down across from her niece. She poured herself a cup of tea and sighed with contentment. "Oh, Mikey does love his morning bath. He's already sound asleep." She took a sip of tea. "You're sure quiet. Anything on your mind?"

"Hmm?"

"You didn't hear a word I said, Rosalynn dear. Whatever are you thinking about?"

Rosalynn snapped to attention. "I'm sorry, Aunt Dottie. I was just wondering how in the world I'm going to clean Pale Flower's room with a mouse on the loose, or worse, an infestation of mice! You know how mice are—they appear right out of the blue and startle the wits out of a body." Rosalynn sank down in her chair.

"What mouse, dear?"

"What mouse? Why, the mouse you saw squeeze under the door!"

"I didn't see a mouse squeeze under the door," Dorothy said nonchalantly. "What a notion, Rosalynn."

"You did too see a mouse!" Rosalynn rose in her seat, facing her aunt head on. "I distinctly heard you say that you saw a mouse squeeze under Pale Flower's bedroom door! You scared us all half to death when you screamed."

Dorothy burst out laughing, and it suddenly dawned on Rosalynn. "You didn't see a mouse, did you, auntie?"

"I told you I didn't, dear."

"Why, you trickster!" Rosalynn laughed so hard that her stomach hurt. "You told a falsehood, and I love you for it!"

"It was the only way I could think of to get Lone Wolf to open the door. I knew he would hunt down a dangerous mouse for you." Dorothy winked playfully.

"Thanks for letting me in on the ruse," Rosalynn said, dashing the tears from her cheeks. "Look, you made me laugh so hard, I'm crying."

"I didn't want you giving it away. You are a poor liar, dear. I wanted Lone Wolf to see the expression I knew would be on your face."

"All that trouble, and the door was open all this time," Rosalynn laughed. "Oh well, at least we got permission to air it out."

Rosalynn worked in Pale Flower's bedroom and sitting room most of the day. First, she removed the old ashes from the fireplace and scrubbed the hearth, then stacked new kindling and wood in a large basket next to the fireplace. She took the curtains down and washed and ironed them. Next, she aired the mattress in the warm sunshine and refilled it with clean-smelling straw. She swept, mopped, and polished the hardwood floors. The furniture shone after a good dusting, and the knick-knacks were carefully replaced.

Rosalynn looked around at her handiwork. The bedroom and adjoining sitting room were neat and clean and smelled sunshine fresh. She would ask the girls to pick wildflowers tomorrow while she went to meet Pale Flower's stagecoach.

By the time she went in the kitchen to check on dinner, Rosalynn was exhausted. Hopefully, Lone Wolf would be happy with the simple dinner she had prepared. She quickly threw together a bread pudding for dessert and shoved it in the oven.

Rosalynn kept nodding off during dinner, but afterward she managed to gather enough energy to play a song on the piano for the children, then have family scripture time and dessert. When bedtime neared, she was thankful she was able to stop and rest before retiring. As Lone Wolf started out to check on the animals, she stopped him.

"Lone Wolf, would you mind butchering a couple of rabbits for dinner tomorrow night? And maybe you could catch some fish if you have time."

"Yes, Roz-lynn, I can butcher and dress them out in the morning before heading for the fields. The fish are easy to catch. I made a special trap that I place under the cascading water. When the fish swim over the falls, they drop into the box. The small ones swim through the slats, but the larger ones are caught in the trap."

"How smart of you, Lone Wolf," replied Rosalynn. "You'll have to show me how so that I don't have to bother you."

"It is no bother, Roz-lynn. I enjoy pleasing you."

When Lone Wolf returned from the barn he found the house quiet. He couldn't wait to spend some time alone with Rosalynn. This was his favorite time of the day.

Lone Wolf grabbed a lit lamp from the dining room table and was heading for the stairs when he saw his mother's bedroom door ajar. He went to shut the door, but looked inside first. The furniture and hardwood floors shone a warm, honey brown against the lamp's illuminated flames. The rooms smelled fresh and clean, not musty as they had earlier when he looked for the dreaded mouse.

How thoughtful of Rosalynn to clean these rooms, Lone Wolf reflected as he fingered his mother's turquoise hair combs. He held her pearl-handled brush and recalled brushing her long, black hair as a child. Lone Wolf replaced the brush on the dressing table. As he turned to leave he felt powerful emotions swell inside him and then suddenly burst like a dam. Tears flooded down his cheeks, and he sat on the edge of the bed and cried. He cried for the past and all that was lost. He cried for what couldn't be. Though he tried to stifle his sobs with the back of his hand, the tears continued to flow in rivulets down his cheeks.

Great Spirit, please take this pain from my heart. I miss my mother, but I love Rosalynn and the children, too. How can we all be a family together, Great Spirit? Please, find a way for us to be a family.

It was some time before Lone Wolf trusted his emotions enough to join Rosalynn upstairs. He tapped on her door, but there was no answer. He slowly opened the door and peeked inside.

A candle on a small table cast a rosy glow in the darkened room. He glanced toward the bed, but Rosalynn wasn't there. When he entered the sitting room, he found her sound asleep, snuggled under a thick quilt in the rocking chair by the fireplace.

He crept closer and whispered her name. When he received no response, he gently scooped Rosalynn into his arms and carried her to bed. Then he sat down beside her sleeping form and traced his fingers over her jawline, noticing a soft sprinkling of freckles across her nose. He marveled at her beauty as he brushed back the hair from her face. Gently, he bent down and placed a kiss on her forehead.

Rosalynn woke and stretched her aching body. Quickly, she recoiled, her sore muscles reminding her that she had overdone it the day before. Today she planned to cook a feast in honor of Pale Flower's return. What did the Bible say about the prodigal son? They had no fatted calf, but Lone Wolf had promised rabbits and fresh fish. *He has no idea why*, Rosalynn grinned.

As she lay in bed, she remembered that she had fallen asleep in the parlor. She made a mental note to ask Lone Wolf how she got into her own bed. Now she forced herself out of bed and donned a clean dress. She brushed her hair and plaited it into one thick braid down her back.

Rosalynn hummed as she put the rice and raisins on to boil. What they didn't eat for breakfast, she would make into rice pudding later.

When she went into the cellar, she saw that Lone Wolf had already butchered the rabbits and caught a nice batch of fish. She grabbed what she needed for breakfast and started preparing the meal. She put the pan-fried potatoes on first and then made some pancake batter. Then she sliced some leftover ham, placed it in a skillet to warm, and set it on the back of the stove.

While the pancakes cooked, Rosalynn made a batter for cornmeal muffins. She sautéed diced ham and onions and added them to the cornmeal batter. She knew she wouldn't have time to fix a mid-morning snack for Lone Wolf and Joshua, so the hearty muffins would have to do.

Everything was ready when Lone Wolf returned from the barn with the morning milk. As he did each morning now, he poured some warm milk into a dish on the back porch for the kittens. Then he placed the milk pail on the counter for Rosalynn to strain and took a deep sniff. "Good morning, Roz-lynn. Breakfast smells good. I was not hungry until I smelled the food, and now I cannot wait to eat." Lone Wolf laughed as he washed his hands.

"Hopefully, it tastes as good as it smells," Rosalynn teased, checking the muffins in the oven.

Lone Wolf sat down at the table and then Rosalynn offered grace. She hoped that someday Lone Wolf would feel comfortable blessing the food.

Lone Wolf stacked his plate high with pancakes, fried potatoes, and ham. Rosalynn slid a platter of fried eggs toward him, then scooped him up a bowl of rice and raisins and poured him a glass of milk.

"I need to go to town today," she said casually. "We have surplus eggs again."

"Let me know when you plan on leaving and I'll hitch up the team."

"I can manage, thanks. I've done it for years." Rosalynn held her breath, afraid her plan might go awry. "By the way, how did I get in my own bed last night?"

"I put you there, Roz-lynn." Lone Wolf smiled, and then stuffed his mouth with pancakes.

"Thank you. I guess I fell asleep waiting for you. I was extra tired last night."

"No wonder you were tired. I looked in my mother's room and saw what you did. That was kind of you, Roz-lynn."

Rosalynn shrugged her shoulders. "It was nothing." Then she squirmed under his gaze. "I'm sending a mid-morning snack with you. The noon meal may be a little late today. I'll send Joshua to fetch you when it's ready. Is that agreeable with you?"

Frightened that Lone Wolf would read the excitement in her face, Rosalynn jumped up from the table. She quickly wrapped the muffins in a tea towel and placed them in a lard bucket. Next, she grabbed several handfuls of oatmeal cookies and a wedge of cheese and placed them in the bucket with the muffins. She filled one jug with fresh water and the other with cold milk.

"I hope this is enough for you and Joshua." Rosalynn chewed on her lower lip, her hands on her hips.

"I told you, Roz-lynn, you are going to make me fat," Lone Wolf chuckled. "I am so full now I will not be able to do my chores."

Lone Wolf grabbed a pancake, then plopped an egg and a slice of ham on top and folded it in half.

"What kind of a sandwich is that?"

"A good one!" Lone Wolf smacked his lips and winked.

The children filed down the stairs, hugged Lone Wolf and Rosalynn, and sat down at the table, still half asleep. When they saw Lone Wolf eating his "sandwich," they all wanted one, and Rosalynn couldn't help but laugh as the egg yolk ran down their arms.

Dorothy joined them and asked, "Rosalynn, dear, may I invite Jeb to dinner? He gets so lonely and he hates his own cooking."

"You need never ask, Aunt Dottie," Rosalynn replied. "Jeb can visit us anytime. How about you, Lone Wolf? Do you mind if Jeb comes over?"

"Jeb is always welcome here. I'll send Joshua over as soon as his chores are done." Lone Wolf kissed Rosalynn before leaving for the fields.

As soon as her other chores were finished, Rosalynn started on the noon meal. She would have loved to be able to sit back and rest and hold the baby, but she had to make sure everything was ready for Pale Flower. *Please, Father, let her be on the stagecoach!*

Rosalynn cut the rabbits into serving pieces and then seasoned them with salt and pepper. Next, she dredged them in flour and began to brown them in a skillet.

"The girls are watching the baby in the parlor. What do you need me to do?" Dorothy rolled up her sleeves and tied on an apron.

"If you could make some rolls, it would be a great help."

Dorothy nodded and grabbed a large wooden bowl designated for bread making. "What else have you planned for this special dinner, dear?"

Rosalynn took the browned meat from the skillet and placed

it in a large roaster. She then filled the skillet with more floured rabbit. "Let's see, we're having fricasseed rabbit with sage stuffing, creamed potatoes, fresh steamed asparagus, and baked fish. And your delicious rolls, of course. I'm planning on pumpkin pie and applesauce cake for dessert."

"We do have our work cut out for us then, don't we?" Dorothy laughed as she kneaded the bread dough.

"It shouldn't be too bad, auntie. The rabbit and dressing will slow-cook in the oven. Baked fish is a snap. We can peel and slice the potatoes early, and you can finish them while I go pick up Pale Flower. The pumpkin is already steamed and mashed in the cellar. One of us can make the pies while the other makes the cake. But we'll have to jostle the food with just one oven."

"I'm sure it will work out, dear." Dorothy covered the bread dough with a clean tea towel and placed the bowl on top of the warming oven. "I'll make the cake now while the oven is free. Then it will have time to cool before I frost it."

"Good idea." Rosalynn cast her aunt a grateful smile.

Rosalynn and Dorothy worked all morning. When it was time to hitch the team, Rosalynn was freshly dressed in a simple peach frock trimmed with lace. She pulled her hair back into a bun and secured it with hairpins. Lone Wolf would disapprove, but she wanted to make a good impression on her mother-in-law. *Please, Lord, let this work. Please let Pale Flower like us, for Lone Wolf's sake.*

Rosalynn stood in front of the stagecoach office, fuming. "Why is the stage so late?" she asked Ida, who stood beside her.

Ida smiled sympathetically. "The noon stage is always late."

"Why do they call it the noon stage, then?"

"I guess they had to call it something," Ida giggled from behind her hand. "By the way, thanks for the eggs. The first batch went fast, and I'm sure this one will, too. Do you want the money to go on your account again?"

"Uh-huh." Rosalynn turned toward Ida. "Oh, I hope I did the right thing by bringing Pale Flower here without Lone Wolf's approval. I can't bear the thought of hurting him."

"Sounds like you're growing attached to Lone Wolf."

"I am." Rosalynn turned away. "Part of me wants to trust him, and part of me is still afraid to trust any man."

"What are you afraid of, Rosalynn?"

"It's hard to explain, Ida." Rosalynn glanced around, not wanting their conversation to be overheard. "I guess I'm afraid of the commitment. I'm also worried that Lone Wolf won't stick around if hard times hit. Is he going to—" Rosalynn stopped herself. "My first marriage wasn't a happy one, Ida. I'm afraid to trust."

Ida put her arms around Rosalynn. "I don't know what your first husband did to you, but don't let him ruin your chance for true happiness with Lone Wolf. Trust in the Lord. He brought you here for a reason, and I think that reason is Lone Wolf. If the Lord trusts Lone Wolf, you can bet that you can also."

"Thanks, Ida. I need reassuring every once in a while," said Rosalynn with a weak smile. "Sometimes, I feel so happy that I worry that it can't last. Something will happen, I'll wake up, and this will all have been a dream."

"Take one day at a time, Rosalynn. That's all any of us can do. That's part of putting our trust and faith in God."

Rosalynn hugged Ida. "Thanks, Ida. I'll try."

Finally, the stage rolled into town. Rosalynn could feel her heart pump as if it were in her throat. Her palms felt cold and clammy, and she tried to calm herself down. *Dear Father, let Pale Flower be on the stage!*

The passengers departed, but no Pale Flower.

"Oh, Ida, she didn't come. Pale Flower didn't come." Rosalynn fought back tears, her voice quivering.

"I am Pale Flower," a smooth, soft voice said from behind them.

Rosalynn spun around. A beautiful woman with creamy, copper skin and dark brown eyes examined her. Her black, braided hair was coiled around her head like a beautiful halo. She wasn't dressed in buckskins as Rosalynn had expected. Instead, Pale Flower wore a black skirt with a white waist shirt. A beautifully woven shawl in bold, striking colors was wrapped around her shoulders.

"You're Pale Flower Larson?" Rosalynn asked incredulously.

Pale Flower's eyes darted around them. "Yes, and who are you? Where is my son, Lone Wolf?"

Rosalynn felt elated. She rushed toward Pale Flower and

threw her arms around her. "You came! I'm so happy you came! Did Black Hawk come, too?"

Confused, Pale Flower pointed.

Rosalynn turned and saw a tall, lean Indian man retrieving the luggage. "I didn't see him get off of the stagecoach."

"He rode in the back with the luggage," Pale Flower explained, a puzzled look on her countenance.

Rosalynn's brows knit together. "Wasn't there room in the coach for him to ride?"

"Yes, but he is Lakota. The other passengers were uncomfortable with him in the coach, so he had to ride in the back."

"When will people stop being so prejudiced?" Rosalynn turned to Ida in distress. "It's so stupid to judge a person by the color of his skin."

Turning back to Pale Flower, Rosalynn remembered her manners. "My name is Rosalynn, and this is Ida Nelson. Do you remember her?"

Pale Flower smiled at Ida. "Yes, I remember Ida very well. It's nice to see you again."

"Welcome home, Pale Flower." Ida embraced her. "It's been too long."

Black Hawk strode over to Pale Flower, his eyes cautiously taking in the surroundings. His features were striking, as those of a full-blooded Lakota ought to be. He had a lean face with a hawk-like nose and dark, almost black eyes. A long scar ran across one cheekbone, and Rosalynn wondered how he had acquired it. He was handsome in a wild sort of way, Rosalynn mused.

Black Hawk wore buckskin leggings, a bright multi-colored skirt, and a bright-red cotton shirt. His long, black hair was tied back with a red cloth band wrapped around his forehead. He stood close to Pale Flower as if to protect her.

"Welcome to Peaceful, Black Hawk," Rosalynn said, offering her hand.

Black Hawk took Rosalynn's hand briefly and then stepped back next to Pale Flower.

"Where is my son?" Pale Flower asked for the second time.

"Lone Wolf is at the farm," Rosalynn started to explain, but saw that they were causing quite a stir among the genteel residents of Peaceful. "Would you please follow me to the mercantile? I have a wagon waiting there."

Pale Flower nodded, and she and Black Hawk followed Rosalynn and Ida.

When they reached the mercantile, Rosalynn hugged Ida good-bye. "Thank you for your help, Ida. I would have been a nervous wreck without you."

Ida returned the embrace and whispered, "Good luck."

Black Hawk helped Pale Flower climb onto the wagon seat and then loaded the luggage before he jumped into the back.

Rosalynn gathered her skirts and climbed up next to Pale Flower. She grabbed the reins and coaxed the team to start down the street, but she waited until they were out of town before offering an explanation.

"I'm sorry that I couldn't explain in town. I didn't want to give those old biddies any more fat to chew."

Pale Flower nodded. "Not much has changed since I left, I see."

"Unfortunately, not for some people, but we can hope they will soften their hearts someday," Rosalynn smiled. "Did you receive a letter from Lone Wolf about Mike?"

"Yes, I was grieved to hear that he took his own life. I knew the marriage would not work, but never thought it would end the way it did."

"I don't know how to explain everything to you, Pale Flower.

Please, just listen to what I have to say before forming an opinion."

With a frown, Pale Flower agreed.

Rosalynn took a deep breath. "Susan is my sister." Rosalynn saw the startled look on Pale Flower's face. "My aunt and I came to Peaceful to help Susan with the baby, but when we arrived she was gone and the children were living in town."

"Lone Wolf did not tell me this. Where is Susan now? Where are the children?"

"We have no idea where Susan went, and frankly, I hope I never see her again. The children are fine and they are living on the farm." Rosalynn slapped the reins to hurry the team and then continued. "Lone Wolf explained to me how Susan had treated him and you. I'm so ashamed that she is my own flesh and blood. I don't understand why she turned out the way she did. I'm deeply sorry, Pale Flower, for the way Susan treated you. I hope you don't judge me by my sister's actions."

"Why would you care one way or another what I feel or think? You are a wasichu, and I am nothing but a Lakota squaw."

Rosalynn winced. "Please don't say that, Pale Flower. I do care very much. I've prayed we can be friends."

"Why?" Pale Flower's mouth was set in a grim line.

Rosalynn could hear the suspicion in Pale Flower's voice, so she took a deep breath and said a silent prayer. "Because Lone Wolf and I are married. He misses you desperately, and I'm hoping you will decide to stay on the farm with us."

Pale Flower's dark eyes glared straight ahead. "Lone Wolf married a wasichu? I do not believe you." The older woman held her head high in defiance.

Rosalynn felt her courage wane. *Please, Lord, give me strength.*

"It's true, Pale Flower, I promise." Rosalynn tried to smile.

"Lone Wolf has told me how much he loves and misses you. I brought you here hoping you would be happy with us."

"Am I to believe that Lone Wolf does not know I am coming?"

"No, he doesn't." Rosalynn saw a scowl form on Pale Flower's beautiful face and hurried to explain. "I didn't tell him because I didn't know if you would really come. If you hadn't come, he would have been so disappointed. I couldn't bear to see him hurt. I will protect Lone Wolf at all costs."

Pale Flower sat rigid beside Rosalynn, her gaze unfaltering, her emotions masked.

"Please try to make this work for Lone Wolf's sake. It would make him so happy to have you safe on the farm with us," Rosalynn said.

"Why did you bring Black Hawk here?" Pale Flower asked, ignoring Rosalynn's plea.

"Lone Wolf told me how terrible life is on the reservation. His desire was to teach Black Hawk how to farm, and at the same time, Black Hawk could help him with the planting season. With Mike gone, Lone Wolf has had to work long, hard hours. It gives him very little time to rest and enjoy his family."

Rosalynn lapsed into silence, deciding that no amount of explaining or pleading would sway Pale Flower. Rosalynn would have to leave the rest in the Lord's hands. *Please, Lord, help me to be strong and understanding. Please soften Pale Flower's heart. Let her know I am sincere.*

Rosalynn guided the team down the drive. When they arrived at the farm, Joshua was perched on the fence rail and jumped down to greet them as she stopped the wagon.

"Who do you have with you, Ma?" Joshua asked in excitement. "Aunt Dottie said for me to wait for you." Joshua then belted out, "Aunt Dottie, Ma's home." Turning back to Rosalynn, he continued with his endless questions. "She said you were bringing someone home with you. Are they friends of Pa's?"

Rosalynn couldn't help but laugh at his exuberance. It certainly lightened up a tense situation. "Joshua, go to the field and bring back Lone Wolf. Don't tell him we have guests, though. It's a surprise." She then cautioned again, "Remember, it's a surprise."

"I will, Ma," Joshua yelled as he dashed for the fields beyond the barn.

Rosalynn climbed down from the wagon and looked up at Pale Flower. "Do you want to wait for Lone Wolf here, or in the house?"

Black Hawk jumped from the back of the wagon and then helped Pale Flower down. Pale Flower looked around, her expression composed.

"This is still your home, Pale Flower. It will always be your home." Rosalynn placed her hand on Pale Flower's arm in a show of friendship.

"I would like to wait for my son." Pale Flower stepped away from Rosalynn.

Rosalynn's courage started to falter again but she tried to stay positive. "Whatever you feel is best. I'm sure Lone Wolf won't be long."

Somehow, her cheery statement didn't calm her troubled soul. Rosalynn could feel her stomach churn with apprehension. She glanced at Black Hawk and managed a smile. He glared back through narrow slits, and Rosalynn again asked herself if she had done the right thing by bringing them to Peaceful without Lone Wolf's consent.

It wasn't long before they saw Lone Wolf and Joshua walking toward the house. Rosalynn could feel her heart pounding, and her stomach tightened into a hard knot. Lone Wolf smiled and then waved at Rosalynn. Then Pale Flower and Black Hawk stepped out from behind the team and turned to look at Lone Wolf.

Lone Wolf stopped, a look of utter shock on his face. Then Pale Flower called out to him in the Lakota language, and he began to run.

A few feet from his mother, Lone Wolf stopped, his eyes darting from Rosalynn to Pale Flower. Then his face lit up with happiness and he embraced his mother.

Rosalynn felt hot tears trail down her cheeks. She took Joshua's hand and went into the house to give Lone Wolf time alone with his family.

Lone Wolf embraced Pale Flower, afraid she would vanish if he let her go. *How can this be, Great One? How can my mother and Black Hawk be here?*

Lone Wolf felt tears streaming down his cheeks. His body shook with emotion. "Mother," was all he could manage without sobbing.

"Lone Wolf, my beloved son. I have been so worried about you," Pale Flower cried out.

He released her, tears still coursing down his face, and then placed an arm around Black Hawk. "My friend, thank you for bringing my mother to me. Why did you not write and tell me you were coming?"

"You were the one who sent for us, my brother. At least that is what the telegram stated." Black Hawk smiled and patted Lone Wolf on the back.

Lone Wolf looked from Pale Flower to Black Hawk. "I did not send for you. But I am happy you are here."

"It was the wasichu," Pale Flower said bitterly. "She sent for us pretending to be you. She cannot be trusted after such a lie."

"Roz-lynn sent for you?" Lone Wolf asked.

"That is her name. She said you married her. This cannot be, my son. You know what happened to Mike."

"Roz-lynn is my wife, Mother. She is not like the wasichu. She is kind and loving. You will see once you get to know her."

"I will not be here that long, my son. This is not my home as long as the wasichu live here. She says she is Susan's sister. That is enough for me to mistrust her."

"Give her a chance, please, Mother. Then if you want to leave, I will pay for your fare back to the reservation." Lone Wolf then addressed Black Hawk. "If you do not like it here, my friend, I will give you a horse so you can go back to the reservation also. All I ask is for you to give us a chance."

"I will give your wife a chance, Lone Wolf," said Black Hawk. "She brought us here and treated us with respect. I will not condemn her without cause."

"Thank you, Black Hawk. You are welcome here as long as you wish to stay. You will be a big help to me, and I can teach you much."

"I will reserve my judgment on your wife," Pale Flower put in. "I will know in my heart if she is sincere. But first tell me, my son, why you married a wasichu. And where are Mike's children?"

Rosalynn gathered the children into the family parlor and explained them who their special company was. "We need to make them feel welcome."

"Is Pale Flower our grandma?" Joshua asked.

"Yes, she is your grandma," Rosalynn smiled at the surprised looks on the children's faces. "Won't it be nice to have a grandma?"

"Yes!" the children cried out in unison.

"What about Black Hawk? What do we call him?"

"Just call him Black Hawk, Joshua, unless he says otherwise."

"Are they going to stay long?" Joshua wondered.

"We hope they do. We hope Pale Flower will live here with us. This was her home first and we hope she will like us enough to live here again."

Rosalynn and Dorothy were setting the table when they heard the screen door slam shut. Rosalynn cast her aunt a nervous smile as she clutched the back of the chair. The children came bursting into the dining room just as Lone Wolf entered through the kitchen. Rosalynn was afraid to look at him, afraid at what she might read on his face.

Lone Wolf came up to her and with a gentle touch tilted her face until their eyes locked. "Thank you, Roz-lynn. Thank you for sending for my mother and Black Hawk."

"You're not mad at me for not telling you?" Rosalynn asked, almost whispering. She searched his face with her eyes.

"I could never be mad at you, Roz-lynn. I think I know why you kept it a secret."

Rosalynn's eyes grew large. "You do?"

"Yes. You were afraid I would say no because I did not think my mother would come. Am I right, Roz-lynn?"

"Partly," Rosalynn answered with a smile. "I was also afraid if they said no, you would be hurt. I didn't want to see you hurt again."

Lone Wolf bent down and kissed Rosalynn on the lips. His soft lips coaxed hers to respond and Rosalynn felt her body go weak under his touch. She wrapped her arms around him and returned his kiss with tender abandonment. When they drew apart, everyone was staring at them.

"Roz-lynn taught me to kiss," Lone Wolf said proudly to his stunned mother and friend.

"It is nice to see the wasichu can finally teach us something of worth," Black Hawk responded with a wink.

The ice was broken, and everyone joined in the laughter. Black Hawk and Pale Flower were ushered into the company parlor and were immediately surrounded by excited children. Rosalynn noticed that Pale Flower's gaze didn't miss a thing as she look around the house.

The children crowded around Pale Flower as she sat next to the fireplace. A smile played across her lips.

"You're our grandma. Did you know that?" Gretchen said shyly.

"My goodness, what a lucky grandmother I am." Pale Flower smiled as she looked from one child to another. "You will have to introduce yourselves."

The children eagerly spouted out their names, each trying to shout over the other.

Rosalynn laughed as she intervened. "Okay, children, Pale Flower can't hear you when you holler. Let me introduce all of you."

One by one, Rosalynn introduced the children to Pale Flower and Black Hawk. She then introduced Dorothy.

Dorothy went up to Pale Flower and shook her hand. "You are very welcome, Pale Flower. I hope you will agree to live here with us. It's a bit noisy, but it's a happy home." Dorothy then handed the baby to Pale Flower. "Here is Michael Adrian Larson, your grandson."

Pale Flower's eyes filled with tears. "You named the baby after your father and brother, Gabriel?"

"Roz-lynn named the baby," Lone Wolf explained, smiling at Rosalynn.

Pale Flower looked at Rosalynn with admiration. "Thank you, Roz-lynn."

Rosalynn returned Pale Flower's smile, a lump forming in her throat. *Thank you, Lord.* She placed her hand on Lone Wolf's shoulder and was surprised when he folded his warm hand over hers.

A knock sounded on the door, and Rosalynn watched Dorothy leave to answer it. When she returned, Jeb followed her. In his arms squirmed a black and tan puppy. The children ran to Jeb and begged to hold the puppy.

"This here is Lone Wolf's pup. He asked me to bring him over when he was weaned."

Lone Wolf walked over and took the puppy, rubbing it behind the ears. Then he handed the dog to Joshua. "This is your pup, Joshua. You must take good care of him. His life will depend on you."

"Do you really mean it, Pa? Is he really mine?" Joshua's eyes grew round and sparkled with excitement. "Ma said it was okay for me to have a dog of my own?"

Rosalynn interjected gently. "Whatever Lone Wolf gives you or tells you, Joshua, is okay with me. Don't question him."

"Thanks, Ma." Joshua ran over to hug Rosalynn and then Lone Wolf. "Thanks, Pa! You're the best pa in the whole world."

Lone Wolf tousled Joshua's hair affectionately. "Take your pup outside and fix him a bed to sleep in. He cannot sleep in the house."

"That's right, no pets in the house. I don't want any accidents on our clean floors," Rosalynn said with wink at Pale Flower.

Rosalynn and Dorothy placed the hot food on the table and everyone filed in and found a seat. Once everyone was settled,

Rosalynn bowed her head and started to bless the meal, but Lone Wolf interrupted her.

"I would like to bless the meal, Roz-lynn."

She felt her jaw drop but managed to mumble, "I would be honored for you to offer the blessing, Lone Wolf."

Lone Wolf stood, looking at all of the smiling faces. He bowed his head and blessed the meal. "Great Spirit, we thank You for the bounty You have given us. Please bless the food that it may strengthen us with wisdom. Thank You, Great Spirit, for joining my family and friends here tonight. I thank You for bringing my mother and friend here in safety. Thank you, Great One, for our blessings, and may we be grateful for them. My world is complete. Amen."

Dinner was a success, with everyone apparently enjoying the food and the company. Rosalynn insisted on cleaning up so that Pale Flower could retire early and so that Dorothy and Jeb could sit on the front porch swing under the sweetheart's moon.

Before retiring, Rosalynn went to Lone Wolf and told him that Black Hawk could use her room. "I can sleep with Aunt Dottie," she explained.

"No, Roz-lynn, Black Hawk wants to sleep in my cabin."

"Are you sure? I don't want him to feel like he isn't welcome in your home."

"He will enjoy the solitude. Remember, he is not accustomed to living in a house with so many people."

"You know what's best, Lone Wolf. I'm going to turn in then. The baby is asleep in his crib in Aunt Dottie's room."

"Good night, Roz-lynn. Thank you again for bringing my mother and Black Hawk here."

"Seeing you so happy is thanks enough. Good night."

Before Rosalynn could leave, Lone Wolf took hold of her arm. "I need my good night kiss, Roz-lynn."

Rosalynn blushed but conceded willingly. The kiss was soft yet stayed with her until she fell asleep.

Chapter
Fifteen

The weeks passed quickly for Rosalynn. Pale Flower was reserved at first, but she slowly warmed to Dorothy and Rosalynn. Rosalynn watched her blossom like her namesake, and it wasn't long before Pale Flower seemed to feel at home once again.

With the extra help from Black Hawk, the planting was finally finished. The garden was seeded and doing well, and the fences were mended. Lone Wolf and Black Hawk serviced the plow and sharpened the tools. Not a day went by without them preparing for a long, harsh Minnesota winter.

Once Lone Wolf caught up with the planting and the odd chores around the farm, he had more time to spend with his family. Joshua followed him everywhere, and Lone Wolf made the boy a small bow and a quiver with arrows and taught him how to hunt.

In the evenings, after the family read from the Bible, the women worked on their sewing and Lone Wolf carved his wooden creations. Soon Black Hawk and Joshua wanted to learn to carve, so Lone Wolf taught them.

Pale Flower often cooked dinner, which allowed Rosalynn more time in the large garden. It felt nice to work in the rich earth with the sun's rays warming her back. Rosalynn loved to garden and took advantage of any spare time that allowed her to do it. She felt a great satisfaction in watching the small seeds sprout and then leaf into plants. Soon, the family would be eating fresh greens, and later they would preserve them for winter.

One day in the garden, Rosalynn stood and rubbed her sore knees. She had been weeding for several hours, and her body now told her that it was time to stop for the day.

All of a sudden she heard several gunshots in the distance. She stood still, listening. She often heard Lone Wolf shoot at night to scare off coyotes that came sneaking in for the chickens, but daytime was another matter.

The farm was set in a large valley, and Lone Wolf owned the land far into the trees. No one hunted on his property without asking for permission.

As Rosalynn headed for the house to investigate, Joshua came running through the trees, almost knocking her down.

"Whoa, son," Rosalynn said, grabbing her son to keep from falling. "Why are you in such a hurry?" Then, seeing the boy's pale face, she asked shrilly, "What is wrong?"

Joshua was out of wind and took several big gulps of air before he was able to speak. "Pa's been shot!"

Shot! Rosalynn's head began to swim and she nearly fainted. "Lone Wolf shot? How? Where?" Not waiting for a reply, she took off running in the direction Joshua indicated. "Where is he, Joshua?" she cried out over her shoulder.

Joshua ran to catch up with his mother. "He's at the house, Ma."

Rosalynn ran pell-mell toward the house, praying all the way. She took the porch steps two at a time and crashed through the back door, causing Pale Flower to jump.

Pale Flower opened her mouth to speak, but Rosalynn interrupted her. "Where is he? Where is Lone Wolf?"

Then Rosalynn turned toward the dining room and saw Lone Wolf sitting at the table, with Black Hawk standing next to him. She started toward him, then stopped abruptly when she saw the blood on his shirt and the soaked rags on the table. Her eyes brimmed with tears, and she absently brushed them aside with the back of her hand, leaving a dirty trail across her cheek.

"Are you all right? What happened? We need to send for a doctor!" she cried.

"I'm fine, Roz-lynn." Lone Wolf tried to reassure her as he offered her his hand. "It is only a flesh wound."

"Flesh wound, my eye!" Rosalynn said hysterically. "Look at all of that blood! It looks like Dodge City on a Saturday night."

As Lone Wolf tried to suppress a grin, Rosalynn became angry. "What happened, Lone Wolf? For pity's sake, explain what's going on."

"I will when you calm down, Roz-lynn," he said.

Rosalynn stood over Lone Wolf, hands on her hips as she waited for him to continue. When he didn't, she finally relented. "Okay, I'm calm."

"Sit down here, next to me." Lone Wolf patted the chair. After Rosalynn sank into it, he continued. "I am fine. The bullet only grazed my arm. Someone must have been out hunting and I just happened to be in the wrong spot. It was an accident, Roz-lynn."

"Are you sure you're all right?" Rosalynn looked anxiously at Pale Flower.

"Gabriel will be fine." Pale Flower took a cloth from a hot pot of dark brew and placed it over the wound. "I'm cleaning the wound first with a special healing tea made of oak bark and wild geranium. After it soaks a while, I'll remove the cloth, and the wound should be clean of any dirt."

Lone Wolf flinched when the hot cloth touched the wound, but he made no sound. Rosalynn quickly moved closer to him and took his hand in hers.

"Is it too hot, Lone Wolf?" Rosalynn looked at Pale Flower. "I think it's too hot for him."

"It has to be hot in order to clean the wound," Pale Flower explained calmly. "I have done this many times for wounded warriors."

Rosalynn looked back at Lone Wolf, amazed at his bravery. The only indication that he was in pain was the sweat that rolled down his face and the tense muscles in his jaw as he gritted his teeth.

Pale Flower brought a small bag filled with dried herbs and poured some into a small bowl made from a hollowed rock. She took a long, thin rock and began to smash them. Once she had pulverized the herbs, Pale Flower added some boiling water and stirred the concoction.

Rosalynn frowned. "What are you making, Pale Flower?"

"This is a poultice of dried comfrey roots. It will help the wound heal quickly. After the wound begins to heal, I will make a salve from dried calendula flowers and lard. The salve will help keep the wound from scarring too much."

"Will he be all right, then?" Rosalynn bit her lower lip to keep the tears at bay.

"He will need to rest for a few days." Pale Flower smiled and then patted Rosalynn on the arm.

"I cannot lie around like a spoiled and pampered cat. I have things to do!" Lone Wolf blustered.

"It's no use arguing, Lone Wolf. Your mother is right, and I agree with her. Now tell me how it happened."

Lone Wolf leaned back in his chair. "Black Hawk and I were working on the calving pens when we heard several shots. One whizzed past us, but I caught the second one in the shoulder."

"This should be reported." Rosalynn face was pale but firm.

"It will do no good. Sheriff Lord cannot do anything about it," Lone Wolf stated calmly. "It will be better to forget what happened."

Rosalynn ached inside, wanting to demand that someone do something, but she decided to trust Lone Wolf's instincts. "I disagree, but I'll do as you say, Lone Wolf. I think it's mighty fishy that someone was hunting on your property and then didn't have the common courtesy to check and see if you were all right." Rosalynn stood up, exasperated. "I need to clean up and change my clothes. Do you want to rest for a while?"

Lone Wolf smiled. "No, Mother needs to dress the wound. I will be fine."

As Rosalynn headed for the stairs, she saw Dorothy and the children peering into the dining room from the parlor. "Lone Wolf is fine. But we need to take very good care of him for a couple of days."

"We help Papa," Hannah piped up, sidling over to Lone Wolf.

"I'm a good helper, Auntie Rosalynn. I can help Uncle Gabe," Gretchen volunteered, her arms around Lone Wolf's good arm.

"I can help Black Hawk with the chores, Ma," Joshua said.

Rosalynn glanced at Lone Wolf and could tell he was overwhelmed with the display of affection.

"Come on, chickens," Rosalynn called to the children. "Let's wash for dinner."

Rosalynn and Dorothy scooted the children into the pantry, where the tub and washbasin were stored. Black Hawk helped haul water to the tub so that Rosalynn could take a quick bath before dinner.

Once Rosalynn, Dorothy, and the children were out of earshot, Black Hawk spoke to Lone Wolf. "Your woman loves you very much, my friend. The Great Spirit has blessed you."

"Roz-lynn loves me?"

"Of course Rosalynn loves you, my son," Pale Flower interjected as she cleaned his wound. "Can you not see it in her eyes and hear it in her voice?"

"Roz-lynn cares for everyone. She does not love me. She married me for other reasons, not for love." Lone Wolf couldn't bring himself to tell Black Hawk and his mother what he had overheard that bleak night so many weeks ago.

"That may have been true then, Gabriel, but she loves you now." Pale Flower's words were soft.

"Listen to your mother, Lone Wolf," Black Hawk insisted. "Your Rosalynn loves you very much."

Lone Wolf shook his head. *Can it be true, Great Spirit? Does Roz-lynn love me? Has she let go of the past?*

"Court her in the way of our people, my friend, and you will discover the truth," Black Hawk challenged.

Lone Wolf paused, then said with a faint smile, "Yes, I will court her the Lakota way."

"I will milk the cow tonight and feed the animals," Black Hawk offered, grinning. "You stay and rest."

Lone Wolf placed his hand on Black Hawk's forearm. "Be careful, Black Hawk. I do not want any more accidents to happen."

"What accident, Lone Wolf? You and I both know the gunshots were intentional. A stray bullet in your valley? No, I do not think so." Black Hawk's voice was low with anger.

"Neither do I, but I do not want Roz-lynn and the children to worry. We must be cautious for a while."

Pale Flower cleaned up the bloody bandages and scoured the

table. "Will we have to return to the reservation, Gabriel? Will I lose my home and family again?"

"No, Mother, we will not leave our home. The wasichu will have to accept us here. I will die before I leave."

"That is what I am afraid of," Black Hawk muttered under his breath.

"We will leave it to the Great Spirit." Pale Flower put one arm around Lone Wolf and one around Black Hawk as she spoke. "He brought us here. Rosalynn went through much trouble to bring us together. The other wasichu will change eventually."

"Roz-lynn is not like the other wasichu," said Lone Wolf. "She is special."

"Yes," Pale Flower responded, "Rosalynn is special. We must protect her, Dorothy, and the children. We will find who this person is and let the law punish him. We must obey the wasichu's laws if we are to live among them."

All evening Rosalynn could feel Lone Wolf's eyes on her. *He is so handsome*, she mused, peering at him through half-closed lids. His long, ebony hair cascaded over his shoulders, and Rosalynn ached to touch it. His lean face and high cheekbones were flawless, his deep brown eyes warm and trusting.

It was becoming increasingly difficult for Rosalynn to deny the feelings she had for Lone Wolf. If only he'd give some kind of sign that he wanted more in their relationship.

As they sat in front of the fireplace in their sitting room, Rosalynn crocheted and Lone Wolf worked on a carving. When she glanced up, she noticed that Lone Wolf's cheeks were unusually red. She put her crocheting down and went to him.

"Are you in pain? You don't look well." She didn't wait for a response and placed her palm on his brow. "You're running a fever."

"My shoulder hurts, but I will be fine. Do not worry, Roz-lynn."

Rosalynn left the sitting room and returned moments later with a glass of water. "Here, drink this."

Lone Wolf's dark brows knit together. "What is it?"

"It's just headache powder mixed with water. It will help relieve the pain."

Lone Wolf put his hand up to halt her. "No, Roz-lynn. I do not trust the wasichu's medicine."

"Do you trust me?" Rosalynn felt her skin prick when Lone Wolf's eyes locked with hers. "Do you?"

Lone Wolf sighed and then took the glass and drank the liquid down.

"See, it wasn't that bad," Rosalynn sighed.

Lone Wolf grunted, and then gathered the wood shavings that had fallen on the floor and threw them into the flames.

Rosalynn put her crocheting into the basket by her chair and rose to leave. "You need your rest. I think I'll turn in too."

"Before you leave, Roz-lynn, please comb my hair. I cannot raise my arm." Lone Wolf walked over to a small dresser and brought back a handmade wooden comb.

Rosalynn took the comb and looked at it carefully. "Did you make this?"

Lone Wolf nodded.

"Does it pull the hair?"

He nodded again. "Yes, but I am used to it."

Rosalynn left and returned with her brush. "May I use my brush? I might hurt you with the comb."

"I'm a Lakota brave. I am tough."

"A head is a head, Lone Wolf," Rosalynn insisted as she sat in her chair before the fire.

Grinning, he sat on the floor in front of Rosalynn.

Taking the brush, she made gentle stokes down the back of his head. Using her fingertips, she softly brushed the hair from his face. She noticed that his thick, shiny hair, had a coarse, strong texture yet was soft to the touch.

Rosalynn brushed long strokes down the thick mane, using her fingertips to guide her. "You have beautiful hair, Lone Wolf."

"I am glad you did not ask me to cut it. As I told you before, the Lakota's long hair is important to us."

"I would never ask you to change." Rosalynn continued brushing, not wanting the moment to end. It felt right somehow, the two of them together.

Lone Wolf's head slowly tilted to one side and he jerked it back erect. Rosalynn continued to brush his hair and watched as his head started to tip again. She knew he was fighting sleep; the headache powder probably made him feel drowsy.

Rosalynn put the brush aside and slid from the chair without disturbing Lone Wolf. She unfolded his bedding and made a bed on the floor in front of the fireplace. Half asleep, Lone Wolf crawled onto the pallet and Rosalynn covered him with a thick quilt, and he appeared to be sound asleep as soon as he rested his head on the pillow.

For the first time, Rosalynn could examine Lone Wolf without restraint. She traced her fingertips along his jawline and across his cheeks. Then she ran her fingers over his dark brows and marveled at his thick, black lashes as they lay across his copper skin. She bent over and brushed a gentle kiss on his lips. "Good night, darling."

—◦—

The next few days passed uneventfully. Rosalynn enjoyed spending more time with Lone Wolf, but she could tell it nearly drove him crazy to sit around rather than work from sunup to sundown. Soon, his shoulder healed enough that he could to return to his normal schedule.

The days grew hotter as summer wore on. Often, Rosalynn, Dorothy, and Pale Flower packed a lunch and took the children to the waterfall, where they spent lazy afternoons enjoying the outdoors and each other's company. Lone Wolf and Black Hawk occasionally took a break from their chores and joined the group for a quick lunch and a refreshing swim.

When Black Hawk first arrived, he was skeptical of the wasichu ways. However, under Lone Wolf's tutelage, he soon discovered that his people could benefit from farming. Rosalynn noticed how patiently Lone Wolf treated Black Hawk, and she was proud of her husband. Her feelings for Lone Wolf seemed to grow in leaps and bounds, and he never disappointed her—never treated her with disrespect and never gave her a moment's worry that he would ever resort to violence with her or the children.

About a month after the shooting, several dozen head of livestock escaped from their pastures. With some searching, Lone Wolf and Black Hawk found that some fence had been cut. They repaired the fence and then set out to gather the livestock, and it was late when they finally came in for supper.

While the men washed on the back porch, Rosalynn set the food on the table. Because of the heat, she had made fried chicken and potato salad early that morning, so she retrieved the leftovers from the cellar, then sliced tomatoes, cucumbers, and bread and placed everything on the table.

Listening to the men talk as they ate, she asked, "Who do you think cut the fences?"

Lone Wolf shrugged his shoulders. "I do not know. It could be some kids from Peaceful. I will ask Jeb if he is having the same kind of problems."

"Do you think the cut fences have anything to do with you

being shot?" Rosalynn tried to keep her voice calm.

Lone Wolf glanced at Black Hawk. "No, I do not think they are related."

When the men came in for breakfast the next morning, Rosalynn sensed that something was wrong. She dished cornmeal mush into a serving bowl and placed it on the table and watched the men scoop the hot cereal into their bowls and add butter and cream. Then she took the food from the warming oven and placed it on the table, looking back and forth between Lone Wolf and Black Hawk.

After the breakfast blessing, the men piled their plates with pancakes, fried eggs, and thick, crisp bacon. Rosalynn filled their glasses with milk and then waited for them to speak.

"The wasichu eat good," Black Hawk said with relish. "Soon I can teach the Lakota on the reservation how to farm. Their bellies will be full. That is good."

Lone Wolf ate silently.

"Okay, out with it," Rosalynn demanded. "I know something is wrong, and I want to know what it is before Aunt Dottie and the children wake up." She threw the dish towel on the table and plopped down in a chair across from Lone Wolf.

"Something has happened again, hasn't it?" As she spoke the question, Rosalynn heard a door open, and soon Pale Flower stood next to her.

Lone Wolf put his fork down and looked at the two women. "Someone shot several of the sheep, including a lamb. It must have been early this morning, because they were still warm when we found them."

"Oh, no!" Rosalynn brought her hand to her mouth. "Who would do such a cruel thing? Who would hate us enough to kill innocent animals?"

"I do not know, Roz-lynn," replied Lone Wolf. "Black Hawk

233

and I were able to save the meat. We will keep some to eat now and I will take the rest into Peaceful. Todd and Arlene will buy it for the café. Hopefully, I can replace the sheep."

"It's a blessing you were able to save the meat, but what a shame to lose good ewes," Rosalynn said with a sigh.

"Will you go into Peaceful alone, son?"

"Yes, Mother. I think it will be best to leave Black Hawk here in case this person returns."

"May I go with you?" asked Rosalynn. "I have some eggs for the merc."

"It may not be safe, Roz-lynn," Lone Wolf said.

"I'll be fine as long as I'm with you. Besides, if this person is just a prankster, he won't dare do anything to us in the light of day and in front of witnesses. Maybe I can find out from Ida if there's been any talk."

"I can ask around also," Lone Wolf returned. "You can come, but we must leave right after breakfast. I need to get back and help Black Hawk and then ride over to Jeb's."

Leaving Pale Flower and Dorothy to serve breakfast to the children, Rosalynn soon let her husband help her onto the wagon seat and then watched him take his place beside her. The trip to town seemed to take forever. When they finally arrived at the cafe, Arlene gladly bought the meat and the eggs, but said she hadn't heard any talk against them. Ida and Swede hadn't heard anything either. Some of the citizens didn't like the fact that Pale Flower and Black Hawk had joined Lone Wolf on the farm, but none had made any public threats.

When they arrived back at the farm, Lone Wolf headed off for Jeb's, and Black Hawk and Joshua stacked wood for the winter. Then Rosalynn decided to wash clothes and, with Black Hawk's help, got a fire started outside to heat the water. She brought the tubs out and then gathered the clothes and lye soap.

Pale Flower and Dorothy started roasting the lamb in the summer kitchen that Lone Wolf had built alongside the house, and Pale Flower prepared new potatoes in a cream sauce. Using fresh lettuce and green onions, Dorothy made a wilted lettuce salad. Rosalynn had made fresh bread and strawberry rhubarb pies early that morning. With the surplus of milk, they made cottage cheese and put it in the cellar.

In the yard, Rosalynn was up to her elbows in hot, sudsy water when she glanced up and saw what looked like smoke. She stopped, and with the back of her hand, shaded her eyes against the glaring sun. Yes, it was smoke, and it was coming from the chicken coop.

Rosalynn wiped her hands on her apron and started for the barn to investigate. When she was halfway there, she saw flames leaping into the air, so she quickly ran back to the house, shouting for Black Hawk. Frantic, she grabbed the milk pail and headed back to the hen house.

By the time Black Hawk and Rosalynn reached the chicken coop, flames had engulfed the small building. The only thing they could do was to prevent the fire from spreading to other buildings and to the dry grass and shrubs.

The building was still burning when Lone Wolf and Jeb came riding through the trees.

"What happened?" Lone Wolf asked crossly as he quickly dismounted to survey the damage.

He searched Rosalynn's countenance as if demanding an explanation. His jet black eyes narrowed into angry slits, and the intensity of his gaze made her shudder.

"I don't know how it started," Rosalynn replied, her face blanching. "I just happened to look up and see smoke."

As Lone Wolf ran his hand through his long hair, Rosalynn felt her stomach grip. Would he blame her? Would he take his anger out on her as Jeffery always had? She just couldn't bear it if that happened! Panicked, she abruptly ran from the scene, refusing to stop when everyone called after her.

When Rosalynn stopped running, she found herself at the waterfall. She was out of breath and gasping for air. Her legs felt weak, and she fell to the ground at the edge of the water. *Please, Lord, don't let Lone Wolf blame me. Please don't let him be like Jeffery.*

She didn't hear Lone Wolf until he knelt down beside her. He put his hands on her shoulders.

"Roz-lynn, are you hurt? What is the matter?"

Her eyes pinched shut, but the rebellious tears managed to squeeze through and stream down her cheeks. "Go away, Lone Wolf. Please go away."

Rosalynn felt his hands slip from her shoulders, but she kept her eyes clamped shut, afraid to see the expression on his face. She screamed inside at the injustice of what had happened to her. All at once, like a dam breaking, she cried out in agony and despair. "Why, Lord? Why do I have to keep suffering? Why can't I trust? Help me, God. Help me heal and be whole again."

Rosalynn covered her face with her hands and continued to sob until she was too weak to continue. When she finally opened her eyes, Lone Wolf was gone, and she felt lost and alone. She had pushed away the only man she would ever love.

—————

Lone Wolf's heart felt like lead. Rosalynn had made it quite clear that she didn't want him around. How could he have been foolish enough to think she cared for him? She was beautiful and loving, a treasure any man would want. Why would she want a half-breed?

Rosalynn liked him—that was clear enough—but she didn't

love him as a woman loves a man. Yet Lone Wolf sensed that her refusal went deeper than she would admit. Something had happened to her, and Lone Wolf was sure it had to do with her first husband. She had never explained why she divorced Jeffery, but Lone Wolf knew her well enough now to know that she wasn't at fault. *Give me patience, Great Spirit. I love Roz-lynn. Help her to love me.*

Chapter Sixteen

When Lone Wolf and Black Hawk went into Peaceful to buy lumber to rebuild the chicken coop, they visited the sheriff's office. Lone Wolf told the sheriff about the shooting, the fence cutting, the murdered animals, and the fire. As expected, the sheriff said he couldn't do anything about the crimes without evidence as to who committed them.

For the next few days, Rosalynn kept to herself. She was ashamed of the way she had treated Lone Wolf the day of the fire, but still couldn't bring herself to talk about what Jeffery had done to her. How could she tell Lone Wolf she was afraid that he too might hit her? Her body had healed from Jeffery's abuse, and all she could do was pray that, in time, her heart would also mend.

On Sunday, after she prepared breakfast for the family, Rosalynn slipped upstairs to dress for church. She was grateful for the Sabbath, knowing that she needed time in the Lord's house to reenergize her heart and soul. There, she could reflect on her blessings and ask God to purge her soul of its troubles.

As always, Reverend Baker gave an uplifting sermon, and Rosalynn felt as if it had been prepared just for her. *Perhaps the Lord revealed my troubled heart to the reverend*, she thought as she sat with her family in the pew.

"Today's sermon is about trusting in the Lord. Give your problems to God and then forget them, brothers and sisters. Trust in Him, and your burdens shall be lifted." Reverend Baker spoke calmly and lovingly. "God doesn't discriminate by the color of your skin. We are all His children and He loves us very much."

Rosalynn noticed that Lone Wolf, Black Hawk, and Pale Flower seemed to listen intently to Reverend Baker's words. Then Rosalynn glanced around the congregation and wondered if the person responsible for their recent bad luck was among the parishioners. *Please, Lord, soften the hearts around us. Reassure them that we mean no harm but only want to live in peace and harmony.*

At the end of the services, Reverend Baker blessed the food they would enjoy at the picnic, and then everyone left the building and walked across to the park. As Rosalynn helped place the food on one of the quilts, she kept looking in her husband's direction. They had grown apart since her breakdown at the waterfall, and he no longer joined them for the noon meal or chatted with her in the evenings in their sitting room. And since that fateful day, Lone Wolf hadn't come to bed until after Rosalynn was already asleep.

Soon Rosalynn sat down on a quilt near Ida's and watched the girls and Joshua play with the other children. "It's so peaceful here," Rosalynn said to no one in particular. "What a beautiful Sunday." She glanced around at several young couples that snuggled close together.

"It is a beautiful Sunday," Ida agreed. "It's good to have a day of rest for our minds as well as our bodies."

"I agree," Arlene commented. "It's nice to get together with friends and just enjoy each other's company."

"I like the cooking, too," Jeb added as he dug into his plate of food. "I sure do get tired of my own cooking."

Everyone laughed. Jeb took a bit of fried chicken and moaned with pleasure.

"You need a wife, Jeb. You've been a bachelor too long," Todd teased.

"Aunt Dottie is a wonderful cook, Jeb." Rosalynn winked at Ida.

"Rosalynn!" Dorothy exclaimed, her face reddening.

"I just might have to come a-courtin'," Jeb winked at Dorothy. "If Miss Dorothy doesn't mind an old cuss like me hanging around."

"Not at all, Jeb. You're welcome anytime. Isn't he, Rosalynn and Lone Wolf?" Dorothy pled, glancing from Rosalynn to Lone Wolf, then at Pale Flower and Black Hawk. "You wouldn't mind, would you?" Everyone laughed, and Rosalynn couldn't help but join in.

All too soon, it was time to start home. The evening chores waited and the children grew tired. Lone Wolf and Rosalynn rode in one wagon along with Pale Flower, Mikey, and Joshua. Black Hawk rode in Jeb's wagon with Dorothy and the girls.

Sitting next to Lone Wolf, Rosalynn yearned to apologize for her outburst at the waterfall, but didn't know how to begin, so she remained miserably silent. They were almost home when they heard several gunshots. Rosalynn heard the bullets whiz past them, barely missing her and Lone Wolf.

Lone Wolf shouted for everyone to get down and pulled the team to a stop. Rosalynn crawled into the back of the wagon, pulling Joshua down with her.

"Lone Wolf—the girls and Aunt Dottie!" she cried.

"They are safe, Roz-lynn. Jeb will have them lie down in the back of the wagon. Stay here."

Lone Wolf grabbed the rifle he kept on the floorboard and jumped from the wagon. Rosalynn's heart pounded so hard she could barely think. Pale Flower lay quiet with Mikey in her arms. Rosalynn could hear the girls crying and Dorothy trying to soothe them. Joshua wanted to go with Lone Wolf, and Rosalynn had to force him to stay in the wagon. *Please, Lord, keep them safe!* she begged.

Several long minutes passed before Lone Wolf and Black Hawk returned to the wagons. Lone Wolf called out when they drew near, "It is clear. You can get up now."

Everyone peeked over the top of the wagons and then slowly rose.

Rosalynn glanced around. "Did you see anyone?"

"No, but we found hoof prints. Whoever it was took off through the forest. There was no way we could follow him on foot."

"Why is someone doing this to us?" Rosalynn implored. "I don't understand!"

"Whoever he is, he could have shot any of us if he really wanted to," Black Hawk said. "He was close enough. I think he is just trying to scare us."

"But why?" Pale Flower rocked the baby in her arms.

Black Hawk scanned the area, his body tense. "He will let us know when he is ready to."

Rosalynn put her arms around the weeping girls. "The children are frightened, Lone Wolf. We need to get them home. We can discuss this after they are asleep."

Lone Wolf nodded as Dorothy ushered the girls back into Jeb's wagon. After ensuring that Joshua, Pale Flower, and Mikey again lay safely in the back of the wagon, Lone Wolf helped Rosalynn onto the wagon seat, then climbed up himself. "Roz-lynn, you drive the team. I will watch." Lone Wolf laid the rifle across his lap, his finger on the trigger.

Rosalynn took the reins and started the horses down the dirt road. She glanced behind them, relieved that Dorothy and the girls were safe in the back of Jeb's wagon. Black Hawk rode shotgun for Jeb. *Please, Father, see us home safely.*

When they pulled up next to the house, Rosalynn watched as Lone Wolf quickly canvassed the area for anything out of the ordinary. Joshua jumped from the wagon and began calling for his puppy. Toby finally popped his head out from under the porch.

"That's funny, Ma. Toby never goes under the porch unless he's scared."

Joshua coaxed the frightened puppy out from under the porch far enough that he could grab him. "Ma, Pa!" the boy suddenly shouted. "Toby's hurt!"

Lone Wolf ran to Joshua's side and knelt down to examine the gangly dog. Toby's back was laid open in a long gash. "Someone whipped him," Lone Wolf said, his face tightening.

"Why, Pa? Why would anyone want to hurt Toby? He's just a puppy."

As she approached, Rosalynn saw tears running down her son's cheeks, making trails on his dusty face. Rosalynn bent over him and gasped when she saw the bloody wound on Toby's back. "Oh, the poor thing! What happened?"

"Someone whipped Toby, Ma. Just like my old pa whipped you."

Rosalynn recoiled, drawing her hand to her throat. *Dear Lord, does Joshua remember?* Glancing at Lone Wolf, she prayed he hadn't heard Joshua's words.

Lone Wolf patted the dog's head and then placed his hand on Joshua's shoulder. "My mother can help Toby, Joshua. He will live."

Rising from his feet, Lone Wolf motioned for Black Hawk to follow him. They spoke in hushed tones and then Black Hawk headed for the barn. Lone Wolf called out to Jeb to stay with the women and the children, and then he headed for the house.

The baby began to fret, so Rosalynn took him from Pale Flower, then changed his wet diaper and gave him a piece of jerky to suck on. Dorothy found some cookies that were left over from the picnic and gave them to the girls, who had started to whine.

Lone Wolf finally came out of the house and joined them by the wagon. "The children can go in, Roz-lynn. The house is safe."

Rosalynn let out a sigh of relief, and Pale Flower and Dorothy ushered the children into the house. Jeb decided it was safe for him to leave them and headed home. Rosalynn waited outside with Lone Wolf. When Black Hawk returned from the barn, he told them the animals were unharmed.

———

Later that evening, after the children had gone to bed, the adults sat around the dining room table, discussing the events of the day.

"All of this is so unnerving," Dorothy stated, shaking her head in dismay. "Rosalynn and I faced persecution in St. Louis, but it was always out in the open, not sneaky like this."

"We weren't threatened with bodily harm, either," Rosalynn added, staring into her cup of tea.

"In all of the years I lived here, nothing like this ever happened," Pale Flower said. "The wasichu's lips smile, but their eyes bite, even now when I go into Peaceful."

"I have not seen the back of a head since I have been here," Black Hawk growled.

"None of us have really been welcome in Peaceful," Rosalynn said, glancing around the table. "Granted, a few families we've gotten acquainted with are friendly, but as a whole, the residents of Peaceful don't want any of us here. Thank goodness the

Swedish families are friendly."

"They are basically in the same position as we are. They were not wanted either." Pale Flower's voice was touched with gloom. "I remember the old days when my husband first came here. The local families would not so much as help him with a meal when his first wife died. That is why I decided to marry him. He came to our camp begging someone to help him with his small children. I knew then that it was to be my destiny to love and care for him."

"Weren't any of the Swedish families willing to help?" Dorothy wondered.

"Thirty years ago, there were only a handful of Swedes here, and they had just as many hardships as Adrian. There were no single women then, and he needed someone to move into the house with him."

Lone Wolf listened in silence, trying to decide what to do. Clearly, they were dealing with someone who was deranged and dangerous.

"You are quiet, Gabriel. What is on your mind, son?"

Lone Wolf glanced at his mother. "Whoever this madman is, he skulks in the shadows like a rattler. He is afraid to face us out in the open. We must all be very careful." Lone Wolf looked at each person in turn. "Black Hawk and I must not leave the farm unattended. This madman could burn the house down next time."

Then Lone Wolf directed his attention to Rosalynn. "You must keep the children close to the house." Then, glancing at all three women, he added, "None of you should go outside without Black Hawk or myself with you."

"Lone Wolf and I have been taking turns watching the house at night," Black Hawk explained. "Now, I think I will sleep in the barn for a while."

"That is a good idea, Black Hawk," Lone Wolf responded. "I will sleep outside for a while."

"Do you really think all of these precautions are necessary?" Rosalynn asked.

"Yes, Roz-lynn, I do. This person is trying to scare us for a reason. He could have killed any of us by now. I want to be ready when he finally does make his move."

Lone Wolf saw Rosalynn shudder. He knew the women were frightened; they had good reason to be. "Please, go to bed," he said, trying to smile. "Black Hawk and I will stand watch. We will be safe, I promise."

———

Rosalynn hated going to bed knowing that Lone Wolf wouldn't be in the next room, but she understood his reasons for sleeping outside of the house. After looking in on the children, she checked the windows before retiring to her bedroom. As she opened the door, Rosalynn felt a little apprehensive about entering the darkened room. She quickly lit a lamp and glanced around, relieved to see that everything was just as she had left it that morning.

Rosalynn set the lamp down on a little stand by the door. Grabbing her nightgown, she hurried to undress. She took the pins from her hair and placed them on her small dressing table. Rosalynn felt around for her brush, but she couldn't find it, so she retrieved the lamp and placed it on the dressing table. When she looked into the illuminated mirror, she screamed.

Within seconds, Lone Wolf was standing beside her. "Roz-lynn, what is the matter?" He grabbed her by the shoulders and looked into her terrified face.

She pointed to the mirror. Someone had written the word *TRAMP* across it in big, red letters. Rosalynn's body began to tremble uncontrollably. "Someone was in here!"

Lone Wolf put his rifle down, folded his arms around her, and held her, not saying a word. Dorothy and Pale Flower dashed into the room, frightened by Rosalynn's scream. Both glanced at the crude word scrawled across the mirror.

Furiously, Lone Wolf swiped at the word with the back of his hand. An angry red smear trailed across the mirror, casting an eerie chill in the room. Dorothy examined the smudged word and told Lone Wolf that it had been written with lip rouge. "I make this lip rouge, but Rosalynn and I don't use it."

"Where did it come from, then?" Lone Wolf asked, Rosalynn still nestled in his arms.

"It was Susan's," Rosalynn explained, stepping away from Lone Wolf. She picked up a small pot from the vanity. "I found it among her things and placed it here on the dressing table."

"Well, now we know this person has been in the house," Dorothy commented with a shiver in her voice.

"Why would he call me a tramp? I don't understand." Rosalynn's voice trailed off to a whisper.

"There is nothing to understand, Roz-lynn," Lone Wolf started. "This person is insane. One cannot find logical answers when dealing with a crazed person."

Dorothy went downstairs and prepared a pot of tea, then brought a cup to her niece. Rosalynn drank it gratefully and felt a bit calmer. Lone Wolf promised to stay just outside her room until she felt safe. As she lay in bed, Rosalynn heard music. Leaning on one elbow, she cocked her head and listened.

It was flute music, but different from any she had ever heard. It had an ethereal, low, almost haunting sound. Rosalynn felt her body relax, and she closed her eyes. As she focused her attention on the music, her fears vanished and she fell into a restful slumber.

In the following weeks, Lone Wolf and Black Hawk stayed close to the farm. Black Hawk remained at home on Sundays to keep an eye on the house and barnyard while Lone Wolf took the women and children to church. During the week, Lone Wolf and Black Hawk busied themselves cutting and stacking wood for the winter. They also used the time to catch up on the odd jobs Mike had neglected through the years. They painted the house inside and out and repaired the broken windows. They also replaced the old picket fence around the yard and helped Rosalynn and Pale Flower turn the ugly weed patch into a flower garden.

Lone Wolf cleaned the smokehouse in preparation for the fall, when they would slaughter animals and smoke the meat for the winter. One day, he found a beehive and brought home several large pieces of honeycomb. The honey was bottled and the beeswax stored to make candles. The women picked the strawberries and raspberries in the garden and made jam, and when they ran out of berries, they made soap for the winter.

Lone Wolf often helped Rosalynn in the vegetable garden, and she enjoyed the time they spent together. Still, she longed to just sit and talk with him like they used to do each evening in the sitting room. But since the day by the waterfall when she had told him to leave her alone, he had been distant. Polite, but distant. Something was missing in their relationship.

One evening, Rosalynn hummed absently as she washed the dinner dishes. Dorothy was preparing the children for bed, and Pale Flower was clearing the dishes from the table.

When the kitchen was finally clean, Rosalynn rinsed the sink with hot water and hung the wash pan on a nail on the back porch. It was much cooler outside and she stood there for a moment to enjoy the breeze. She didn't hear Pale Flower come up behind her until she spoke. "It is a beautiful night."

"Yes," Rosalynn leaned against the doorframe gazing up into the star-filled sky. Fireflies swirled in the darkness like little fairies. In the distant, she heard the melodious flute music that she had come to love.

"Do you hear music, Pale Flower?" Rosalynn asked dreamily. "I hear it every night when I go to sleep. I pretend that only I can hear it, that it's only for me."

"But it is, child," Pale Flower said with a smile. "The music is for you only. Did you not know that?"

Rosalynn turned to face her. "I don't understand. What do you mean it's for me?"

"My people, the Lakota, are very romantic. We do not shower affection publicly like the wasichu, but privately. A young brave makes a flute from river cane and plays it for the maiden he wishes to court. Gabriel plays his flute for you, the way of the Lakota."

Staring at Pale Flower, Rosalynn blurted out, "I wish it were true, Pale Flower. Lone Wolf has made it pretty plain he wants a marriage in name only."

"You both have eyes but cannot see what is in front of you. My son loves you, Rosalynn. He may not say it in words but he feels it in his heart." Pale Flower embraced Rosalynn. "Go to him. He waits for you."

As Rosalynn thought of meeting Lone Wolf under the romance of the stars, her stomach filled with butterflies and her pulse quickened.

"Look at the moon, Rosalynn. It is a sweetheart's moon. Your love waits for you."

"I . . . I don't know what to do . . . what to say to Lone Wolf."

"Let your heart be your guide. Now go to him. He waits."

Pale Flower nudged Rosalynn from the porch. As if in a trance, Rosalynn followed the flute music into the yard. Colorful roses lined the path, their intoxicating fragrance filling the air. The sky lit up with thousands of stars, and a full moon hung overhead.

Suddenly, from the shadows, a figure emerged. The music stopped and Lone Wolf stood before her.

"Roz-lynn, you came." His voice was full of affection.

She glanced into his eyes and then quickly turned away. "Yes, Lone Wolf, I came. Don't ask me why, but I came." Rosalynn breathed her words out in short gasps.

"I was wondering when my music would bring you to me." Lone Wolf pivoted Rosalynn around to face him, then wiped a wavy strand of hair from her flushed face.

Wringing her hands nervously, she mumbled, "Pale Flower just told me why you were playing it. I thought I was dreaming the music until now."

Lone Wolf cupped Rosalynn's chin in his hand and gently raised her head until she was looking at him. "I was hoping it would help you sleep and dream happy thoughts."

She felt giddy at his touch. "It did."

"Then let us walk together under the sweetheart's moon, my wife. There is magic in the air on nights like this."

Rosalynn allowed Lone Wolf to guide her, not caring where they went as long as they were together. It wasn't until she heard the rushing water that she knew he had taken her to the falls. Hand in hand, they stopped, and each searched the other's countenance.

"Tell me, my Roz-lynn, if you would make a wish under the sweetheart's moon, what would it be?"

The moon illuminated Lone Wolf's face and for a moment, Rosalynn thought she saw love reflected there. She ran her fingers across his glossy, black hair. She paused and then trailed her touch across his cheek and then along his jaw. She ran both hands down his broad chest to his narrow waist.

She felt Lone Wolf take a deep breath as though he enjoyed her touch as much as she enjoyed touching him. She gazed again into his eyes. She drew close, a breath away, and could smell wood smoke, mint, and sandalwood mingled together.

"I dream that you love me and we become one here in our special place under the sweetheart's moon." Rosalynn couldn't believe she was so bold, but her heart knew no bounds.

Lone Wolf's breath caught in jagged gulps. "Then it is destiny, my wife."

He brought his mouth down on her lips. His kiss was sweet and gentle at first but soon became more fervent. Rosalynn responded, bringing her body so close to his that their hearts seemed to beat as one. And there under the sweetheart's moon, Lone Wolf and Rosalynn became one.

When six weeks passed without any suspicious incidents, Lone Wolf and Black Hawk started the fall harvest. Jeb offered to help, and Lone Wolf accepted with a promise to return the favor when the crops were stored. Once the cut hay dried in the sun, the men raked it into large piles, loaded the piles onto wagons, and stored the loose hay in the loft of the barn. Everyone helped pick the field corn, and once it dried, they stored it in the silo. The men dried the cornstalks, tied them in bundles, and stored them for winter feed for the cattle and horses.

Rosalynn, Dorothy, and Pale Flower started the winter preserving. Everything from the garden that they didn't eat fresh was either dried or canned and carefully stored in the pantry or cellar. They picked the peaches, pears, and apples and spent long hours canning jams, jellies, applesauce, and sliced fruit. They stored the extra apples in the cellar, where they would last for at least a few months, and the extra peaches and pears in the pantry.

Rosalynn enjoyed the fall season, especially watching the shelves fill with food for the long winter ahead. With so much to preserve, she felt incredibly blessed. Her little kitchen garden in St. Louis couldn't hold a candle to the garden they had here.

When she went to the falls, Rosalynn gathered fresh mint and carefully rinsed it in the clear water of the creek. Then she tied the mint into bundles and hung them from the rafters on the back porch.

Pale Flower showed her where to find wild hazelnuts and black walnuts, and they collected the nuts together. The two of them also sliced apples, apricots, peaches, and pears, then carefully strung the slices on fishing line and hung them on the outside walls of the smokehouse to dry.

With Lone Wolf's help, Rosalynn carefully maintained the five-acre garden. She loved to work in the rich earth. She had grown brown as a nut and more freckles appeared across her nose despite her wearing a bonnet, but she didn't care. She marveled at how much food they had harvested over the summer. Tomatoes, cabbage, cucumbers, and squash still grew, and soon the root vegetables would be ready to dig up.

One afternoon in late August, Rosalynn noticed that the

blueberries and grapes were ready to harvest, and she gave a little squeal at the thought of fresh blueberry pie. Then she glanced at the hot sun and realized it was time to start dinner, so she quickly picked enough greens, tomatoes, and cucumbers to make a nice salad. She would miss the taste of fresh vegetables during the winter months and wanted to enjoy them as long as possible.

Brushing the dirt from her overalls and straightening her straw hat, Rosalynn paused. *It's so hot,* she thought. *How nice it would be to take a quick dip at the falls!* Surely, she would be safe, she reasoned, since they hadn't had an incident in so long. She had gone to the falls many times recently with Lone Wolf, and the memory of what they did there brought a pink stain to her cheeks. The thought of Lone Wolf's copper body gliding through the water, him washing her back with his gentle hands . . . Rosalynn couldn't stand the temptation any longer. Lone Wolf would be coming soon to bathe at the falls, and they would have a few moments together.

Rosalynn set the basket of vegetables near the garden gate and headed for the falls. She heard the rushing water long before she saw the creek. Anticipation hurried her along the trail. When she reached the falls, she sat down near the edge of the water, then removed her straw hat and placed it next to her. She then took her handkerchief and swirled it in the cool water, then washed her face.

As she sat deep in thought, she suddenly felt a sharp sting on her back. Letting out a loud cry, she jumped to her feet and turned to see what had hit her.

No more than ten feet away she saw an outline of a man. The bright sun obscured her vision, so she placed her hand over her eyes to block the sun's rays.

"Don't you recognize me, Rosalynn?"

Bile rose in her throat as she recognized the voice. She must be dreaming—it couldn't be!

"Surely the welt on your back should remind you who I am. Or does your new husband whip you into submission as well?"

"Jeffery?" Rosalynn's voice quivered.

"That's right, it's me. I bet you never expected to see me in this old cowtown."

Jeffery's cruel laugh sent chills down Rosalynn's spine. "How—how did you find me?" Rosalynn asked as she backed away. She glanced around and saw Jeffery's horse tethered in the trees behind him.

"It wasn't hard. You don't have many relatives."

"Susan? How could Susan tell you we were coming here? She left St. Louis five years ago, and I didn't even know where she was until recently."

"Questions, questions," Jeffery laughed. "I guess I can tell you now. I came to Peaceful quite by accident. I was traveling on a steamer when it docked here. I happened to see Susan on the waterfront with some unsavory fellows. Seems she lived two lives in Peaceful."

Rosalynn didn't need Jeffery to go into detail; she knew what he meant.

"It was then she told me she always fancied me—loved me, if you like." Jeffery shrugged.

"I'm leaving with someone I've loved for a long time . . ." The words from Susan's letter to Lone Wolf finally made sense.

"I ran into a bit of bad luck and Susan bailed me out by paying some of my gambling debts. All she wanted in return was to leave this horrible place."

"Then why are you here? You and Susan got what you wanted . . . or should I say what you deserved." Rosalynn tried to keep the conversation going, praying that Lone Wolf would arrive soon.

"Yes, we did get what we wanted. Too bad that stupid husband of hers had to die before signing the land over to her. So now we need a new stake."

Rosalynn flinched at Jeffery's coldness regarding Mike's demise. "I don't understand. What's that got to do with me?"

"You never were very smart, were you?" Jeffery growled. "I guess I'll have to spell it out for you. Susan says that half-breed husband of yours—" Jeffery spat on the ground "—has a lot of money stuck away in the bank. We want it and we want the farm. Now that you've fixed the place up, I can get a good price for it."

Rosalynn stared at him in disbelief. "You're crazy, Jeffery. There's no way you can scare Lone Wolf in giving you his farm."

"His farm and his money, don't forget. I think I can persuade him," he sighed then snapped his whip inches from her face.

While she tried to appear calm, Rosalynn was screaming inside. "Lone Wolf isn't afraid of you, Jeffery. You're no longer dealing with a scared woman with two small children."

"Oh, I wasn't planning on whipping him, you twit. You'll do nicely."

"Go ahead and whip me. I won't let Lone Wolf give up his farm to the likes of you and Susan. You took my home away. I'll not let you do the same to Lone Wolf."

"You underestimate me, Rosalynn. I have it in my power to take Susan's children from you. I also have it in my power to have Lone Wolf taken care of for good. After all, if he dies, Susan will legally own the place."

From hard experience, Rosalynn knew that Jeffery didn't make idle threats. She also knew him well enough to know he wouldn't fight fair; he always had a card up his sleeve. He scared her, but Rosalynn was determined not to show it. "I don't believe you. We have the law on our side."

"The law on your side," he laughed. "A half-breed savage and his tramp squaw."

"Tramp?" Rosalynn's head began to swim. "You're the one who has been terrorizing us!"

"You just figured that out? Thinking was never your strong suit, was it?"

Rosalynn trembled with fear. Just the crazed look on Jeffery's face almost made her faint. Memories of the past rushed through her brain, and she felt as if her head were spinning. *Please, God, don't let him hurt me again. I can't keep this up much longer. Send Lone Wolf! I can't face my demons alone; I need Lone Wolf. Oh, Lord, I have trusted him all along—I just didn't know it!*

Almost as soon as she uttered this silent prayer, Rosalynn felt a calmness come over her. Yes, she was afraid, but she was no longer a young girl browbeaten by Jeffery's presence. He no longer had a hold on her soul. She would not back down to him—ever.

Rosalynn held her head high and looked Jeffery straight in the eye. "Go ahead and hit me. I'm not afraid of you now. I'm much stronger with Lone Wolf at my side, because he has shown me what real love is." She swallowed hard and continued, "I'm no longer ashamed of the fact that you hit me and mistreated me. It wasn't my fault, and I won't continue to hide it from others. If you harm me or anyone in my family, I'll go straight to Sheriff Lord."

"We'll see about that. Tell Lone Wolf I want the deed signed over and all of his savings tomorrow or he will live to regret my wrath."

"Why don't you tell him yourself? Or are you afraid of facing a real man?"

"Oh, I'll face him all right, but I'm white, and he's a savage. Who do you think the town will side with?"

"You're the savage, Jeffery. Lone Wolf is the kindest man I know."

"Yes," Jeffery broke in. "I've seen your savage husband with you down here at the falls. I've seen what a gentleman he is."

Rosalynn's hands balled up into tight fists at her sides, and the jeering grin on Jeffery's face only added to her anger. She would not let him make something ugly out of the love she shared with Lone Wolf. "Go ahead and say what you want. We have God on our side, and He is stronger than you or the town."

"Don't be spouting that Bible-thumping drivel to me. Give Lone Wolf my message." Jeffery paused, then added, "To show I mean business, I'm going to leave him my calling card."

How could I have loved such a man? Rosalynn thought with horror. Then she watched as Jeffery drew his whip back and snapped it, grazing her left cheek. She screamed out in pain and quickly drew her hand over the slash, feeling the blood bead and then trickle down her cheek.

Prepared for the next snap of the whip, she put her hand out to ward off the blow. The tip of the whip caught the back of her hand and laid out a wide gash. Rosalynn bit her lower lip until she tasted blood. Sweat beaded on her forehead and then ran down her neck as she fought against the pain. Turning from Jeffery, she started to leave. Repeatedly, she felt the snap of his whip on her back. *Please, Father, help me endure the pain. Don't let me give in!* She knew that Jeffery expected her to cower before him and beg him to stop—just as she always had—but she vowed not to cry out. He would never have power over her mind again.

"If my whip isn't good enough anymore," he finally shouted, "I'll take you from Lone Wolf." Jeffery grabbed Rosalynn by the arm and dragged her to where his horse was tethered. Clutching the reins, he ordered her to mount. The horse whinnied and pranced, and Jeffery let go of Rosalynn to steady the animal.

Rosalynn seized the opportunity and slapped the horse's flank as hard as she could. The horse jerked his head back and reared up on his hind legs, forcing the reins from Jeffery's grip. Rosalynn took off on a dead run through the dense forest. Soon she heard the horse crashing through the underbrush and knew that Jeffery would stop at nothing to catch her, and that she would be lucky if she survived.

Lord, I can't make it back to the house. What should I do? Suddenly she knew exactly what to do, and she quickly backtracked to the falls by a different route. Stumbling from the pain, Rosalynn ran to the falls and jumped into the rushing water, then entered the hidden cave. Through the flowing water of the waterfall, she watched Jeffery on horseback, trying to pick up her tracks. She stepped back into the cave as far as she could and pressed her back against the rough wall. Her body shivered but she was burning inside. As she slid down the wall to the cave floor, she lost consciousness.

"Did you find Rosalynn?" Dorothy asked when Pale Flower returned from the garden.

"No, and I looked everywhere for her. The only thing I found was this basket of vegetables on the ground by the garden gate. I called her name many times, but she did not answer."

"I'm worried, Pale Flower. It's not like Rosalynn to go off alone without telling anyone, especially since strange things started happening around here."

"Let us not panic yet. She may be with Gabriel."

"That's a good idea. I didn't think of Lone Wolf." Dorothy's face brightened. "I guess I don't think rationally when it comes to Rosalynn. She's more like a daughter to me than a niece. She's had it rough all of her life, so I tend to be overly protective."

"You can never love too much, Dorothy," Pale Flower said with a smile and then patted Dorothy's arm.

Chapter
Eighteen

Lone Wolf peeled the husk back and took a bite of sweet corn. It would be a bumper crop this year. He heard someone call out his name and glanced up to see Pale Flower waving as she approached him. He handed the corn to Black Hawk and went to meet his mother.

"Is Rosalynn here with you?" Pale Flower asked, glancing through the tall cornstalks.

"No, I have not seen Roz-lynn since the noon meal. Is she not at the house?"

"No, and I have looked everywhere for her. She left to work in the garden, but that was hours ago. I am frightened for her."

Lone Wolf felt his stomach twist with dread. Without saying a word, he headed for the house with Black Hawk and Pale Flower trailing behind him. They searched the barn and all of the outbuildings with no luck. Lone Wolf began to panic and headed for the house in a dead run. "Black Hawk, bring me my horse."

Black Hawk ran back to the barn while Lone Wolf continued toward the house. Dorothy was waiting on the back porch with Mikey in her arms. "Rosalynn isn't with you, Lone Wolf?"

"You are sure she is not in the house?" Lone Wolf asked.

"I'm positive. We've searched everywhere for her."

When Black Hawk arrived with the horse, Lone Wolf quickly mounted. He looked down at his friend pleadingly.

"Do not fear, my friend, I will stay with your family." Black Hawk slapped Lone Wolf on the leg. "Go find your woman. May the Great Spirit guide your steps."

Lone Wolf dug his heels into the mare's sides and raced toward the garden. Rosalynn was nowhere to be seen. Next, he galloped toward the cabin and called out her name, but there was no answer. He jumped from the horse and quickly searched the cabin.

Something is wrong, thought Lone Wolf. *Great Spirit, help me find Roz-lynn. Keep her safe.*

Lone Wolf ran back to his horse and mounted again. Where would his wife go? Recently they had met at the creek several times a week for a few minutes of privacy. *Yes! She must be at the falls!* Lone Wolf cursed himself for not thinking of it sooner.

Within minutes, he arrived at the falls, then slid from his horse and ran to the bank. Next to the pond lay Rosalynn's straw hat. Lone Wolf searched the area, but found no other sign of her. He called out her name. No answer.

Lone Wolf squatted to examine Rosalynn's tracks in the wet sand. She had been sitting next to the water. But more of her tracks faced the opposite direction. He slowly walked in the direction that she had faced, and found evidence of a horse tethered in the bushes. Kneeling, Lone Wolf found two sets of human tracks. There had been a struggle! The smaller footprints led into the forest, and he knew they must be Rosalynn's.

Lone Wolf followed the tracks on foot and realized that Rosalynn had been pursued by someone on horseback. The adrenalin surged through his veins. *Who would do this?* he thought, his breath coming in shallow gasps as he ran. Soon the footprints backtracked toward the falls, but the horse's hoof prints turned off into the forest; obviously, the rider was no tracker. Lone Wolf sprinted back to the falls, his side aching.

The footprints led to the edge of the water next to the falls. Did she go downstream or swim to the other side of the pond? He then remembered Rosalynn's fascination with the small cave. Lone Wolf jumped into the pond and swam to the falls, his heart pounding. He crashed through the rushing water and brushed the hair from his face. Immediately, he called out her name, but the raging water drowned out his voice. It took several seconds for his eyes to grow accustomed to the semi-darkness.

As he felt his way along the wall to the back of the cave, Lone Wolf stumbled over something. Reaching down, he felt a body. *Rosalynn!* He quickly knelt and lifted her head, then cradled her in his arms.

"Roz-lynn, Roz-lynn!" His voice was strained with fear. "Darling."

Lone Wolf heard Rosalynn moan and felt her body shudder. He called out her name again. Suddenly, she screamed and tried to pry herself from Lone Wolf's arms. She screamed again, kicking and scratching him. "Don't whip me again!"

"Roz-lynn, it is Lone Wolf. Do not be afraid," Lone Wolf soothed, then gently laid her down again. Soon, she stopped struggling and lapsed back into unconsciousness.

Lone Wolf lifted Rosalynn into his arms and carried her through the falls, shielding her from the pounding water as best he could. Once they were on dry land, he placed Rosalynn on the grass and examined her condition. He saw blood seeping from her cheek, and blood on her torn clothing—a great deal of blood. When he felt her face, he discovered that she was burning up with fever. *What happened to my woman, Great One? Please don't take her spirit. It is not her time to die.*

Lone Wolf carefully lifted Rosalynn and carried her to the

horse. He draped her across the mare's back, mounted, and then headed for the house. When they drew near, Lone Wolf saw Jeb's horse tied behind the house. He shouted for Black Hawk and within minutes, Black Hawk and Jeb were at his side.

"Jeb, go to town for the doctor. Hurry!" Lone Wolf ordered.

Jeb nodded, climbed on his horse, and dashed toward town at a gallop.

Black Hawk steadied the mare while Lone Wolf carefully dismounted. Then he gently gathered his wife in his arms and carried her into the house.

"Is she alive?" Dorothy asked as she scurried frantically behind Lone Wolf.

"She lives. I need your help to remove her wet clothing."

Over his shoulder, Lone Wolf called, "Mother, put water on to boil and bring bandages."

Joshua and Hannah tried to get close to their mother, while the baby cried hysterically and Gretchen stood off to the side, pale and silent.

"Children, your mama is very ill," Lone Wolf explained as calmly as he could. "We must be quiet. I will let you see her after we care for her."

"I'll help Grandma, Pa," Joshua said, choking back tears.

"Mama! I want my mama," cried Hannah.

Pale Flower went to Hannah and picked her up. "Your Pa will let you see your mama as soon as she is better. You must be a big girl, Hannah."

Hannah sobbed, clutching Pale Flower. Dorothy ran ahead of Lone Wolf and pulled the quilts back on Rosalynn's bed. "We must get her undressed," she said.

While Dorothy undressed her niece, Lone Wolf went in search of a nightgown. When he returned, he placed the nightgown on the bed and then went into the sitting room to build a fire. He pushed the coals back and placed several large bricks in the hearth to heat. Then he waited anxiously until Dorothy called to him.

"I couldn't put Rosalynn's nightgown on her. She has some deep welts on her back, so I left her undressed. But I put a towel underneath her." Dorothy's voice was strained with concern.

Kneeling next to Rosalynn, Lone Wolf dried her hair with a towel. He then asked Dorothy to go downstairs and bring back hot water and bandages.

Lone Wolf smoothed Rosalynn's hair from her face and felt her flushed brow. She still burned with fever, but her limbs were as cold as ice.

When Dorothy returned, Joshua was with her. He saw the deep gash on his mother's cheek and his eyes grew large. "Pa, does Ma have any more wounds?"

"Yes, she does," Dorothy answered. "I found them when I undressed her."

"Can I see them?" Joshua asked quietly.

Lone Wolf placed his hand on Joshua's shoulder. "Not now, Joshua. The doctor will be here soon."

Joshua craned his head back so he could look up at Lone Wolf. "Please, Pa. It's important."

Lone Wolf's heart filled with compassion for the small boy. He looked at Dorothy. "Help me with Roz-lynn."

Dorothy held the quilts in place over Rosalynn while Lone Wolf lifted her into a sitting position. Long, thin welts crisscrossed her back, and oozing blood stained her pale skin. Already the towel was nearly soaked with blood.

A strangled cry escaped Lone Wolf. "What happened to her?"

"I don't know," Dorothy said. "It looks like she fell and cut herself. She has the same kind of mark across the back of one of her hands."

Angrily, Lone Wolf started, "These marks are not from falling. They are—"

"She was whipped!" Joshua interrupted as he stared at the ugly marks on his mother's back.

Dorothy replaced the soiled towel and then helped Lone Wolf ease Rosalynn back onto the pillow.

"What makes you think so, Joshua?" Dorothy inquired with her hand on the boy's small shoulder.

Joshua looked back and forth between his aunt and Lone Wolf. "Ma was whipped, and I know who did it. It was my old pa. He whipped her!"

Lone Wolf squatted down next to Joshua, noticing the pain in the boy's eyes. "How do you know this?"

"I saw my old Pa whip Ma many times when we lived on the farm in St. Louis. When he got drunk, he'd get mad and whip her with his riding crop. I would try to stop him, and he would try to whip me too, but Ma wouldn't let him. Instead, she took the whipping herself. Look," he said, pointing, "you can still see the marks. She has them on her legs, too." Joshua's face was white.

Dorothy started to cry. "Why didn't she tell me? She suffered so much and didn't say a word. My poor baby!"

"You are brave, Joshua, for taking care of your mother," Lone Wolf said. "Did you dress the wounds?"

"Yes, I helped Ma the best I could, but I couldn't stop him from hurting her." Broken sobs shook the small body. "I wanted to hurt him back, but Ma said we can't do that. She said I should feel sorry for him."

Joshua's face glistened with tears and his slender frame shook. "You're not going to let Jeffery hurt Ma again, are you, Pa? He was mean to her and I don't want him to hurt her anymore."

"No, son, I will not let him hurt her again." Lone Wolf felt the Lakota blood surge through his veins, demanding revenge, and prayed that he would have the strength to let the wasichu law punish Jeffery. "You and your aunt need to leave now and let her rest. I will watch over her until the doctor comes."

Lone Wolf wrapped the hot bricks in thick towels and placed them at the foot of the bed. He rubbed Rosalynn's feet until they warmed. He then slipped heavy socks on her feet, and placed her feet next to the covered bricks. He rubbed her arms and legs vigorously to warm them.

Undressing down to his loincloth, Lone Wolf pulled the heavy quilts back, leaving the sheet over Rosalynn, and crawled in next to her. She felt like a slab of ice as he wrapped himself around her. Soon, she began to warm from the heat of his body.

As Lone Wolf lay next to Rosalynn, his heart filled with compassion. She felt so small, so vulnerable. How could this have happened? Before he realized it, Lone Wolf's pent up emotions flooded his body, and he wept.

Was Joshua right? Had Jeffery beaten her? Why would he want to hurt sweet Rosalynn? Only she could answer his questions, and right now she could not.

When Rosalynn's body was finally warm, Lone Wolf slipped out of the bed and dressed again. He went to the bowl and pitcher and wet a washcloth. As he placed the cool cloth on her burning brow, he heard the doctor downstairs.

Everyone waited outside the door while the doctor examined Rosalynn. When he finished, he allowed Lone Wolf, Dorothy, and Pale Flower to enter the room. Black Hawk and Jeb stayed downstairs and fed the children their dinner.

"I don't know who hurt this little lady, but she's suffered a great deal. Jeb informed me she was lost. At any rate, it's a good thing you found her when you did. She would have been dead by morning."

Dorothy gasped and broke down in tears. Pale Flower

embraced her.

"I applied some salve to the wounds, and if you keep them clean, they should heal." The doctor said, taking another look at his patient. "I'm sure your herbs will benefit her as well, Pale Flower."

"I gave her something for the fever and left an envelope on the vanity with more powder in it. Give her two pinches of powder in a glass of water. It wouldn't hurt to give her an alcohol rub, but keep her warm if you do." The doctor picked up his bag. "I noticed that you placed hot bricks by her feet. Keep doing that until the fever breaks."

"Thank you for coming so quickly." Lone Wolf shook the doctor's hand. "I will stop by your office and pay you the next time I am in town."

"That's fine, Mr. Larson. I'll come by again tomorrow to see how she's doing." The doctor started to leave, and then hesitated. "I'm going to contact the sheriff and let him know what happened. We can't have a madman running loose whipping innocent women."

"So they are whip marks?" Lone Wolf asked.

"I'd stake my reputation on it," the doctor said with a sigh. "And by the looks of the scars on her body, it's not the first time this has happened to her."

Lone Wolf stayed by Rosalynn's side day and night, personally tending and dressing her wounds and keeping hot bricks by her feet. As promised, the doctor came the next day and said there was nothing else he could do for her. If she did not acquire an infection, she would live. Otherwise, it was in the Lord's hands.

Reverend and Mrs. Baker came to inquire after Rosalynn, bringing hot dishes of food from concerned parishioners. Arlene and Ida also drove out to check on Rosalynn, their arms full of food.

After two agonizing days, Rosalynn's fever finally broke. It was four days before she opened her eyes. She drank some broth and then fell into another restless slumber.

Black Hawk took over the chores so that Lone Wolf could stay by Rosalynn's side. Lone Wolf refused to leave Rosalynn and only slept when he was so tired that his body refused to continue. He ate little, and he looked haggard and worn. But with the entire family praying for Rosalynn almost constantly, he had great hope that she would recover.

The children were quietly ushered in every day for a brief peek at her. Finally, on the sixth day, Rosalynn was coherent and could stay awake for longer periods. She ate a little, but didn't talk about what had happened to her. Lone Wolf wouldn't let anyone press her, not even the sheriff. She would talk when she was ready.

Just past midnight on the seventh day, Lone Wolf heard Rosalynn stir, so he hurried to her side. Gently placing his hand on her forehead, he made sure the fever hadn't returned. He felt the bricks to make sure they were still warm, then tucked the quilt snugly around her body. Then he returned to the rocking chair and picked up his flute. Soon a low, melodious tune filled the room.

"Lone Wolf." Rosalynn's voice was barely above a whisper.

Again, he rushed to her side. "Roz-lynn, are you awake? How do you feel?"

"Thirsty," she croaked.

Lone Wolf poured a glass of water from a pitcher on the nightstand. He lifted Rosalynn's head and watched as she drank.

Rosalynn laid her head back onto the pillow and winced. "Why do I hurt so bad?"

"You do not remember, Roz-lynn? I found you in the small cave behind the waterfall."

Rosalynn went silent for several seconds and then sighed, "I remember now."

"You are safe now, Roz-lynn. You must tell me what happened."

Grimacing, she exclaimed, "I . . . I can't. I can't tell anyone! I'm too ashamed. Please don't make me talk about it." She turned her face to the wall.

Lone Wolf thought a moment. He didn't want to cause Rosalynn more pain, but he needed to know what had happened if he was to protect her. *Great Spirit, guide my words so that I may help Roz-lynn.*

"Roz-lynn, did Jeffery do this to you? Is he the one who whipped you?"

Her eyes flew open and she turned toward him again. "How did you know? Did Jeffery try to harm you? Did he take Mikey and Gretchen away?"

"No, Roz-lynn. Joshua told us how Jeffery used to whip you. We all assumed it must have been him."

"Joshua remembers." It was more of a statement than a question. "He was so small." Tears rolled down the sides of her face and puddled on the pillow. "I tried so hard to protect Joshua and Hannah from Jeffery. I'm so ashamed that Joshua remembers."

Short sobs escaped her lips and she turned away from her husband. "Please, Lone Wolf, don't look at me. I can't bear to see pity and disgust in your eyes. I'm a stupid, worthless . . ."

The desire for revenge boiled up in Lone Wolf's heart. "Do not say such things, Roz-lynn," he said vehemently. "Jeffery is stupid and worthless. I will kill him for what he has done to you."

Rosalynn quickly looked at Lone Wolf, fear in her eyes. "No,

Lone Wolf, you mustn't kill Jeffery. Promise me you won't do anything to him."

"Why, Roz-lynn? Why do you protect him? Do you still care for him? Do you still love him?" Lone Wolf backed away from the bed, but Rosalynn grabbed his arm.

"Listen to me, Lone Wolf. I despise Jeffery. But if you kill him, God will punish you. One of His commandments is 'Thou shall not kill.' I'm trying to protect you, not him. Can't you see that?"

"I do not understand why the Great Spirit would become angry with me after what Jeffery has done. My mother's people would not allow him to get away with what he did to you. He has no right to harm you, Joshua, or Hannah. You are my family now."

Rosalynn's face softened. "Lone Wolf, please kneel here next to me."

He grunted indignantly but did as Rosalynn asked.

"Lone Wolf, it is you that I love." She smiled shyly. "I've loved you all along, but I was afraid—afraid to trust a man again. I felt I wasn't good enough for you. But you kept proving yourself to me, proving you weren't like Jeffery.

"When I saw him down by the falls, I was terrified. I felt worthless again, and I didn't know how I could survive the whipping I knew was coming. Then, suddenly, I thought of you. Knowing you were my husband gave me the courage to face Jeffery. I will never forget how he has treated me, but I won't live my life by it. Lone Wolf, I know now that I can freely love you without fear that you will treat me badly.

"If you seek revenge, then Jeffery wins and we lose. This town would hang you in a heartbeat if you harmed him. They're just looking for an excuse to get rid of you."

Lone Wolf couldn't believe he was hearing correctly. Rosalynn loved him! *Great Spirit, Roz-lynn loves me!* "Say it again, Roz-lynn."

"Say what, darling?" Rosalynn raised her arm and brushed the long, black hair from his face.

Lone Wolf put his hand over hers and held it against his cheek. "Tell me again that you love me."

Rosalynn laughed. "I love you, Gabriel Lone Wolf Larson. You make me so happy, I'm afraid I'm going to wake and find you're only a dream. I want to spend my life with you. I want to have your babies. I never want you to leave my side."

Tears slipped down her cheeks. "Hold me, Lone Wolf. Hold me and never let me go."

He embraced her, careful not to touch her wounds. Tears of happiness streamed down his face. "I love you, Roz-lynn, my wife. I need you as the fish need the water, as the night needs the stars. You are the air that I breathe, the food that I eat. I cannot live without you."

"Oh, Lone Wolf. Kiss me, my darling husband."

He gently cradled her face with his hands and then kissed her sweet lips.

"Lone Wolf, don't leave me. Stay here with me. We are man and wife in the eyes of the Lord. Let us live as man and wife from this time forth."

"I will never live apart from you, Roz-lynn. I will stay by your side day and night. We will live and breathe as one."

Chapter
Nineteen

When Rosalynn woke the following morning, Lone Wolf was lying next to her. She looked into his warm, brown eyes and smiled. Her heart filled with love and she knew she would always feel this way for her husband.

"Good morning, my wife." He reached over and weaved his finger in her long tresses as they spilled across the pillow. "How are you feeling?"

"I'm feeling much better, thank you," she said cheerily, then feigned a frown. "I'm also starving to death."

Lone Wolf laughed and placed a kiss on her cheek. "I will go down and tell Mother and Dorothy that you will be eating breakfast this morning. They will be relieved to know you are better. We have all been very worried about you."

While Lone Wolf was downstairs, Rosalynn slowly got out of bed, relieved herself, and pushed the chamber pot back under the bed. She washed her face and hands, trying not to get the bandage wet, then brushed her teeth. Not having the strength to fix her hair properly, she simply combed it and let it cascade over her shoulders. Next she walked slowly to the dresser and found a clean nightgown. When she looked up and saw herself in the mirror, she gasped. The gash along her cheekbone was red and swollen and ugly. In addition to the bandage on her hand, she saw bandages on her back and legs. No wonder she hurt so much! At least her wounds were healing, as she could see a scab forming over the cut on her face.

After carefully slipping on her nightgown, Rosalynn crawled back into bed and gingerly propped the pillows behind her back. Then she thought about Lone Wolf and how happy it made her to express her love to him! She had been so afraid of exposing her feelings—afraid of rejection and ridicule—but he had offered neither. Now, remembering the Source of her happiness, she bowed her head. *I thank Thee, Lord, for my many blessings. I thank Thee for my husband and for bringing me here. I thank Thee for teaching me that I could trust and love him. Thou hadst a plan for me all along, and I'm so very grateful. Now, what should I do about Jeffery . . .?*

Lone Wolf entered the room carrying a cup of steaming tea, but Rosalynn didn't hear him until he spoke.

"Roz-lynn, I brought you some of my Indian tea. It will make you strong."

"Thank you, my dear."

He set the tea on the little stand next to the bed. "Mother and Black Hawk are the only ones awake. Mother asked me to tell you she will come up as soon as she has breakfast ready. When your aunt and the children wake, they will want to see you too."

"I'm grateful to Pale Flower. She has been a godsend." Rosalynn took a sip of tea, then drew in a deep breath and set the teacup back on the nightstand. "Lone Wolf, I need to talk with you before the children wake. Can you please shut the door and come sit next to me?" She patted the edge of the bed.

"What is it, Roz-lynn, that puts such a frown on your beautiful face?" Lone Wolf stroked her cheek affectionately.

"I need to explain some things to you. It's going to be difficult, so please bear with me."

Rosalynn took Lone Wolf's large hand in hers and kissed it, then held it in her lap for moral support. Sighing, she began to tell him about her life with Jeffery—about the beatings and about Jeffery selling their farm out from under her.

"It wasn't easy, but Aunt Dottie and I made ends meet. Somehow, the Lord always blessed us. But I was a divorced woman. As if that wasn't shame enough in and of itself, the town shunned me for it, too.

"I never told anyone how Jeffery whipped me and put me down. I was disgraced. I was ashamed of what he had done and humiliated that I allowed him to do it. He put me down so much that I began to believe him. I felt stupid and worthless. I guess when a person is told enough times that they are nothing, they lose their self-respect."

Rosalynn brushed her hand against Lone Wolf's cheek. "It wasn't until I met you that I felt hope. I wanted to believe you so very much, but in the back of my mind I kept telling myself that you were just being kind to a stranger in need. I believed you married me only to get Mike's children and to have a housekeeper. I didn't think you would ever consider me as anything but a servant. Nevertheless, I couldn't help but fall in love with you.

"When your mother told me that you were courting me with your flute music, I was so happy. I felt, for the first time, that you might love me a little bit."

Lone Wolf kissed the palm of Rosalynn's hand and smiled sheepishly. "I, too, have a confession to make, Roz-lynn. I suggested marriage only so that I could keep you here with me. You were special, and I wanted you for my wife. I asked the Great Spirit to bring me a wife and then you came into my life. I knew it was my destiny to marry you.

"You treated me as a man, a human, not as a savage. You came to my defense more than once, and my love for you just kept growing until I thought I would burst. We were two lonely people until the Great Spirit brought us together."

Tears sprang to Rosalynn's eyes. "I feel the same way, Lone Wolf. The Lord meant for us to be together. I put my trust in God, and He found a way for our foolish pride and stubbornness to disappear." She clasped Lone Wolf's hand in hers and sighed. "But we both know our troubles aren't over just because we finally declared our love to each other. Jeffery is still out there. He told me that he came here to get you to give him your savings and the deed to the farm. He wanted me to talk you into doing as he said. When I refused, he whipped me. When that didn't work, he threatened to kidnap me and force you to give him what he wanted. I got away, but with him on horseback, I knew I'd never make it to the house without him catching me. That's when I remembered the cave behind the falls, and the Spirit told me to go there. So I backtracked and hid in the cave. When I saw Jeffery leave, I was still too frightened to leave the cave. I think I finally passed out, for I don't remember anything until this morning."

"You were burning with fever when I found you. But I do not understand how he knows that I have money in the bank and the deed to the farm." Lone Wolf's brows came together as he frowned.

"Jeffery and Susan are together," Rosalynn explained. "Apparently, they were seeing each other while Mike was still alive. The man that Susan referred to in her letter to you was Jeffery. He was the man she had been in love with for a long time. Anyway, Susan ran off with him and they've spent all of the money she took from Mike's accounts. Susan told Jeffery about your money and the deed."

"Is Susan with him here in Peaceful?"

"I don't know. But I know one thing for sure—Jeffery won't

give up. I know him well enough to be certain that he'll do anything to get what he wants. He made threats against you, and threats to take Mikey and Gretchen away from us."

"Do not worry, Roz-lynn. I have done nothing wrong and the children are legally ours now. I will go to town and tell Sheriff Lord what is going on. Maybe we can find Jeffery."

"Oh, Lone Wolf, I don't want anyone to know what Jeffery did to me. And if you tell the sheriff, the whole town of Peaceful will know."

Lone Wolf held Rosalynn, stroking her hair. "This is not your shame, my beautiful wife, it is his shame."

"I still couldn't bear anyone knowing that I was whipped like an animal," she said, gripping her husband tight.

Lone Wolf released her and gazed into her eyes, glittering with unshed tears. "Some of the townspeople already know that someone hurt you."

Rosalynn cried out, hot tears escaping down her face. "How did they find out?"

"The doctor said that he had to make a report to Sheriff Lord. Reverend and Mrs. Baker have been here several times asking about you. So have Todd, Arlene, Ida, and Swede." Lone Wolf wiped the tears away from her pale cheeks. "Many of the parishioners have brought food. Everyone is concerned for you."

Rosalynn sat back against the pillows, suddenly too tired to move. "I don't know what to say. I've been shunned for so long, I forgot what it feels like to be accepted."

"I feel the same way. We both have stood against the odds for our convictions. Maybe now all of Peaceful will accept us."

She reached for Lone Wolf's outstretched hand. "That would be nice, but as long as we have each other and our friends and family, I will consider myself very blessed."

The children refused to leave Rosalynn's side for several days. Pale Flower and Dorothy spoiled and pampered her until she almost felt guilty. Rosalynn wanted to get back to her normal routine, yet it was so nice having everyone look after her for a change.

Lone Wolf reported to Sheriff Lord what had happened, and the sheriff promptly sent his deputies out with Lone Wolf to search for Jeffery. They searched the wharf where the sternwheelers docked, figuring that Jeffery was holed up there. But riffraff and crime abounded at the wharf, and no one was talking. Lone Wolf and the deputies searched the rest of the town with no luck. Now all that the family could do was keep an eye out for Jeffery and pray that if he returned, the Lord would protect them from him.

Rosalynn soon healed enough to resume her chores. Some of the scars were fading, thanks to a salve that Pale Flower had made.

The last of the garden was harvested, and the cellar brimmed with good food for the long winter ahead. Lone Wolf and Black Hawk finished the fall butchering, and the women helped smoke the meat. They rendered the pork fat into lard and stored the cracklings. The women made headcheese and ground pork into sausage. Soon the smokehouse was full of meat for the winter.

Lone Wolf, Black Hawk, and Jeb spent long hours harvesting the crops. The women dried the sweet corn and the field corn. Most of the field corn was hauled into Peaceful to be shipped and sold elsewhere. When their harvesting was over, Lone Wolf and Black Hawk went to Jeb's farm and helped him with his harvest.

Finally, everything was ready for the coming winter. Lone Wolf gave Black Hawk his share of the profits and then loaded a pack mule with meat for Black Hawk to take back to the reservation. They would all miss him, but were happy to know that he would be back in the spring.

With Black Hawk gone and the harvest finished, Lone Wolf spent more time close to the house. He used this time to gather wood that he could carve during the long winter months.

At the mercantile, Rosalynn used her egg credit to buy fabric and other goods for making Christmas presents. She decided to make Pale Flower a quilt using the Amish star design. The vivid Lakota colors would look beautiful against the black background.

Deciding to make dolls for the girls, Rosalynn ordered china heads and glazed arms and legs. She would make the dolls' bodies, stuff them with sawdust, and use scrap fabric for the clothing. Joshua wanted a pony, so Lone Wolf bought him one and hid it on Jeb's farm.

Jeb had proposed to Dorothy, so Rosalynn decided to make Dorothy a crocheted tablecloth. For Lone Wolf, she would make warm flannel shirts and thick wool socks. Everyone would get a new hat, mufflers, and gloves from her homespun wool. As for their friends in town, she and Dorothy planned to make gift baskets filled with homemade cookies and candies and Dorothy's handmade toiletries.

The weather was changing, but the house was warm and snug. Rosalynn looked forward to the long winter ahead. Lone Wolf would be inside more, and she had so many plans for keeping the family busy.

Preparations for the wedding began. Rosalynn and Dorothy spent an entire day cleaning Jeb's small two-story farmhouse, which had never seen a woman's touch. Soon it was presentable enough for him to bring his bride home.

That day, as they pulled the buckboard back into the drive,

Rosalynn said to her aunt, "I'm starved. I sure hope Pale Flower has fixed lunch."

"Speaking of Pale Flower, I see her standing on the back porch." Dorothy waved, but withdrew her hand as they pulled to a stop outside the back gate. "I think something is wrong!"

Rosalynn pulled the brake and tied the reins to the brake handle. She looked up just as Pale Flower came running towards them, Mikey in her arms. Pale Flower's eyes were wide, and tears streamed down her cheeks.

Jumping from the wagon, Rosalynn ran to Pale Flower and grabbed the shaking woman by the shoulders to help steady her. "What's wrong, Pale Flower? What's happened now?"

Gretchen and Hannah heard Rosalynn's voice and ran from the house. Joshua ran to his mother, tears streaming down his dusty cheeks, and clutched her tightly.

"For pity's sake, what has happened?" Rosalynn asked sharply, dread filling her very soul. "Tell me what is going on before I go mad!"

"Pa's gone," Joshua cried out in agony.

Rosalynn searched Pale Flower's face. "Please, Pale Flower, what's happened? Where is Lone Wolf? Where is my husband?"

"They took Gabriel. They are going to hang him."

Rosalynn took the baby from Pale Flower's arms and handed him to her aunt. Hannah and Gretchen clung to her, screaming with terror.

Feeling faint, Rosalynn placed one hand against her forehead, while the other clutched her throat. She closed her eyes and felt her body reel. *This can't be happening, Lord*, she prayed. *Please don't let this be true.* Then Rosalynn took a deep breath and tried to force herself to calm down. She opened her eyes and tried to focus on Pale Flower. "Please, what are you saying? Who took Lone Wolf?"

"A mob of men from Peaceful came to the farm and demanded that Lone Wolf go with them. They said he had murdered Mike—his own brother. They said they were going to hang him."

Hang Lone Wolf? "Mike committed suicide!" Rosalynn cried out. "Lone Wolf loved Mike. He would never harm him! I can't believe Sheriff Lord would think such a foolish thing."

"The sheriff was not with the mob. We must do something to save my son." Pale Flower broke down in tears again.

Rosalynn held her head in her hands, trying to think. Suddenly, she ran toward the house, shouting at Joshua as she went. "Joshua, unhitch one of the horses! I'll ride him bareback."

She raced into the house and up the stairs to her room, then pulled open her desk drawer and flung the contents onto the floor. Finding what she was looking for, she quickly grabbed it and tucked it into her waistband.

She ran outside, grabbed the horse's mane, and climbed onto its back. "Joshua, ride over to Jeb's and tell him I need him in town right now!" Without another word, Rosalynn kicked the horse's sides and galloped off towards town. *This can't be happening!* she thought. But it was. Her heart beat so fast that she thought her head would explode. When her eyes blurred, she swiped the tears away with the back of her hand.

The journey into town seemed like forever, and Rosalynn prayed aloud the entire trip. *I can't lose him, Father. I couldn't bear to go on without him. Protect him until I get there. Please, Father, I beg Thee!*

When Rosalynn finely reached Peaceful, she spotted Ida and Arlene huddled together in the middle of Main Street. As she approached them on horseback, she noticed their terrified expressions and turned to follow their stares. A small group of men stood under the willow tree where Rosalynn's family had rested when they arrived in town all those months ago.

When Rosalynn spotted Lone Wolf, a strangled scream erupted from her throat. He stood in the back of a buckboard with a noose around his neck and his hands tied behind his back. A man stood next to him, yelling at the crowd.

Rosalynn screamed, and Ida and Arlene ran towards her. "Rosalynn, thanks heavens you're here!" Ida exclaimed as she gasped for air.

"They're going to hang Lone Wolf!" Arlene cried out as she grabbed the horse's bridle. "We've got to stop them!"

Rosalynn's heart pounded so loudly in her chest that she couldn't think. How could three women stop a horde of men from hanging Lone Wolf? *Please, Heavenly Father, help me. Please help me save my husband!*

"Find Sheriff Lord," Rosalynn shouted as she urged her horse forward.

Ida ran after Rosalynn as the horse headed for the willow tree. "The sheriff is out of town, and he took Todd and Swede with him."

Barely able to breathe, Rosalynn raced toward the mob, her eyes focused on Lone Wolf. When she reached the willow tree, she quickly dismounted then fought her way through a throng of men. Several grabbed her, one tearing her sleeve, but she managed to pull away from them. She could feel her adrenaline pumping through her veins as she neared the wagon. Then, she got a closer look at Lone Wolf. Deep gashes on his face oozed blood, and his face was twisted in pain. As their eyes locked, Lone Wolf shook his head at her.

"Go, back, Roz-lynn," was all she could make out before one of the men standing next to Lone Wolf punched him in the stomach with his fist.

When Rosalynn finally reached the wagon, she saw Reverend Baker standing before the crowd, his back towards Lone Wolf.

"Please, in the name of God, stop this insanity! Wait for Sheriff Lord to return," the reverend pleaded with his hands in the air.

Choking down tears of gratitude, Rosalynn ran to Reverend Baker's side and grabbed his arm. "What's going on? Why do they want to hurt Lone Wolf?"

"Rosalynn, you must leave now! These men are serious. They think Lone Wolf started an Indian uprising. Now go! I can't protect both of you."

Lone Wolf start an uprising? Impossible! He was the gentlest man that Rosalynn had ever met. *Where did they get such a crazy idea?* she wondered, her mind racing.

Then, realizing that it wouldn't help to panic, Rosalynn put on a brave face and turned to the crowd. She recognized several faces from the barbershop—men that had taunted Lone Wolf when she first came to Peaceful. The rest of the men were strangers.

"Please, I beg you, don't harm Lone Wolf! He is innocent of the accusations. He would never harm anyone. I know this. Please believe me!"

Ignoring her, the men continued to shout and shake their fists in the air. Some even waved shotguns or pistols above their heads, and at this sight Rosalynn gasped. She glanced at Reverend Baker, whose face looked strained and white and whose voice was becoming hoarse from attempting to yell over the roar of the crowd. Rosalynn lifted her skirts and quickly climbed into the wagon.

One of the men guarding Lone Wolf grabbed Rosalynn when she tried to approach her husband. They both went down, and the man grabbed her by the hair of her head and forced her to the bottom of the wagon.

"Hang the white squaw along with her redskin husband!" a voice called out from the crowd.

Rosalynn turned to Lone Wolf and saw an ugly, red welt

around his neck.

"Get out of here, Roz-lynn, while you have a chance. Leave me," Lone Wolf mumbled through the blood that slowly dripped down his face.

"I won't leave you, my darling," Rosalynn whispered in a long, shuddering breath.

"Lice makes nits! I say hang them both!" the man holding Rosalynn yelled out.

When the crowd cheered madly, the man grinned and bowed. Then he reached up and tightened the noose around Lone Wolf's neck. Lone Wolf's face went red as he struggled to push the man away with his shoulders.

The cries from the crowd made Rosalynn's blood run cold. *This can't happen! God led me to Lone Wolf, and I know it wasn't meant to end like this.*

She tried to jerk free but the man held his grip. *What can I do? Lord, please help us!* Rosalynn thought. Then it came to her. The only hope they had was their faith.

Facing Lone Wolf with tear-filled eyes, she said, "Don't give up, dear. God is with us. Do you believe that?"

Lone Wolf nodded, tears coursing down his cheeks.

She grabbed him by the legs and held him, praying the noose wouldn't get any tighter. It was then she saw the gleam of steel concealed in one of his moccasin boots. *The knife!* Rosalynn waited for the right opportunity, and it came when the man turned from her and Lone Wolf again to boast to the crowd how he was going to hang them both. Carefully, Rosalynn pulled the knife from its hiding place, leaped up, and cut the rope above the noose. Gasping for air, Lone Wolf sunk to the wagon floor.

Before the man in the wagon knew what was happening, Rosalynn cut the cords binding Lone Wolf's hands. As Lone Wolf lay in Rosalynn's arms, several Swedish farmers she recognized from church grabbed the man in the wagon and dragged him to the ground.

"This has gone far enough," one of the farmers said, facing the crowd of men. "We need to wait for the sheriff to return before committing frontier justice. Lone Wolf has the right to justice just as much as any other man does."

"A redskin isn't a person, he's vermin!" a lone voice shouted.

"What about Mike's death? Are you good people going to let this redskin get away with murder?" another called.

Rosalynn's skin crawled as she recognized Jeffery's voice above the din of the mob. She swiped the tears from her face and turned to the crowd. Walking toward her was Jeffery, with Susan on his arm.

"Susan?" Rosalynn uttered in shock. "I never thought I'd see you again!"

"Like I wrote in my letter," Susan said, tipping her head toward Jeffery, "there was someone I'd loved for a long time, and—"

"Yes, I know," Rosalynn interrupted. "Jeffery told me."

"I deserve to be happy, don't I? He makes me happy."

"Susan, I'm glad I'm not with Jeffery anymore. But please, don't let him manipulate you as he did me. You know as well as I do that Lone Wolf didn't kill Mike. He loved his brother."

"I—I—," Susan stammered, looking at Jeffery.

Rosalynn saw the fear on Susan's face and pitied her. She knew all too well what Jeffery would do if Susan didn't back him up. "Susan, please tell these men the truth. Sheriff Lord is a good man—he'll protect you from Jeffery."

Reverend Baker then spoke. "Susan, if you know the truth about Mike and the accusations against Lone Wolf about the alleged uprising, you need to tell us—now. If you don't speak up and Lone Wolf is hung unjustly, you will be an accomplice to murder. Do you really want to live with that on your conscience?

Do you want to spend the rest of your life in jail?"

"Susan doesn't have anything to fear," Jeffery interjected, glaring at Reverend Baker and then at Rosalynn.

Turning to Susan, he said with forced sweetness, "Susan, darling, tell the citizens of Peaceful how you watched Lone Wolf kill your poor husband." Then turning toward the mob, Jeffery went on. "Lone Wolf threatened to kill Susan if she told anyone that he killed Mike. She was so terrified that Lone Wolf would harm her that she fled from Peaceful."

"You're a liar, Jeffery," Rosalynn said, trying to keep her voice even. "You know that Mike committed suicide because Susan was leaving him and taking his money when she left. That wasn't enough, was it, Jeffery? Now you're back for Lone Wolf's money and his farm. You're nothing but a greedy coward."

"The crowd isn't interested in what you have to say, Rosalynn. They want justice," Jeffery replied with a sneer.

"We can't let Lone Wolf get away with murder," a man shouted. "Either produce evidence that he's innocent, or we're hanging him."

Looking at the man who shouted, Rosalynn could see that he was not a resident of Peaceful. He was clearly a river rat from the wharfs—a ringer to help Jeffery keep the townspeople riled!

"Yes, Rosalynn prove your lies or hang with your half-breed husband," Jeffery yelled, escalating the shouts from the mob.

"Do not harm Roz-lynn! It is me you hate," Lone Wolf called in a pleading voice.

Rosalynn looked down at Jeffery. "You want proof? I have proof." She slipped the small book from her waist shirt and held it over her head for all to see. "I have proof Lone Wolf didn't kill his brother."

Susan saw the diary and her face grew pale. "Please, Rosalynn, don't do this. You know what Jeffery will do to me."

"Yes, Susan, I know what Jeffery is capable of doing. Please, tell the truth to save yourself as well as our lives. I'm your sister, Susan, doesn't that count for anything? I've protected you all of your life."

"What's going on here?" Jeffery demanded. "What does she have, Susan?"

"This is Susan's diary, written in her hand. In this diary, she explains how she watched Mike as he hung himself in the barn. Don't take my word for it, take Susan's." Rosalynn thumbed through the entries, then read a passage aloud. "*I can't believe my good fortune. I went out to the barn tonight,*" Rosalynn paused, waiting for the noise of the crowd to die down, "*to have it out with Mike, when I saw him crawl onto a barrel and hang himself. I won't have to divorce that wimp now. I'm free! I'll get rid of the brats and clean out Mike's accounts. My lover waits for me and I can't wait to leave this disgusting little town. I now have a dirty little secret to keep . . .*"

The crowd went silent all eyes pinned on Susan.

Jeffery nudged Susan in the ribs. "You fool, what in blue blazes possessed you to write down those things? You've ruined everything!"

Susan backed away from Jeffery, and Rosalynn cringed at the murderous look in his eyes. Tears streaming down her cheeks, Susan cried, "Jeffery, I can't do this any longer. I can't let you kill my sister and Lone Wolf." Susan wiped the tears from her face. "I thought you loved me! You promised to take me places I've always dreamed of if I took Mike's money and left my children. I realize now what a fool I was to believe you."

"Keep your mouth shut, Susan," Jeffery growled, "unless you want the same fate as your husband."

Susan panicked. "Tell them the truth, Jeffery. If you don't, I'll tell them it was really you who hanged Mike!"

An audible gasp went up from the mob. Even Rosalynn was shocked, and she knew Lone Wolf felt the same as he squeezed her hand tightly.

Jeffery drew a small derringer from his breast pocket and brandished it before the mob. "How can all of you believe this woman's lies? Can't you see she's just trying to protect her own skin?"

Jeffery slowly backed away from the crowd. "Do what you want with the redskin. I'm leaving and don't try and stop me. Susan, come on we're leaving."

"No, Jeffery, I'm staying here."

"Oh, no you're not," Jeffery snarled, grabbing Susan by the arm. "You're not talking to the law. Either you come with me or I'll shoot you where you stand."

As Susan screamed and tried to pull from Jeffery's grasp, Rosalynn jumped from the wagon to try to protect her sister. Before she could reach Susan, however, a gunshot pierced the air.

Surprised, Jeffery looked up, and at that moment two of the Swedish farmers threw him to the ground and grabbed his gun.

Rosalynn saw four riders coming toward them. As the riders dismounted near Jeffery and Susan, Rosalynn saw that it was Sheriff Lord, Todd, Swede, and Jeb. She heaved a great sigh of relief and would have fallen if Lone Wolf had not reached up to support her.

The sheriff grabbed Jeffery and pulled him to his feet. "Come on, I have a nice cell waiting for you." Sheriff Lord then looked at Susan. "Mrs. Larson, I need to interview you at the jail. Please follow me."

Rosalynn reached out to Susan and hugged her close. "Thank you, Susan, for telling the truth. I need to attend to Lone Wolf, and then I'll come to the jail and tell Sheriff Lord that you helped prevent a hanging."

Susan burst into tears. "I hope you can forgive me someday, Rosalynn. I've treated you and Aunt Dottie horribly, and then I abandoned my children . . . I didn't know Jeffery planned to hang Mike, but once it was done I went along with his scheme. I'm ashamed of myself."

Rosalynn smiled at Susan. "Put it in God's hands, Susan. Tell Sheriff Lord the truth, and God will help you."

Rosalynn watched as Susan left with Sheriff Lord. Then Rosalynn rejoined Lone Wolf.

"I am glad Mike did not take his own life. I know it saddens the Great Spirit when any of His children choose to die that way. It will be a long while before I can forgive Jeffery."

"God is patient and loving. He knows how difficult it is to forgive when someone commits such a heinous crime against us. You will heal, Lone Wolf but in your own time."

"The letter Mike left . . ." Lone Wolf started.

Rosalynn pressed her fingertips to his lips. "Susan and Jeffery must have staged the letter to cover their tracks. Mike can rest in peace now."

Jeb walked up to them and slapped Lone Wolf on the shoulder. "Sorry, I was almost too late," Jeb drawled, scratching his head.

Rosalynn could have kissed Jeb. She looked down at Lone Wolf. "Did you know Jeb was here?"

"Yes, I watched him ride up with Sheriff Lord, Todd, and Swede.

Lone Wolf rose from the ground and shook hands with Jeb. "I owe you, Jeb."

"Ah, it was nothing," Jeb reddened. "It was only one gunshot. I came as quickly as I could."

"No complaints on our part," Rosalynn laughed with tears in her eyes.

Ida, Swede, Arlene, Todd, and Reverend and Mrs. Baker surrounded Rosalynn and Lone Wolf. Each person hugged the couple in turn, then expressed their relief.

Dorothy drove up in the wagon with Pale Flower and the children, and they all ran to Lone Wolf and Rosalynn and embraced them, shedding happy tears. Pale Flower handed Mikey to Dorothy and then embraced Lone Wolf.

"My son, you are safe." She then turned to Rosalynn with tears glistening in her eyes. "Dear Rosalynn, how can I ever thank you for saving my son? You have done so much for Lone Wolf and me. I love you, my daughter."

Rosalynn's heart was so full of joy that words escaped her, so she simply hugged her mother-in-law. Dorothy wrapped her free arm around Pale Flower while balancing Mikey on her hip. "Rosalynn speaks for me too, Pale Flower."

As the three women spoke, the children surrounded Lone Wolf, each trying to secure his attention. Finally, Pale Flower and Dorothy gathered the children and went to stand with Reverend and Mrs. Baker, giving Lone Wolf and Rosalynn time alone.

Rosalynn put her arms around Lone Wolf and pressed her face to his chest for several moments, then raised her head to look into his eyes. "We have been so blessed today, Lone Wolf. And you are no longer alone, for you have me and the children."

Lone Wolf placed a kiss on his wife's lips. "There is one thing I still need, Roz-lynn."

Feigning a frown, Rosalynn asked, "What else could you possibly want?"

"A baby with you. A child formed from our love."

Rosalynn's throat tightened. "Maybe in the spring, my darling, you will get your wish. Anything is possible under a sweetheart's moon."

Epilogue

Rosalynn examined the table, making sure there were enough place settings for their Christmas-dinner guests. The combined aromas of turkey, fresh baked bread, and cinnamon filled the house. Wisely, Aunt Dorothy had hid the freshly baked pies in the pantry until after dinner. Rosalynn sighed contentedly and then checked the turkey. Everything was ready.

"Rosalynn, come join us," Aunt Dorothy called from the parlor.

When Rosalynn entered the parlor, her eyes stung with unshed tears. *My cup runneth over, Father.* For the first time, she understood those words.

Aunt Dorothy and Jeb sat together on the settee next to the fireplace, playing with little Mikey. Lone Wolf patiently explained to Joshua how to take care of his new rifle. Susan was playing dolls with the girls on the floor.

Yes, Rosalynn felt truly blessed this Christmas Day. It had only been a short while since Jeffrey's greed had almost destroyed her life with Lone Wolf and the children. Fortunately, Judge Warner had spared Susan from prison for her testimony against Jeffery. Susan had testified that Jeffery killed Mike and terrorized Rosalynn and Lone Wolf out of pure selfishness and greed.

Rosalynn was happy that Susan had decided to stay for the holidays before returning to the life she loved on the riverboats—a life of gambling and seeing new places. Susan had admitted privately to Rosalynn and Lone Wolf that she loved her children but was not able to live the life they deserved. Rosalynn and Lone Wolf were both relieved when Susan asked them to continue raising Gretchen and Mikey.

Walking over to Lone Wolf, Rosalynn sat down beside him. "Dinner is ready, darling. We only need to wait for the Olsons, Reverend and Mrs. Baker, and Todd and Arlene to arrive."

"I do not know if I can wait that long," Lone Wolf groaned. "Can't I have just one piece of apple pie while I wait?"

Rosalynn laughed and kissed him. "No, because if you eat a piece of pie, the children will all want a piece too."

"If I cannot have any pie," Lone Wolf began with a sly smile, "can I have the Christmas present you promised me?"

Rosalynn blushed. "I'm afraid you won't get your Christmas present until summer. Seven months, to be more precise."

"Seven months? What could you give me in seven months?"

Rosalynn touched her husband's cheek tenderly. "I'll tell you under the sweetheart's moon tonight, my darling."